Dark Drink

AN ABSOLUTELY GRIPPING PSYCHOLOGICAL THRILLER FULL OF TWISTS

DARK SERIES
BOOK ONE
IN THE DARKNESS UNIVERSE

TINA O'HAILEY

Black Rose Writing | Texas

ISBN: 978-1-68433-977-8
PUBLISHED BY BLACK ROSE WRITING
www.blackrosewriting.com

Printed in the United States of America
Suggested Retail Price (SRP) $22.95

Dark Drink is printed in Garamond

*As a planet-friendly publisher, Black Rose Writing does its best to
eliminate unnecessary waste to reduce paper usage and energy
costs, while never compromising the reading experience. As a result,
the final word count vs. page count may not meet common
expectations.

For Aunt Sandy. I'll miss your snark.
1947 – 2020

ACKNOWLEDGMENTS

Writing Group: Enormous bushel baskets full of thanks to my Apocalypse Writing Group. Via zoom during 2020, we focused our efforts on becoming better writers. Basically, it was a master class in writing by Joseph Carrabis and the rest of us attempted to edit too. Thank you: Joseph Carrabis, S.M. Stevens, Joe Della Rosa, Rox Burkey. You will forever be the editing voices in my ear. Of course, the story couldn't have formed without a zoom cocktail session with Matt Maloney (from the Sh!ddy Writers' Group). We can see the influence of his love of story and cocktail creation in these pages.

Alpha Readers: Unending thanks to eagle-eye proof readers James Burns, Dr. Denise Smith, S.M. Stevens, alpha readers: Leslie Lytle (fellow author who helped me with story points while we scrambled deep in a cave), Myrna Attaway (I am proud to have maintained the title of twisted bitch to her), Joseph and Daniel O'Hailey (my muses), and of course—John O'Hailey.

Without Mr. O'Hailey's everlasting love, support, and understanding—I would not be.

Dark Drink

1 - 151 WAYS TO DIE

'I'm going to die because of a watermelon. Fuck me.'

I can't stop my fall. My legs are distant. My arms do not respond. They ignore my insistent demands: Protect your head! Hold on to something! Brace for impact!

Not even a twitch, just— *'Good luck to you and your brain holder.'*

The world moves in slow motion. Outside, I glimpse Mercedez slumped against the railing. Is she okay? A bizarre strangled sound comes from my throat instead of the yell I intend. I don't feel the floor when I hit.

My brain records one last high-definition mental image: That goddamned watermelon sitting above me on the counter. A sticker pasted onto the sweating rind encourages all to, *'Enjoy Summer!'*. It's late September.

My favorite German steel-core knife—which according to Amazon is *'great for rocking while chopping'* but has a *'sometimes uncomfortable grip'*—sticks out of said malignant watermelon at a jaunty angle.

A handsomely manicured hand grabs the knife; yanks it free.

The pulp in the air smells sweet. A drop of juice—not yet mixed with the tequila I intended for it—falls onto my face.

My brain issues one last somewhat coherent thought before checking out, plunging me into darkness, *'151 Ways to Die? Well, here's to 152. Heh.'*

151 WAYS TO DIE

Recipe notes from Jude's journal.

Pour equal parts into desired vessel:

- Bacardi 151 rum
- Whiskey or Rye
- Everclear alcohol
- Tequila

Usually delivered in a shot glass, unless someone is trying to put it in a watermelon. Because—'reasons. In retrospect, if I had ditched the watermelon, maybe I could have avoided the whole getting murdered thing.

2 - APPLE PIE MOONSHINE

Mercedez—my tech-savvy, best-friend since grade-school—rips the flip-phone from my back pocket and proclaims, "Jude! You need to get into this century. Sweet Sally. *What*, might I ask, is *this*?"

"My vibrator." Obviously, she's been struck blind by the homemade moonshine recipe I am trying to perfect. "Sorry you lost your eyesight. Must be the turpentine."

I pour a jigger of vodka into the mixture and eye it for the right amount of light amber color before adding the real kick to it.

"Seriously. How do you even keep up with work with this antique thing? Don't they have to ping you all the time with location updates of POTUS or something?"

I ignore the dig. "Okay, so I need to put the grain alcohol in here."

"How long did it take to make that?" Mercedez pulls her long hair behind her shoulder and sniffs the clear 190-proof liquid.

"Not as long as you think. It only takes about ten days to ferment." I pour the acid—which if distilled one more time could be used as car fuel, seriously—into a cooled apple-cider-allspice-ginger-brown-sugar slurry.

"Do you have a permit for making that?" Mercedez eyeballs me as if she hasn't known my straight-up-can't-break-a-rule-self for a gazillion years.

"And risk my security clearance? Of course I have a permit." I hold my hands up for her to stand back and strain my creation into a jug.

"Isn't your security clearance re-up coming soon?" she asks.

"It isn't the cocktail-making that worries me. Focus here." I point to the drink at hand.

Mercedez gets down eyeball-level with the marble countertop and gives an approving nod. "I do like to be part of your test kitchen. It's cheaper than the bars."

"Less drama too," I say and wiggle my eyebrow knowingly.

She glares at me and changes the subject—which she brought up to begin with, "Where is this batch going?"

"There's a get-together at work and I want to bring in something for the team," I answer.

Mercedez stands to her full height, which isn't much—yet amplifies her glare as if she were on stilts. The amount of reserve and poise in this tiny woman still astounds me even after twenty-five years.

"Stop it. I like my team. It is not a big deal I am the only girl there. Not all men are weird," I say and avoid looking at her judging eyes.

Mercedez has a history of being hurt and is wary of most men; a long story that's not mine to tell. I will say, when we were growing up in California, she was hurt by everyone. I stood up for her when no one else would.

She knows we are safe in D.C. with no one from our past except me. No friends, no family, no anything from back then. Most of all, no psychopaths.

I pour two small drinks with a flourish.

"Tada," I say. "One for you. One for me."

"Can't be sloppy for work," Mercedez warns, raising the glass to the light.

"Can't drink after 10 pm." I ride a motorcycle in the VP motorcade and am paid to be hyper-aware of surroundings. I can't have a hangover or be fuzzy in the slightest. Bad shit happens when you get fuzzy.

I sniff the sweet light-amber liquid; decide it would look better with a little whipped cream and some graham cracker crumbles on top.

"That's nice. You should take a picture." Mercedez looks at my flip-phone disapprovingly, "Oh, wait. You can't. 'Cause this phone is from 2000. How does it even still work?"

She takes pictures with her fancy phone from various angles; pulls out some clip-on lenses or such nonsense from her purse and takes more pictures. I have to sit down because when Mercedez gets into taking pictures—it might be a minute. This is her job. Making things look good for social media.

"Damn. It's going to ferment. More," I complain.

"You don't appreciate me." Mercedez pouts. She puts her phone down so we can finally taste the drink.

"It's just too sweet for me. I want something as bitter as my soul," Mercedez says, then drinks more.

"I agree. There's a sharp bite behind that sweet though." I top off Mercedez's mason jar—appropriate glassware for moonshine—and take another tentative sniff at the jug in my hand.

I point to Mercedez's phone. "That takes great pictures and all, but I like the simple life." I hold up my flip phone. Black gaffer's tape holds the back of the phone—and the containing battery—in place. "I miss the pagers we had on the unit. Get a page, read it, done."

Mercedez relaxes back into the overstuffed couch and takes my phone, pats it like a pitiful stray, tosses it into the nearby recliner. It bounces and the lights of D.C., barely visible through the window, wink across the phone's cracked display.

She smooths out imaginary wrinkles in her slacks. Her maroon fingernail polish is the same shade of dried blood as her shoes.

Mercedez interrupts my morose train of thought, "Petal, I gotta get you something better. No friend of mine is going to walk around looking like 1996. Think of my reputation."

Mercedez picks at imaginary dust on her cashmere sweater. It bulges and cinches at all the right places to accentuate her slight figure.

She works night and day as a social media marketing something-or-another. I don't understand the details, but it involves a lot of reading things on her phone, using her thumbs, and swearing.

I finish my glass of moonshine, sweeter than I like. "I don't like change."

"You're in a rut, you mean." Mercedez takes my empty glass and places it into the mostly empty dishwasher.

"I am not." I straighten the one newspaper on the coffee table. My own blank face stares back at me from a faded article titled "Women of the Vice President Motorcycle Motorcade."

It's a grueling job. I love it.

"I know. It's a comfortable rut." Mercedez smiles at me as only a best friend can.

I like my rut: safe and mostly predictable. After the trauma of our childhoods—don't we deserve safe and predictable?

APPLE-PIE MOONSHINE

Recipe notes from Jude's journal.

Shopping list:

- 64 oz. apple juice
- 2 ½ cups brown sugar
- Ginger
- Allspice
- Cinnamon sticks
- Grain alcohol
- Vodka

Grain alcohol–180 proof
10 days Tried to cut this by a 1/10ʰ.

- 25 lb corn meal or 25 lb shelled whole corn
- 100 lb sugar (sucrose)
- 100 gallons water
- 6 oz yeast

This one takes concentration. People love it though. Too sweet for me.

3 - MERCEDEZ JONES

"Ms. Jones, do you need unlimited text and data with this?" The clerk's overly friendly voice annoys me.

"Probably not." I consider if Jude will use this phone at all. Sweet Sally, I'll drag her into modern times, if it kills me.

Debbie, according to the name tag on her shirt, continues to press for her commission. "What about damage protection?"

I think about my fearless, rough-and-tumble Jude. "Absolutely. And tell me a little bit about these smart watches. Do you have one in purple?"

***

The first time I met Jude was on the playground, middle school. My bully of the day was Billy Barnes. I think there was a bully sign-up sheet somewhere. He had stolen the peanut butter and jelly sandwich from my lunch box and was holding it over my head. That mushed mess was my only meal for the day.

I did my best to ignore Billy Barnes while he taunted and teased, and my stomach grumbled. The lunch itself came from the neighborhood church's free lunch program. More fuel for my minor-league bullies: free lunches, skinny, poor black kid. That's what the bullies saw. They had it wrong. Raised by my aunt after my adoptive parents died, I was more forgotten than poor. She tried her best.

Billy balanced the sandwich on my buzz-cut. When I'd reach up to get it, he'd snatch it away again and sling slurs my way with an apprentice's precision.

I opened my tattered paperback, gave it my full attention. Dangerous move. Bullies dislike being ignored. Now, he had to get a rise out of me. He couldn't just turn and walk away. His face turned a brighter and brighter red, sweat beaded on his forehead, his eye twitched. He was near a boiling point and rage would go somewhere, breaking something, probably my book.

That's when Jude appeared at my side.

She sat down right next to me, squinted up at Billy, addressed him matter-of-factly, "Little man."

Gnats buzzed around our sweaty faces. Jude's hands were draped between her bruised and skinned knees. She leaned toward me, poking my leg with her finger, and said, "Peanut butter and jelly. So lame. Don't you think?"

The world and all of its problems disappeared in an instant. Lonely mornings waiting for Aunt Sue to get home from a double shift, hungry evenings when she couldn't get to the grocery store, drunk boyfriends snoring in the living room, taunting bullies, a body that didn't fit right on my own skeleton—it all became distant. I felt seen for the first time ever. I just smiled stupidly at her; Billy and my sandwich long forgotten.

"I have a BLT. Split it with me?" she asked.

A BLT. Someone loved her enough to spend time making bacon and buying fresh produce.

Jude grabbed my hand and we walked away from Billy to share a sandwich. He was mad enough to spit nails. Boy, I'd pay for that later on. But for one moment, he may as well have been on the moon.

"This phone has that face ID feature."

I'm distracted playing with my new smart watch. I deserve a little gift. "What's that?"

"Your friend can unlock her phone with her face," the clerk explains.

"The phone will be better than she is at that. She's face blind."

Miss Perky looks confused.

"Doesn't do too well with faces," I add.

I'll stop and pick up dinner for Jude. If I distract her with pizza, maybe it will make this new gadget a little easier to digest.

It damn near takes an act of murder to get her to change up anything.

4 - BIBLE BELT

The upcoming security clearance renewal for work is stressing me.

'Who pulled the trigger?'

Imaginary interview questions the psych evaluator will never ask plague my brain.

'Were you there when he shot himself?'

I quicken my steps up the stairs to my apartment, trying to outrun my thoughts.

'Do you think you are fooling anyone? You killed him didn't you?'

I just drive the bike out in front of the motorcade. Keep traffic out of the way.

'Are you fit to be on this motorcade?'

They will not ask me these questions.

'Let's not forget—you are __not__ an agent. In the off chance actual agents are not near, could you protect the Vice President? Her family?'

But the imaginary interviewer in my head, he is relentless. I fear him.

Upset with myself for once again torturing me, I slam the stairwell door.

'Fuck.'

I cringe and look down the hallway, instantly regretting making noise. Betty's door is ajar. Betty—the crazy lady from down the hall. She's no match to the sickos from my childhood, but definitely unhinged.

She listens for people like a trapdoor spider. A shadow hunched on the other side of the door, waiting to spring out at the unsuspecting bug.

The apartment unit between us is on its third tenant this year, thanks to Betty.

I slip into my apartment, hoping to avoid the spider. One last glance over my shoulder; nothing moves in the hallway. Now to drown my imagined interviewer in a steamy shower.

This is my third security clearance renewal. I have nothing to worry about. I turn the hot water up to somewhere between lava and skin peeling.

Nice. My brain quiets for a moment and stays in neutral. I focus on breathing and nothing else. Quiet. Good.

Just as I step onto the soft gray bathmat and grab a robe, I hear a knock at the door.

'Goddammit.'

I open the door to find Betty in her pajamas, wet hair, towel around her neck.

"I locked myself out. Can I use your phone, Jude?" she says, her southern accent laid on thick, dripping with honey.

Against my better judgment, I open the door wider.

"Sure. I don't have a landline. You'll have to use my cell phone." I produce my ancient flip-phone. She eyes it suspiciously.

Is everyone opinionated about my old-tech ways?

I consider offering to help her out since I have lock picks in my wallet and could probably open her door without breaking a sweat. (That's not a skill I learned in the uniformed division of the secret service—my Dad was a hobby locksmith and got a kick out of teaching his six-year-old girl how to pick locks.)

Something about Betty's demeanor—the spider-trap door being opened, and the fresh-out-of-the-shower look but not smelling daisy-fresh—makes me hesitate.

Out of habit, I don't want to reveal anything about myself to her. Growing up the way I did, learning to read psychopaths' moods and being face-blind: I have to trust my instincts.

"Are you a Christian?" she asks. Her fake smile widens but doesn't touch her scorn-filled eyes.

'Ah. Where is this conversation going to go?'

Perhaps Betty is going to launch into the "You are a sinner" conversation. People often think I'm a lesbian because I have short hair and don't wear makeup. Appearing in a uniform with a gun on my hip seals the look. Plus, surely she has seen Mercedez come into the apartment. No, we are not an item. Eww. We get confused for partners often though.

'Good-holy-fuck.' I decide to lay on the charm. "I was raised in all denominations, in fact."

She doesn't respond, doesn't move. Is she holding her breath?

Unconsciously, I read her from top to bottom. That profiling training we all had to endure—even though we at the UD, don't forget, are *not* agents—comes in handy sometimes.

I see: 70-plus, blue-tinted hair, worn flat spot on her thumb from a book. A bible maybe? Or an avid reader? Cross necklace. Bible, then. Her car in the parking lot still has Kentucky plates. Southern accent. I bet she's an *old-timey* Southern Baptist. Sometimes they don't take well to other faiths, skin types, or sexual orientation. Best to play up to that.

"But I was baptized in the Baptist church." I lie so smoothly you can feel the baptismal water go up your nose. "Come on in." Uggh. I invite her in like a stupid-head and point to the bar stools.

She takes a deep breath. Her lip curls as if she is about to lash out but she pauses, mulling over my story. Her eyes suddenly twinkle as her thoughts shift gears. "The neighbors aren't Christians at all. I asked my preacher if I could get an extra prayer book for them." She sits down and opens my phone.

A corner of the tape holding the battery in place has lifted and catches on her hand.

"They didn't take it. Said they were Catholics." She looks like she is about to spit. Her face contorts as she grimaces. "I'll pray for them."

Before I can ask if she needs the number to a locksmith, she produces a dog-eared business card from her housecoat pocket and dials the number.

Who needs a locksmith that much?

She holds the phone out, shakes it a little, and tries to get her finger free from the tape—which has pulled even further off the back of the phone.

The small screen is dark and blank. She didn't dial a number at all. Well, this woman's bread isn't completely buttered.

One last yank and the tape pulls free from her finger, taking a small piece of skin as its price. She puts the finger to her mouth, sucking at the bleeding tear.

"Oh hell," I yelp and go to the kitchen to get a hand towel. How did that even happen? Tissue for skin?

Talking around the bleeding finger, she discusses her predicament with an imaginary locksmith.

After a moment, she "hangs up" and holds the phone out to me. I use the kitchen towel to grab it, put it on the counter, hand the towel out to her.

"You can keep the towel. Sorry about the tape. That back broke off a long…" I pause, looking at the tape and thinking about her skin on it. I'm not squeamish, but well, come on—that's gross.

Betty interrupts my grossing out, "Would you like to pray with me?" She reaches forward to take my hands.

Blood drips off her finger. I stare at it. What's grosser than gross? North of her finger, brown grime streaks the side of her hand. Above that rests a plastic hand-beaded bracelet. The bracelet looks like something a kid would make from a dollar-store kit. Little faded blue crosses sit between letters spelling out her name.

"Betty, what a lovely bracelet you have there. Where did you get it?" I distract her and stay on the other side of the counter, keeping the bar between us.

"Oh, this was given to me by a missionary visiting from Haiti." She points to the B—half of it a dark, chunky brown.

That's grosser than gross. I don't want to think about the origin.

"This is made from jade," Betty says.

It is plastic. Shit covered plastic. And Betty doesn't live in the same reality that you and I do.

Heavens, she must not have met Mercedez yet. It's a safe bet a young and energetic black-trans-woman just might set Betty off. I would like to avoid a crazy shade of drama if I could.

Okay, let's not question her reality or point out anything that might upset her.

"Well, I will pray for the neighbors too," I say—walking toward the door and opening it.

She follows me to the door and says, "I should go wait at the front steps. They won't be able to get into the building"

I don't point out our apartment building has a locked entry door and she needs her keys to get back inside. The keys she said she left in her apartment. The keys are actually in her house-coat's pocket. They weigh the thin material down so it hangs lower than the right side. Right-handed, my noisy brain catalogs.

She needs to go. And I need to bleach the door handles. And my phone.

"See you later, Betty!" I jump when she tries to grab my hand again. I slip away from her grasp, put my hand almost on the back of her shoulders—but not quite touching—and will her out the door. "Best of luck with the locksmith."

"I'll get a prayer book for you too," she says as I shut the door.

Holy-get-the-god-damned-bleach. I shiver and dance in place with a full-on case of the heebie-jeebies.

I have to disinfect my phone.

I'm slathering the phone with sanitizing gel when Mercedez opens the apartment door. She has pizza in one hand, a shiny white box in the other.

"OK, Luddite-Lucy, we're going to get you hooked up into the new world," she says.

How can I fight pepperoni and bacon pizza? She even got mushrooms on my half.

Plus, at this moment my slide-phone is a biohazard and I am ready to give it up.

"You just missed a show." I fill her in on the Betty incident.

"Oh, I run the other way before she can berate me." Mercedez unwraps the new phone and pulls off the protective plastic cover. She fiddles and plinks. The weird little device lights up and beeps in response to her cajoling.

"Do you think she is dangerous?" I ask. "I mean, what if she hurts herself? Confuses bleach for apple juice. How would we even know?" I adjust my hold on the plate to keep the pizza slices from sliding off. "Here's yours." Mercedez takes the plate from me without glancing up. I continue, "I don't think she has family."

"I guess we'll know something's up when weird things stop happening to the neighbors," Mercedez answers and continues to twiddle with the phone. "Remember when she flooded that couple?"

"From Venezuela?"

"Drug a hose over, stuck it through the shared air-conditioning handler closet and watered them good."

"Hid everything before the HOA investigator got there."

"Yeah. When weird stuff like that stops, we'll know she drank the Lysol."

"She's creative."

"Let me show you how to use this." Mercedez proudly walks me through features I'll never remember.

"Here, I've made a Facebook account for you. I'll make up a name for you—security clearance blah, blah, blah—you'll probably say. Your 21st century social media name will be Jude Lawz. That's funny," she mumbles around mouthfuls of pizza, "and I'll send you a friend request."

Jude Lawz. Yeah, that's not funny. I do not—and never will—wear a badge. My Dad would spin in his grave.

Mercedez gets silent, lost in phone-land. I sit back, determined to finish the apple-pie moonshine so I can move back to just plain smoky whiskey.

Mercedez interrupts my peace saying, "I joined you into the caving group and followed this funny mixologist. I'll bet you'll love him…"

I tune her out, nod at the appropriate places. She doesn't need my approval to continue on. Mercedez—she self entertains. She picks me up when I am down. In return, I talk her off of ledges when she needs to be saved from herself.

"…in this weekend?"

Darn it, she requires words from me. "Huh?"

I'm eloquent like that sometimes.

"We still going to Caver's Heaven this weekend?" Mercedez phone buzzes like an angry hornets' nest. We both jump. She picks up the pink iridescent beast and grimaces. "Damn. I gotta sit down and handle this Instagram campaign that's got a type-o in it. Hold on, Penelope-Plum."

Just for the record, Mercedez is not from the south. She transplanted from Ohio to the Valley when we were in fourth grade. That same year *Forrest Gump* came out and Mercedez watched it 5,000 times. She doesn't exactly have a drawl, but her alliterations are totally south of the Mason-Dixon line.

Crisis averted—she experiences those hourly—she looks at me expectedly.

Mercedez has trust issues with me and plans. My job needs me sometimes at a moment's notice and I have to drop everything. It's a valid question if we still have weekend plans.

"Well, of course. It's a three-day weekend! I've got caves to visit. No local VP detail. She's in China," I assure her.

If I'm not on a motorcycle, I love to cave. Mercedez does not do either. She doesn't do dirt. You'll never find a speck of grime on her.

She *does* like to sit up there in the woods and read through a stack of paperbacks—oddly no electronic reader for Ms. 21st century—while yours truly leaves in the wee hours and returns in the evening as a battered, muddy, and bruised mess. Caving is fun that way.

I continue to explain my plans for the weekend, "I want to take the Triumph out for a spin and dust some cobwebs out of him."

For what I do not own in trinkets or hair products I make up for in motorcycles. I have three at the moment. Two stored at a friend's house up in the mountains and one here in the city. I don't even own a car. Given that my job is to drive a motorcycle no matter the weather—one gets used to driving in anything.

I also don't get asked to help people move: Win. Win.

At night the white-dragon-phone beeps and blinks at me. I glance at it a few times to see what the commotion is about. I got to get some sleep. Got to arrive at work buttoned-up. The psych-eval is just one part of a stress-me-out performance evaluation. I'm not senior and I am not in the Johnson club. Have to be tip-top, rested, and shiny—always.

'You killed him didn't you?'

Facebook profile written by Mercedez Jones
User id: Jude Lawz
Works at: Motorcycle Club for Men
Interest: Mixologist, Caving, Motorcycles
Quote: "Taste this for me—is this too sweet?"
Friends: Mercedez Jones

BIBLE BELT COCKTAIL

Recipe notes from Jude's journal.

Shake gently in shaker with ice until chilled.
Equal parts:

- Smooth whiskey of choice
- Sour mix (equal parts lemon + simple syrup)
- Half part Cointreau

Strain over ice, judging is optional.

- Garnish with lime wedges.

5 - GREEN HICK FAIRY

The alarm clock—which I won off a radio call-in contest when I was fourteen—flips to 5 a.m. and bleats. I eye the new phone suspiciously, wondering if Mercedez will notice if I keep using my flip-phone. Yes. She'll notice. I can't *not* use it. Yuck.

And further yuck, I hate mornings. But here I am, type-A personality, getting up to run before work. After a quick dash of coffee and a piece of toast, I head out to the streets.

Traffic is light. I jog through sprawling, sleepy suburbia. I keep my eyes down and avoid looking at the slim pickings of people on the street.

I accidentally make eye contact with one old lady sweeping her sidewalk. Her face swims and blurs. Look at the ground, damn it.

Face-blindness, it's a thing. Nothing registers on a face as it should. My brain tries to offer up suggestions—all wrong—I might know this person, or maybe that person. Not quite being able to trust how your brain pieces information together causes some 'hella strong social anxiety. I keep it at bay by exercising: endorphins. And keeping my eyes down.

The burn in my legs intensifies and I push a little further, setting my sights on reaching the Lincoln Memorial as my turnaround point. The burning fades and those lovely endorphins kick in. Yes.

The heat of the day hasn't reached broiling yet. I rest on the wide marble steps—not yet filled with tourists—to enjoy the moment. Maybe there are some good things about early mornings, like beat the heat and the crowds.

Some early birds climb the steps, take selfies trying to capture the Washington Monument in the distance.

What does face-blind mean? I can see people. Their hair, their physical markers, but the bits on their face don't record together. I've never remembered an eye color in my life. Unless they have an enormous nose, huge creases around their mouth, or maybe remarkable eyebrows—my brain records nothing.

Actually, I didn't even know about it for most of my life. I thought I was just an asshole and didn't care about people, really. Secretly, I worried maybe I was a closet psychopath; maybe it's in the genes, you know? I mixed friends up all the time and always get anxious when in crowds. As a defense mechanism, I stay away and keep to myself.

I found out years ago in FLETC training (Federal Law Enforcement Training Center) being face-blind can be a benefit—except for the anxiety.

I was in my late twenties. We had a recall exercise. This is where someone busts into the room you are receiving a lecture in and tells everyone to drop to the floor. Usually they are holding a gun.

A toy gun. Much of the group I was with were once police officers. Jaded as fuck. They burst out laughing at the toy gun. It lasted for only a second.

The agent lecturing at the front of the room bellowed, "Down. Now."

The guy at the front with the orange tipped toy gun added, "You're dead. All of you motherfuckers are dead! Face down!"

The older fellows griped as they got to the ground. I was already there, smelling the musty carpet.

He couldn't have been there for 5 seconds, yelling and waving his toy before he left. The agent took command at the front of the room and we all sat back in our chairs.

"Describe the invader," he said.

"Twat with a toy pistol."

"Rookie, did you see anything from your advanced position on the carpet?" the agent asked me.

"Not quite six foot. Red Washington National's ball cap. New. Bald or shaved head. Caucasian. White, scuffed Reebok tennis shoes. Missing eyelet on the left shoe: outside, second hole." I answered without looking up.

"Anything else?"

"Gun was in the left hand. Right hand holding the butt wasn't closed all the way. Hurt ring finger. Sprain, cut, or arthritis, maybe. Oh, black gloves." I dared to look up at the agent and try to read his expression.

Blank. Nothing. Light eyebrows in a neutral position. No creases to read on his face. I dropped my eyes.

That evening we had a pot-luck dinner at someone's hotel room: brought in our favorite foods, stood around the single beds, spilled out onto the patio. During training, they housed us in nearby hotels.

I set up a large thermos of margaritas on the dormant wall A/C unit. Even back then, I had a thing for making drinks for everyone. It made them happy—who doesn't want to give happiness to their friends? My friend Darren came up and poured himself a drink. He was smiling from ear to ear.

"What did you think? Convincing?" He asked. His grin grew even wider.

I had no idea what he was talking about so I poured myself a drink hoping he would give me some more clues.

He continued, "You know I'm not left handed so that isn't impressive. The missing eyelet on the shoe and the arthritic ring finger—that's impressive."

I smiled to mask my surprise. The guy I had known for months had been the intruder in the training room earlier. Darren, the guy who had been my sparring partner in hand-to-hand combat class more often than not. Darren, the guy who had been the first to master handcuffing techniques and offered to show me pointers (in a non-creepy way). I hadn't recognized him. He picked up on my surprise.

"You didn't know it was me did you?"

"Nope."

"Well, it was a quick look." He smiled. "And this handsome mug was behind a mask."

I grimaced good-naturedly and we laughed it off. Everyone had a good time bonding that night. The Margaritas were a hit. Not a single drop was left.

How can you tell your friends, "Hey, I can't recognize you right away. But give me a sec, I'll put it together." Meanwhile, you stand there like the village idiot looking at your best friend blankly until you recognize how they move.

Darren holds his nose up when he talks.

Every time I admit to someone I'm face-blind, they look at me like I'm lying. How could I not recognize someone I've known for years? It's a blow to the self-esteem. Theirs and mine.

It didn't take long for me to realize I remember everyone on context clues: body movement, hairstyles, body type, voice, etc.

I recognize people from the back of their heads and looking at their ears more quickly than looking at their faces. It's impossible when everyone has the same buzz cut and wears the same uniform.

A group of middle-schoolers in matching uniforms bustle toward me on the steps. I cringe. They are a moving group of sameness. Similar heights, hairstyles, clothing, energy. The only thing I can see is variations of hair color and one little kid who hangs back. She's not with the other kids. I look at their faces, but they almost appear blurry to me, no features stand out; some teeth filled smiles, that's all. The slower little girl stops in front of me and I smile at her. Mistake. Her face is more than a blur. It is a flesh mask. I can see no features. Perhaps she's fair-haired or lacks eyebrows. I look again. No face. It makes me sick to my stomach. I look away quickly.

I've learned to live with it. And avoid eye contact. It didn't get in the way of my FLETC training for the UD. And hasn't affected my job. Yet.

***

Friday, finally. I'm looking forward to a three-day weekend. Caving and riding motorcycles around twisty mountain roads for me. Maybe I can stop worrying about the psych eval for a few days. Having finished all my paperwork, requisition forms, etc., there's one last thing to do—polish my bike.

I jaunt down to the unit's garage where the smells of steel and grease sooth me. Reminds me of my Dad's shop. Many of the guys are already there doing the last detail on the bikes before heading out for the weekend. A few of them look my way and nod when I walk in.

I like to keep my bikes sparkling clean. At work, it's a mandate.

A dog-eared poster from the 80s hangs next to the lockers. It reads, *Buttoned-up for the Unit!'* Next to it hangs a Polaroid hall of shame. Artful and faded pictures of windshields with bird shit, pipes with scuffs, and one smiling dude with a melting ice cream cone on his helmet. I haven't made it to the wall, yet.

One hour to polish and I'm out of here. I pat my HOG, promising her a good shine. I've put 150,000 hard-earned miles on this Harley Davidson. She's a beauty. A little thick across the hips. But her chrome is spotless, her windshield is haze-free, and the presidential seal on the front fender is shitless.

My locker sticks a little, so I yank up to open it. Inside, at eye-level, my wire basket of cleaning supplies is missing a few things.

Fuck. Those guys.

There is a difference between torturing someone and hazing a team member. I think the picking on me comes in as the latter. That's what I tell myself, anyway. I look around the room slyly, noting no one makes eye contact. Some hold helmets in front of their faces to hide wide smiles.

On top of the lockers—well above my head—sits my favorite soft, fuzzy, yellow polishing rag. Undeterred, I pull over a stool and a windshield squeegee. The stool's metal feet squeak against the concrete floor as I stand on it. Using the handle, I retrieve the rag without dropping it to the ground—making it a scratching rag and not a polishing rag.

Where's that purple spray can? It gets kidnapped often. Looks like something from the dollar store. The guys can't get enough of making fun of it.

At first I don't see it. Scott—wide and square dude—stops polishing his bike, looks above him. Thanks for the clue. Next beer is on me. There it is, on a steel rafter fifteen feet above us. Sitting there. Not just sitting there. Duct taped there. Stepping up their game, I see.

I know what they are expecting. They are expecting me to break out a rope and climb up to retrieve the spray, caver style. Last time it was in the A/C vent, ten feet back. I had to wiggle in to get it.

With a flourish, I open a gym bag in my locker and pull out a spare can.

One of the nearby guys smacks his bike seat and says, "Aw Jude, that's cheating."

I smile smugly and polish. The poster on the wall scolds me, *'Buttoned-up for the Unit!'* I can't leave the can up there. We'll get docked points in an inspection and everyone knows whose can that is.

I wait till the bay clears and go back to my locker. It's quiet. Every noise is twenty times too loud. Inside my bag, next to the extra purple can of Sparkling Shine, I keep a 30-foot length of green webbing. I don't know why. It goes into my cave pack on the weekends. You never know when you need to climb or descend, right?

I tie knots with loops hanging off every thirteen inches. Almost silently, I throw the webbing over the rafter and tie the dangling end to a nearby paint-chipped hydraulic lift. As an afterthought, I put a helmet on—I mean, safety first—and stick my foot into the lowest loop. The webbing sways as I climb toward the kidnapped spray can.

"I saw that," Darren says from the shadows. The same Darren who once pulled a toy gun on us in training, and I didn't recognize him. His left foot turns in slightly, walks on the outside of the foot. Bunion is my guess. Must hurt like hell when he's on a watch assignment and has to stand for nine hours straight—on a short day.

Unhitching my webbing, I say, "Just another day on the UD."

UD stands for Uniformed Division or Ugly Dicks, depends on my mood.

"The guys like to pick on you." Darren holds out his hand for the spray can. He pulls the duct tape off while I finish braiding the length of webbing. "We're all going out for some dinner. Want to join?"

Usually, I don't go out with the team. I always feel like I'm putting a damper on their conversations. Though, honestly, I don't think they pull any punches or avoid any topic of conversation on my account, come to think of it. Even if it was a group of women I'd probably think the same thing. Honestly, I just don't enjoy hanging out with people.

The face-blind thing, that's part of it. Besides, I just like to be quiet and be on my own. People think I'm a snob because of it. Working in a team of men—well that doesn't help me win friends over.

I agree to go.

It isn't so bad after all, not really. We all gather at a nearby hole-in-the-wall bar. This place is fabulous, old, the walls look like they hold secrets.

I'm down to the final French fry on my plate and sopping up the last morsel of ketchup when Darren asks about my upcoming caving plans.

I get super jazzed when I talk about caving. I also get very self-conscious about my excitement. But, he asked.

"I'm not doing much, really. Going to bounce some pits on Saturday."

"How deep?" Bobby, a tall guy, late thirties, slouches when he sits, has a long-haired cat, and a scar on the inside of his finger from a childhood injury.

"185, I think."

"Do you ever go alone?" Scott. His chest is wide and square—a football player in his youth.

"You are not supposed to. That way you have someone to help if you fall."

"You ever fallen?" Darren offers his half-eaten plate of fries to me.

I accept the offered fries. "Yes. It was hilarious."

And it was. I tell them the story of this amazing fall I took and came out completely unscratched.

I was out with one other caver and we were trying to find a passage called the step across. We had visited the cave two other times and each time we couldn't find this passage. Frank, my caving partner, had gone up ahead of me to see if the passage was through this narrow opening. I stayed on the outside of the opening on a ledge. The ledge was about seven feet up in the air. The rocks jutted out a bit so you could climb up.

So I was standing there, my head ducked a little into the rock doorway, calling to Frank and asking if he had found anything. The way ahead was narrow and I couldn't see him. The passage had turned to the right.

Just then, I heard a bat coming at me, and caught a glimpse of it in my light. These bats are cute. Not scary at all. They are just little things, like a cute mouse with wings. I knew I was in his way. I decided to duck down so the bat could fly over my head and out into the bigger passage. The air was very still and super dark except for my helmet. I couldn't even hear Frank, and he probably wasn't even thirty feet away from me. I ducked down, but as I ducked I took a step backwards. Only problem was—there was nothing behind me. So I took a Nestle-tea-plunge right off the ledge.

Three things happened at the same time. One, my right toes somehow caught in a rock crack and wedged in. Two, my left foot caught on a rock outcrop. Miraculously, my boot-heel hung on the edge of the rock. Three, my left arm grasped a boulder. And. Did. Not. Let. Go. All three points of contact stopped my fall.

My helmet stopped three inches from the rock ground. I would have broken my neck. My legs hurt like hell screaming for release from their weird pinning. My right shin screamed the loudest, and for a hot second I thought I might have cracked the leg. That's the first foot I freed, while still holding onto that rock with my left arm's steadfast grip. Then I freed the left foot. I lowered my feet to the ground and just stood there amazed. I took a beat to pat myself down, make sure I wasn't missing any message from an appendage bent at the wrong angle or something. But everything was just as it should be.

I climbed back up the rock face and popped through that little tunnel and called out to Frank saying, "You won't believe what I just did."

He popped his head into the passage from an opening at the top, his head upside down, and said, "I found the step-over. Get your webbing."

It's hard to talk about caving to people who haven't done it. They look at you like you are crazy. And these are guys who literally drill in hand-to-hand combat and endurance testing. We all balance on a two-wheeled vehicle for hours on end no matter if it is ice, high-wind, rain, hail. We've learned how to ditch our bike safely, jump off, pick it back up again and carry on as if nothing ever happened. Hell, we could probably shoot a moving target while doing it. And if I think that one out loud some son-of-a-bitch will make a training scenario for it.

By the end of my story, Darren, Scott and the others are staring at me, their food forgotten.

"Are my antennae showing?" I ask.

"You could have broke your neck." Darren motions for the server to bring the check. She is already on it.

"We could break our necks on our motorcycles everyday. No different."

"Way different."

I shrug. "I'll take any of you to a cave if you want to check one out."

No one makes eye contact.

"I don't like camping," Scott says.

"You don't have to camp to cave." I give a credit card to the server. "Besides, you should see the camper Mercedez has parked up there. We glamp."

There are mumbles of encouragement and someone at the other end of the table comments about the game. Conversations shift. A sinking sensation of alien-ness settles to the pit of my stomach, an unwanted condiment for the French fries. No one knows what to say when I talk about caving. Maybe the Mercedez reference weirds them out? They aren't like that, are they?

Square peg in a round hole—that's me. Unless I'm in my element, maybe, like a three-day weekend at Caver's Heaven.

"What the hell is that?" Mercedez has her fuzzy pink slippers resting on a log destined for the fire. She is often confused about what items are and requires clarification.

A gathering of five caver friends circles the small camper's pop up tiki bar. The nearby fire roars and crackles. Having devoured a ton of hamburgers and hot-dogs we retire to the tiki bar, complete with carved totems and plastic tiki cups.

If ever there were a definition of class and poise, it is Mercedez. I don't think dirt sticks to her. Imagine such a perfectly poised person in the middle of a camping ground behind a tiki bar hanging off the side of our small camper. She owns the place and exudes power from her petite frame.

If you are guessing the tiki bar has a rug thrown down on the grass—you have a great imagination and are correct. Having Mercedez around is like having a themed camping event with spontaneous social media trending commentary at all times.

I'm setting up a bottle of green liquor when Mercedez rudely interrupts me to ask for explanations. I turn to the group in front of us, "This is absinthe made from moonshine. You can make it from vodka or according to the website I found this recipe on: pure ethanol."

Cathy leans forward, "What makes it green? Is it lime?" Cathy: average-height, small scar on her eyebrow which interrupts the hair growth and always makes her look like she is asking a question. Likes baking. Dislikes exposed rock-climbs. Sews.

"Two ingredients make it green: Lemon balm and Hyssop. Lemon balm is a kind of mint herb. Hyssop is a minty thing too. I used to think it was lavender. Except it doesn't smell like lavender." I hold the bottle to the light and admire the green glow of the liquor within. "It tastes just the same with or without the green."

I place a row of small glasses on the bar, complete with small silver spoons over the top of them. "You put the sugar cube on the spoon." I hold up a spoon. "See, it has a bat cut out of the center. Brandy made them for me with a little jewelry saw."

"Wait." Mercedez jumps out of her chair. "That's a good picture." She moves my hand, adjusts a candle, squats, mumbles, and finally takes a few pictures. "I'm going to make a hashtag for you. Spelunking Bartender."

I groan audibly.

"I know, it's a derogatory term. Cavers rescue spelunkers. Yaddata, yaddata." She waves her hand at me in annoyance and goes back to her seat, holding her phone in the air and muttering to the one bar of reception, "Maybe Speleo Bartender. Speleo Sauce. Sauced Spelunker." Her thumbs tap and she stares deeply into her phone, looking at what I can only assume is a place that creates hashtags. Is there a hashtag store?

The spoon clinks when I pour the green absinthe over the sugar cubes, sweetening the drink.

We all take the glasses and hand them around.

Cathy toasts, "To dark holes."

We all beam, looking forward to the dark holes we will explore in the morning.

"To dark holes!" everyone cries in unison.

I warn, "Sip. Sip. Don't chug."

We sip to the toast and everyone looks at the green liquid with suspicion before trying a second sip.

The night goes by and not once do I feel awkward. This group, we're all types. Doesn't matter where they are from, what they do, what they believe in. We're just cavers sitting around the fire. There's no other feeling like it.

Those are my different circles. The UD division in D.C. where I love my job, love to ride, have an excellent team, but don't feel a part of anything—and my caving family in Tennessee where people unify through their craziness of wanting to crawl into muddy holes. Through it all, Mercedez is my stable constant.

***

The next day, I leave Mercedez to read her stack of trashy paperbacks and meet my friends to bounce pits.

Brandy calls out from the bottom of the pit, "OFF ROPE!" With her gear unclipped from the rope, she steps out of the way.

My turn. "I swear, I never come to this damn pit unless it is hot as blazes outside. Why is that?" I take hold of the rope while standing two body lengths away from the edge of the pit.

Mark stands further away from the rock ledge awaiting his turn. His yellow rain slicker flaps at his side where duct tape has given way. "We like to sweat."

"ON ROPE!" I yell to Brandy and Susan below then turn back to Mark and say, "See you at the bottom."

He smiles and quips, "Safe travels."

Mark, Brandy, and Susan are a good bunch of cavers. I like going out with them. We mesh. I think Brandy and Susan are from north Florida, maybe? Mark is from somewhere up here in TAG. (Tennessee, Alabama, Georgia: where all the caves are.)

I clip in, test my rappel rack, and descend into the pit. Just as I sit into my harness and lean back, I notice Mark has his camera out. I smile and he takes the picture.

"I'll give this to Mercedez," he calls out. "She'll put it to good use."

Uggh, I'm sure I look like a goober in his picture. Photogenic—that's NOT me. I think. I actually wouldn't know since I can't see my own face.

I sit further back into my seat harness. God, I love this part. Just when my feet are on the edge of the pit and I'm hanging out over nothing. The blue sky goes on forever as the darkness does below. I've never done it at night—bet that would be wonderful. Just being there in nothing and then descending into the open air pit with nothing around you. The rope makes a whizzing sound as it goes through the metal rack. I keep my left hand on the rack to apply pressure—like a brake—so I can go slow and take in the sites.

Flying. That's what I like about motorcycles and being on rope. It's as close to flying without wings as I can get.

We all get to the bottom and Mark breaks out his camera again. We ham it up for few pictures and then queue up to take our turn climbing out of the cave.

Climbing out of a cave isn't hand over hand on a rope like you did—or tried to do—in gym class. We have clips of various types that either pin our feet to the rope so we can use walking type steps to climb, or we have a clip at our waist and we use a sit-stand motion with foot-loops to climb up the rope.

No matter how much cardio I do, I still have to take breaks on the way up. Brandy is on the other rope near me. She takes breaks alongside of me so we can chat.

No big deal—chatting, 150-plus feet off the ground.

"I have my security clearance re-up coming up. They want a list of friends and acquaintances to interview. Would you mind being on that list?" I ask Brandy.

"Sure thing! I like it when G-men come visit me." She looks down at Mark and Susan below us. "Half the time I get put on someone's friend list the G-men don't show though."

"It should be no big deal." Though it is a big deal in my head. I look up ahead, trying to guess how many breaks I can take. Cardio. I gotta do more cardio. I run. But it's different. Perhaps I fear the heights and it doesn't register. Maybe adrenaline is sapping my strength. I worry more about the climbing up than the descending. Because the climbing up has to do solely with my strength. What if I run out of umph? Descending. Don't fall. Almost anyone can do that.

We talk, chat. She's met someone new recently but hasn't heard from him in a while.

"Maybe he has another girlfriend or something," Brandy says as we near the top of the climb. "I feel stupid worrying."

"It's been a while since you chanced a relationship." I look above us, fifty feet left. "One more break?"

"Sure. What about you?"

"If I get lonely, I'll get a dog."

"I like Mercedez's cat. What's her name?"

"Whiskers. Yeah, a cat would be better." I move up the rope a few inches and Brandy matches my climb. "A cat isn't much trouble."

***

That night around the fire, my body aches in an amazing way. It's different from a normal workout. This type of workout uses so many parts of your body you just don't think about. That, and the adrenalin I suppose you get from hanging 200 feet in the air, does a body good.

I stretch and settle into my lounge chair.

Mercedez levels a gaze at me. "When are you going to move up here? It suits you better than the city."

"I can't stay on the motorcycle motorcade forever. I'll have to give it up one day, I suppose." I must not come across as convincing because Mercedez shrugs then glares at me.

"You don't worry about things when you are up here. Have you worried about your psych eval since we've been here?"

I don't answer. Damn, but she makes valid points.

"Stop looking at me in that tone of voice." I try to level the gaze back. I just don't have that much judgment in me.

She softens. "Do you want me to show you how to post a pic on Facebook?"

I don't, but also don't have the guts to tell her that. We post the pic Mark took on Facebook. Now the world can see me.

Facebook friend request for Jude Lawz:
- MercedezJones– Accepted
- Brandy Bayents– Accepted
- Susan Gibbons – Accepted
- Mark Oliver – Accepted
- Darren J. – Accept or Ignore?

First post: *We spent the day trying to find a pit. Finally found it.* [Picture shows Jude, on rope, in a pit, looking up at the photographer, Mark.]

Privacy set to friends only.

Comments:
"Great day as always!" —Mark
2 likes from Brandy and Mercedez

GREEN HICK FAIRY

Recipe notes from Jude's journal.

Absinthe from moonshine

Shopping list:

- Moonshine (80-85%) – 1 liter
- Bitter wormwood (dried) – 100 gr
- Anise seeds – 50 gr
- Fennel seeds – 50 gr
- Lemon balm – 5 gr (for shade)
- Hyssop – 10 gr (for shade)

Oh look, I don't have to cut this recipe down by 1/100th! Tastes like licorice. This one takes a lot of dedication.

6 - RANKINGS

It took all morning for me to come up with a proper strategy for Jude and her love of mixing drinks. I think she should get out there, show the world this crazy magic she can do with a handful of liquids.

The campground is quiet. The cavers have headed out to the woods to get muddy together, and I have the place to myself. I read a little. Work a little (on fun stuff) then read some more.

The reception is spotty and I have no email or Instagram campaigns running this weekend so I can relax. Today, I'm blue-skying ideas for Jude. Watching her make the drinks last night for everyone got me to thinking. She should start a YouTube channel or an Instagram, or both.

I stand to stretch my legs. The quiet and solitude comforts me. A distant sound of a four-wheel Mule bounces through the trees; the campground owner making the rounds.

I walk to the bathhouse, past little camp sites, a communal fire-pit, and the path towards the nude hot-tub. I don't go there. I couldn't imagine being that exposed.

I wash my face in the sink. My reflection stares back at me. The hum of the fluorescent light buzzes.

I am not trying to change Jude. I made that mistake once.

"Jude, sit here and let me give you a makeover," I had demanded. This was probably right after her mom died, and before her brother shot himself. But before I got the shit beat out of me, a direct result of witnessing something horrible. Macabre time markers.

"Uggh," she protested, but sat.

I turned her on the bar stool so she faced the plastic-framed mirror in her mom's dining room. It needed dusting.

"My cousin gave me all of her old make-up. Some of it is brand new. Look." I held out a treasure trove of mismatched cosmetics.

Politely she examined them then said, "I never wear that stuff. Feels heavy."

I placed a glamour magazine on the table and pointed to Minnie Driver. "We could make you look like that."

Jude wrinkled her nose and shrugged. "I can curl my hair like that. I'll show you. Mom taught me."

"Ok," I answered.

Together we applied mascara, blush, contouring, straightened and curled hair resulting in a poor attempt to match the magazine picture.

"Tada," I spun her back towards the mirror.

I wish she had burst into tears. She didn't. Instead, she shrunk into herself, almost afraid.

Jude tried to say something, only a strangled whimper escaped her glossy, ruby red lips.

Knowing now what we didn't know then about her face-blindness, I realize we created a face she did not know and it made her extremely uncomfortable.

Experiencing crushing dysphoria for not feeling right in your body. I get that.

I still feel bad about that sometimes. I shouldn't have tried to "make her pretty." She's beautiful without any help. She has the kind of soul that is unapologetically its own.

My phone chimes. It's a picture of Jude on rope from Mark. Perfect. I'll show her how to post this to Facebook tonight. She's so happy. That smile. Hanging over an expanse. I don't know how deep that pit is, and she's beaming from ear to ear.

I hope me bringing Jude into the open doesn't backfire like that makeover. I think she needs to come up in her own rankings, that's all. I want to shine a light on who she is and what she does. I want people to see her and love her as much as I do.

Things in the digital world can't hurt you, right?

7 - JOLLY JELLY SHOTS

Mercedez and I pack on Monday for the drive back to D.C.

"Can you check that the tiki bar is locked up?" Mercedez asks.

"I did. Also put the leftover booze over at the gazebo with a note. Someone will love it," I answer.

"Well, the drive is sure better from DC than when we lived in California."

"Makes me happy to get out here to TAG more now." I pat the camper. It stays here at the campground, always waiting for us. "I didn't get any of the bikes out this weekend. Well, next trip."

Before Mercedez can draw her next breath, I know what she is going to say.

"We could be here all the time, you know," she says.

"What would I do? Go back into fancy fake security like I did in California?" I gesture to the woods. "There's a severe lack of famous people needing a flashy bodyguard detail here."

My boss, when I worked for a security firm in L.A., once looked at me and said, "One day you are going to walk in and give me a pink slip saying you're leaving for Tennessee."

He wasn't wrong. I did ditch everything to apply for the Uniformed Division so I could do my favorite thing: ride a motorcycle, get paid for it, be closer to the caves of TAG.

"Obviously, I'd move with you to Tennessee just like I moved with you to D.C." Mercedez turns from the car, looks at me.

I know that look. For a moment, all the strength and gusto she has—cracks, and I see that nine-year-old kid fighting to fit in, afraid of being shunned. It breaks my heart. If she only knew how amazing she is.

"Of course I want you to be here with me in Tennessee. I never want to be without you." I take the keys from Mercedez. "Here, I'll take the first shift until lunch."

It was my idea to move to D.C. and Mercedez jumped at the chance of putting the old memories behind. Everyone at my old security job thought I was crazy. They didn't say it out loud, but they thought it was a fool's dream. No girl was going to make it onto the UD.

FYI: I'm not the first woman in the division, but I have the bathroom to myself. The security team couldn't understand why I would leave a cushy job of getting paid top dollar to babysit pretty people with money and make them feel safe.

Traffic is light. We drive with the top down on Mercedez's silver Miata. I'm looking forward to this upcoming week. We have a few details moving the VP around and I picked up an extra detail escorting a visiting dignitary.

I try not to think about the psych eval.

'Did you pull the trigger?'

Mindless driving. Moving. Keeping my brain on the moment. Staying safe. Caving on the weekends once or so a month. This life is good. It can't get much better.

I'm perfectly happy with zoning out while being perfectly attuned to the moment. Motorcycles and caving. You can't think of anything else, can't be distracted by anything else. You can only focus on what you are doing and what your surroundings are. Otherwise—you or someone else gets hurt.

My work phone buzzes and I hand it to Mercedez.

She reads it silently for a minute then summarizes, "Your psych eval has been scheduled in three weeks. You need to do your physical eval first."

I say nothing. All the wind leaves my body.

"Want me to reply?" she asks.

"Write 'received'."

We drive in silence.

"You've passed all the ones before. I wish you wouldn't get keyed up about this," Mercedez finally says.

"I can't help it. There's a list of weird things that could be used against me being fit," I say. I point to an upcoming exit and ask, "Hungry yet?"

"Not yet. Name them," she answers.

"Face-blindness."

"So you see people like Sherlock Holmes, all their little bits. Like, every single little detail."

"He is an asshole. I could be labeled as an adrenaline seeker. You know, caving." I look longingly at the exit signs for food. We'll need gas in another 100 miles. Food then.

"I think everyone that rides the motorcycles fits into that category. Keep reaching," Mercedez answers and looks at the passing cars.

"Okay. The drinks. Making drinks as a hobby and sharing them with friends makes me another type of psychological risk: an enabler." I grasp as test anxiety grips me.

Mercedez groans and side-eyes me.

"How exactly did your brother die?"

The invisible interviewer steps into my consciousness and takes over my peaceful drive.

"You are unfit to hold a firearm and protect anyone," he says.

I know it makes me vulnerable and a risk.

Buried past. Yup, that's me.

***

Three weeks later, Mercedez buzzes into my apartment without even knocking. She has a key. But what if—I mean, just for a second think—what if I was walking around naked? She wouldn't care, I suppose, and neither would I. She knows I don't date so there's no chance of her finding me riding cowboy or something. I'm not interested. I hear there's a term for it nowadays that isn't "broken" as I was led to understand growing up. The kids call it "Ace". Who knew?

"I got the gelatin. Why don't you ask for anything normal?" She plops a small brown bag on the countertop.

I am elbow deep in making a mess as Mercedez breezes in smelling of lilacs. "I'm trying to make shot glasses with Jolly Ranchers. I saw this guy on Facebook do it."

"Ha! I told you you'd like him!" Mercedez beams.

"Okay. Okay. You were right. I like some things about this century. Now stop gloating and hand me that gelatin. I ran out." I have three glass mixing bowls lined up with vodka infused with Jolly Ranchers: red, green, and blue.

"Gelatin." Mercedez slaps the box of gelatin into my open palm like a dutiful nurse. She pokes on her phone, then places it on the counter to watch my energetic argument with gravity, gelatin, and vodka.

I mix, stir, and cuss; pour the mixtures into the awaiting plastic Dixie cup molds. The green one goes perfectly. The red and blue tip over, spilling their contents all over the pumpkin colored counter.

"Son of a holy mess." I yelp and grab the nearest towel, a sacrifice to the food coloring gods.

"My phone!" Mercedez saves her device. It is nowhere near in danger. Perceptions are a reality—whatever.

"Well, I'll have to try that one again. Thanks for the gelatin. We have at least two shot glasses." I put them in the fridge to set. "While that sets, I got a crock-pot going. You want some chicken and rice?" I hold out a steaming spoonful for Mercedez's approval.

We fill bowls with steaming rice and I hope she won't remember what had been on my schedule for the day.

No such luck, Mercedez has a fine memory. She asks, "So, how did the interview go today?"

"Oh, that was a train wreck. I don't want to talk about it." My heart sinks to consider talking about it. "It was just the first psych eval. It's not over yet. I don't even know what their findings were. The senior reviewer will compile everything together and then interview me next week."

Mercedez doesn't say a word. She goes to the fridge to check the firmness of the Jell-O shot.

I keep blathering, "All this time I hoped the face-blind thing was going to get in the way, or the booze, or caving. But it was the worst. They actually asked questions about my brother. Like I'm unstable or something."

I can't talk anymore about it. I knew it would get me, eventually.

'Who pulled the trigger?'

Instead I ask, "How's the firmness?" I point towards the two congealing Jell-O shots in the fridge.

"Almost." She pulls out a carton of chocolate chip cookie dough ice cream. "We could just go straight for this, huh?"

And we do. She doesn't ask anymore questions. I avoid bursting into tears.

My brother. I don't talk about my past. I have no one. Parents are dead. Mom when I was 15—cancer. Dad when I was 20—heart attack. My one brother—dead too. Suicide. I was there.

Yeah. That stuff—you don't talk about it.

We end up hatching a plan for our next visit to Tennessee. Mercedez gets a lot of frequent flyer miles and she likes to spoil me.

"Let's do a high-end weekend. No dirt?" Mercedez begs. "I can rent a cabin in the woods, or at that Smokey Inn place on the bluff. You can go ride your bike around the twisty roads and clear your head. What do ya' say, Sally Sugar?"

"I can pitch in for the cabin."

***

Less than 48 hours later, we are in the same positions around a kitchen counter in a rented cabin on a Tennessee bluff. I am setting up to make Jell-O shots again.

"Wait." Mercedez holds up her dainty hand. "Let's make a video of you making these."

I can't argue. She is already pulling out a travel tripod and a clip-on circle of LED lights.

"Do you always pack that?" I ask.

"Do you always pack caving gear?" she parries.

She isn't wrong.

"You never know when you need to check out a cave."

I set everything up on the counter so her camera can capture it all. She moves everything and shoos me out of the way.

"I finally came up with just the right hashtag, by the way. The Tipsy Caver." She pauses and looks at me. "Stand here and lean in a little."

"I dunno. Don't know if I speak for all cavers." I watch Mercedez line up her camera. "Keep my face out of it. Security clearance and all. You know, if I haven't already blown it." Self pity, my finest feature.

"What was that article about you when you made the UD team?" Mercedez asks, pushing the Jell-O molds closer together.

"Dykes on bikes."

Mercedez looks at me harshly until I answer, "Wonder Women of the UD." I grimace, cause who doesn't love getting a headline because you own a vagina.

"Mmmmhmmmm. Your stock is high. And you have a spotless record." Mercedez pokes at the app on her phone, adjusts the LED lights to shine warmer; stands back, gives a nod and says, "You didn't blow the psych eval. No negative thoughts allowed. Okay, girl. Big, deep breath. We're not in D.C. right now. We are in your favorite place on earth. Just talk to me about the drink you are making."

"My face?" I can't tell where the evil blinky light and its lens points.

"Getting you from the cleavage to the table only."

"Uggh." My cleavage is scant. I'm pretty much built like a box, not a lot of curves, thicker butt and thighs—unlike Mercedez. She paid for those fair and square.

I stare at her.

"Oh, good lord. I'm going to look out the window here to this gorgeous sunset. Look at this! This as an opening shot."

We both look out at the sun setting over the valley. The cabin we rented is on a bluff overlooking a state forest. It is amazing how quiet it is outside—and how deafening. So many crickets and frogs and I-don't-know-what-else yammering on.

"I think I should buy a place up here," I whisper. "Maybe one day I'll need to have a safe place to go to and start all over again. I don't know what I'd do to make ends meet—but I could start all over again here for sure."

Mercedez opens the French doors and walks out onto the porch to get a better shot of the trees blowing in the breeze. "It's pretty peaceful up here. You know, I can do my job from anywhere. Just sayin'."

We stand in silence and watch the sun slip away until there is nothing left but a burning glow behind the purple horizon. I take my position behind the counter, ready to make the drinks.

Mercedez points her phone towards the sorbet sky then turns it towards me, trying to get the best shot of the flasks and candies I had scattered on the marble counter.

"Show me how to make a Jolly Jello Shot," she says, "and don't worry about your voice. Since we don't see your face, we can do a voice over later. Just use graceful hands to show the camera the steps."

"I have man hands."

Whiskers, Mercedez's cat, jumps onto the counter near us. We brought her for this civilized weekend trip inside. I hold a

Jolly Rancher out to she so she can sniff it. She gives her approval and sits down to watch the show.

Mercedez adjusts her camera position to get the cat in the frame. Her long black and white fur fluffs out around her majestically.

I use powdered Jell-O mixes this time and set up three glass mixing bowls with red, green, and blue concoctions. Whiskers asks to sniff the vodka shot and grimaces slightly when I hold the shot glass out for her.

"Wait, do that again. I want a close-up."

I hold the shot glass out again and Whiskers sniffs slightly but otherwise ignores me. She slumps on the counter and folds her feet under her body, full loaf mode.

Mercedez and her phone follow my every move as I pull the Jell-O shot glasses out of the refrigerator and carefully take them from their molds. They jiggle gleefully. I dab the edges of the jiggly brightly colored shot glasses in corn syrup and roll them in crushed up Jolly Ranchers.

"Close-up," Mercedez whispers.

I accommodate her. Whiskers bats at her long hair.

"The last step," I continue to narrate, "is to pour in the liquor of your choice. We're going to use a green-apple vodka."

I pour the vodka into the shot glasses and line them up on a white serving tray Mercedez had bought at the—gasp—dollar store. There aren't many places to shop when you have a state forest in your front yard.

"We probably should have some legal disclaimer or something posted in the comments," Mercedez mumbles.

"Use your noggin' and drink responsibly. Read the doobly-doo in the comments."

Mercedez smirks. "Doobly-doo?" She positions for a good shot of the glasses and the cat.

"Doo-hickey?"

Whiskers takes a keen interest in the shot glasses and I set a Jell-O shot glass closer to her.

"What do you think, Whiskers?" I ask.

Whiskers stares at the Jell-O shot glass. She paws at it and it wiggles about. Then, in one deft swoop, she pushes it off the counter and it splashes to the floor.

We both stand stock still, then burst out laughing. Mercedez puts down the phone and picks the cat up. "Holy crap, Whiskers. Don't cost me my security deposit!"

"Tipsy caver? More like Tipsy Kitty," I say.

***

The stars hang like perfectly blazing diamonds. We rock leisurely in the rocking chairs on the porch, a gentle breeze in our face. The weather isn't too uncomfortable for July, 70 degrees. D.C. will be another story when we return.

"Do you want to talk about it yet?" Mercedez ventures. She holds up the half-eaten shot glass. "This wasn't half bad."

"Thanks. And—no. It does me no good to worry about something I can't control. The subject has come up before and I passed the review and they deemed me as 'stable' enough. No reason it should cause a problem this time."

"But?"

"But, he asked questions they didn't ask last time. He kept drilling in on if I went to therapy afterwards. Did I bury the trauma? How did I process it? What if I find myself in the same situation again—what if someone was holding a gun on themselves, or on a protectorate, or me? Would I freeze?"

"That was twenty years ago." Mercedez reaches over and holds my hand.

We rock in silence for a while. Mercedez knows. She was there.

The phone in her lap buzzes and she squeezes my hand before letting go to look at the beast. After a few moments, she mumbles to herself in tech talk. Something must have broken and needs fixing. Either Mercedez is really bad at her job or she's really good at fixing someone else's bad job.

I tune her out and try not to relive the past—and fail.

The psych evaluator had asked me the wrong questions. He only asked about my brother's suicide and how it affects me. He didn't ask why as a 15-year-old I was so happy Jackson blew his fucking brains out. I could have only been happier if I had pulled the trigger myself.

***

Mom had just died of cancer. It, thankfully, was a quick battle. By the time she noticed, or admitted, that something was going on, the doctors gave her less than a month to live. She lasted two weeks. Hospice set her up with care and a hospital bed at home. She slept in her favorite fancy sitting room—right next to the entryway. She could see out the bay windows into the yard. Dad was by her side when she died. It was as peaceful as one could hope for in the situation.

Jackson was older than me by five years. To say he was always troubled is an understatement. I was ten and he was fifteen when Mom died. Dad was a detective, didn't talk about it at home. It wore at him. After Mom died, he took his pension and opened a driving school for semi-truck drivers with a long-haul truck-driving buddy. It became a hangout for his friends in blue. On the weekends, four times a year, he taught a motorcycle safety course. Jackson was my babysitter mostly. Dad trusted him to keep me out of trouble.

Jackson, however, was the trouble.

He hid it well from everyone, his weird deviations. I knew. He showed his true self to me.

And—I never told.

There was a small drainage ditch with a concrete landing and an access cover near the three-bedroom house we tried to make a home. When he was 11, Jackson showed me the secrets he hid in the drainage syphon. He swore me to secrecy. He was very convincing.

Being before the internet, streaming television, or the movie IT, we played near that concrete drain and watched with fascination as it devoured anything we floated towards it. Pinecones. Leaves. Sticks. Mud-pies would disintegrate in the water and clump around the metal bars before falling into the abyss. Mother would have our hides if we sent anything down that "wasn't from nature".

"You want to see what is in there, don't you?" he asked. "You aren't too scared?"

I firmly set my jaw and declared as bravely as a 6-year-old could, "I'm not scared." Of course I was. I wasn't going to let him know.

"You can't tell anyone." His eyes grew cold and his voice stern.

I pulled my hand out of his for a moment and hesitated. That cold voice could be followed by a hard slap if I didn't tread lightly.

He softened his tone, but his eyes did not soften. "You don't want to see me get in trouble? Right?" He tugged at my hand. "Come on. You have to see what's in there."

I once lost a Barbie doll to the drain and stuck my arm in as far as I could to retrieve it. I never once considered opening the access cover up. Mom forbade it. I was a straight arrow even then.

Jackson had a short crowbar in hand and maneuvered the cover off. Being of slight build, he grunted with the effort.

I'm sure my eyes were as big as the access cover and sweat poured into them. I secretly hoped he would get caught, for any adult to look our way and see him for the creature he was. Arrest him. Get him in trouble. They never saw. I was too afraid of him to make them see.

I had learned how to read his fluctuating moods, his intentions before they became actions. It had been a steep learning curve. Now, his eyes warned I should not make a peep. Or else.

"You have to get closer to see." He got down on his belly and poked his head into the open hole.

I did as he did. The gravel crunched on my belly where my t-shirt had ridden up. I tried to pull it back down to protect my bare skin from the freezing, hard concrete. At first I couldn't see anything in the dark hole. The smell was wetness filled with a sweet-rotten odor grasping with long tendrils snaking into your sinuses. You knew that smell wasn't going to leave you for a while. I didn't know it was the rotten stench of death.

Jackson clicked on a small flashlight and illuminated the carcasses at the bottom of the dark hole. "I keep them here."

The sickly, pale light made the horrible sight more gruesome. I couldn't count how many dead animals there were. I couldn't even tell what they were. Rabbits. Dogs. Cats. All of their heads removed from their bodies.

Jackson's words crooned and echoed into the dark, "Can you hear them whisper?"

The flashlight bounced on the lapping water and sparkled on the dark wet patches which squirmed and moved with maggots and things I could not define. It was as if the mound of death had coagulated into a new life form and threatened to inch its way up the mold covered wall towards us. It throbbed and lulled. Dead eyes glared. Skulls and teeth barred. Matted fur clotted and pulled back to reveal bone. Viscera pulsing with lower forms of life.

"That's where I'll put you." He flashed the light in my face. I winced from the glare. "If you ever tell."

I couldn't tear my eyes from the glaring skulls, accusing me of telling and begging me to at the same time.

"Fuzzy Bunny is over there." He pointed to a far corner.

My pet rabbit had disappeared a year ago, Mr. Fuzzy Bunny. (Kids are so good at coming up with original names.) "You're lying," I retorted as only a little sister can. Bold for a kid who was going to have their insolence rewarded by being buried with the molding dead.

He merely smirked at me. A "I'm better than you" smirk that to this day irrationally pisses me off when I see it on someone's face.

I looked but couldn't see anything in the stinky carcass mass.

He turned the flashlight and clicked it so a higher beam shone brightly. It focused into a smaller disk of light and reflected off a small collar. Grime covered the faded collar, the color barely discernable. The tag on it—pitted and no longer shiny—had an engraving on it. I couldn't read it, but I knew what it said. When we had bought the tag, I was inconsolable Fuzzy Bunny couldn't fit on it. We put "Fuzzy" on one side and "Bunny" on the other. That poor rabbit probably did not want to wear a collar or be in a rabbit hutch. I loved him dearly for about four months before he disappeared. The cage door had still been closed.

I screamed and got up from my prone position to run. Jackson was on me within a second. He grabbed me by the shoulders and held my squirming body towards the gaping hole. "Remember. You can't tell or I'll throw you in there to sleep with Mr. Fuzzy Bunny in the dark. Maggots will crawl in your ears."

His fingernails dug into my skin as he sang, "The worms crawl in. The worms crawl out."

I'm sure I whimpered something, but I don't remember it. I just remember the fear I had of being put in a dark, wet, maggot-infested hole and seeing Mr. Fuzzy Bunny's zombie body crawl towards me with its jaw gapping and slime covered bugs oozing from it.

***

I shiver. Mercedez looks at me. "Do you have nightmares about any of it?" she asks.

"Oddly, I don't." I pause. "Well, not anymore. When I was a kid—I was plagued with them. Walked in my sleep. Had night terrors."

"Did your parents send you to therapy?"

"My Dad wasn't the type to see that as an option. And he didn't know the whole of it, so…" I shrug. "He did his best."

On the porch, we rock some more until the moon comes into view. The world is quiet. No city noise. No city lights. Bugs. Birds. Frogs. Lighting bugs. Crickets. Stars. Stars for miles. I wish myself small in all that vastness. Diminish until nothing can reach me.

***

On Saturday, we drop by Cathy's house, not too far from our rented cabin. I pull the Triumph out of its storage shed to go for a late morning ride.

As I roll the bike down the wooden plank, the shed's door swings on its hinges and squeaks. I peek through a small crescent moon—a friend's idea of a joke—cut into the door and see Mercedez pulling out of the drive off to her own adventure today. I hope the bike starts.

I scrawl a message on a battered chalkboard: "Out for a spin, Jude." Cathy doesn't do smart phones, or texting. I'm not the only Luddite. A cacophony of barks and whines emit from the nearby house, a ton of foster dogs. One oversized gray dog—who knows what type—leaves a strand of drool on the kitchen door when he woofs.

I pull on my black leather jacket. It fits snuggly and gives in all the right places. The hard plates sewn into the lining move stiffly on my body and I find it comforting. It creaks and groans as I lace up my boots.

The Triumph kicks over without complaint, a thrumming, a promise for escape.

"Do you have repressed memories?" the interviewer had asked.

"I hardly think about it. It was so long ago," I had lied.

What type of happy-horse-shit-type of question was that anyway? I have a spotless record. It isn't like I have to guard a protectorate. I drive the bike. Who cares what is in my head?

I am the clearest when I'm riding.

Flying. Freedom. Escape.

I learned to ride a motorcycle when I was very young. My dad had brought home a Coleman mini-bike for us to ride around in the backwoods of the subdivision. It looked like it had a lawn mower engine in it, big fat huge tires, and an uncomfortable seat.

I loved it.

As a kid, you know that neat feeling when you hop on something that takes you away from your parents and away from adults? Yeah, that. Add getting away from Jackson. On my own and in the woods away from everyone, this time not on a bicycle with a clacking loose chain, but on a mini-bike that went a whopping five miles an hour!

Oh, I was in love. Within the first ten minutes I hit a rock and flew head over heels over the handlebars. I picked myself up, inspected my skinned knees briefly, but was more worried I had broken the brand new mini-bike. I didn't want to get my Dad upset. It seemed unhurt. I put some mud on my knees and elbows to cover the scrapes. I didn't know I had also hit my head, had a good scrape above my eyebrow.

"You okay, Rocket?" Dad eyed me curiously but probably couldn't muster concern when he saw the grin split across my skull.

I jumped off the bike and gave him the biggest hug, jumping up and grabbing his shoulders and wrapping my legs around him, "I LOVE it! Thank you."

I wasn't a crazy motorcycle driver, even when I was little. I was very careful and followed all the rules, etc. Crashed a few times. Picked myself back up again and kept going. I usually rode alone. Back then, no one worried about kids on their own as much.

For me, it meant my brother couldn't find me. I was on that bike—and the ones that would eventually replace it—every moment of the day I could.

The suburban area we lived in didn't care too much for my constant motorcycling around in the backwoods. There were complaints. I got older and started hanging out at Dad's work instead and riding on the obstacle course there. The neighbors sighed with relief. I learned to drive a semi there too. Who wouldn't take advantage of semis sitting around?

On top of that, I drove every motorcycle that came into the place. His friends would literally bring their bikes in just to see his little Rocket—who stood all of 5'5"—throw her leg over it and swoop around any cone course they could set up. I liked to make Dad proud.

An added bonus: Jackson didn't like to hang out at Dad's work. Now, I realize it was because those guys—many of them police officers and detectives—would have probably seen right through his charming veneer. It was a place I was safe from him.

***

I click my turn signal on as my turn comes up and follow the windy road back to the Cookie Shelf, a restaurant hidden amidst rolling hills and overlooking a 150-year-old dairy. Dust on the gravel road, kicked up by the bike's tires, drifts across the crowded parking lot.

I get used to the looks when I pull up on my own. The bike usually gets looks too. It's a beauty. Triumph Bonneville Bobber 1200cc from 2017. The rake is 25.8" and the seat height is 27.2". I can ride a bike with a seat height taller than my inseam, but I prefer not to. The seat looks like they ran out of material. It is miniscule and makes the back fender look exposed and huge. I've never been into custom paint jobs or anything, but I bought this one used and it came with a paint job I couldn't get rid of: midnight blue with iridescent blue accents on the tank. I put a plastic disc under the kickstand so it won't sink into the gravel parking lot.

I order a cup of coffee and a slice of coconut cake, carry them to the porch filled with rocking chairs and checker boards. I choose a seat at the far end, sit, and tune out everything.

Consider this, at work I have to be on my toes and alert for everything; keeping my head on a swivel at all times. My face-blindness causes me to take extra care looking at people. I can't miss anything that could be a potential threat.

Here watching the hills, the cows, the clouds, the tourists, enjoying a good cup of coffee and an amazing slice of cake—I don't have to watch for anything. I can totally relax. Well, as best as I can relax that is. No bad guys here. No one to protect. Just cows, coffee, cake.

The world falls far away from me until it is something otherworldly. Wonder how Mercedez is doing in Nashville?

A notification on the phone beeps. Something Mercedez had put in my feed—or whatever you call that—has a new video. I can't help it. I watch, though there is barely one bar of reception. Cows don't need the internet.

The video shows the Tipsy Barkeep cutting a hole into a watermelon rind, inserting a mixer and liquefying the insides.

Intriguing. What things you could do with that as a base. What drinks you could make. That's pretty cool, actually.

I click and then share it, add my own comments. All five of my friends might be interested in this for a caving camping event.

I scroll for a bit and get another cup of coffee. The afternoon crowd thins and Jen, a server I have talked to before, comes out onto the porch.

"You were here last month. I remember the bike." She offers a piece of gum, I take it.

"Yeah." I lift the empty plate. "I love the cake."

"Jen." She holds out her hand. No wedding ring. Chews her fingernails. Three earrings in one ear. One in the other. Tattoo just visible at her collar bone over her heart. I'll bet she's lost someone, and that tattoo says something about someone who died in the past two years. Semi colon tattoo on her inner left wrist, hidden by a rubber bracelet with WWJD on it.

"Jude." I shake her hand and then we both stare off into the clouds for a while.

"You should follow us on Facebook. We give away free cakes now and again."

I think the shock in my eyes must have shown. Like something? She smiles and is about to say something else when the door opens and someone from inside hollers, "Jen, we need some help in the kitchen."

"Gotta go." She smiles and ducks back in.

It takes another cup of coffee, but I figure out how to find and like the Cookie Shelf's page. Sure enough a coconut cake giveaway just happened hours ago.

Maybe this getting connected to things in the 21st century isn't all bad after all.

***

Facebook followers for new page Tippsy Kitty, created by Jude Lawz: 10

First post: *Jolly Rancher Shots with Tippsy Kitty!* [Video recipe] Privacy set to global.

Comments:
"I love this!"—Brandy
"Why is Tipsy spelled wrong?"—Mark
"Yum!"—Susan
"Sweet drinks. [heart] [heart] [smiley face]"—mom62460
"Bellissimo!"— 1825Salieri
"When I was younger, I wood make...."—jake_not_from_SF
5 other comments

JOLLY JELLO SHOTS

Recipe notes from Jude's journal.

Start with 3 flasks of Vodka infused with jolly ranchers. (red, green, blue)

- Use hot water and gelatin or buy Jolly Rancher Jell-O mix.
- Only use ½ the water the recipe calls for.
- Use infused vodka as the other ½ of liquid required.
- Pour into molds and let set in the fridge.
- Fill shot glass with more infused vodka.

Super fancy—roll edge of shot glass in corn syrup and then crunched up Jolly Ranchers.

8 - TIGERS

I have kept so much from Jude. In the beginning, I was too young to know Jackson for what he was.

I was probably 6 or 7 when I first visited Jude's house. Jude's Mom went out of her way to make me feel at home and though I smiled and nodded at all the right places, I couldn't help but feel unwanted.

It wasn't Mrs. Morris's fault. I felt unwanted and wrong in my own skin. No amount of chocolate chip cookies and milk from a mother figure with a warm smile was going to erase that.

Jude excused herself from the table for a moment, saying, "I'm going to get my sticker book. Be right back."

She ran off. I sat there at the table feeling awkward and alone. Her Mom had her back to me as she washed the dishes.

"Mom says we can watch *Forrest Gump* on laser disk," Jude called out from her room.

I loved *Forrest Gump*. That day was the first time I saw it. Since then, I must have watched that film 500 times.

Jackson came in the front door. I could see him from where I sat at the kitchen table, in the same seat Jude would sit in years later and watch Jackson's body get rolled out of the house in a black body bag.

Jackson was looking at something in his hand, a Polaroid, then slipped it into his inside pocket. The look on his face was disturbing. He looked hungry for whatever was in the picture. His eyes lifted and met mine. For a split second he looked startled, then blazingly angry. He blinked the heated anger away and his eyes went dead cold. A large lifeless smile spread across his face and he came towards me.

I felt nauseated looking at his smile. All teeth. I imagined rows and rows of razor teeth with gangrenous meat stuck in them like a shark. Dead black shark eyes. I had no experience yet in life to know to listen to your instincts.

"You must be new to town." He looked down the hallway where Jude appeared with a 3-ring binder hugged to her chest. "New friend, Jude?" he asked.

Jude rolled her eyes at him and did not reply.

"Mom, Jude is being rude," he whined. Those dark eyes of his became depths where no light could escape as he continued to stare at me. His death grin stretched wider.

"Jude. Introduce your friend to Jackson," Mom called from the sink without turning around.

Jude rolled her eyes again and frowned at Jackson; introduced us by pointing at each person with her notebook, then opened the book and turned to me. "This is my favorite sticker. Touch it. It's squishy."

Jackson stood there a while longer while we ignored him. Eventually he leaned in close to Jude, his lips almost touching her ears, and whispered, "I'm going to go feed Fuzzy Bunny. Want to watch?"

Jude took in a breath and froze. I didn't know at the time about the years of taunts and manipulation that went beyond normal sibling rivalry. All I knew was Jude looked like a tiny mouse caught in a tiger's grasp, like I had seen on Wonderful World of Nature.

Jude's Mom intervened, "Jackson, go away. Fuzzy Bunny is Jude's responsibility. Go on now. Leave the kids alone."

She stood behind Jude and smoothed her hair while Jackson slunk down the hallway and out of sight.

That night, I told my aunt I wanted to make my hair look like Jenny's from *Forrest Gump* and she laughed, touching her own thinning brown hair, then mine. "Got that Haiti hair." She slumped further on the couch, too exhausted to keep her eyes open. "Good luck with that, goldilocks."

***

Awkward moments with Jackson filled the following years. Times where Jackson waited until Jude left the room so he could come talk to me, sit close to me, touch my knee.

It all seemed innocent, but it made me sick to my stomach. I was too young to know those danger signals. Those signals were not something discussed when we were kids. I only knew I felt uneasy around Jackson. When he got together with his friends, it was even worse.

Jude and I did our best to avoid Jackson and his friends. She had that mini-bike as an escape. Even then, I didn't like dirt or bugs, but I would ride on the back long enough for her to drop me off in the woods. I'd drag along the thickest book I could find and read while she buzzed about. I guess people don't change.

The bug spray was probably poisonous back then. The bug spray. I would lay it on so thick it dripped off of my thin, bony elbows.

Once, Jude showed up at my front door, tears streaking down her dirt covered face, wearing no helmet, carrying a backpack full of cold drinks and sandwiches.

"Spray up buttercup," Jude said, "and grab a book."

I didn't ask her to explain, the look in her eyes said there would be no further discussion. The tiger had batted the mouse about, taunted it, left it dazed and breathing rapidly in a dark corner. Meanwhile, the tiger waited for the mouse to have a hope of escape, only then would it pounce and renew the game.

I drowned myself in bug spray, grabbed my huge, tattered copy of the *Chronicles of Narnia*, all ten books bound into something heavy enough for self-defense or hours in the woods. Days in the woods, even.

I jumped on the back of Jude's bike and held on for dear life as only a scrawny 10-year-old can. We had many escapes like this.

That was the day the new kid in town found me in the woods. My own tiger who would taunt and torture my little mouse soul.

I was halfway through the book, nose buried deep, keeping an ear out for Jude as she buzzed through the trails, when a noise in the woods caught my attention. The obnoxious gray smoke from her two-stroke engine left a haze that hung in the air, making it difficult to see who was approaching.

"What you reading?" a voice called from the fog.

No one had ever followed us into this abandoned area behind suburbia land, at the foot of the hills. In the distance I could hear Jude buzzing through the trails, maybe ten minutes, forever, away. Alone in the woods can be a wonderful feeling, away from everyone, no one there. Until you realize you are alone in the woods, away from everyone, and you are not alone.

I looked up to see a teenager I had never seen before break through the haze. Dark curly hair hung down over his eyes and he brushed it away with a hand. His nails, cut perfectly, buffed, covered with clear polish, shone in the midday sun. I had never seen a boy with a manicure. His face broke out in a grin when he saw the direction of my gaze. The grin was friendly and warm, unlike Jackson's.

"Mom wants me to be a hand model." He smiled wider, stepped a little closer. "I'm Zack."

I introduced myself and then asked, "Why are you out here?"

"We just moved into town. Mom and me. I'm wandering around. Heard the bike, thought I'd see who was tearing up the trails," Zack said. He nonchalantly leaned against a tree.

I relaxed. He wasn't coming any closer and didn't seem to have any ill intent.

"That's Jude." I pointed over my shoulder in the general direction of the hills behind us.

"You don't ride?"

"Me? No. I don't have a mini-bike." I didn't even have a normal bike.

He looked at me closer, nodded as if understanding more than what I had said. Heat rose to my cheeks. I wasn't used to being looked at, being seen.

Zack patted down his pants pockets, looking for something, then retrieved a silver packet. "Gum?" he asked.

He moved closer, squatted down, and held the pack towards me. I took the offered piece. Closer, I could see the rash of pimples across his forehead covered by his dark hair. They screamed in angry defiance to his flawless hands.

"Have you had any modeling jobs?" I asked.

He shrugged and looked away. "Not yet." He unwrapped a piece of gum, took a moment to inspect it, put it in his mouth.

He didn't look at me when he said, "Mom used to be a beauty queen. She wanted a daughter. Got me instead."

We fell silent together. In the distance, Jude was jumping her bike over small dunes; the engine revving and switching gears when she caught a little air. She'd do that for hours, hoping to take flight, leave the gravitational pull of this dark earth.

"I was an accident," I admitted. "Born clutching the IUD in my hand."

"Metal," he said.

Why did I admit that to him? He was easily five years older than me and paying attention to me. That easy going smile and charm made me feel taller somehow, bigger. Keeping some secrets to myself, I didn't disclose being adopted by a suburban white couple who died when I was four. He'd never see my aunt. I rarely saw her.

We chatted about school, the teachers, where the best video game store in town was, who was in the snob group, the nerd group, etc. I spoke more to Zack in those 30 minutes than I probably had to anyone besides Jude in my entire life.

"You ever been to the old Chrysler plant that shut down?" he asked.

"No." I had heard of it but straight-laced Jude and I would never dream of going inside a closed factory.

"It's only been closed a few years, but there are parts that have been derelict for decades." He raised his hands and wiggled his fingers. "Spooky place."

"Don't they have security?" I asked, imagining guards with guns, red lights, sirens.

"Not in the back part. I have an office there." He grinned and nodded. "It's kinda cool."

I looked at him skeptically.

"I have some old paperbacks and magazines you can read."

"What type?" I asked.

"Some kinda naughty," he said, then pointed to the *Chronicles of Narnia* book clasped to my bird chest. "A far cry less religious than that."

I looked at him questioningly.

He answered, "There's a lot of symbolism going on in there. Have you made it to the crucifixion yet?"

It took a moment before my naïve ten-year-old brain could put it together. My eyes grew wide. "Oh!" I said.

"I can sneak other books from the older kid's section of the library, if you want," Zack offered.

I was speechless. The librarian thwarted all of my efforts to gain access to higher-level books. She said I could get them if I had a note from my parents. She might as well have asked for a million dollars.

I'd like to say I hesitated, that some part of me thought this might be a bad idea. I did not. Zack just wanted to show me a cool factory, his "office", and raise my reading level. What could be bad about that?

"That would be cool," I mooned.

"I have to get. I have an audition to go to." Zack said, pointing towards the sound of Jude through the woods. "Don't tell anyone about the factory. Our secret."

"I won't."

"Cool. Meet me Friday after school at the 7-11. I'll bring some subs. You like Italian subs?"

"Yes." I had never had one.

"Gotcha. See you then."

I nibbled on the PB&J sandwiches Jude had brought and read the same paragraph fifty times over and over until the mini-bike carrying wild-haired Jude appeared.

The tires kicked up dust when she screeched to a halt.

"Hey stranger," she said. "Anything happen while I was gone?"

I nodded back and held out a sandwich to her and lied, the first of many, "Nope."

We ate for a while, then she said while mournfully looking towards the path home, "I guess we need to head back."

I'd like to say I felt guilty for lying to Jude about Zack. But I didn't. It was something special. Something all my own. Then it became my personal nightmare. I couldn't tell Jude after that. I couldn't tell anyone.

***

"This one is naughty," Zack said, holding out a battered paperback. "Don't get caught reading it."

I gingerly held the book as if it would bite. "What's it about?"

"Erotica."

"What's that?"

"Sex and stuff."

"Oh." I shrugged, knowingly. "I know about that."

"Gay sex."

The words hung in the air.

"My aunt says that's illegal."

Zack snorted. "If you don't want it." He motioned towards the small fire as if to throw the book into the flames.

Snatching the book, I tried to act detached. "Don't burn a book. That's ignorant."

We had been meeting at the factory for a couple of weeks. Mostly I read while Zack fiddled with an 8-track he had pulled out of a supply closet. Most Friday evenings Zack was in a jovial mood. This night he was dour and sulking.

"Something up?" I asked.

"You're boring me."

Tears threatened to well up.

"I'll pay you a dollar to climb up on that catwalk and do a handstand." He sat back in the squeaky office chair and put his feet on the dilapidated desk, nodded to the ladder just outside of the office.

The catwalk at the top of the ladder extended over the factory floor.

"I'll fall."

"Five dollars."

The ladder was solid enough, though the catwalk swayed as I stepped onto it. My sweaty hands shook on the rust-pitted railing.

"Show me the Lincoln," I called out. "I'm not doing it until you show me you got five bucks."

Slowly, he pulled open his wallet and extracted the money. Held it up in front of his face. "Go on, wimpy boy. Show me what you got."

Far below me, twisted metal scraps and a row of open metal lined pits filled the factory floor. Dozens of pits hulked, most of them empty, except for the largest. Dark sludge filled that one.

"Five bucks? Promise?"

"Twenty if you do it naked."

"Funny."

Zack stood in the doorway and looked out at the factory floor, an unconcerned foreman. "Just kidding. Five bucks. Promise."

My knobby knees threatened to knock together. The floor's diamond grating bit into my palms as I put my weight on them. "Ok, it will take me a sec. Gotta use my elbows."

The metal bit into my head uncomfortably, though I couldn't have weighed more than 80 pounds with rocks in my pockets. Knees on elbows, I balanced then kicked one foot up. It swayed wildly and hit the railing with a clank. The clatter reverberated around me, causing my head to ache with it. I kicked the other leg up and managed to hold steady.

"That's a headstand, not a handstand," Zack called from below me. His shadow coiled around the twisted metal on the floor.

"Come on, man. It's close."

"Hand. Stand."

My shoe, one size too big, slipped off and fell with a thunk behind me as I clumped to the catwalk floor. More clattering and something fell in the distance.

Zack leaned forward and smiled. "I won't let anything happen to you."

I curled my fingers into the diamond holes, gripping with all my tiny might, extended my arms and kicked my feet up. What a sight it must have been, my bony legs in the air, white tube socks pulled up to my calves. Tears leaked from my squeezed eyelids.

Zack kicked the ladder, hard.

The sound was like a cannon blast. My eyes shot open. Violently, the floor beneath me lurched. I crumpled onto my elbow. My feet tangled in the railing. Clattering all around vibrated through my skull.

Below me, Zack guffawed. "Kid, your face."

"That wasn't funny!"

"You did good."

He ducked when I half heartedly threw my sneaker at him. The loose sole flapped as it hit the ground and bounced.

"I could have fell."

"You're overreacting."

I sat on the floor to put my shoe on and to hide how badly my hands were shaking.

"Here. Ten dollars." He held out the money and smirked. "Hell, get some new shoes. Doesn't your aunt love you enough to buy you decent shoes?"

"She doesn't know."

"Why not?"

Wanting to shrink and hide. Shaking. Anger turned to humiliation. I pulled my feet underneath me, hiding the shoes.

"I get it. She works hard and you don't want to bother her." He turned and walked back to the office.

Zack was right. She worked two jobs. I was already an unexpected burden to her.

"I got some shoes that should fit you. Have barely any wear on them. I'll bring them next Friday."

And he did. I was too stupid to know I was being played. Every Friday was filled with dares, mercurial moods, and rewards if I did what he said. It was attention, and I shrugged off the bizarre requests.

Things got weirder when a handful of older friends became regular visitors. Two skinny twins and one blond girl. Brad, Chad, and Janet.

One night, I was doing my best to disappear into the background when Janet handed something to me.

"Will you paint my toenails?" she asked, wiggling her naked toes in dust covered sandals.

"I've never done that before."

"It's not that hard. I'll teach you. Here. I'll do yours first." She pulled at my new shoes. "Take off those tube socks. They look uncomfortable on you."

We perched on the sagging couch, and she patiently taught me the art of applying multiple coats.

Brad and Chad rolled in with a couple of middle-school kids in tow. "See. Told you it's a neat place," one twin said.

Zack entered the room to see the new victims. The group enjoyed playing pranks, harmless mostly, on little kids. Somehow they did not prank me, nor was I asked to take part.

"Janet, jump in here," Zack directed.

"Can't. Got wet nails." She wiggled her bright red nails at him.

He looked at the bright red dots at the end of my small feet. Raised an eyebrow. I took a deep breath, expecting to be mocked.

"I like it," Janet said and pointed at my feet. "We all have our thing." She waved Zack away.

I busily blew on the nails, both proud and embarrassed at how they looked.

"Playing pranks on kids is getting old," Janet whispered and rolled her eyes.

Zack turned to Brad and Chad. "Let's get them up on the catwalks. Play pirates."

Brad dared the kids to walk the plank across the largest sludge-filled pit. The pits' original use for the factory was lost on us and a subject of much conversation as to the depth and purpose.

Chad jeered at the kids and then rewarded their bravery with candy. Sometimes the reward was cigarettes or nudey magazines. Stupid things like that.

"Here, don't spend it all in one place," he said and cackled like it was the most original thing anyone could say.

Those shenanigans fizzled out and general partying continued. Kegs. Dares. Janet making out with Zack. The twins spray painting and sneaking peeks at the couple when they went off to another office away from me.

Jude had ROTC on Friday nights. She never suspected I had this second life. I don't know why I stayed there. I was like a mascot. I'll admit I was jealous to not have Zack to myself, and relieved to not be his puppet.

Then Jackson joined the ranks. Bringing Jackson in was like pouring gasoline onto an open flame.

I wasn't there the night Janet brought Jackson in to play a prank on him. I heard a fight broke out. After that Jackson joined the group.

Imagine my shock when I arrived one Friday night and everyone had black eyes, split lips, and busted eyebrows. The fight must have been a real duster. Worse yet was finding Jackson sitting on the dilapidated couch where Janet had painted my toenails.

I froze in my tracks when Jackson's eyes met mine.

"Hi ya," he said. Shark teeth grin firmly in place.

Zack came out of his "office". The twins had spray painted "King Shit" on the door in bright florescent orange. "Runt. You know Jackson, right?"

I couldn't talk. The Koontz book, which was tucked up under my arm, slipped and clumped to the floor.

Zack picked it up and handed the book to me. "Here kid, I got a project for you." Zack put a video camera on top of the book. The camera was second hand and held together with duct tape. "You can have it. Bring it when you come out here. Don't forget to charge it," he told me, then turned to the group. "We're going to set up a haunted house."

The haunted house was lame. Everyone got too stoned to care. The twins forgot to invite anyone. I had worked hard on the decorations and even had dry ice. No one gave two shits. I was disappointed and questioned why I hung out with this group, when lame turned to…

***

Things happened after the haunted house. I saw it all. I recorded it all.

The last thing Zack said to me after backhanding my face was, "If you tell, I'll tell everyone *what* you are." He loomed over me. Behind him, bloody evidence dripped to the factory floor.

I held my hand to the newly forming bruise and swore an oath I would take this secret to the grave.

Silently, demanding, Zack held his hand out.

I handed the video camera to him. My hands shook. The camera rattled.

He ejected the home-movie of debauchery and smiled. Turned. Threw the camera into the green scum pit of dark, inky water. The camera sunk, disappearing the same as the broken body that had gone before it.

Janet's broken body.

I stopped sleeping, unable to un-see the horror. My grades tanked. Jude noticed I was becoming distant. I couldn't tell her and hid from Zack and Jackson as best I could. I didn't want to end up like Janet. The look in her eyes when…

It was an accident, what had happened to Janet. It was. But I saw the gleam in Zack's eyes and the bulge in his pants. He liked it.

Except for a few other unavoidable occasions, I didn't see Zack again until probably right after Jude's Mom died of cancer. Jackson and Zack caught up with us on our way back from watching the truck drivers practice backing their 52-footers between two cones at Jude's Dad's new semi-trucker driving school.

They pulled up in an old blue beater van. Zack was driving, being the only one with a license. The rusted hulk, complete with belching blue smoke and missing muffler, rattled loudly. Scratchy music escaped from the tinny speakers, the soundtrack from that old '80s film *Amadeus*. It was an odd combination, blue smoke, a woman screeching in Italian, and these pimple faced sadists.

Jackson leaned forward in the passenger seat. His gaunt face came into the light as he turned the volume down. "We're going to get ice cream, want to come?" Blood-shot eyes rimmed with purple luggage met mine.

I did not go to the factory after that night, no one would have after what I had witnessed. I heard the twins never went back. It was only Jackson and Zack now. Ever since Zack got the rusted panel van for his birthday, the two teens trolled the malls constantly.

I tried not to look at the pair. Sharks on the prowl. It was hot out and I would have loved ice cream, but anything to do with those two was out of the question. I could feel Zack thinking the last words he had said to me, "If you tell, I'll tell everyone *what* you are."

"No thanks," we quietly answered. Jude nervously looked back the way we came, towards her Dad's work. Probably wondering if we could out race them to the safety of that cinder-block building.

Zack leaned forward on the steering wheel and glared at us over his mirrored sunglasses. He leaned even further towards Jackson so he could level a steady gaze on me. His head was an unruly dark wavy mass. His eyes showed no sign of sleepless nights plagued with nightmares. Though he had put on a little weight, his puffiness added to his menacing hulk.

Jackson jeered, "Zack said he'd treat."

Zack nodded his head, never taking his eyes off of me.

"We rented some movies. Ice cream and movies," Jackson continued to cajole.

Zack touched his shoulder and said dismissively, "Don't waste your time on them."

Jackson eyed us up and down greedily, "Yeah. Waste of time." He leaned back and added, "More for us."

Zack gunned it. The muffler clattered loudly. Jackson shouted, "Later faggots."

Fun times.

She asked, "Want to go to Dad's shop? There's a new bartending school next door."

I didn't want to. I was busy re-living the haunted house of horrors in my head.

"Sure," I answered absently.

"They have all these neat books. We can go in 'cause it isn't an actual bar," my rule-loving Jude said.

9 - CAMPFIRE MARTINI

Back from the mountain and buttoned-up on a bright Monday, I check with my supervisor. "Hey boss." I try to be nonchalant and fail miserably. He can read me like a neon sign.

"No, I haven't heard anything back about your security clearance." Boss leans back in his squeaky chair and eyeballs me—hard.

I don't shrink under his glare. I wait for him to give more info. You don't rush this man.

"They get backed up and it takes longer than you want it to." Boss pinches the bridge of his nose, a stress indicator. "We have a big detail coming up this week. Put it out of your head. Worrying drains your energy."

He is right and I am being overly concerned, which is a sign there should be concern. I might as well write "I HAVE A GUILTY CONSCIENCE" on my forehead.

"Psych eval rattled me a little." I am honest.

"They rattle you on purpose." He looks at me pointedly.

Crap. "You probably have to weigh in on my reactions to it then." I'm so dense some days.

He nods then says, "I've never seen anything knock your focus on the job. I'd be worried if he didn't rattle you and," he pushes up from the desk and stands with his hands on his hips, "you being honest about your reaction to it shows emotional awareness and maturity."

He's somewhat of a philosopher—I hope I'm not blushing.

"You're a tough cookie. Time to focus. We have some weather coming in, a potential picketing on one of our routes, and a spontaneous dignitary that likes to avoid the secret service."

"Yes, sir."

"We good?"

"Yes, sir."

***

Tuesday and it is pissing rain. I am 100% glamorous in my yellow rain suit. Am I 300 pounds? 200? A man? A gorilla? You'd never know. I'm dry, that's what matters. The rain is supposed to stay wicked all day with a strong potential for hail. That shit hurts when it hits you on the bike.

"You get the new route?" Darren asks. He slips on his helmet, muffling his last words.

"Yeah. We've adjusted to get a back door for Mr. Dignitary." I answer and snap my helmet visor shut.

"He's three sheets to the wind, I heard." Darren points to his earpiece. "Agents had a hell of a time getting him away from the VP."

"Hold up." I say as I hold up a finger and listen to the chatter in the earpiece. Darren gets a faraway look, listening in.

"Constitution Ave for three miles to 14th Street," says the patient but persistent agent in charge.

"Joan of Arc is secure," the voice of an agent intones. Code for the VP is in her limo.

Chatter goes back and forth as the VP and dignitary get tucked away in various limos.

"Check. Ducks out."

Deco limos deployed with officers in tow.

"Check. Wheels forward." Our group rolls out in front of the procession.

Darren triggers the microphone in his helmet with a press of his jaw and says, "Roger that. Wheels forward."

We pull onto the street and lead the procession through the heart of D.C. taking the alternate route as directed by the secret service.

We turn onto Constitution Ave and thankfully the picketers have stayed under the awnings to avoid most of the weather. Our original concerns were unfounded.

The weather is challenging. The rain pelts us and the wind buffets at me, trying to blow me sideways. I lean in and counter steer against the pressing wind. Well, I'm not going to hydroplane at least. Can't get enough speed to do that.

My teen years spent riding enduro dirt bikes taught me how to keep my balance at even the slowest of crawls. (Enduro dirt-bikes have itty-bitty seats and you basically climb rocks and sides of hills without putting your feet down. It's all balance and being one with your bike.) But I still worry about putting my foot on the center line or any marking on the road. Those get very slippery.

I scan the crowded sidewalk unconsciously. Just in front of me, a picketer drops their sign into traffic and jumps into the lane to grab it.

I pull hard on the brakes and put my foot down on the slippery pavement. Sure as shit, my foot lands directly on the painted yellow line. My boot slips and I instantly shift my weight to the left, catching the weight of the bike and pull it back. It looks graceful. No one but my heart rate knows for a split-second my foot did not find solid purchase and this 800-plus pounds of steel was ready to go to the right straight towards the ground. My heart knocks on the back of my front teeth.

Normally, I'd curse. But in things like this, that part of my brain turns off. I process instead. The picketer looks at me as she picks up her soaked sign. I nod my head slightly as she jumps back onto the sidewalk.

I don't even hear the chatter going on in my ear. Agents checking and triple checking if there is a problem in the crowd.

"All clear." I hear someone say. "Picketer dropped a sign."

We drop our bikes. It happens. In order to pass the test for the motorcade, you have to be able to pick your bike up if it drops. Your bike might get pushed over by a crowd. They'll have burns from the pipes, but they can push up against your bike and dump you over. Doesn't happen often, but it can. Of course cars, weather, etc., anything can take the bike out from underneath you, including picketers who drop signs.

We are all doing our full best to keep the bikes upright and crawl through the streets, stopping traffic as we go along. Four bikes break formation, split up and stop the cross street of traffic while the other four stay in front of the limo.

Darren and I peel off to stop the oncoming traffic from 17th street. My heart is still pounding. I will it to slow down while scanning the cars and people around me without moving my head. Night-driving polarized glasses keep my eyes hidden and allow me to see with clarity.

Something in one of the cars catches my eye. But what? Better safe than sorry.

"Darren, on my three, anything off in that white sedan to you?" I say over the helmet mike.

The earplug squawks a response, "Driver in a striped shirt, mid-forties, balding. Sweating excessively for this weather."

A secret service agent responds, "Jarrett, take a look."

There is silence for a moment while the motorcade passes us. The sweating man's knuckles tighten on the steering wheel when the limo comes into his vision. The flags' reflection ripples across his windshield. They dance translucently on his forehead. Two of the front motorcycles from the unit peel off and stop between the white sedan and the procession.

The man jumps when a secret service agent raps his knuckle on the window.

I can barely hear him over the wind say, "Sir would you mind..." The wind carries the rest of his words away.

Two other agents surround the car and place keen eyes on the fellow.

His eyes are wide. Sweat pours down his face. He holds up his hands in plain view. An agent opens the door, but he does not get out of the car.

The limo passes, the trailing officer motorcycles with it. We pause for a moment, waiting for our order to stay or go.

Darren and I keep our eyes straight ahead as agents tense and move closer to the car.

"Make a hole." An order comes through and a dark SUV pulls up.

Within two seconds, agents transfer the man to the back of the SUV. An agent pulls the white car to the curb and we receive the order, "All clear."

The dark sedan pulls one way across traffic. We pull in the opposite way and line up behind the procession.

The rest of the trip is uneventful. We deposit the drunk dignitary at his hotel via a back entrance. The Vice President whisks off to her next appointment.

We gather at the bar that evening. The conversation is light.

"SHCCCCCK—Darren, do you see anything off in that car over there? SHCCCCCK" Scotty calls in a falsetto before taking a swig of his beer. Foam clings to his lip.

"THHHBBBT—I think that guy has to take a shit— THHHBBBT," Bob answers. He gives a deep laugh that escalates into a high-pitched giggle.

"Roger that. Better send in the secret service to take a whiff." Darren snorts and wipes the foam off of his own lip. Points to Scotty's lip for him to do the same.

Everyone congratulates me on spotting "the great shitter", "Mr. Danger-Poop", and the like.

Apparently the strange look I had picked up on was this poor man, stopped by our motorcade while in a blind panic to make it home for his constitutional, losing the battle and shitting his pants.

When the agent opened the door, the stench hit him directly between the eyes. The driver merely said, "I'm sorry."

Just to be sure it was an "innocent shit" and not a reaction to stress because he was about to do something nefarious, they took the fellow to an undisclosed location for questioning; soiled pants and all.

"Better to call 'em all," I say and giggle along with the guys. We'd all rather be sitting around talking about a missed call versus recuperating after something bad; or worse, post-mortem meetings after something extremely bad happened that we missed.

Molly brings a double of whiskey and sets it in front of me.

"I didn't order that," I protest.

"Robert bought it for you," she says and shrugs.

Darren looks at the drink then me and says, "The new guy?"

"I haven't met him yet." What the hell do you do when someone buys you a drink? "Molly, put his next drink on my tab." I hold the whisky up and mouth, "Thanks!"

Robert, the new guy, nods my way. Doesn't smile.

I turn to Darren. "He wasn't on today's detail."

"Nope. He's been on paperwork all week. Hasn't spoken to anyone," Darren informs me. He clinks his beer bottle against my highball glass and says, "Has his eye on you, I guess."

I turn my head so Robert can not see my face and say, "Gross."

"Can't fault a guy for hoping." Darren darts his eyes towards me and smiles.

I smile back and change the subject. "I'll have to sober up a bit before I drive home if I drink this."

My phone beeps. I peek at it.

Darren smiles. "That Mercedez?" he asks.

"Yeah. She's swinging by."

The door swings open and Mercedez walks in.

"Nope, she's here," I answer.

"What type of backpack is that?" Darren asks.

Mercedez spins to show off her backpack and its occupant. Whiskers peeks out at everyone via a round dome. Whiskers looks fairly complacent for a furry alien visiting a bar filled with people.

"Get you anything?" Molly appears behind me and asks. "Cat want a vodka?"

Whiskers paws at Molly's fingers as she taps the glass.

"No thanks. We're on our way to a cat-match-up social thing." Mercedez sets her backpack on a stool so everyone can eyeball Whiskers.

Molly points to the backpack and says, "Tippsy Kitty."

Mercedez beams, "Have you seen it?"

"Yeah. I saw an Instagram ad. Whiskers is a tough critic." Molly unconsciously wipes the bar with a rag.

"Wait. What's a cat-match-up?" I hold my hands up to slow the conversations. "And what's Tippsy Kitty?"

Mercedez points to a sticker on Whisker's plastic dome. "See."

The pink and purple sticker sparkles 'Tippsy Kitty'. Cat's eyes peer out of the double P. A martini glass stands in place of the Y. "What do you think?"

"What's it for? Is that spelled wrong? One p. And we're circling back to the cat-date thing," I say.

Mercedez rolls her eyes at me as if I'm an imbecile and turns to Molly, "This is the logo for the YouTube channel. One p was taken. Worked better for the logo. You like it?"

"Very cute." Molly nods in approval. "I saw the jolly Jell-O rancher drink. That's your first recipe right?"

"Yeah. We just made it over the weekend." Mercedez looks at me. "It's trending already so we should make some more soon."

I don't even know what that means.

"Sip?" I hand my whisky to her. "New guy at the end bought it for me."

"Uggh." Mercedez sips at the whiskey then hands it back. "Oh, isn't he giving me the hairy eyeball? Don't look."

I spin on my barstool, simultaneously swigging the rest of the whiskey and taking a glance at Robert. The darkness doesn't help me read his face, but I can tell he isn't blinking and he isn't breaking eye contact with Mercedez. Like—damn creepy eye contact.

Of course, she did just drink the whiskey he sent my way. The warmth of the drink makes me smile. I swing back.

"Can you say, creepy death glare?" I say.

"Sweety, I'll see you tomorrow. I got a date. You okay to go home?" Mercedez asks.

"Sure. Wait. What's the cat date thing?" I glance at Darren and he looks at his empty beer bottle.

"We all bring our cats and mingle," Mercedez says.

"God, it isn't called something horrible, is it?" Darren asks.

Mercedez smiles secretively.

"Forget I asked." Darren blushes.

"You good?" she asks again.

"In good company. I'll hang out a little till I clear up." I point to Darren and we both grin.

Mercedez waves and leaves. Bouncing in the backpack, Whiskers looks a little sad she didn't get to at least sniff a drink. Darren watches Mercedez walk out the door, or maybe he's watching the cat.

Out of the corner of my eye I see Robert stand, place a $20 on the bar, and walk towards the door. My heart rate jumps up and I bristle. He's not going to fuck with Mercedez is he?

Darren puts a hand on my shoulder, "I see it. I'll make sure she makes it to her car okay." He stands and calls back over his shoulder, "Be right back."

Better to call them all.

***

I pull in to my apartment's garage and replay the evening's events in my head. Darren reported back Robert had disappeared, and Mercedez was merrily unaware of our concern. Still, what a weird vibe from that guy.

I park in my assigned slot and lock the fork of the bike with a click. This beauty is a 2015 Honda Shadow Phantom I bought off of a buddy. It's matte black and everything on it is black, even the pipes. She's a little heavy and small, good for going back and forth to work on. If she gets dinged or stolen, I won't care.

I stow my helmet in the dingy locker hanging on the wall. This locker was the chief selling point of this place. I can store my helmet and rain gear in the garage. This leaves my hands free to bring in the limited groceries I can fit in my bike's hard bags.

It is late. The garage is quiet. Betty's car is in its usual parking space sporting American flags hanging out of the windows.

They sag, lopsided, from the tops of the passenger windows, as if they've been there since 9/11.

My footsteps echo and the grit underneath my boot scrapes loudly. I almost reach the door when—I swear—the air changes. I don't adjust my walk or move my head perceptibly, but I listen with all fibers. Something moved in the space, shifting the air. I know someone has moved. Maybe there was a sound and I don't realize I heard it?

Better to call them all, right?

On instinct, I abruptly about-face with a "Oh, I forgot" hand gesture and walk towards the locker.

Nothing.

Actually, I do want to bring up a map book of Tennessee to pine over. I unlock the locker and rummage around for it.

A slight creaking noise to my right. Carefully, I close the locker and turn around.

Is it my imagination or have the flags on Betty's car changed the slightest position? One has shifted a millimeter, the edge of the flag hangs slightly more to the left.

Is someone in there? Good heavens, who knows what weird stuff she keeps in that car. Boxes of prayer books. Razor blades for apples. I should just disregard it.

I don't listen to anyone—even me.

The windows are heavily—illegally—tinted, and I can't see into the vehicle. I need a flashlight. The lights on the car blink and the horn beeps, causing me to jump a half-step back.

"Oh hey," a voice calls out.

A tall, wiry man walks into the garage from the outside guest parking lot. He carries a heavy box; the cardboard lids flop with each step he takes.

"Hello," I answer shortly. I have never seen this guy. Could be new to the apartment building. I mean, something like 80 people live in this small building. I don't know everyone.

He turns to check out the bike and does the raise-the-eyebrow-a-girl-rides-a-motorcycle look which immediately makes me want to drop kick his gonads into his ear canals.

He must sense the burn from my eyes and keeps his comment to, "Nice bike."

"Thanks. I bought if from a buddy who had to pay for his Vegas wedding." True story.

"Did it last?"

"Two weeks."

"You won that one."

"Sometimes you eat the bear." My body is tense. I must have unconsciously put the map book down to free my hands. Don't remember doing that. My body prepares for this guy to strike. Heart beat thrumming. Feet planted for balance. I'm on guard after the whole Robert thing.

The new guy isn't going to strike. He stands there holding his box and looking at the black beauty. This gives me a chance to size him up. Button-up shirt. Ironed. Sleeveless T-shirt underneath. Khaki pants. Plain brown belt. He's lost weight or the belt is a hand-me-down. The hole above the one he is currently using is worn. Shoes are expensive running shoes. They look lightweight and brand new. I can't get a good view of his hands because they are under the box. Clean-shaven face. Dimple. Dark hair. Cowlick waves over his left eye. He looks up at the ceiling over my bike, exposing a small scar on his forehead hidden by that cowlick.

"What's that hanging up there?"

"A ramp if I ever need to put the bike on a trailer." Oh, the fight I had with the HOA to get permission to use all the space in my parking space. They finally had acquiesced, stating if it fell, it would harm my property and no one else's. Mensa folk, these people. "Moving in?" I nod to the boxes.

"Oh." He lifts the box slightly. "Betty has me out getting things from the storage unit for her. Preplanning for the holidays."

"Betty in 4C?" I give the wrong unit number. We don't even use letters. All of our units are numbers.

His smile broadens and warms. "Ah. No really. I'm here staying with her." He shifts the weight of the box and holds up a key chain with one silver key and a black key fob. The fob lets you get into the gated garage and the front door. A silver cross complete with crucified man dangle from the key chain. Next to Jesus hangs a small circle tag with the apartment number 214, Betty's.

I find myself smiling in return, though the hairs on the back of my neck continue to stand on end. Long day. I'm jumpy. "K-then," I answer and tilt my chin slightly.

We turn together and walk towards the elevator. A natural thing to do, walk to the elevator together—but—my suspicious sensor is on and I can't get over it. I pause, turn back and pick up the map. He keeps walking and doesn't look back. That makes me feel better for some weird reason. He holds his black key-fob to the pad and calls the elevator. The door opens, and he holds it for me. My brain reaches for a reason to not get into the elevator, to not let him know where I live.

Stupid. If he's helping Betty, we're bound to run into each other. She's probably told him everything one can glean about me from peeking through a cracked door at the end of the hall.

I let out a breath and let go of my willies. What happened the last time I thought something was off about someone? We interrogated someone who shit their pants. I smirk at the memory and the wiry fellow looks at me questioningly.

"Oh. I'm Dirk." He shifts the box so it rests on the elevator railing and holds out his hand.

The light overhead in the elevator casts long flickering shadows across us.

"Jude." I shake the offered hand: warm, small, soft. Firm handshake.

We ride in silence and then part at my door where we exchange some pleasantries and I don't think of him anymore.

I love the smell of my apartment. There's a lot of wood and it relaxes me the second I close the door. My phone binks.

Damn it. Oh wait, is Mercedez okay?

She's fine. Her text reads, *"OMG you have to check this link!"*

I put the phone away and don't click on the link. I want to make a chocolate martini in the worst way. Something fudgy and sweet with a dash of adult sin.

Mercedez texts again, *"I'm coming over. Make me one too."*

I text, *"You don't even know what I'm making."*

"Does it matter?"

It doesn't.

Liquors are mixed. Chocolate drizzled in martini glasses. Chocolaty alcohol poured.

"Better yet." I turn to Mercedez without saying hello when she enters. "Chocolate filled marshmallows soaked in chocolate vodka should float on top and set ablaze." I call back over my shoulder, "Have a good cat switch date?"

"Couldn't have said it better myself. And no. The event was a dud." Mercedez lets Whiskers out of the backpack and she takes up residence on a bar stool immediately. Mercedez pulls out her phone and says, "Tell me what you are making, champ."

I am so into the drink creation at this point I don't bat an eye. "This is a Chocolate—wait I'm going to light it on fire—a Campfire Martini!"

"Is there lots of chocolate?" Mercedez scoots in closer to get a close-up. With the hand off-camera, she points to the marshmallow bag.

Taking the cue, I pull out two chocolate-filled marshmallows. "These are a little square-er and squatter-er than your typical campfire marshmallow." I squeeze them in front of the camera. "Don't body shame them. They have something your s'mores marshmallow don't have," I plunge my thumbs into the centers and chocolate oozes out, "chocolate."

I pull a bowl in front of the camera. "And these chocolate filled marshmallows have been soaked in vanilla vodka." I place them gently on top of the chocolate martinis, add shaved chocolate and announce, "Now we set them ablaze."

Mercedez reaches in front of the camera with the long lighter and lights the marshmallows. Quite talented for someone who also is holding a camera and trying to record.

She pulls back for a wide shot, still taking care to keep my face off-camera.

"Whiskers, what do you think?" I ask.

"Genius," Mercedez says and moves to get a reaction shot with Whiskers.

"Not too close," I warn.

"I know."

Whiskers glares at the flames.

"Whiskers is not impressed," I say.

We clink glasses, blow out the flames, and sip at the chocolaty goodness. Perfect for the end of a weird day.

"Oh, you didn't click on that link, did you?"

"Nope, what was it?" I ask.

"Your YouTube video of the Jolly Jell-O Shot was reposted by the *Huffington Post*. On their blog." Mercedez pokes at the marshmallow with her manicured fingernails.

"Cool. Hold up. What YouTube video? And what does that mean reposted?"

"Honey. You went viral today."

"Is that bad?"

"Noob. You have an Instagram, a Facebook page, a Twitter, and a YouTube channel for 'The Tippsy Kitty'. You need some more content too. Hope you don't mind, I dropped the Caver bit. The 'Kitty' was easier to brand."

I am speechless about having so many things I don't know about. I sip the chocolate instead. Too sweet, but tonight this is what I want.

Mercedez explains in *noob* terms what each of the social media platforms are for, how they interact, and what I should do to keep them filled with content.

I'm not up for this.

Then she takes my phone and clicks on the link she had texted earlier. "See?"

I don't at first. She points out the blog article titled "This Week's Top People Who Know How to Unwind." The second image is my headless body holding a Jolly Jell-O shot and Whiskers the cat mid strike, knocking a Jell-O shot off onto the ground. She's pretty photogenic, I have to say.

"I'll get you the stats soon, but this went to millions. You're probably already seeing traffic to your site. I need to post something right away to give them something else to look at." Mercedez goes into techno-crisis-mumble to herself and buries her nose into her device.

Suddenly she looks up. "Do you feel like making some more drinks?" She holds up her phone. "For science?"

"Uh, I guess?"

"You get set up. Do you have work tomorrow?"

"Yes. But no details. Should be an office day."

"Up for a late night tonight?"

I smile and say, "You're only young and viral once, I suppose?"

It is a late night and with Whiskers judging, smelling, ignoring, and two other times swiping drinks to the floor, we make four videos.

I sneak out early in the morning to go to work, leaving a sleeping Mercedez in my guest bedroom.

I peek in on her. She keeps a small amount of clothes and toiletries at my place for sleepovers. Whiskers is curled up on her shoulder. She eyes me with one sleepy eye, then snuggles back into Mercedez's mass of hair. I quietly close the door and can still hear snoring on the other side.

She left a post-it note on the counter: "Awesome work! I got it all scheduled to post."

Excerpt from *The Huffington Post's* blog article: *"Top People Who Know How to Unwind"*

This mystery lady has everything you could want to unwind: a cabin, a mountain view, Jell-O shots, and a teetotaling cat. Viewers want to know more about the Tippsy Kitty and can't get enough of Whiskers. Click here to view the video. [CLICK HERE]

Comment on the article:

"Yummy! Must have now!"—Rachel382

"This looks fabulous! Plus I love cats."— _can_do_24

"WHISKERS the DESTROYER!"— craft2cardsMe

"Wish I was there."— KingBarbour90

"No Drink for You!!"— roRollins8

+2.4K more comments

CAMPFIRE MARTINI

Recipe notes from Jude's journal.

- Drizzle chocolate syrup on inside of glass

Mix in shaker with ice until chilled.
Equal parts:

- Irish cream
- Chocolate liqueur
- Vodka (vanilla or chocolate)

Top with shaved chocolate. (Optional—but why would you skip that?)

Also top with chocolate filled marshmallows that have been soaked in vodka.

Drizzle more chocolate syrup on top.

Use a long lighter to toast those marshmallows.

Make sure the cat's tail is nowhere nearby

10 - TRIPLE THREAT

"Were you there when he pulled the trigger?" the interviewer had asked.

'Hell, yes I was,' I thought but said, "I was outside and heard the shot." I've said that lie so many times it almost feels like it is true, except for the horrible memory of Jackson pointing the gun at me as I stood in the hallway.

I swing by the boss's office and poke my head in. Before I can open my mouth he says, "No word yet."

My phone buzzes.

"I need to ask a question, boss."

"Shoot."

Internally I wince and hear a memory of a gunshot, flat and dull. So, I might need a little therapy. I'm not an agent and do not need to use a gun. I have one. I drive the bike. I don't need therapy.

My phone buzzes again.

"I have this online thing that I do. It isn't huge, and I don't show my face. Don't use my name either." Honest and not a rule breaker, always me.

Boss looks over his glasses at me. I don't think he even knows what online things are. He sets the bar for Luddites.

"Feels like something I should tell you about," I say.

Buzz. Buzz. My phone wants attention.

"Does it get in the way of your job?" he asks.

"Nope."

Buzz. Buzz. Buzz.

"Ok then," he says and drops his gaze to a stack of paperwork on a desk from 1974, with no computer in sight.

In the hallway, I check the phone. The front screen is littered with notifications, I don't even know what for.

I text Mercedez, *"My phone won't stop buzzing. Help me turn off these notifications tonight?"* I take five minutes to type the message and make twenty mistakes.

Her response, *"K."*

***

Back at my desk, I overhear the guys talking.

"She sure makes a lot of sweet drinks."

"I saw a whisky one the other night that looked good."

"Hey, Jude—there's this chick on the YouTube that has a recipe kinda like your apple-pie moonshine you made a while back," Darren calls from his cubicle.

I stand up from my bare cubicle and look at Darren, keeping my smile hidden behind the wall.

'Holy shit.'

"I'll have to check it out," I say, then return to my computer and hit submit, sending a request for two days off next month to my boss—who will ignore it until I put a printed version on his desk. I half-heartedly listen to everyone and hope my face doesn't give away my secret.

A literal shadow falls over me and I look up to see Robert, six foot three, greasy hair, bright blue eyes, slight asymmetry to his mouth—but it is hard to tell 'cause he has a slight sneer plastered there. It is like the sneer has pulled his smile off balance and it stuck.

"I think you have a secret," he whispers to me.

My mouth, always quicker to engage than my head, quips, "Oh, I have many." I look up at Mr. Sneer to see what he is getting at. "Don't think we have been properly introduced. I'm Jude," I say and hold out my hand.

He stares at me knowingly and does not take my offered hand. Seriously, we learned interrogation tactics in training. I stare back—refusing to fill in the silence.

He blinks first, rolls his eyes and grumps, "Whiskers."

I tilt my head and think, *'So?'*

He misunderstands my indifference as confusion. "The cat," he man-splains.

He must have gotten close to Mercedez the other night in order to see Whiskers. Creep-o-rama.

To my left, Darren stands up in his cubicle.

I can't help myself. I toy with the guy. "What cat?" I look around as if there might be one underfoot, then look at him questioningly.

He purses his lips and glares at me. His death-glare up close is pretty impressive. He draws back and then jabs a finger at me. "I know your type…"

Darren rounds the corner of the cubicle and steps mostly in front of Robert, interrupting him. Look at that body language tactic; we learned that in training too. It is funny when we trot these techniques out on each other. I wonder if Robert realizes.

Surely, he does, right? Of course, I think he must have skipped the How Not to be a Jackass class.

"Hey, we on for helping Wyatt move tonight?" Darren asks me.

Robert steps back and grimaces.

We do not know a Wyatt.

"Yeah. Should I pick up boxes?" I ask.

"He's got them," Darren answers and leans into my cubicle, putting his body between Robert and me. "Here's the address." He grabs a post-it note and pen off of my desk and scribbles.

Robert turns and walks away.

"What was that?" Darren asks.

"I've never even met the dude up close before," I say. "Kind of a dick."

Darren watches Robert leave the floor. "He's about to lose his shit then."

"Why?" I ask.

"Let's just say, the team has welcomed him in their own special way," Darren answers and hands the post-it note to me. It's a drawing of a cat walking away, tail and butthole in view.

"Oh shit. He's going to go nuclear." I push Darren out of my cubicle. "Let's go watch."

We make it to the garage just as Robert is shouting, "Where the hell is my log book?"

I know all the hiding places and locate the spiral-bound book in a split second. There it is—duct-taped to the rafters—dead center.

Robert's face turns red. He swears, "Son of a bitch. Don't touch my stuff." He sounds like a three-year-old. "I'll have your balls for this."

He pivots quickly and covers the ground between us in two loud steps. "I'm not kidding," he says. I hold my ground against his sour breath.

"Hold on there, Sparkey," Darren interjects.

Robert faces the garage. "Where's a ladder?" he asks.

Darren leans over to me and whispers, "Damn. That guy is wound tight."

We all stand back to watch the show. Robert stomps, curses, and drags a ladder out. It clinks and clanks. Finally, he gets it into place. He takes three steps onto it before realizing it is too short. I could have told him that.

Rage renewed, he spits a new batch of colorful cursing. Some combinations are impressive. He must have Australian friends—I've not heard these phrases before. I should take notes.

His eyes bulge as he yells, "You bunch of deadshit dog-cunts," and kicks the ladder with a solid thunk.

"Fuck," I yelp as I and three other guys lunge forward to catch the flung ladder as it topples towards a parked motorcycle.

Gravity and the ladder win. The ladder bounces on the gas tank, denting it in. In slow motion, it succumbs to the pull of the earth—scratching the tank with a sickening screech on its crash course with the ground. Dead silence.

Lashing out is uncalled for, but the unit has a zero tolerance policy towards property damage. I've seen the guys close ranks around someone who was truly having a shitty day. Scott punched a hole through a wall when he heard his wife had died while he was on a detail. The team fixed it before the end of the day and no one was the wiser.

We protect our group. People have shitty days. Robert isn't one of us yet, and no one moves to help him.

Lighten up. How many times has my purple Sparkling Shine made it to the rafters? It's just good fun—a group of big brothers all picking on each other. It's kind of nice having healthy, not psychotic, not animal killer, not child molesting brothers for a change.

One by one, the guys disappear from the room. Boss walks in, sizes up the situation in a glance, points to the bulletin board and the shelf next to it, and says, "Incident form is there. It goes on my desk. I expect to see you in an hour with it completed."

He turns and walks out.

Robert glares at the group then at me, "I know you were behind this, kitty."

I attract them, the crazies. It's like I got a magnet.

At the bar later, we all giggle like schoolgirls.

"Kitty? What's that mean, anyway? Was he trying to call you a c..."

"Don't you say it..." I interrupt.

Darren smiles, and Scott laughs under his breath, but neither one finishes the word.

"...you dog-cunts," I finish and we all smile. Banter. It makes their world go round. "Never heard that one before." I sober, "Can I be honest with you guys?"

Molly is near. I lean over the bar and whisper in her ear. She smiles and says, "O.K."

She lifts the wooden flap for me, and I get behind the bar. I set up a martini glass, a few bottles, and mix a nice dry Orange Martini.

"This is my favorite Martini garnish." I peel off a slice of orange rind and hold a flame under it for a moment. The guys watch with blank faces.

I twist the orange rind and rub it across the martini glass, then present the drink with my hands like a game-show host.

Blank faces.

"Darren," I say.

"Huh?"

"Say Meow."

"Meow." He looks at me as if I've lost my mind.

I place an empty martini glass in front of him, put a dash of liquor in it and say, "Knock it over."

Realization dawns on his face.

They all speak at once.

"You're?"

"That's you?"

"I love your show!" Darren yelps.

"Yeah, well, Robert there thinks he has one over on me."

"Your face doesn't show. I mean, we didn't recognize you at all!" Darren says.

"I told the boss this morning." I taste the Martini, not half bad.

"Yeah, but he doesn't really know about the digital world. Did he understand what you were talking about?" Scott asks.

"True. I don't think it's a big deal though. Like, twenty people and you all see those videos." I say.

"How did he figure it out?" Scotty asks. He's looking at the videos on his phone and catching up everyone around him.

"Mercedez," Darren says and grabs some pretzels from a nearby bowl. "He followed her the other night. She had Whiskers with her."

"Oh yeah, I saw the logo on the backpack," Molly quips as she takes the empty glasses away. "Cute kitty."

"Anyone know where he came from?" I ask.

No one knows.

We hang out a little more. I make my excuses to leave. Mercedez is waiting for me to come home and make some videos. I look around as I leave the bar, just to make sure Robert isn't lurking in the shadows.

A nearby car backfires, traveling through me like a bullet. I flinch. Cool under fire—that's me.

"You know, when Whiskers knocks something over we should do a give-a-way. I made merch." Mercedez beams and holds up a glass tumbler with the Tippsy Kitty logo engraved on it.

This is her thing. It exhausts me, all the moving parts—but it is a cool glass. I nod my head yes and say, "Whatever you think is best. I trust you."

"Don't act so bored. Gosh," Mercedez warns.

"I just like to make the drinks."

Mercedez sets up her camera and I place my bottles. When she's ready she says, "What'cha making tonight, Rocket?"

I smile. My Dad used to call me that.

"This one is called Triple Threat," I tell the camera. "Most recipes of this drink have peach schnapps in it. If I ever ask for peach schnapps, that's code for 'I've been kidnapped.'"

I hold bottles out to Whiskers for a sniff.

"This version has gin, tequila, vodka, grenadine, and sour mix."

Whiskers obliges and comes close to supervise my pours.

"You know what we should do?" Mercedez positions a LED light so the back of Whisker's luxurious black and white fur is highlighted in a rim light. "We should do a recording in front of an audience. That would be neat."

'Holy shit, yuck.'

A gentle knock on the door interrupts this horrible idea from going any further.

"Who is it?" I call.

Mercedez gives me a weird look. "You expecting trouble?"

"Weird stuff at work. I'll tell you later. Got me over thinking," I answer.

"Me. Dee," a small voice answers.

This month's installment of neighbor between me and Betty is a research librarian who works part-time at the library of congress and lectures part-time at George Washington University. I don't quite understand her area of study. Something to do with birds.

"Hiya, Dee," I chirp. I like her. She's smart and a quiet neighbor.

"Hi, Jude." She leans in, "Mercedez."

"Howdy." Mercedez picks up Whiskers to keep her from bolting out the door, though she has no interest of ever moving quickly.

Dee asks, "Betty left something weird at my door this morning. Do you know what this means?"

Without missing a beat—having been through this before with the previous neighbors—we take guesses, "Well, let's see is it a prayer book, crucifix…"

"Dried fruit." Mercedez adds. "Moldy."

I continue, "Moving boxes, a dead fern."

Mercedez holds the door in one hand and the cat in the other adding, "Once there was a bunch of oily rags. I don't know what that was about."

"Oh." A worried look scrunches Dee's eyebrows. "That sounds kinda gross."

"Hose through the wall? Oh man, she hasn't moved on to—like—bodily fluids, has she?" That's gross. The brown smeared plastic bracelet. Why is there so much badly placed shit in my life?

Dee holds up a "Get Well Soon" card.

"Oh." I stare blankly at it.

There is one obvious question to ask. I don't ask it. I just look at Dee in all of her obvious health and prettiness. She's a runner. Goes out running just about the same time I get in from mine. Slight build. Shorter than me. Maybe 5'2". Light brown hair pulled in a perpetual ponytail. Tiny gold ball earrings. No other jewelry. Manicured fingernails, light pink polish, little gold stars. Accent is from further up north. Michigan or thereabouts, I think.

"I've not been sick," she says.

Mercedez takes the card, opens it up to see the scrawled signature inside.

"Thinking of you in this trying time. —Betty"

"That is weird."

"I know, right?"

I roll my eyes, "She's a piece of work."

We peek down the hall to see if her door is open a crack. Not today. Maybe the spider is out getting groceries or doing her laundry in the community laundry room.

"She doesn't have a grasp on reality. I don't know if it is Alzheimer's, dementia, or just your average day psychotic." I say.

"Does she ever get visitors? Like, who's going to take care of her when she's unable to take care of herself?"

I take the card from Mercedez and give it a once over. Nothing else to see. On the front is a sad-looking cartoon cat in bed with a red hot-water bag like you see in old cartoons.

"I ran into some guy in the garage the other day carrying a box of stuff in. Said he was helping her get some things from storage. I didn't ask if he was related to her or not. I didn't really want to talk to him."

In unison, we look towards the end of the hall at her closed door.

"Weird."

"Right?"

"Wanna come in and have a drink?"

"I'll pass. Thanks, though. I got an early start in the morning."

We say our goodbyes and she bounds off, get well card in hand.

Mercedez and I finish recording the drink and Mercedez gets quiet on the couch for an hour, clicking away on her device.

"Do you think we should have them post a video of themselves saying why their drink will be Kitty approved? Or why their drink will be the one Kitty knocks over?"

When Mercedez asks for input questions like this, it is best to just make noises. "Uuuuuuh. Mmmmmmm." I pretend to think.

"You're right. I don't want to come across like we're judging people on how they look." She clicks some more and nods to herself. "I can just screen them for weird-o vibes by looking at their social media presence."

"Where is this taking place?" *'Why on earth would someone want to come to this?'*

"I was thinking we'd rent that cabin again and then the one next to it."

"Mercedez, how much is this going to cost?" *'No really, why on earth anyone would care and want to be there?'*

"I have some frequent flyer miles that are going to expire soon and you make some dough from the YouTube."

"I do?"

Mercedez smiles. She had said there was funding coming in. But, God love her, she takes care of it all and could rob me blind. I'd never know. It all feels like make believe money to me.

"Plus you have some sponsorship now."

"I do?"

"You have sponsorship ads and click-throughs make money." Mercedez bounces with excitement.

"Uuhhhhhh." How do you even respond to something like this?

"Baby Betty, you are big. You just don't realize it. You are one of my biggest clients."

"But I'm just having fun making drinks."

"And people can't get enough of the mystery woman and her cat." She swivels the screen of her laptop towards me. "This is the stats on the traffic you get across the sites." She points to something on the screen that makes her happy. "And this," she clicks and the screen changes, "is the amount you get for the merch you sell."

"Who knew?" I am impressed but still not quite getting the concept of everything. "It can't last forever."

Debby Doubtful—that's me.

"No. But it will last a pretty long time with me as your PR agent." Mercedez—the tech wizard—beams.

I remember when Mercedez got into tech. She was always trying to figure things out. I was on my way to ROTC practice— it made my Dad happy—and swung by the science building to see Mercedez.

"You here?" I called. Soldering guns filled the room, waiting in their holders on long burn-pocked tables. All else was quiet.

"I'm heading off to march. In the heat. While wearing—God, I think this is wool." Those uniforms itched something awful.

A clattering noise in the back storage closet startled me. "Fuck. Mercedez?"

"Army Alice," Mercedez crooned. Her face was flushed. She was busy stuffing something in her backpack.

"Drugs?" I asked, knowing it wasn't—but not sure what she was up to.

She fumbled a bit and flustered. "I just." She looked down at her shoes. "I'm fixing up something."

"What?" I tried to peek into her backpack.

Mercedez looked like she might cry. I backed off.

"Sorry. You don't have to show me," I said.

"Promise you won't make fun of me?" Mercedez held the backpack protectively to her chest. There was actual sweat on her forehead.

"If you don't show me, I'll totally think it's a bong." The week before, I had caught Jackson in the shed with a bong. He'd backhanded me for my transgression. Unconsciously, I touched my jaw where the bruise from "falling off my bike" was still tender.

"I fixed your alarm clock." She carefully reached into her backpack, without opening the zipper too far, and pulled out my favorite alarm clock.

"The one I won last year!" I was so happy, I hugged Mercedez—crushing the alarm clock between us. "How'd you fix it?"

Jackson had hurled it against the wall after it came in the mail. "What a stupid thing to win," he had said.

She pointed to the long tables in the room. "A little glue, a little solder, and I made a new face for it out of some bulletproof glass."

"What the hell?"

"There's a pile of scraps in here." Mercedez pointed to the storage closet. Behind her a rack of Betamax and 3/4" editing equipment blinked. "Over there." She corrected my gaze to the right.

Five bins of various scraps from Plexiglas, a small bucket of bulletproof glass, and a barrel of actual glass gathered dust.

"I had fun grinding it down in the workshop next door," she said.

"This is the best thing ever," I said and hugged her again.

"I have to go march in the heat. See you after school?" I asked.

"I'll walk you there," she said. "Oops. Hang on." She went back into the closet and powered down the editing rack.

"They should name this room after you," I said. "You're in here all the time."

Mercedez smiled and hurried me out of the room as if it would catch on fire. "Don't be late for practice."

"You okay?" I asked.

"Sure. See you after school," she said and hurried off to her next class, forgetting her offer of walking me to ROTC. I was kind of sad about that.

Then, that afternoon, Mercedez called me in a panic. I was just getting out of Algebra II, ducked into the bathroom to take the call. Mercedez's voice, on the other end, was difficult to hear—she was crying her heart out.

"I can't hear you, Mercedez. Slow down. Breathe," I said.

All I could hear was deep soul-shuddering sobbing.

I was already scheming on how to kill whoever was behind making Mercedez cry.

"Come get me?" she finally managed.

"Where?"

"Donut shop."

It meant skipping the rest of my classes. "Hang on. I'll be right there," I said without hesitation.

By the time I got to the donut shop, Mercedez had stopped crying and emerged from the backroom where she had locked herself in for safety. Daryl—a friend of ours—worked there at the time and had hid Mercedez.

The place was empty except for us three. Mercedez huddled in the back corner, an uneaten chocolate éclair in front of her.

"Mercedez wouldn't let me call the cops." Daryl let me know the second I walked in the door.

She was a mess. Bloody nose. Black eye. Gash on her forehead. Ripped shirt. She held her arm protectively to her side.

Daryl filled me in on the details. Mercedez stared at the éclair and wouldn't lift her eyes. I scooted into the booth and put my arm around her. She winced. There was more damage I couldn't see.

She had ridden her bicycle to the donut shop to hang out with Daryl. They weren't a thing. Daryl, our albino-punk-but-buff-gay-but-looked-straight friend, was never Mercedez's type.

"White-bread," she'd call him.

She had been in the parking lot chaining up her bike to the bike rack when three guys jumped her. Right there in broad daylight. There were the racial slurs, the gay slurs, and the normal verbal fuckery you expect from assholes. They beat the crap out of Mercedez and when she was on the ground, they finished the job with a short 2x4 they had pulled from the bed of their truck.

"Who was it? Did you know them?" I asked them both.

"It was over so quick. I was pulling donuts out of the proofer when I heard the noise. Couldn't see who it was. Didn't recognize the truck," Daryl said. He put cups of coffee in front of us.

Pickup truck, rebel flag, the whole thing. Stereotype? Yes. They lived up to the image. She'd wanted a donut and instead got beat up for being different.

Daryl twisted the hand towel. It made a rasping noise against his dry, red hands. "They screeched off. Lots of smoke from their tires. I couldn't see the plate."

I had noticed the trail of black on the tarmac when I walked in.

"We should call the cops," I said.

Mercedez shook her head and winced from the movement. "No," she croaked.

"Your arm could be broken," Daryl said.

"And a few ribs." I stroked her unbroken arm gently.

She wouldn't hear of it. I drove her home, and she hid in her room.

A couple weeks later, after school, I stopped by her house as I had every day since the donut shop. Her aunt was sitting on the porch.

"You empty the locker?" she asked.

Mercedez had dropped out of school.

I held up a battered box filled with notebooks, parts of computers, a broken keyboard.

"I don't know what to do with that kid. He's not coming out of the bedroom," she said and hitched a thumb over her shoulder towards the back bedroom.

To this day Mercedez's aunt still calls her a he and dead names her. She never really understood.

I went in and knocked on the door. "I brought your stuff."

"Thanks," Mercedez said through the door. She hadn't opened it for me yet.

I sat in the hallway and made myself comfortable. "Mr. Erdles from school sent some spare parts he had. Said you can have them to finish building your PC."

"That's nice." She was on the other side of the door.

I didn't ask anything more about the donut shop or why she had been weird that day. I figured she'd tell me when she was ready.

Facebook post on "Tippsy Kitty" created by Mercedez:

"Win a two-day—one-night stay in the gorgeous mountains of Tennessee and a seat at a live recording session of Tippsy Kitty. She'll make YOUR drink for the show.

*can not be allergic to cats

*meals not included

*Absolutely no photos will be allowed during the event. Phones will be collected at the door.

To enter— put a picture of the drink you want to see made on the show and list the basic ingredients."

5K Likes, Happy faces, Hearts, and Wow emojis.

3K comments

1.4K Shares

Comments:

"what a great idea! Here's a pic of my favorite dirty martini."— little.miss.chockablock

"*I want a Blow Job. The drink I mean. Hahaha. [smiley emoji]*"—crustiersteve

"*This is my boyfriend's favorite drink a Dirty Harry.*"—nicolez170b9ekl

"*Gin Gin mule*"— mom62460

"*You gotta love a PainKiller [martini emoji, skull emoji]*" — KingBarbour90

"*I love me a Boulevardier with a tangerine twist*"—gilbertine.victorine

"*All is the same time has gone by some day you come some day you'll die someone has died long time ago.*"—1825Salieri

"*Banana Daiquiri will be your next favorite drink*"—frank.likes.bang

"*Why don't you like beer?*"—jack93ozumvjfse

"*Show us your face, bitch!*" — thswhtshesd22

Reply FtGrlsNd0Apply69: "*I'll bet she's a dog.*"

Reply from thswhtshesd22: "*Show us your tits!*"

Twenty direct messages all fitting the same description:

Profile pick is a smiling selfie of a 30-50 something dude [pick one]:

in military fatigues
in front of a boat
in front of a car
on a beach wearing no shirt
in bed

Border of profile pic includes [pick one]:
Hearts
Flowers

American flags

Message begins with, "Hello [pick one]:
Beautiful
My friend
Lovely
Gorgeous
Hon, Hun, Honn

Message ends with, ..." [pick one]:
How are you today?
May be misspelled or filled with poor grammar, examples:
Haw today? How you too? You today?

Bonus points for [pick one]:
Gif of flowers
Gif of cute animal with flowers
Gif of heart animation
Dick pick

Repeat messages may include [pick one]:
Hello?!?
Are you ignoring me?
Why won't you talk to me?
I just want to be your friend.
Didn't you like the pic I sent you?

Continued ignoring may devolve into unimaginative slurs and suggestions of self fornication.

If also accompanied by a friend request—a quick look reveals:

Profile Banner includes [pick one]:
Bonus round – repick from selfie list above and add
Group picture with military group
Group picture with outdoorsman group
A picture ripped off from google. An image search reveals:
Dog from "How long will your Irish Setter live?"
Kid from "Parenting Strategies"
Car from "This year's best rides"
Food from "10 dishes for summer"
Outdoors from REI's website.

TRIPLE THREAT COCKTAIL

Recipe notes from Jude's journal.

Mix in shaker with ice until chilled. Strain over ice.
Equal parts:

- Gin
- Sour mix (lemon and lime with simple syrup)
- Tequila
- Vodka (got any Jolly Rancher infused vodka left?)
- Dash of grenadine
- Dash of orange bitters
- Four parts orange juice
- Garnish with orange rind

I like this one better than anything that uses peach schnapps.
(Yuck!)

11 - DONUTS AND GUNS

Getting beaten up at the donut shop was the best bad thing that ever happened to me. Everyone misinterpreted why I was beat up. I didn't correct them. To everyone it looked like I didn't fit into a myopic, mouth-breathing, dimwit's view of the world. It put me into a cocoon for years, followed by self-defense classes, gun range practice, and transitioning. What emerged was me.

"This tape won't play!" Zack all but hissed in my face.

He cornered me behind the gym. In the distance, the coach's whistle warned P.E. participants to keep moving.

"You need a SX player," I squeaked, wanting to puke, run, hide, and die all in the same breath. I did not want to be there. Did not want to remember. Did not want any of this. Dark thoughts of self-harm filled my head. I wanted this to stop.

"It says SP on it," he snarled.

"The recorder was an SX." The recorder he threw into the open pit. Where Janet was. Both dead and lost in the murk. I lost my battle and vomited, barely missing his shoes.

He smiled, unbothered by the stench.

"Make a copy that will play." He grabbed my shirt and yanked me up. "You're going to do it, or I'm going to put Jude in that pit with Janet."

I heaved a dry belch, grabbed the nearby wall to steady myself. I should be somewhere reading, studying world history, not living this nightmare.

A vomit string hung from my bottom lip as I blubbered, "It will take me a couple days. I have to get into the engineering room." I wiped my lip and continued, "When no one is there."

Zack shook me hard by the collar of my shirt. The seam pulled against my armpit. "I can come watch." His eyes gleamed.

The thought of Zack hovering over me, reliving that night, brought renewed bile to my throat.

I filled in the silence, unnecessarily. "Tape duping is boring," I said between hiccupping sobs that brewed deep in my chest. "It doesn't show on the TV."

He leaned in close, scanning my eyes for deception, said nothing.

Years of defending myself from bullies kicked in. Survival mode. A cold, detached part of me took over motor functions while my mind screamed in circles. My hands gently grasped his wrists, my voice said, "Your hands. Don't you have a commercial to do this weekend?"

He loosened his grip on my faded shirt. "Donut shop. Friday. 1 pm."

"I've got class," I whimpered.

Zack glared at me. My shoulders hitched with each breath.

My brain screamed, *'He's going to kill me. He's going to kill me. Just like Janet.'*

Zack stood up straight, pulled his t-shirt at the hem, and that smooth, suave congenial mask lit up his face. He said, "1 pm. The copy and the original. Or you'll wish you were never born. Jude, too. Right, kid-o?"

My hiccups turned to a shudder coursing from head to toe. That 'how are you old buddy' tone and smile with a promise of a painful death

—*like Janet*— caused my stomach to churn.

***

Friday, at the donut shop, Billy Barnes drove up. Remember him from when I first met Jude? The very same Billy, now all grown up and driving a red-neck special, skidded to a stop inches from my bike.

"Back from juvie?" I called. Bold for a scrawny little gay boy bound to be pummeled. I couldn't hold on to being scared any longer. Convinced I was going to die and channeling my inner Jude, I decided to go out with the last word. Fuck them.

"Look at this scrawny faggot," Billy drawled then slammed his door shut.

Jackson and one other kid I didn't recognize jumped out of the truck bed and fell in line behind Billy. Zack sauntered from the passenger side of the truck and stood in front of Billy. The rebel flag in the truck's back window presented a gruesome backdrop.

"Got them?" Zack asked.

"Both," I whispered. I handed a battered paper bag tied shut with rubber bands to him. Two rectangular shapes bulged against the sides.

He took it without saying a word. Confusion swept across the others behind him. Zack held the bag to his chest, inspected the contents, threw it into the truck's open window.

Billy asked, "What's that about?"

"Fucker stole something from me," Zack said. His tone dropped. "Let's show him what happens to sons-a-bitches that steal from us."

Zack stood back while Billy, Jackson, and the other guy used me as their personal punching bag. Through swollen and bleeding eyes, I saw Zack reach into the truck bed and pull out a 2X4.

Zack leaned in close and hissed in my ear so the others couldn't hear, "If I find out you made a copy for yourself, or you go to the police, I'll enjoy killing you and Jude." He stood. "Might anyway. Just for fun." He handed the plank of wood to Billy. "Here," he said. His eyes were cold, black. His smile—vicious.

Sharks.

I curled into a ball, holding my backpack to my stomach, and tried to disappear as the hits rained down. I don't remember much until Jude and Daryl were hovering over me in the donut shop. The chocolate éclair in front of me smelled sickeningly sweet.

When we stood to leave, Daryl reached into the booth, "Don't forget your pack."

God, I had almost forgotten it. Jude reached for it and I snatched it from her, though it hurt me to do so. The thought of her touching that bag, even without its unclean contents, horrified me. "I got it," I said.

Jude supported me gently over her shoulder and helped me to her ugly blue car. How that thing rattled. Every time she shifted gears the frame shook and my cracked ribs screamed.

***

July and Jude's vacation weekend has arrived. I stop by the local range while Jude goes out caving. I was nervous the first time I came here. A small thing like me going into a range where potential mouth-breathers gather.

"Mornin' Mercedez!" the owner shouts a greeting as I walk in.

This range is women-owned, and I love it.

"Good morning, Meg." I pat the bag hanging over my shoulder. "Got room on the range?"

"Sure. Quiet today."

Jude has always been an excellent shot. Her Dad taught her. After high school, Jude helped me get back on my feet by going to the range and taking self-defense lessons. She helped me get strong.

Now, going to a range by myself makes me feel like a superwoman.

I pay for some ammo. The bell on the door behind me jangles as a customer walks in.

"Mornin'," Meg calls out. "Help ya' with somethin'?"

The guy pauses and looks from Meg to me and then back again, smiles an affable grin. "I was hoping to get a 9 mil."

I don't mean to look him up and down, but the smile intrigues me. Looks like a nice guy, not my type though. Dark, wavy hair and a goofy grin.

He leans against the glass display counter and takes in all the guns.

"I like the silver slide on that one." He points out a shiny Glock.

I wave and walk towards the basement door where the range hides under the floorboards. Meg nods my way then turns back to the man and answers, "I have a used one like that over here if you want a better deal. G43 not the G43X."

I hear little more, the thick door to the basement range closes behind me.

Meg was right, dead quiet on the range. No one else is around. The range is small, only five lanes. I like the one closest to the right wall, furthest from the door. The sound proof lining on the wall is flaking, having taken a lot of abuse over the years. It silts the ground with every round shot. It smells in here, musty mildew mixed with gunpowder, and sweat.

I set my gear out, hang up my target, pull on my ear protection. With a button click, it whizzes to the end of my lane. I'm shooting with my favorite Glock today. It fits snugly in my hand. I'm careful to not touch the trigger. Glocks don't have a traditional safety; the only safety is to keep it unchambered. I chamber it, aim, slip my finger into the double-action trigger and squeeze. It kicks, re-chambers. My shot is low.

'Damn.'

The guy looking at the 9 mils must have bought one. I am into my second target when he comes in and takes a stance two lanes down from me. Keeping my eye on the target, I don't acknowledge him. Breathe, squeeze the trigger, hold as firmly as I can so the gun doesn't buck. My heart pounds. I fear this gun. It scares me and comforts me at the same time. Makes me feel safe in a dank place like this and also fearful I'll regret holding this metal death.

That's always the fear. Fear I'll drop it, point it in the wrong direction, forget to clear the chamber, forget to even chamber it, or it will misfire.

As if conjured by thought, the new guy's slide kicks back and sticks open after his last round. It nicks his thumb, blood drips down the side of his hand. He stands there and looks at his hand in shock.

Blood drips on the faded linoleum.

What am I going to do if he passes out? He's bigger than me, I can't catch him.

His head swivels slowly. He recovers and smiles, pulls his ear protection off one ear. "Well, damn. That's embarrassing."

"Looks like your round jammed. Is that the used 9 mil?" I ask, lifting my ear protection to gauge my voice level.

"Yeah. Needs cleaning, I guess." He pops the stuck round. It pings to the ground.

I stay in my lane and watch him pick up the bullet and put it in his pocket.

A stray memory of Zack intrudes. *He casually picks up the nearest one and puts it in his pocket.*

I push the memory away and focus on my target, press the button. The battered target whirrs towards me.

"Nice grouping," Mr. Six-Foot says.

I hate small talk. "Thanks," I reply and look at the disintegrated target, all at the center of the neck. Low, but consistently low. I should be happy with it.

He puts his gun down on the counter and holds out his hand, "Kurt." Blood drips from his thumb.

"Mercedez," I answer and point to the blood. "You're bleeding."

"Oh, shit." He fumbles.

I hand him a packet of tissues from my purse.

"Thanks." He takes a few and holds them to his hand. "You from around here?" he asks, nodding at my small gun case as I zip it closed.

I don't know why I lie, but my mouth opens and these words pop out, "Yes. On the other side of the mountain going towards Nashville."

"I'm just passing through," he says and pats the gun on the counter. "On an extended construction gig. Thought I'd pick up a souvenir."

"Well, I hope you enjoy your stay."

Suddenly, I want to get out of there. Like when you turn the lights off and have to run up the stairs before the boogey man gets you.

He smiles and brushes his dark hair out of his face, knocking the safety goggles. They almost slide off his nose. Kurt catches them and rights them. A quick dimple-filled smile blooms on his face.

He looks at his bleeding thumb again, "Guess I'm done for the day. Do you recommend any places around here for lunch?"

"There isn't much to pick from." I walk past him to get to the door. "The mom and pop place across the street has an actual cappuccino machine and linen tablecloths."

"That beats Taco Bell. Thanks for the suggestion, Mercedez," he answers. The gun case clunks out of his hand as he tries not to bleed on it. "Shit," he says.

"Can I help?" I ask and move closer.

He looks helpless. "I'd appreciate it. I don't think that lady up there wants me bleeding on her guns." He laughs nervously.

I take the gun and case from him.

He continues to babble, "I'd be afraid to bleed on her guns." He looks at the linoleum and startles. "Hell." He wipes up the blood with a tissue. "I don't want to bleed on her floor either."

I put the gun into the foam lined case and say, "Your Glock is bigger than my Glock." *'Good God, that's stupid.'* "I've got the 26 model. It's smaller." I zip the case closed, wishing I could zip my mouth.

"I uhh, would it be stupid to ask if you come here often?" he says. "Does she have good prices?" He points to the gun.

"Best in town. Also, the only place in town." I hand the gun case to him and think to myself, *That's enough small talk. Time to end this conversation.'*

As if reading my mind, he touches my hand as he takes the gun case from me. "I got this. Thanks. I don't want to keep you away from anything."

"You sure?" I ask. I feel bad for wanting to get away from him.

"Yeah. See you next time?" He smiles and opens the door for me.

"Hey." I reach into my purse and pull out a business card. "Here's my email. Well, one of them." I look at the card. This one has the Tippsy Kitty information on it. "Let me know next time you're in town. We can go shooting together." I point to his hand and say, "Maybe next time you'll bleed less."

12 - SUICIDE SHOT

"You're going to need to be honest with me." Boss looks at me across his desk. His coffee mug—which looks like it hasn't been washed since a peanut farmer was in office—clinks on the desk.

I am unsure where this is going and think the worst. I must be out. This is it. The psychiatrist has reported I am an unstable team player because of my past. Or my face-blindness is a weakness. I take too many three-day weekends like the one I've just returned from. Or...

A collection of weaknesses and problems lists itself in my head. Imposter syndrome doesn't go away, I guess. I've been in the division for nearly 8 years. You'd think I'd feel like I belong here at some point.

"Robert has put in a complaint with HR about you making this an uncomfortable workplace."

"Uhhhhh." Articulate as always. Thanks, brain.

I don't want to take the rap for a log book being duct taped to the rafters. I've never taken part in the very harmless hazing pranks the group does. But if I open my mouth and say I didn't do it, I'll have to say who did.

I don't want to lie. I don't want to tell the truth either.

'This is some bullshit.'

"OK, boss. What happens when someone makes a complaint?" Might as well just jump in and see this one through. It can't be that hard a knock. Can it?

Boss sips at his mug again. Dried drips of coffee from days gone by stain the side. "It puts a ding on your record. I have to fill the check boxes. Talk to you."

"That's it?" I ask, somewhat stunned.

"Yeah. Verbal warning. It's not like you had a mad fit and did $500 damage to a bike tank." He hides a smile with his coffee cup.

"Roger that." I guess Robert is going to be in hot water. "Have you met with him yet on that?" I don't want to be around after the meeting in case he wants to start trouble.

"Why don't you take the afternoon off. Think about what you did." Boss smiles again, his eyes crinkle up.

"Yes, sir." I stand and leave.

"Look whipped on your way out for me, would 'ya?" he calls after me.

I hang my head as I suit up for the ride home. No one approaches me and Robert is nowhere. I feel like I won but suspect this fight is just getting started. Robert probably fights dirty.

***

I park my Phantom at the condo garage. The pipes are warm and the engine ticks ever so quietly while it cools down. It's the only sound.

I look around and spot Betty's car a few spots over. The flag still hangs at the same angle as before. I walk over to the car. A fine layer of pollen and dust is on it. It hasn't moved in a couple weeks, maybe even a month. In fact, I haven't physically seen her in a while, have I? She's had her door cracked open, now and then. Small weird gifts have continued to show up on Dee's doorstep as usual. But I haven't actually seen her.

Maybe that dude, Kurt, has been helping her out and getting groceries for her so she doesn't need to go out.

Maybe I should check on her. Go knock on her door. She might be crazy, but she's a human. I stop by the mailbox first.

"What the hell is this?" I pull magazine after magazine from my mailbox. They each have brown paper wrappers over the cover. That's not a good sign.

Porn magazines. All lesbian porn and one obscure mag that apparently involves animals. They have that? Each is addressed to "Jude F.U. Lawz." That's dedicated revenge there, and awareness of my Facebook name. Creepy.

My phone rings, but it is an unfamiliar ring. What the hell? I drop half of the magazines while pulling out my phone. They plop open to expose their imagery in a flash of flesh.

"Good God." I grimace. How much do these subscriptions cost, anyway?

The phone beeps away. I juggle it and close the magazines at the same time while guiltily scanning the lobby. Surely someone will come around the corner at any moment and get an eyeful of this debauchery.

Who wants to see animal genitals draped in lace? Really? Who funds that? We could be curing cancer. One magazine falls out of my hand and hits the ground. BDSM. Interesting outfits, creative. There's some craft there, I have to admit. But damn, not my thing at all.

The phone beeps and cajoles. I tame the flesh rags and look at the phone screen—an incoming Facebook video call?

Someone from Morocco? What the hell is this? You can make video calls? I decline it.

I make it to my door, look down the hallway to check on Betty's door. Closed. Maybe I should go knock? Let's put these magazines down first. That would be a hilarious greeting. "Hi, Betty. Came to check on you. Want a magazine on—let's see here—pig porn?"

I fumble my way into the condo and before I can put the magazines on the counter another Facebook video call comes in from India this time.

What the actual fuck?'

Forget Betty, how do I turn this off? I can't ask Mercedez, she is out for a night clubbing or whatever you call it nowadays. She rarely goes out on the town, but now and then she gets an idea in her head she is missing something. Usually they end with a late night call.

Sure enough, the phone rings at 2 am.

"Your job is to talk me out of going out. I regret it every time." Mercedez's voice is quiet and husky over the phone.

"You okay?" I try my best to not sound groggy.

"Just drama and jerks," she says.

"That's why Whiskers is the best boyfriend." I shouldn't pick on her and instantly regret it.

"You're not wrong." Rustling as she shifts the phone from one ear to the other. "I gotta quit looking for Mr. Right in all the wrong places."

I sit up in bed to keep from nodding off. "Well."

"Yeah." She gets quiet. Moments go by and we listen to each other breathing. "I need a change of scenery."

My phone buzzes again—another video call from Facebook. "What's that?" she asks.

"I keep getting these weird video calls via Facebook from all sorts of weird places." I decline the call and put the phone back to my ear.

"I'll help you get that turned off tomorrow."

"Thanks. Let's turn off any and all notifications. That stuff bugs me," I beg.

"We heading back to TN soon?"

"Yeah. I need to run the bikes and maybe bounce a pit or two." Plus, I want to get away from my mailbox, and the drama at work. I won't tell Mercedez about any of my drama. She doesn't need that right now. I slide back down into bed.

"What happened?" She knows me too well.

"S'ok. I'll fill you in tomorrow. Nothing major. I just need to clear my head."

The phone beeps again with a video call.

"Damn it." I drop the phone on my face as I hit decline. "Fuck-all." Luckily, my face doesn't hit accept. That would suck.

"Price of fame, chick-a-dee." Mercedez blows her nose and sniffs demurely.

"I'm not famous."

"Your show is. Whiskers is. She has his own line of merch now."

"Seriously?"

"Yes."

"You've been busy." I'm in awe of how she gets all these things done. "And amazing. I'm proud I figured out how to order something on Amazon. Got a nice chef's knife. It had great reviews."

"It's what I do. And, look at you. Told you you'd like this century. We can expense that." She pauses and I can tell she wants to say more. "Thanks, babe."

"It's what I do," I return. "I'm going to turn this phone off. If you need me, call my work phone."

"Got it," she says.

A loud text wakes me up at 6 am. I worry it might be Mercedez.

"Meet with me at 8:30 am"—a text from the boss.

'Shit.'

That's never a good text to get.

***

I cut my morning workout short, just body weight stuff in the apartment with little colorful, nearly useless dumbbells.

Betty's door is open a crack. Damn, I forgot to check on her last night.

I got to get in and deal with whatever is blowing up at work. If there is a situation with Betty, I don't have time to deal with it. She must be okay and up to her normal shenanigans if her door is open. Just because I haven't actually seen her means nothing.

The hallway is deathly quiet as I walk through it towards the garage.

I just about had myself convinced the psych eval went okay. Maybe something I said raised a red flag. They poked at it differently this time.

Traffic is backed up, I'll turn up 20th street to avoid it.

I certify on the range every month with flying colors. I mean, I started shooting after high school. All right, that wasn't the most healthy thing to do. I admit. Who starts shooting at the range the second they turn old enough—right after their brother shoots himself?

I had come home from school and was looking forward to getting to Dad's trucker school and trying out someone's Hayabusa motorcycle—a fast bike. It will jump right out from underneath you. Dad set the training track up with cones and obstacles. I could spend hours out there and usually did. I'd pay for the gas I used and it usually ended up being $2 for the couple of hours. You can't find cheaper entertainment. Cheap and safe away from Jackson.

I think since Mom died, Dad liked me there with him most times and he didn't have to worry. Needed to get my boots at the house, having forgotten them that morning. Thick-soled boots give me a better purchase on the ground when sitting on a taller bike. Short legs—so me.

The house was quiet. I didn't know Jackson was home. He shouldn't have been. He was supposed to be at the gas station working. We found out later he had stopped showing up two weeks earlier.

"She was never proud of me." In the silence of the house, his hoarse whisper was deafening.

I jumped and dropped my book bag. The contents—algebra, chemistry, and civics books—spilled out into the hallway.

"Jackson. Why aren't you at work?" My question was sharp and needling.

No one else was home. Fear pricked at the base of my spine. I considered what my options of escape could be.

I got curious when he didn't answer. Oh, but being curious about what Jackson is up to has never led to anything good. I've walked in on him setting fires to his mattress, taping the cat's eyes closed, destroying mother's pretty blue Sunday school dress, cutting my Barbie dolls' heads off.

What's worse is when he invites you to come look at what he is doing, to bear witness—like showing me the dead animals in the sewer.

Recently he had called out to me from his room, "Come see. You'll like it!"

I thought he was going to show me something neat, like a rock or a new model airplane. Instead, when I walked into his room, I witnessed him diddling a ten-year-old kid. The poor kid didn't know what to think, and I didn't know what to do. Jackson just smiled smugly at me.

"Kid, get out of here," I yelled. But he didn't move. He stared at Jackson, waiting for the tiger to strike him down.

"I'll set you on fire in your bed, if you say anything." He looked at me and then the kid. "Get out of here. Both of you."

We ran. The kid took off. I never knew his name. I kept my door locked every night after that.

I'm sure Jackson did more than what I knew of. I heard rumors, knew he'd done more. I suspected he was just getting warmed up. He was growing into a monster, and I feared him.

Did Mom and Dad know? They ignored Jackson. We all ignored this growing demon in our midst. Ignored him like a bad water stain on the ceiling no one wants to fix.

I didn't want to see what he was up to this time. The hairs stood up on the back of my neck.

His voice sounded like a small, frightened boy when he repeated, "She never was proud of me."

I sighed, took the bait, and walked into the front sitting room. This was Mom's favorite room for "receiving guests". We were not allowed in this room. When Mom was alive, she would sit in there—all poise and grace—with her lady friends. They would legitimately have tea and cookies and talk as if it were something out of the 50s.

A year ago, Dad closed the curtains in there. The room was slightly dusty. No one had been in it since Mom died. We had put the hospice bed in there so Mom could look out the big bay window and see the trees outside. Even in those last few weeks her friends came over and they drank tea and ate cookies in there as if Mom wasn't frail sticks covered with pale skin and half glazed from the morphine. She'd smile and Dad would put lipstick on her and brush her hair. I hadn't even looked in that room since she died.

Jackson had perched himself on the formal couch—the white one we were never allowed to sit on. He hugged Mom's urn to his chest. The silver vase gleamed in the dim room. His muddy feet were on the pale-pink carpet. Only grown-ups could go in that room—they wouldn't get it dirty. No kids allowed in here.

I wanted to tell him he shouldn't be in there. Mom wouldn't like it. And he should put Mom down. What if he spilled her? On the pale-pink champagne carpet? How would we fix that? But the look of Jackson sitting there on the white couch stopped me. His eyes were wide and staring ahead at nothing. Tears streamed down his face. Snot bubbled and ran from his nose. I had never seen Jackson show any emotion but contempt and rage. I had never seen him show remorse of any type, ever. This frightened me more than anything.

He raised the gun. Half-heartedly pointed it at me. "She loved you." Pointed the barrel of the gun at his chest. "She never loved me." He limply dropped the gun to the couch. His hand still had a loose grip on it.

What do you do in a situation like this? Run. Call for help. Get the hell out of there. A sane person would probably do that. Not me. My fifteen-year-old brain had frozen and locked onto the urn filled with Mom's ashes. I didn't want her spilled. That would hurt Dad too much.

Is that a rational thought? No. When you're fifteen, you don't have enough experience with problem solving to know which problem is actually more pressing. At that moment my safety didn't matter, because I didn't actually believe he would shoot me. He didn't seem like he wanted to shoot me. I hadn't registered the gun was an actual honest to goodness threat, yet.

We had all learned gun safety and even shot down at the range with Dad. Guns weren't a shock. Surely he was being dramatic with a dry gun. We didn't keep loaded guns in the house. Hell, I didn't even know where Dad kept the ammunition. We'd always buy the ammo at the range and shoot it all there.

The gun became an issue when I heard him pull the hammer back. That click made my insides turn to liquid, not because it was so loud, but because it was so silent.

Click.

Sweat beaded on the small of my back. The hairs on my arms stood on end. I was both freezing cold and flushed hot at the same time. My voice babbled, "What's going on Jackson? Tell me about it."

I really didn't want to hear. This monster was hitting rock bottom and he would probably spill mom. Dad was going to lose his shit, and I'd have to clean it all up. But he'd be gone. One less monster in the world. A flush of heat blossomed on my chest and crept up my neck. My fingers tingled from the rush of adrenaline as it hit my veins.

Jackson glared at me hatefully. His hand twitched on the sofa and the cocked gun rocked slightly, but stayed safely pointed away

"I made her sick." He moaned. "She died because of me."

"You didn't cause her breast cancer." My eyes ping-ponged from Mom's urn to the gun—two dull silver totems.

"I prayed for her to die." He snorted and the line of snot, previously glistening on his upper-lip, disappeared.

"You're that powerful you prayed her to have cancer." Fifteen-year-old me—zero tact.

His eyes zeroed in on me. "You were her favorite."

Considering the amount of whupping I received growing up, I begged to differ, but held my opinion to myself. The gun still stayed on the couch and I was trying to figure out what to do.

"What are you planning to do with the gun, Jackson?" I took a step into the doorway of the sitting room. There was nothing to hide behind.

Jackson stood. I jumped back a half step. That hint of fright lit him up. With flat eyes, he smiled. "I could take you with me." This time he lifted the gun and pointed it at me.

I could have run. I could have turned and fled out the door. Maybe he would have missed me. Maybe he would have chased me. I didn't. Instead, an epiphany came over me. He smiled when I became frightened. Gained strength when I got scared.

It was all a power trip—bringing me to see the dead animals in the sewer, my pet rabbit. The countless times he had manipulated me to believe he would cause me harm if I didn't keep his secrets like that poor kid in his bedroom.

Anger broiled my thoughts. I took a step forward and the voice that came from me was not one I had ever heard. Cold. Harsh. Strong. Cutting. "You know what. You did kill mom. She found out about what you did in the sewers with the animals. She couldn't take the sight of you. It caused the cancer to eat her alive."

I took another step towards him. He stood with his mouth agape and the gun drooped towards the ground. "Uhhhhh…"

"She heard you were molesting little boys and taking Polaroids," I said.

I was making things up. I had never seen the Polaroids, but the camera had always been out. I had picked it up once and Jackson nearly broke a toe running through the hall and tackling me to get it out of my hands. His precious camera. But I never saw the photos.

"She found them." My voice—sharp and hoarse—scared me.

Jackson's eyes darted to the bookshelf.

'Gotcha.'

"She was having tea with her friends and they were admiring the bookshelf. The pictures fell out of a book right there on top of the marmalade cookies. It horrified Mom. She couldn't look at you again."

Jackson staggered back and dropped onto the sofa. The gun fell to the floor. "You're lying." He didn't sound convinced.

"She told me she wished you had never been born." I couldn't stop my mouth. I had him broken. I wanted him gone. "You should pick that gun up and just blow your head off."

He stared at me.

"Save us all the fucking hardship of having to look at you every day." What was coming from me? Anger. Pent up rage. Things I had felt and wanted to say since I was six.

He blinked and his mouth worked, no words came out.

"You should put Mom down first. You fuck-up. Don't you dare spill her." I pointed to the ground.

Jackson wordlessly put the urn on the floor between his feet.

We stared at each other in silence. The air conditioner kicked in and a hum filled the house. I was in a flop-sweat and my skin was ice cold. The words that had issued from me were unearthly, and I regretted I could be such a fiend. Even though he was a horrible monster—I shouldn't talk to anyone like that.

I remembered my bunny. That little boy, wide-eyed when I opened Jackson's bedroom door. How quickly he ran out of the house. Years of torment escalating over the years.

"Get it over with." I nearly spat, turned my back on him and walked out of the sitting room. I almost tripped over my algebra and chemistry books, but stepped over them at the last second. I hadn't made it two steps before the gunshot made me jump.

The shot was loud and dull. The splat of something—I didn't want to know what—hit the wall. I patted my body, looking for wounds. I felt nothing on fire or hurting. In fact, I felt nothing at all. Disbelief, shock—

—and relief.

I couldn't turn around and look. Slowly, I walked to the kitchen and pulled the cordless phone from its base, dialed 911, waited patiently for the dispatcher to come on the line.

"I just got home and I think my brother shot himself. I can't go in there and look. Can someone get my Dad?" I gave them the address of where to get him.

It took them seven minutes to pull up. I stayed at the back of the house and refused to come forward and see. I sat heavily in a kitchen chair as the adrenalin ran through and shook me. My teeth chattered.

I saved the world from a monster—all but pulled that trigger myself.

Every month, for my job, I certify on the range seeing Jackson each time I pull the trigger—every single shot for 2 clips.

The psych evaluators never ask the right questions:

'You took up shooting at the range months after his suicide. That's not healthy, is it?'

'Who do you see when you shoot your gun?'

'You hid who he was from everyone. Including your father. Do you feel guilty about that?'

I did. I hid everything about him. Found all the evidence and burned it all. He was dead; it didn't matter anymore.

As I pull my bike into the employee parking lot, I'm torturing myself with questions and reasons I am in trouble. Surely, these unresolved issues deem me as unfit. The psych evaluators know. They can smell it on me. I'm not clean. Not honest. Guilty.

I know how stupid that sounds, even as I think it. Like I'm the only one walking around with a history with some hidden hate and anger. Some stain on them. Everyone has something like that. It has never—not once—ever gotten in the way of my job. I'm clear as a fucking bell when I work.

Guilty for the lie? Yeah, I know.

It is me wanting to have closure and I probably really needed to go talk it out with a therapist and move on. I know. You don't have to say it.

All of this is spinning in my brain as I open my boss's door. I rock back on my heels when he turns to me and says, "You have breached your security clearance." His voice is flat and emotionless.

"What, boss?"

"It came in anonymously to HR that you have a social media thing going on."

"Boss, I told you about it. I'm not recognizable in that at all. It's not a big thing."

"This person figured it out."

"You mean Robert did and told to get back at me."

Boss looked at me blankly. I would never want to play poker with him.

I give him the silent treatment back.

'Damn it.'

"But he told HR, which means you have to follow protocol," I answer. It isn't a big deal until someone—Robert—makes it a big deal.

I had never paid attention to the technology policies and regulations since I had never been active online. I still don't feel like I'm active online since Mercedez does it all for me.

"I don't manage those accounts. That is all done by a—" I can't stop the stupid, damning words as they come out of my mouth. "—PR manager."

Boss does not waver his gaze.

Yeah. I am proving his point. Who has PR managers? People with large social media presence.

'Damn it.'

"You have a choice to make." He leans back in his chair and holds his hands out, palms up. "Quit that or quit this."

'Fuck. There it is.'

I never imagined this is how the day would come.

"Take the rest of the week to think it over." He is unreadable. Further conversation on this topic will not occur. He can not—will not—give any indication which decision he prefers. It will be my idea. I can't fault him. He's a solid boss.

'Double fuck.'

***

I call Mercedez after I pull into my garage at home. Childishly consider drawing in the dust on Betty's car when Mercedez picks up.

"I have a four-day weekend. Surprise. Want to get away?" I try to sound perky.

"Sure, hon." Mercedez sounds hesitant, but she doesn't press. "Leave in the morning or now?"

I consider if arriving at 3 am would be better than waiting until morning. "I think I have to get away now."

"Give me one hour, sweetie." She hangs up the phone.

I keep silent for much of the drive. How am I going to tell her about this choice I have to make? How can I make it feel like it isn't her fault? I should have thought ahead—realized what the repercussions could be.

Mercedez is unusually quiet on the drive too.

"Want to stop and get provisions for a new recipe?" she asks.

"I don't know," I hem.

"I have something to tell you." Mercedez looks straight ahead at the road. "You have a couple other sponsorship deals and an interview for the local newspaper and local news."

"Seriously?"

"Yes. I didn't say no right away."

"But, I can't."

"Because you can't show your face. But they can work with that, maybe?" She sounds hopeful.

I sigh. "This isn't supposed to be my life. This is getting too surreal." I speak with my head turned to the outside world.

We have the top up—neither one of us feeling carefree enough to have the wind in our hair.

"When do they have to know?"

"Forty-eight hours." Mercedez glances at me and frowns. "Do you want to talk about it?"

I tell her the total mess with Robert at work, the complaint he filed which didn't get me anything more than a write-up, him retaliating by throwing me under the bus and exposing me as the Tippsy Kitty. I blab on and on and end with the Boss's ultimatum.

I say, "I knew better. I should have kept myself out of it. We could have done it with a voiceover. It could have been all you."

"But it is you that makes it."

"Whiskers, you mean."

"No, people like to hear you and want to know about you. You've got a charm and energy that comes across when you talk about the recipes. They love you."

I harrumph.

"Lovely Lucy, we've been through everything together, haven't we?"

I nod, turn my head to hide my tears. It makes me pissed off to have tears making more angry tears fall.

'Triple fuck.'

***

Angry tears rained down my face as I sat in the kitchen after Jackson killed himself. The police stomped through the house. The medical examiner stepped over my chemistry and algebra books in the hallway and gingerly walked onto the pale-pink carpet that was my mother's favorite.

Shock kept me from processing anything except for my anger at Jackson. I couldn't let Dad know the truth about Jackson. It would destroy him.

People were coming and going. Dad walked towards the front door and a group of cops stopped him from walking in. He stared at me. His face wore the same mask of disbelief I wore on mine.

"You don't want to see this. Go around back, Ted," an old officer friend of Dad's said.

"Come on. Rocket's in the kitchen. We'll go around back." Another cop put an arm around Dad's shoulder. Turned him away from the door. I recognized the cop's cauliflower ears. He helped teach the motorcycle training classes.

The others I recognized by their name tags. They had all been around, friends of Dads, but never visited the house on Mom's orders. Now, they milled about, looked uncomfortable, kept their eyes down.

Dad came around to the back door and sat at the kitchen table with me. We watched wordlessly as they wheeled the bulky black bag out on a gurney. The wheels left indents in the carpet.

Mercedez showed up at my elbow. I didn't know who called her. Suddenly, she was there, standing just behind me and waiting for me to invite her into my circle of sorrow.

Mercedez hadn't stepped out of her house since her attack six months before. Yet, there she was, at my elbow. I couldn't believe she had ignored all of her anxiety, her fear, and the trauma she was still recovering from to come help me.

Speechless, I turned to her. I'm sure my eyes were wide and crazed. She was so small and withered. A brisk breeze could blow her over. But under that, she was steel. Old beyond her years.

"I'm going to get your overnight-bag. You're going to stay with me for a couple nights." She squeezed my shoulder and nodded at my Dad. He nodded back.

One of the officers came up and faced us. "I need to take your statement before you go."

I recognized him. He had once brought a fat-boy Harley Davidson to the center for me to ride. It was a huge and heavy motorcycle. Loud and vibrating. Kasinski. Jack Kasinski. He had a younger daughter who played the violin. He hated the violin but loved her dearly.

He sat down in front of Dad and I, placed a hand-held recorder on the table, pressed the red button.

"Tell me what happened." He leaned forward on his knees, looked at the ground briefly before he met my eyes.

I took a deep and shaky breath. Mechanically my brain and mouth engaged in spinning a true, but highly edited retelling of the incident.

"I came in the front door. Jackson was in the sitting room. Something was wrong. He had a gun and Mom's urn and…" I trailed off for a moment.

"Go on," Kasinski urged.

"I was in the hall when I heard the gunshot, right there." I pointed to the spilled book-bag.

"Did you see him pull the trigger?"

Why the hell would you ask that question? Did it matter?

"It's like he waited for me to come home." I shook. "I think he wanted me to see."

Just like every other heinous thing he had done, he wanted me to bear witness. That mother-fucker. Tears of anger swelled and flowed from my eyes uncontrollably. I swiped them away with a harsh hand.

Dad put an arm around me, mistaking my tears for sadness. Jesus, did they never know? Him and Mom? Were they that clueless? Suddenly I had to throw up. I made it to the kitchen sink before my tater tot and yoo-hoo lunch ejected.

Mercedez came into the kitchen and silently held my hair back.

Dad came over and patted my back, "I'm going to the hospital with Jackson. There's paperwork to do. You go with Mercedez."

"I can't leave you." My voice was rough against my sore throat.

"Shush. You go. I'll take care of this and see you in the morning."

We gave our love and I barely remember crawling into the spare bed at Mercedez's house. It felt too much like when Mom had died. The same had happened. He had sent us kids off to our friends' houses and "took care of things." It's what he did. I miss Dad.

"You've always been my rock," I tell Mercedez. Our exit is coming up and she puts the blinker on to get off the highway.

"I'm going to ask you a straight up question." Mercedez smiles.

I mumble the expected response, "From someone who isn't straight."

"If there was nothing stopping you, what would you want your life to be?" She double checks for traffic and merges onto the two-lane road.

A group of college kids from the nearby university slow down in front of us and pull off the road. They pour out of the SUV and bumble into the McDonalds/gas-station.

"I like my job." It sounds defensive—even to me.

"Do you think you took that job to remember your Dad?"

"I'm good at this job."

"The unit is much like your Dad's shop."

"True."

"What did you want to be when you grew up?"

I pause. "I don't think I ever had a clue."

"Maybe it's time to figure out a life for you."

We pull into the deserted camp ground and roll up to our camper. Midweek—only those on the brink of being fired camp midweek.

Self pity—that's me.

"I think I'll make a fire," I say.

"Darlin' I have to go to sleep. It's 2 in the morning," she says.

She leaves me alone with my thoughts about the past and the future. I watch the fire burn to nothing.

In the morning, Mercedez sleeps in while I walk up the road to a nearby friend's house to get my other bike. I don't keep all my motorcycles (eggs) in one basket; I guess. This one is my favorite. I think she's the ugliest bike ever, but she has the best seat-height-to-bike-length-to-fork-rake ratio I find to be perfect for my height. I can ride her in sneakers if I want to. A 1999 BMW R1200C. She's a cruiser with curves.

Yeah, motorcycles remind me of when I was safe with Dad. I rest against the bike for a moment, taking stock of my condition. I'm tired. Shaken. Distracted. Should I be riding? Fuck, yes.

The bike is a little hard to start when she's cold, and today is no exception. I let her run a little and the pipes click loudly. I should get aftermarket pipes to replace that click—but I haven't in 18 years, why bother now?

Maybe Mercedez is right. I'm in a rut. Convinced I'm doing what I want. But I just went where the wind blew. Every time things get a little tough—what do I do? Head for the hills, the bikes, the caves.

The bike warms up, and the clicking ABS warning light finally calms down. She drives like a dream and the boxer engine—which sticks out on either side—keeps my feet warm in the winter.

I ride through the winding roads aimlessly, slightly following my memory towards a waterfall with a short hike. I mean, a short hike. It can't even be a quarter of a mile to the top of the waterfall.

I've never been this way before. I ride along a bluff ridge road and appreciate the view to my right—an expansive valley, and the view to my left—huge ass houses. A sign up ahead points out my turn is coming up.

The "W" road. Odd name. I'll have to look up why it's called that later. Red tail light up ahead. I stop, put my foot down, look ahead to see why the cars have stopped.

The road is narrow and winds tightly as it goes up the steep mountainside. Cars take turns going around the curves. They physically can't keep their vehicles inside the yellow lines to take the curve. Bet that curving looks like a "W", got it.

I'm already in it. Can't turn around. I don't remember seeing this on the map.

'*Distracted.*'

I drive a motorcycle for a living 24/7 in any type of weather. This should be no problem. I take the first curve to the left and my throttle gives a little throaty glub-glub. She sat around for a bit and sludge has built up in the tank. I pull the throttle back a little, keeping the clutch pulled in to blow the debris through the fuel lines, risking clogging the fuel injectors.

The car in front of me stops, waits for another car to come around in the opposite direction so I have to stop. The throttle continues to glub.

Stopping a bike on an incline takes a solid foot placed on the ground and keeping a keen eye on the clutch and gas when you start up the hill. Take the challenge of driving a stick, and starting from a full stop on a hill, now add needing to keep your balance. Fun.

It's my turn to go around the next curve—no problem. I roll the right hand to get some gas, ease off on the clutch, add a little more gas than normal to account for the hill and take off. Curve conquered—no sweat.

The lady in the oncoming car decides she doesn't need to wait for me since I take up less room. Thanks. She takes up half of my lane.

I negotiate the curve without becoming a hood ornament for the impatient old lady in the white Chrysler, get about ten feet up the next incline when the throttle glub-glubbs again. Then dies.

Double damn it.

I put my foot down to stop the fall, but the hefty incline up and the lean to the right wins. The bike gently tips over onto its right side. My foot—magically—does not get caught under the bike. Instead, I do a head over heels roll—landing on my feet in a standing position. From my new vantage point, I look over the two-foot high rock wall.

I kiss my hand and place it on the rock wall between me and the cars twenty feet below—waiting for my dumb ass to get back on the bike and no longer block traffic.

"Hell fire!" I yelp. "That was fuckin' graceful." And I mean it. What a nice dismount. And I didn't go over the twenty-foot drop. Bonus.

First off, it is a misconception that motorcade drivers don't tip their bikes over. It happens. Second, the trick is getting the bike back up and getting it going without missing a beat.

In fact, that is one criterion of the Uniformed Division motorcycle motorcade test. Many fail. Rarely has a woman taken it and passed it. My bike is pretty heavy. But it has a low center of gravity. The trick to lifting it is in the technique. I'm too short, too small, to grab the handlebars and just straight up lift it from there.

I get on the downhill side of the bike, squat, plant my heels firmly and deadlift that side of the bike. It pivots and stands straight up. Now the next tricky part is getting back on and not have it tip back over again—given the incline up and the lean to the right.

Lucky for me, two fellas jumped out of their trucks and are in position to hold the handlebars the second I have it righted. Nice guys. I am moving lighting fast to keep traffic moving, so yell to them a thank you, start the bike and take off. The entire ordeal is over in ten seconds, if that.

As I round the next hard left curve, another old lady—there must be an abundance of them up here—sees my small bike and also takes the curve without waiting. She stops mid-turn in my lane and yells, "You're slowing down traffic!"

I—uncharacteristically losing my cool—flip my visor up, negotiate the left curve around her land barge, while yelling back at her, "Are you helping?"

"You're slowing down traffic!" she repeats and actually shakes her fist at me.

I can't stop-mid turn, but straighten my bike after the turn and continue driving one-handed, giving her the finger with the left hand and yell, "You're the one stopped in the road!"

Thank heavens the engine doesn't glub; with my clutch hand otherwise engaged it would be disastrous.

The old lady can't find words and turns away from me, taking her foot off the brake and motoring down through the tight curves of the "W" road.

'Distracted. Stressed. Reactionary.'

I need to get my cool back. By the time I make it through the very nice residential area and park at the trail-head, I start shaking. Adrenalin is no joke. It's going to happen. You can't fight it. I barely get the kick stand down—my leg is shaking so badly. I sit. Deep breathe. Patiently wait for my body to stop jittering around. It takes a handful of minutes before the calm I like to keep employed comes back. I dig in my saddlebag for a bottle of water and a protein bar. I'll need some energy in the tank to replenish what the adrenaline just burned. How long has this protein bar been in my saddle bag? Years, maybe.

It's a short "hike" and I cover the distance to the top of the waterfall in minutes. Recklessly, I sit at the rock ledge. Per safety rules—I shouldn't go within a body length of a ledge. I dangle my feet over a 100-foot drop and look down.

"Quit that or quit this." Boss had said.

The simple choice is to give up the videos and the Tippsy Kitty. Who cares about it anyway? But it is fun to do. I guess it pays. I just need to make enough to keep out of the sizable savings I earned selling Dad's trucking school, and the house.

The house with Jackson's brains soaked into the carpet.

It is rewarding. I don't even care if people watch it or any of that. I enjoy making the drinks and explaining how to make them to people. What a silly thing to find rewarding, I guess.

Down below my feet, the water crashes and rolls into a stream. There is a dead dog down there; it's sun-bleached ribcage peeks through weeds and wildflowers. Dark fur still on the hide.

Gravel cutting my bare stomach as I look into the sewer. Matted fur clotted and pulled back to reveal bone. Viscera pulsing with lower forms of life.

I hope it wandered there by itself and died of natural causes, but my brain is filling in all the details and it adds up to bad business.

Jackson laughs as he points the flashlight at Fuzzy Bunny's skull. It throbs and lulls. Dead eyes glare. Skulls and teeth bare.

Damn, someone threw a poor dog off the waterfall. Who hurts animals like that?

A mound of death coagulates into a new life form and threatens to inch its way up the mold-covered wall towards us.

He was going to pull the trigger with or without me. I wish I could throw him out of my head, let him rot on the rocks below.

My bike looks sparkly in the small parking lot. A small mist, not even a rain, glitters on its paint. Wonder if there is a route back without the "W" road? Something clatters against the windshield as I lean against the bike to look at my phone.

Weird. A plastic disk wedges against the windshield. It couldn't have been there this whole ride? It's the disk I put under the kickstand—keeps it safe from sinking into gravel or hot pavement. Usually, I keep it in the bike's bags. Maybe it fell out and one of the guys helping me lift the bike earlier placed it there? Odd.

Back at the camper, the black convertible and Mercedez is gone. She left a note, "I've gone to Nashville. Be back tomorrow."

'Left you room to think,' implied.

Just me and the fire. I shoot a few emails and Facebook messages out to local caver friends to set up a caving trip. No one answers. They are probably busy. It's hard sometimes to link up when you aren't a super chatty person and you aren't living near the group.

'*Live here and cave all the time.*' Mercedez is right.

The next morning, I awake refreshed. I can do this. Be here. I'm here all the time, anyway. I take the bike to Rolling Rock Cave and unpack my gear from the saddlebag. Leave my caving permit under the half-moon windshield. The logo of the conservation group that manages the cave at the top in streaky ink.

I use the decadent port-a-potty outside and change in the changing room shed.

"Club med caving," I say to myself as I pull on two layers of non-cotton clothes to keep me toasty warm in the cave.

Outside of the shed a dog pants, waiting for me to pet him. He walks me to the cave entrance—10 feet from the road—and watches as I unlock the gate. The tumblers on the lock freely spin; property manager must have just oiled it. Out of habit, I recite the combination in my head.

"See you in a few hours, doggie," I say, locking the gate behind me and stoop walk into the darkness.

My helmet light doesn't feel bright enough. It never does at first. After a few feet, the ceiling slopes up and I can stand. The silence is wonderful.

I step over a small crevice, taking care to watch where I place my feet. I'm breaking rule number one in caving: never cave alone. If I fall or get hurt, I have no buddy to go for help. No one will realize I'm gone until tomorrow, maybe.

But this cave gets a lot of traffic from boy scout troops, old-time cavers, and newbies. There are multiple cars in the parking area—I'm not exactly alone in the cave. Technically, not alone. Right?

After a minute of walking, I veer to the left and pay my respects to Walt. His family laid his ashes to rest in a rock depression off the path. I didn't know him, but talk to him every time I visit.

"It's always a good day in a cave," I say. "See you on my way out," I tell the rocks and Walt.

Voices up ahead distract me. I choose the stream passage to by-pass them. I can see their headlamps and flashlights from my hidden vantage point fifteen feet below in the stream. The cold water only comes to my ankles. A group of kids with a couple of cavers leading them. I don't want social interaction, so I quietly continue down a different path in the cave and slip around them.

It takes a couple hours of slow and careful movements through the rock passages. I make it to my favorite landmark—a huge rock that looks like a Christmas tree. Too early in the year for the lights to be lit up. I was fortunate once to tag along on a grotto trip where they brought a small battery pack and lit up the Christmas Tree. Well, not so small. It caused considerable negotiations to decide who would lug the battery back to the formation. It's a unique sight.

Even without the lit lights, it is lovely. I find a flat place to sit and catch my breath.

'Dad died without knowing the monster Jackson was becoming, I hope. Did I go to the UD out of guilt?'

I continue through the Suicide Crawl. A crawl through jumbles of rocks—it isn't as horrible as it sounds. After a couple hundred feet, there is a place to sit up. Excited to bring my body upright, I sit up in the area too quickly and bang the back of my head on the rock wall overhang.

"Helmet check. Damn." I see stars and take a moment to collect myself. To my left, someone has spray painted "Slow 15 MPH" on the rock. Yup. Now you tell me. Cave conservationists have cleaned most graffiti from the cave, this one has remained. I move on.

Another 500 feet of hands and knees crawling, broken up with areas that you can walk in. I pop out into a large hall filled with piles of breakdown rock 25 feet tall. A small rock pile with a clay sculpture of a caver sits on the floor marking the passage. I catch my breath and stare at the clay caver. He bears witness to the silent expanse before him. I turn off my lights and listen to the darkness.

Guilt hits me. I am breaking a rule—shouldn't be here alone. Silence fills the surrounding darkness. Boy scouts and tourists don't come back this far.

I tell the clay man, "I'm here already, might as well enjoy myself."

Many cavers turn to the right and head back towards an immense pile of rocks called Mt. Olympus and then continue on another 1,500 feet of more crawling to some awesome formations at the back of the cave.

Instead, I turn left and work my way up a steep rock embankment towards Surprise Waterfall. The climb isn't too tough, but I am slightly tired and take it slowly. I work my way back to a small hole, take off my pack. It scrapes against the rock wall. Dirt drifts onto my boots.

'I hate change though. I'm comfortable. D.C. is a fine place.'

If I get into a scrape down here, no one would think to look this way for a while, being off the preferred path. I take a small piece of neon pink flagging tape from my pack, write my initials on it, wrap it around a rock so it is visible from the main path.

Safety first, says the solo-rule-breaking-caver. I slip into the small hole, pull my pack after me. After some more climbing up large picnic-table sized rocks, I enter an impressive chamber. A waterfall pounds at one end and a mountain of rocks rises above me at the other end.

I find a place out of the water spray to sit and look up—it must be 20 feet tall. The water pounds loudly onto rocks 15 feet below me. I love it.

I turn off my headlamp and listen to the water and the darkness. It's like I don't even exist here. Just a small part of this cave, the water, the dark. My heartbeat, my breath—the only proof I live.

'What do I want my life to look like?'

Pounding water.

'Good God, just decide and do it already.'

Cold mist.

'Let go of the past.'

My outer layer of clothing is damp from the mist. A slight chill has set in. My nose is cold. I need to get moving or risk getting hypothermic. I stumble a little as I stand, feet are going numb too. Stupid-head.

It takes less time to get back to the entrance using the main passage and not the stream route. The boy scouts locked the gate, as they should. The ceiling is low and I have to squat at the gate. I dial in the combination and yank on the lock. It doesn't open.

A breeze rips through the entrance and I'm thankful it's not colder outside. My damp clothes have me chilled enough. Carefully, I dial the combination in again. I'm sure it's the right one. The lock doesn't open.

There's another lock, just in case. I spin the chain around and try the second one. Stuck.

'What the hell?'

Birds chirp outside. I look through the gate to my bike. No other cars. The adjoining camp ground is empty. Who camps during the week except silly girls in trouble at work? No houses for at least half a mile. I literally could scream my head off and no one would hear me.

'Damn it.'

I try the locks again. Jammed. Upon closer inspection, a broken bit of wire jams the shackle of each lock.

'Those little boy scout shits.'

Did they do this? Who the hell would lock someone in a cave.

'Son of a bitch.'

A shiver runs through me. Sitting still in the damp coolness drops my body temperature. I take measure of the gate hinges. Can't pry the pins out. Worse case, I wait until someone realizes I'm gone and comes to find me. Tomorrow morning at the latest, or maybe even tonight, depending on when Mercedez gets back.

I didn't even leave a note. She has no idea what cave I'm at. The permit. They have me on file and eventually someone would figure out I'm here. That will be embarrassing as hell—getting rescued at the entrance of a cave. I bang at the locks again, pinching my finger between the gate bars and the chain. "Damn it!"

I sit in the dirt and stare at the bars. Rocks pile against the bottom of the gate. Deep breaths. With my muddy boots I push at the gate, it barely jiggles. How am I going to get out of here? Like a kid, I kick at the dirt and dislodge a rock. It clinks against the gate's bottom bar, nine inches off the ground.

There's barely any daylight left. Darkness is going to bring a temperature drop. I can ride in any weather, but that doesn't mean I want to. Time to get out of here. I'm not waiting to be rescued in the morning.

Pulling the piled rocks away from the bottom of the gate, I unearth an area small enough to just barely squeeze through. I'm full on cold now and dreading the drive home on the bike. At least I have dry clothes to change into. I'll live.

My helmet fits under the gate. If my helmet fits, I can fit. Laying on my back, I squeeze my head and shoulders under the gate. Piece of cake—my nose barely touches the metal. Thank God for small tits. But fat smooshes—including boobs. I skootch forward on my back, rocks scraping my skin, until my hips enter the equation. Oh, please fit through. Bone against metal. With a free hand I push down behind me, clearing away a small, pointy rock. It gives and opens a trivial bit of room. Twist diagonally. My hips slip forward. Think skinny thoughts. Dig my heels in and push. With a little less skin on my upper thigh than before, I pop through.

'Fuck this shit.'

I slither out and pull my pack through. Five minutes later, I've re-stacked the rocks, changed clothes, and am ready to head up the mountain. I should call the property manager and report the locks.

No cell service.

I'll call in the morning.

***

Back at the campsite, I wash my gear and hang it on a clothesline to dry. Other cavers show up and Mercedez arrives with Chinese food and booze.

"Thought you could use this," she says.

"I don't deserve you," I answer and duck under the LED tiki lights. They jiggle and cast dancing shadows on the ground, festive lights bouncing on everything else.

"Good day?" she asks.

"Quiet." I can't tell her about the locks, she'd just worry more when I cave.

Caving friends, who live nearby, have come in for the evening's fire. The conversation is light and occasionally lulls. We enjoy the quiet company while looking into the night.

My overachieving phone with one bar of service lights up.

"Whose that?" Mercedez asks, a little protective.

"Not work," I grumble and look at the phone. "Weird Facebook messages."

"Oh, I need to turn all those notifications off for you," Mercedez says.

I open one and read it aloud, "'LOVE your show. You should get more cats,' says LoveHugKiss489."

I scrub through some more. "You should visit the beautiful land of Kazakhstan, where I am from."

"You are a sinner and should be ashamed of your indulgences. I will pray for you."

"Hello beautiful. How are you?"

"My favorite gin is Empress 1908. Have you tried it?"

While I scrub an incoming FB video call comes through. I turn the phone towards Mercedez and the group. "I didn't even know you could use that to make video calls. Who calls strangers?"

"Who answers?" Blaine says. He's a caver. Lives nearby and is best known for his homemade brew. Always smiling. Tall. Likes the Grateful Dead.

"I thought I disabled that." Mercedez snatches the phone from my hand and gives it a scowl.

"So, if I can ask," Brandy says from the other side of the campfire. The marshmallows she holds over the dwindling coals catch on fire. She blows the fire out and continues, "You don't come up here during the week very often. What's up?"

Mercedez hands the phone back to me. "I'm pulling out the margarita machine."

It is my turn to scowl. I'm not a fan of margaritas. I like to make the drinks more than drink them—and have opinions about this machine. Turning on an adult icee machine is an abuse of the craft. But I am in the minority as everyone else gives a cheer.

"I saw that scowl," Mercedez says. "There *is* art form to this."

She can read my mind pretty well.

"I have been squeezing limes for hours." She beams. "Sit back and let me make the drinks for a change."

"What does that mean?" Brandy the ever observant.

I explain about the show.

"How cool is that!" Brandy says.

We drink the pitcher of margaritas and I explain about everything. Well, almost everything. I tell them about Robert turning me in for something I didn't even do. And when that didn't result in enough trouble for me, he turned me in for the Tippsy Kitty videos which did make trouble for me. So here I am—on leave with pay—trying to figure out what to do next.

"Well, if it is causing you to think this much about it, then you must want to make the change but can't figure out how to tell yourself to do it." Brandy picks up the pitcher and pours it out into everyone's nearly empty glasses.

"Say that again," I demand. A numb tingly-ness is messing with my hearing.

"If you wanted to stay, you'd have already said you'd quit the videos. Path of least resistance." She eyes the empty pitcher and sits it down on the wood counter.

Mercedez takes the hint and sets out limes for another batch. Brandy and Blaine both grab limes and start squeezing. I jump in and help.

"I love to make drinks. Always have." I salt the rims of the glasses except for Blaine's. He nods a thanks.

Everyone pulls up a small bar stool to listen and squeeze limes.

"Where did you learn?" Blaine asks.

"Next door to my Dad's trucker school was a bartending school. I hung out there a lot as a teen," I answer as I squeeze a slice of lime and rub it on the rim of Blaine's glass.

Mercedez and I exchange a look, remembering the actual reasons we stayed at the training school for almost every single waking hour we weren't in school—our sanctuary.

Just like this place is my sanctuary now, huh? Of course, I'm not running from a psychopath. I don't think Robert is a psychopath. Could Robert have been fucking with me today at the cave? Yesterday at the waterfall?'

An idea—probably formed by tequila—pops into my head. "You know, I noticed no one has bought North Base Camp down there at the base of the mountain," I say.

"The old bar?" Blaine asks.

"Some vets owned it for a few years. Completely set it up, then shut it down," Brandy says. "Hand me another lime, please."

"I drive by it every time I come into town. Lights are always on—looks like it is open for business. But isn't. Realtor sign in the window." I grab a wet rag and wash the sticky off my hands.

Mercedez eyes get huge. "You should buy it! Hell, you could live in the back. Buy it for cash. Invest that inheritance." Mercedez knows all of my secrets. "What do you want to do with your life?"

"Cave. Ride motorcycles. Make drinks. Make people happy," I answer, a little unsteady on my feet.

Now, tequila is an odd thing and I know better. By the time I feel the effects of it, I should have stopped drinking 45 minutes ago. So, I am one margarita in too far when the numbness at the front of my brain starts. I do what any smart person would do— I pour another one in an uncharacteristic display of tying-a-good-one-on.

We drink and talk of caves until the pitcher runs dry.

Brandy giggles and Mercedez catches the giggles from her.

"Sorry I've never seen your show," Brandy finally manages to say between giggles. "I rarely drink."

I nod and say, "Me either. Like to make them though." I turn and the world turns slower than my head. "Mercedez, you could help me, right?" I slur slightly. "Open a bar."

"I would help you," she answers quickly.

"I mean it, you'd help me start a bar," I reiterate.

"I have a bar right here. Let's try." Mercedez holds her hand out to indicate the gleaming orangy-wood bar top.

Brandy and Blaine put their elbows on the bar and sit slightly straighter.

"I'll take whatever you have on tap," Blaine announces.

"I don't have a tap tonight. But I can whip you all up something special," I say.

"Ooh," Brandy coos, "I'll take something special."

Mercedez quips, "Will you all sign releases so I can put you in a video?"

They look at her blankly. Then Blaine answers, "You don't have your cat here."

"I record her in the studio sometimes."

"You have a studio?"

"Well, it's a retrofitted closet, but it's a studio. And where I store my shoes." Mercedez dives into the trailer and materializes her LED light ring and other accessories. Oddly, she barely slurs at all and is only slightly wobbly.

I open the built-in cabinet and take an inventory of the liquor bottles.

"Okay. I can make a Brave Bull with the tequila and coffee liquor or a Suicide Shot with rum and the blue stuff." I move the few bottles around.

"Why choose?" Mercedez positions the camera and points it toward the bar to get a wide shot. I pick up a caving helmet and hold it in front of my face.

"The Suicide Shot is pretty," I answer from behind the helmet, "despite the name."

She comes in for a close up of Brandy and Blaine. "Wave to the audience," she coaxes.

Blaine beams and Brandy shyly waves. Mercedez turns the camera towards the bar and my hands. I have set up two shot glasses and am ready to pour the drink.

"So tonight we're in Caver's Heaven and we're going to make a Suicide Shot," I say.

"Because it's pretty," Blaine interjects.

Mercedez holds up a hand for me to pause, turns her phone to get a shot of the fire and then pans back to my hands.

I try my best to sound sober. "Remember to always drink responsibly. Don't drink and drive."

Brandy giggles.

I continue, "I'm going to pour this shot glass half full with the blue stuff." I can't even begin to attempt to say Curaçao in my state of inebriation.

"Or is it half empty?" Blaine interjects. He's quippy—I love it.

"Then I'll take my long handle twirly spoon and pour the 151 Barcardi Rum on top. It makes a nice layer."

"That's the pretty part," Brandy interjects, getting in on the action.

I can't help but smile. I pour two and push them towards Blaine and Brandy.

"Will you do the honors?" I ask.

Mercedez moves in for a close up. They smile and take the drink. It is a scorcher—I'm sure—but they smile, anyway.

Brandy grimaces slightly. "Ahh," she says.

"But it's a pretty drink," I add, and we laugh.

They clunk the shot glasses down onto the table and thunk them twice.

"Whiskers, what do you think?" I ask and slide a third drink off camera. "Mercedez will edit a spoof shot in later of Whiskers. She's got a library of them."

"It will clearly look like it was from a different location," Mercedez adds. "Part of the hokey charm."

Mercedez still has the camera on Blaine and Brandy. Blaine reaches out and knocks the drink off of the table. We all burst into drunken laughter and Mercedez drops the camera.

"You watch the show?" I say in between hoots of laughter.

Blaine snorts and says, "Of course. I'm one of your biggest fans."

"Holy crap. That's the sweetest thing ever." I help Mercedez up off the ground.

"We have Blaine. No Whiskers needed!" She is laughing uncontrollably, dark mascara streaks down her face with her tears.

A wall of numbness crashes over my skull, and my awareness of the evening's events comes to a decisive stop.

Facebook, YouTube, Instagram, Twitter responses to the uploaded video titled: *"I quit!"*

"You go, girl!" — mom62460

"Tell them where they can stick it!"— jamilynz170b9ek

"We want MORE VIDEOS!!"— denise.likes.adrenal.cortex

"Live your life!"—darkclarktheshark

"You do you!"—hasnazx1fn0q2rc

"More Whiskers! More Whiskers!"— effectualliammeow

"I can't stand tequila."—jack93ozumvjfse

"They don't deserve you."— joseph.the.josef

"Show your tits!"—crustiersteve

"Beautiful lady"— antonthephenomenon

"Make me a sandwhich" — thswhtshesd22

"[skull emoji]" —KingBarbour90

"Don't listen to those jackasses. Pigs."— matilda_jackson_australia

"I'd totally come visit your bar! I mean that in the most platonic, not-creepy way."—cliff93ozumvjfs

"Tippsy Kitty Bar with an Air B&B on the mountain would be rad!"—almondycelina

"With lots of cats!"—rattyhattie

"Can't a guy show appreciation for a lovely lady?"— antonthephenomenon

"*Bitch. You stole my idea.*"— karenu.wxkejt6l0
"*You got this, sister.*"— gerrymander_alexander

45K similar unread messages and responses are posted including one buried response.

It contains five pictures of Jude posted by KingBarbour90:

1. Falling off bike on the "W" Road.
2. Getting back on the bike.
3. Flipping the old lady off.
4. Sitting at the waterfall.
5. Patting a dog's head outside of the Rolling Rock Cave.

SUICIDE SHOT

Recipe notes from Jude's journal.

Equal parts:

- Curaçao Blue
- 151 Bacardi rum
- Dash of tobacco on top

Carefully layer in a shot glass. Blue on the bottom. PTSD may occur.

BRAVE BULL

Equal parts:

- Tequila
- Coffee liquor

Pour over ice. Stir.

- Half part Half and Half (Add on top, do not stir. Optional.)

13 - LADY FINGER

We're all moving a little slow this morning.

"Damn. I forgot to plug my phone in," Mercedez says upon exiting the camper.

"I don't even know where my phone is." I hand a cup of coffee to Mercedez.

"Yum," she says and looks back at the devastation covering the bar. "I'll clean that margarita mess up today."

"It was fun though." I sip at my piping hot coffee and add, "I think."

Susan and Brandy drive up in their truck. Susan, Brandy's friend, leans out of the driver's side window. "Is there a caver chick here that wants to bounce some pits?"

This woman—so energetic. I point to my coffee cup then hold up one finger. *'Hold on a sec.'*

Brandy opens the door and turns to Mercedez, "Wow. We made a mess last night." To Susan she says, "You missed some wild Tippsy Kitty's libations."

We all pitch in cleaning up and I throw my cave gear in the back of Susan's truck.

Susan drives us down the mountain to a nearby town. We pass an old abandoned hospital.

"They do ghost tours and stuff in there," Susan says, pointing out the green awning at the front of the old building. "I'm not going in there."

"I did a Halloween haunted house there years ago. Everyone jumped out at you. It was really neat. Creepy place," Brandy says.

I say nothing. Honestly, I am somewhat hung over and concentrating hard on keeping the coffee down. Little bit of sweat and movement, I'll bounce back.

"There's a good coffee shop over there." Susan points out a small building that looks like it was once a bank drive through. Patio furniture sits under an awning where the drive-up speakers used to be. The lights over the drive-thru lanes are lit up "closed."

"Pity," she says. "I could have a muffin."

Susan continues to drive around the small town and slows down at a squat building with high windows. "There's your place." She gives a knowing glance to Brandy.

At first, I can't remember what she is talking about. Then a memory, dull and distant, surfaces. I talked about opening a Tippsy Kitty bar and buying this place. Crazy drunk talking.

We pause in the parking spot in front of the building. The neon lights are on advertising beer.

"I don't have my phone, can you take a picture of the realtor sign and text it to me?"

"I got it," Susan says.

"It looks like you could just walk in, stock it up, and open shop," Brand says.

"Wait a second," I say. "Which way is the cave?"

Brandy smiles. "Back that way," she says.

"Took the long way 'round, didn't you?" I peer at the front of the building. It looks like it's waiting for someone to unlock the doors and start pouring.

I know nothing about running a bar. And this is a small town. You'd have to be from here, or be related to someone from here to be trusted. I would be a curiosity, sure.

"So what drinks did you make last night?" Susan asks.

"Brandy really loved the Brave Bull," I explain.

"Oh, I just don't drink hard stuff often," she defends herself.

Susan pulls away, makes a U-turn towards the cave on the other side of this three-stoplight town.

I could buy this bar and live in the back. Or maybe find a little place up on the mountain. Why do I stay in D.C.?

Dreams and possibilities fill my head as Susan parks and we climb up the mountain. The pit, named after the town, isn't too far up the hillside.

"How deep is this one?" I ask.

"One hundred and eighty-five feet deep with some passage at the bottom," Susan answers and holds up a huge coil of rope. "I've got a three hundred footer."

"I shouldn't admit this, but I tried to find this pit on my own once and couldn't," I almost whisper.

It happens. Sometimes you don't find the hole in the ground you are looking for. It can be right there in front of your face. To get all Buddhist about it—the cave presents itself to you when you are ready. Today, I am ready to drop that pit.

We locate the cave after a steep hike. Brandy ties the rope to a nearby tree and clips it with a carabiner while I secure my seat harness. Our harnesses clink and whoosh as we silently put on our gear.

Susan clips into the rope by attaching a thing called a QAS which is attached to her seat harness. She tests it and gets closer to the edge than the rest of us, being clipped into a rope and safe.

She ties a loop at the end of the rope and throws the length into the pit. It whisks through the air and then thunks as it catches on a ledge below.

"Damn it," she says. "I can't see the bottom. Can't tell if it reached or not. I think so."

Brandy grunts a reply as she struggles with her seat harness.

"Having issues there, sissy?" Susan calls.

"Shit. I think I put on some weight," Brandy grouses.

"Can't imagine why." Susan approaches and helps Brandy with her purple harness.

I watch from afar and grab the rope. "I'll go down first and check it out."

I clip into the rope and thread it through my aluminum rack.

"On rope," I call.

"OK," Brandy and Susan answer.

I put my feet on the edge of the lip—below me, 185' of darkness beckons. As I lower myself slowly, I watch Brandy and Susan futz with their gear. They make me think of Mercedez and me. Except I couldn't even begin to imagine putting Mercedez on rope. She'd tell me what to do with myself before I got the first bit of rope near her.

Once my butt is in line with my legs, I slowly walk my feet down the rock wall of the pit. It bellies out and I am left free hanging in space.

Caught in this amazing moment of flying in darkness—all thoughts of what I should do with my life leave me.

'Wow, look how beautiful this is.'

The rope slides through the rack's horizontal bars. I push the bars together with my left hand to add friction and control my speed.

Above me the sky is blue punctuated with small puffy white clouds. I open the bars up and slowly whiz down the rope.

The rope trails through my right hand and dangles below me into the darkness. I make sure the rope hasn't snagged on the side of the pit. Sure enough, a snarl comes into sight.

Sixty feet from the bottom of the cave, the rope has tangled itself into a ball of naughtiness. I slow my descent by compressing the bars and stop before the snarl gets too close to my rack.

Far above me I can hear the clink of gear as Brandy and Susan move about. It's the only sound that reaches me in the dimness. Far below me, water drips quietly.

I lock off the rope by pulling it around my rack. It acts like a brake. I can descend no further. I'm safe to take my hands off the rope and deal with the snarl. It is stubborn and takes me a moment to coax it loose.

Brandy and Susan must be getting worried. The rope moves slightly above me, tugged by someone clipping into the rope. They poke their heads over the lip of the pit.

"OK?" They call.

"Snarl!" I yell back.

I argue some more with the rope and finally win, toss the unsnarled rope towards the floor. I keep an eye on the stubborn rope as I descend.

Fifty feet whiz by and I can see the end of the rope below me. There is a loop tied in it to keep one from sliding off the end of the rope.

Unfortunately, it is dangling in the air with the bottom of the cave a couple feet below.

Short roped, damn it.

"Oh, shit!" Susan calls from above me, "I think this is my shorter rope!"

I yell, "Hey, the rope is short."

"I am so sorry!" she calls out.

She'll probably be apologizing for the next year.

"I'll drop another rope," Brandy calls.

I considered changing my gear around to ascending gear—it is all hanging on me just in case of a situation such as this—and climbing back up the rope. Instead, I wait, appreciative of my comfy padded seat harness.

"Come on down. I'll wait," I yell.

"What?"

"It's a good view. Get on rope and come down. I'll wait," I yell louder.

I dangle at the noon position of the cave. A rope slithers down at the 3 o'clock position. This rope hits the ground and coils there like a good rope should.

Brandy hollers, "On. Rope. Two!"

"OK," I and Susan call back.

After a few minutes, Brandy slides down the second rope and stops inline with me.

"Hi ya! Whatcha doing hangin' around in a place like this." Brandy smiles.

"Can I ask you something?"

"Shoot!"

"You ever think about moving up here to TAG permanently?" Because hanging in the air is the place Brandy and I always have heart to hearts.

She looks up at Susan high above us and then back at me, "You know, it's been an extremely crazy year for me. I have a new boyfriend that lives in the area."

I tilt my head; I haven't stayed up with current events lately. "We talked about that a while ago. So you heard from him again?"

Brandy looks down. "Susan's going to get antsy," she says, then descends. "It's a long story. But yes, I'm looking at moving up here. Might as well be closer to everything I love." She squats once her feet hit the ground to gain some slack in the rope, unclips, calls loudly, "Off. Rope!"

"OK," Susan answers from far above.

I slide close to the end of my short rope, lock off my descending rack, and reach for the ground with my toes. Six inches away. I can almost touch a rock with the tip of my shoe.

Susan calls out from above us, "On. Rope!"

"OK," We call up to her.

I put my foot back in the loop at the end of the rope, my knee jams up into my chest. I can't clip into the other rope, Susan is already descending.

"Want me to grab your feet?" Brandy offers. "Or, I could stack some rocks."

"Nah, I'll dangle until she's down. Stay out of the fall zone," I insist. "Should have transferred over before she got on rope."

Susan slows her descent inline with me and says, "Oh, I thought you were off rope." She tilts her head to the side, considering, "Oh no. There was just the one off rope call. I should have waited. Sorry!"

I wait for her to disengage from the rope, then transfer to the longer rope and finish my miniscule descent. Easiest descent ever—a whole six inches. My feet finally touch the ground.

"Fuck me." I laugh and look at the rope. "I just have to get on the right rope."

Susan looks at each of us, bewildered. Brandy catches my meaning, smirks and says, "Yeah. You've been fighting that one for too long. Time to quit and get on the right rope."

"Pictures or it didn't happen," Susan says and we gather round for selfies.

"Is someone on rope?" Brandy asks and looks up.

The rope jiggles back and forth silently behind us.

"Maybe kids messing around with it?"

"Yeah, I had some kids jam the locks on me up at RR yesterday."

"HEY! There's people down here. Leave it alone!" Susan yells.

"I'll climb up first." I grab the shorter rope that isn't being messed with.

We climb fast. I'm winded by the time I reach the top.

"Look." Susan gets over the edge first and points to the rope's rig point.

"You just climbed on that. Holy shit." I gasp. The carabiner, used to lock the rope to itself, hangs free. Only the friction of the rope wrapped around the tree held it in place.

"Pull the rope so Brandy doesn't climb it," I order.

"Your rope looks good"

"Their ass is mine." I get a safe distance from the pit's edge and unclip. "You got Brandy?"

"Yeah."

I run down the trail ready to kick ass. As I near the bottom of the hill, I stand still, listening for kids running.

Nothing.

From my vantage point I can see the small parking lot. Empty except for Susan's truck.

'Where the hell did they go?'

***

Not much later, Mercedez and I are standing in front of North Base Camp before heading back home.

"You could make a go of it," Mercedez whispers. "They have internet here, I could make a go of it." She smiles, cups her hands over her eyes and peers into the bar's windows.

I follow suit. "It looks like it could be open right now. Everything is there."

"Maybe the owner died, and no one wanted to take it over," Mercedez speculates.

After a few hours on the road, I break the silence. "It feels surreal to be thinking about this type of change."

Mercedez is quiet. My brain is full of what ifs and scenarios of caving every weekend and enjoying the mountain life. The shenanigans of the weekend are already a dim memory. Pranks.

Hours pass and we arrive back in D.C. tired, hungry, and excited about this new road.

"See you tomorrow?" Mercedez calls out of the car window.

I look up at my apartment building as I pull my gear out of the trunk. "Yeah. I'm not scheduled for anything this week." I lean down and look at her through the window.

She doesn't ask if I'll quit tomorrow. In fact, she is giving me a lot of space to decide what to do.

"Night."

"Night."

I open my mailbox and cringe. Porn magazines and other odd subscriptions have become the daily norm. Today we have— *Fat Chicks with Dicks* magazine.

The things I didn't know existed. Robert is investing some serious dough to fuck with me. It's kind of impressive.

I pull the envelopes and magazines out of the small cubbyhole. A metal key falls to the floor. A large brown rectangle hangs off the end—a key to a large parcel mailbox.

Nice. My fancy knives. Thank you, Tippsy Kitty. Sure enough, a smiling box waits for me inside the larger mailbox along with a crunched up padded manila mailer envelope.

I stuff envelopes and boxes under my arms along with my gear and head towards the apartment.

Betty's door is open a crack. Guess she's okay if she's back to being a trap-door spider.

A small plastic bag hangs on my door handle. We're not supposed to get solicitors in the building. But sometimes they slip in, tailgate behind someone with a key, leave behind baggies full of Chinese food menus, pain management, you can pawn your things, meet God, etc. I don't mind the Chinese food menus.

Today's solicitation is a blue envelope. A card. Betty. Must be.

I roll my eyes, open the door, and dump everything on the floor. Let's start with the card first. Heavy card stock. An expensive card from Hallmark. The front illustration is a sudsy beer mug with cheerful lettering proclaiming, "CHEERS TO YOU!!!"

Well, that's not something I'd expect from Betty. Inside, equally cheerful lettering reads, "BEST WISHES!!" Underneath—a handwritten signature in angry sharpie slashed writing, "*Cunt.*"

Well, shit. Robert? Oddly poetic. I look around the apartment, suddenly concerned someone might have broken in.

Silly. I unlocked the door just now to get in. My guard was down thinking it was Betty.

I could take it into work and complain. They won't believe me. I have no proof it is Robert.

I set the preposterous card down on the counter.

Well, Robert. I'm out of here. You'll just have to rub your mad spot. Though it kind of feels like he's winning. Fuck. I hate that.

Pushing the card aside, I open the Amazon box and unwrap my new chef knives. They had great reviews and I want something nice to have when chopping things for the drinks and also for murdering steaks on the grill. I've never been one for fancy things unless they are also practical.

I almost forgot about the wrinkled envelope. It could have been in a coat pocket for a year, it is so mangled. Rolled on the floor of a truck. There is no return address. My name—written neatly on the front label. The post mark—

Well, that's weird.

—the postmark is from Nashville, TN. Kind of near Caver's Heaven. Maybe I forgot something there, and they mailed it to me? That would be weird. I go there all the time and I just left. There wasn't enough time from this trip to have something mailed to me and beat me home.

I open the envelope and pull out the plastic bubble wrap. There is something wrapped up inside of the plastic. It takes a moment to get the tape free. I use my keys. Darn, could use my new chef's knife. Wouldn't want to tarnish them on the tape.

I shake the envelope to empty the contents—it's rattling in there.

A meaty thwap—a finger rolls out of the envelope and onto the marble counter. That's one of those fake fingers, right? Something made from latex.

A hell-of-a prank. The pink fingernail polish is a nice touch. Gold stars.

I poke at it. It doesn't jiggle as I would expect. The bone protruding from the end of the finger clinks ever so lightly against the marble.

'Holy. Shit.'

There is not enough bleach to remove this memory. Not enough curse words to describe the maroon blood dried into flakes around the serrated wound.

The brain kicks into neutral and records nightmare fuel for later. A small piece of bubble wrap around a layer of plastic wrap. The inner layer—silky-thin paper with dark blood streaks. Finger stops abruptly at the top knuckle. Sharp cut, nothing sawed. Big butcher knife? Something large and sharp.

I'm so glad I didn't open the package with my new knives. I move them away from the finger, never taking my eye off of it.

Pink nail polish peeks through the gore. The printed paper, it looks like something from a bible or an old dictionary. The paper stock is very thin and silky. A silvery script across the top reads "Daily devotions".

Two-second finger analysis complete, I sit down hard on the bar stool. What is this fresh hell? What type of sick fuck is Robert? Whose finger is this?

On autopilot, I make a few phone calls. Within thirty minutes my open door frames a couple of police officers, a detective, and Mercedez. I didn't call her. Why is she here?

They eye Mercedez wearingly. She is dressed down—sweats and a hoodie.

"Is there a reason you would receive threatening letters?" the detective asks. No name badge. Buzz cut. He has no face to me. Stress makes the face-blindness worse.

While not looking at him in the place where his eyes should be—which surely makes me seem shady as hell—I tell them about the events at work; Robert threatening to expose my YouTube video life and then doing so when I didn't get more than a written warning for the garage shenanigans and his logbook.

"Do you recognize this finger? Anyone you know?" the detective asks.

"Can't say that I do," I say. I don't know of anyone missing a digit lately.

"What about the postmark?"

"That's near where I just was. I go there every month."

They raise their eyebrows and write into their book.

"We'll need a list of people that saw you there."

Fuck. I'm a suspect.

"I wouldn't mail a finger to myself then call you." I say disbelieving.

An FBI agent comes into the room, nods to the detective.

"Ma'am," the FBI agent says. Solid build. Close cut hair. Stereotypical blend in type who looks like he isn't able to fart without filling out five forms. Suit and tie. Pin on the lapel.

I cringe at the salutation. Knowing the drill, I start back from the beginning of my story for him—glad he has something of a face I can see, unlike the detective.

He continues matter-of-factly, "You see everything in this line of business."

Images of a decomposing bunny, the tag still showing "Fuzzy" springs to mind. "I suppose so," I say.

They ask more questions and I answer them with what little I know. They take the card, the finger, the envelope away with them—leaving Mercedez and I to look at the blank counter. Mercedez reaches under the sink to get the bleach spray.

"That will never be clean enough," I say.

"Pink fingernail polish," Mercedez says to herself.

"Not a caver friend, then. Few people I know wear fingernail polish except for you." I look at her fingers.

She counts them off from one to ten. "Not me."

We fall into silence. Mercedez taps away at her phone as I bleach the counter top.

"Oh shit," she says then looks at me with wide eyes.

"Is my day about to get even better on the shitty scale?" I can't even guess what is next on my shitty-day agenda.

"I uploaded a video the other night to Tippsy Kitty," she says.

"The Suicide Shot. Right? Was a little fuzzy." I tilt my head to the side—trying to remember. "Oh yeah, Blaine did a Whiskers and knocked the shot off the bar."

Mercedez connects her phone to the chromecast—a gift from her. The feed displays on the TV. I don't even turn on the TV unless she's with me.

"Here's the video I posted," she says.

On the screen is the paused video of me hiding behind a caving helmet with drinks in front of me.

Mercedez continues, "I couldn't understand the deluge of comments that were going on. My phone kept pinging the entire drive home. Then I re-watched the video."

"Comments?"

"I was coming over to show you. I did this to you. Posted it while I wasn't quite sober. It's my fault."

"I just got a finger in the mail, nothing else could make my day worse." I sit on the couch—not wanting to be near what used to be my favorite place to sit in the apartment. Moving sounds good right about now. I could move.

Mercedez cues up the video to where I am pouring the drinks. The camera shows my hands and the shots. It follows as I push a shot in front of Blaine. He has an extremely grumpy face, sniffs at the shot, then whacks it to the ground.

"That was funny," I say, not feeling funny at all.

The camera shakes as everyone laughs. I take a deep intake of breath when my face on the video almost comes into view. It doesn't. My hair covers my face as I lean forward onto the counter while laughing.

"That was close. Almost showed my face," I say.

"Wait." Mercedez sounds deflated.

The camera steadies and then drunk me in the video turns my head, my face, my has-a-security-clearance-I-should-not-be-seen-on-social-media-face to the camera and says, "You know what. I'm going to quit my day job and do more of these. What can be more fun than hanging out with friends, making people happy, and doing what I love? Huh? You hear that boss? I made my choice. I quit."

The camera swings and Blaine and Brandy cheer heartily.

Drunk me in the video keeps blabbing on, "Come see me in a couple months at my bar. We'll do live recordings like this and there will be lots of kitties. Watch the Tippsy Kitty channel for updates."

The video stops. An icon to re-play appears.

'Well, drunk me did it.'

"I'm so sorry, Jude." Mercedez looks at her hands in her lap. "I can take it down."

'Drunk me—you go, bitch!'

I look back at the counter behind me and then at Mercedez. "I think drunk me was right."

"Really?"

"The cat angle. That's an interesting thought. I've seen coffee shops that have oodles of cats you can sit with. Saw one near the Incline there in Chattanooga just last month." I pat her hand. "Drunk me is a genius. A Tippsy Kitty with lots of cats for people to hang out with. I can see it."

Mercedez brightens. "We could partner with a local animal rescue group."

"Of course, I think we would jump on any idea at this moment," I say. "But I like this one."

Anything to occupy our thoughts and keep us from wondering about the owner of the finger and the butcher who sent it to me.

***

It's early and dead quiet at work. I don't want to see anyone. Maybe slip in—hand in my badge, gun, and phone—then slip out the back door. An Irish exit.

Boss is already there.

Before I can clear the doorway to speak, boss says, "Well, you couldn't have been more clear." He turns an ancient laptop around for me to see.

"New computer, boss?" I ask.

I am expecting to see the Tippsy Kitty YouTube channel. Instead, CNN's home page is on the screen. The trending story of the day is me saying "I quit."

I can't look at it. *'Damn.'*

"Boss, you don't deserve that type of notification," I say. Though a weight—heavier than my bike—lifts from my shoulders.

"I love the job here, boss. I love the team. It's been a rock solid team with the occasional jack asses like Robert. This isn't even his fault. I did this to myself. I take responsibility for that." Boss doesn't invite me to sit. I give my goodbyes, standing at his desk. "It's not the biggest breach, I know. It could be erased, and I'd ride a desk for a few until it blows over. I'm not made for desks, though. It's time for me to move on."

"You're in your prime. I hate to see you go. Usually people leave the motorcade when their health declines. Bad back. Loss of equilibrium..." he trails off.

He is talking about himself. He slipped a disk in his back by moving something at home. Not even anything heroic. Simple moving a large box. It put him down for two years and he rode a desk. Worked his way up. Hated every second of not being on the motorcycle or working any part of the 'cade.

I smile—a large ear-to-ear smile. This is the right choice. I don't want to wait until my health is going to get to where I want to be. Why? Why bother? I have no one to build up an estate for. No one to hand anything down to. So, I am going to be selfish and live for myself. What the hell does it matter?

We shake hands and say goodbye. My hopes for slipping out the back door are squelched when Darren comes up to my locker as I'm cleaning it out and putting my purple cans of spray cleaner in a box to take home.

"Meet me at Branaghan's tonight at 7? The guys want to give you a proper send off. Dinner and everything." He smiles. "Well, burgers and beer. That counts as dinner."

I agree and walk out of the building for the last time.

I am not expecting to have red and blue lights and the attached squad cars around my apartment building when I pull up. It happens. Health issues. Heart attacks. Maybe Betty had a fall? The occasional break-in—rare in our gated building. Usually a break-in is an ex who has a key and forgets their status as ex.

The congregation of cops on my apartment floor is a curiosity. They are not at Betty's door. Nope, the men in blue gather around Dee's door, the librarian neighbor between me and Betty. I put my box down at my door and reach for my badge to flash—yeah; you turned that in this morning, remember?

Damn. That is going to take a while to get used to. Maybe I'll go hit the gym, my brain offers irrationally. I missed the workout this morning.

Creature of habit—that's me. Safety in habits. Not really. Habits put you at risks to observers. What train of thought is my brain on?

I'm snapped back to reality when the closest officer says, "Do you live here, Miss?"

"Yes. What happened to Dee?" I ask.

Before I can get the answer an FBI agent, the one who had visited my apartment for the finger, steps off of the elevator. I see one of the officers briefly roll his eyes. His investigation is about to get taken over. I understand the implications of the agent's arrival before he flashes his badge. Someone is dead.

He introduces himself to the officers and they discuss who's who for a second.

"This crime scene directly connects to a federal crime I am investigating," Agent Worthington says.

The finger in the mail.

Dee.

"Pink fingernail polish." I whisper.

Agent Worthington turns to me as if just realizing I was there—or perhaps surprised I am going off the script he wanted the day to follow.

"I couldn't see much from all the…" I pause briefly wondering what I can say in the hall, "…blood."

"Pink with gold stars," he says flatly.

I look towards her open apartment door where the cops' forensic team stands frozen awaiting their next command. "Is she in there?"

And how long has she been in there? Did it happen there? Did I miss it? Could I have helped? What did I miss?

"Come with me," Agent Worthington curtly orders.

I follow Agent Worthington to Dee's apartment. He blocks my view of the interior by standing in the doorway as we pull paper booties over our shoes. He moves to the side. Watches for my reaction. The inside of Dee's apartment is in shambles. Not the neat, orderly, pristine, and nearly museum quality organization I witnessed on previous visits.

The superintendent stands to one side, a jumble of keys in hand. Balding, comb-over, greasy hair. Nice enough guy. He looks like he was kicked a dozen times a day as a kid and trembles when people look at him. Twitchy. He keeps his eyes cast down and sinks into himself like damp wallpaper. Bet he wants to escape back to the inner sanctum of his apartment. I know the feeling.

In the entryway, overturned books litter the floor. I stop and look back at the door—I can see the scene.

She had gone to the door and unlocked it. Looked out. Door locks are still intact. Invited the person in. No forced entry. After the door was closed, the tune changed and whoever had entered her room—someone she knew, maybe—became a threat. She had backed up and grabbed the first thing at hand—a bookshelf to her left—and hurled books at the intruder. They piled against the door and side of the hallway. She had aimed high, aimed for his/her head and missed, knocking a framed portrait of her at Niagara Falls off the wall. Glass shattered. She was smiling in that picture.

Dee made it to the open area of the kitchen/living room and had stopped. Her foot caught on the white faux fur rug.

Mom's pale-pink carpet. Blood stains would never come out of it. I shake my head to remove the intrusive memory.

The intruder must have tackled her at this point and sent her over the back of the couch. The white fuzzy blanket which usually hung on the couch was on the cushions. She had sailed over the couch and hit her head on the wrought-iron coffee table. Blood and hair stuck to the side of it. Though the coffee table had slid a few inches, it had not suffered damage. Stout. Something had kicked a nearby lamp off of the end table— probably as he/she went over the couch edge with Dee, on top of Dee. He might have hurt himself.

Drag marks of blood. He had pulled her by her heels, her head leaving a bloody streak towards the dining room. Too cramped near the couch and coffee table for him to work. Crouched on the floor, he had done damage to her. A pool of blood oozed further down from the smear of blood left by her head.

I look at it. She was alive when he cut her finger off. Maybe unconscious. Hopefully, unconscious.

Then? There were driblets of blood in long thin streaks that looked like a Jackson Pollock painting. He had lifted her and her hand had swung around, dripping a small stream of blood. The stump had hit the floor here and here as he hefted her weight onto his shoulder. She was a small thing. He had to be bigger to lift her up. Probably not a female assailant.

I stand in the hallway—taking the crime scene—feeling every grunt and scream Dee gave.

Finally, I look at Agent Worthington. He is watching me intensely. Hope he wasn't expecting a girly gasp or such nonsense. Or an admission of guilt.

"Is the body here? Where did he take it?" I ask.

The body. Not Dee. She's a body now. I point to the Jackson Pollock blood spatters on the wood floor in the dining room where he had picked her up.

"Her car is gone. Looks like he dressed her in winter clothes. A ski cap, maybe, to cover the head wound. Gloves. Perhaps, carried her to her car and left," the agent said.

It is a little brisk outside, no one would have noticed the hat and gloves. Carrying her though—

I turn back towards the door. There are security cameras in the hallway and garage.

"The cameras have been out of service. Looks like for a couple of months," Agent Worthington supplies, following my train of thought.

At least he is talking to me like I'm not a suspect. Small victories. What a bad day this was turning out to be. Poor Dee. Is she still alive somewhere? Why was—

"Why did her finger get mailed to you?" the agent asks the very question I am asking myself.

I look at the path of destruction and consider potential answers.

"I got nothing on that. I knew her. She came over the other night to tell me about weird cards she was getting from…" I pause. "Betty. Next door. Has anyone checked on her?"

"We knocked. No answer. Don't have a warrant to search there."

"She's a little unhinged. Leaves weird cards and gifts for whoever rents this apartment. She drives them away," I say.

"How unhinged?" Agent Worthington is curious now, taking notes.

I give a brief history of the gifts, notes, comments, actions by Betty. "I never figured her for an aggressive type. Just passive aggressive. For instance once, she knocked on my door and I didn't answer. I was in the middle of doing something."

Making a video, is what I was doing. Making a Tippsy Kitty video—the start of all my troubles. "I looked out the peep-hole to see who it was. I figured it was her. When I didn't answer, she reached out and knocked over Dee's plant in the hall, then stomped off."

We both look at the superintendent standing in the hallway. He points to the plant. "It's right here. Still standing."

"There's a point of contention between Betty and Dee whether we can have plants in the hallway." I shrug. "Or some stupid penny-enny shit like that. I dunno. I stay to myself and don't care about neighbor squabbles."

I turn back to the blood splatters, imagining what my brother's brains must have looked like on the white couch. The one we weren't supposed to sit on. Yup, sure thing, doc. I'm keeping those memories out of the way. But this isn't my job. Not my pig. Not my farm. I'm just the neighbor that lives next door.

The neighbor that received Dee's finger in the mail.

"You can have plants in the hallway." The super-attendant tries to be helpful and supplies useless information.

"We should do a wellness check on her." He shuts his little black book and looks at the medical examiner. "You got a time on all of this?"

She grimaces behind her eye shields and mask. "Dark blood. It's been here a while. Place is sealed up tight, so lack of flies, bugs, larvae don't give me indicators. Evaporation is the best I can go with. Looks like a week. Two weeks. Maybe as much as three." She looks at the abstract blood drips on the dining room floor. "More like two."

Agent Worthington barks orders to those around him. Get this here. Get that there. Need things back to this point person. Such and such is in charge.

I keep thinking about Dee.

"Let's go to your place and talk about a possible connection," he asks, the orders dispatched.

I numbly nod and we go back to my apartment. For the life of me, I can't see a connection. She visited the other week to show us the "Get Well soon card" and we concluded it was Betty being weird.

"We found that card on her dining room table. Pulling prints from it now," Agent Worthington says.

There is a knock at the door. I had left it open—but the officer is courteous and knocked.

"Boss, we got something. You need to take a look." The officer looks at me and his eyes light up in recognition. "Hey, you're the Tippsy Kitty lady! I love your show."

Agent Worthington's head turns on a swivel and he looks at me expecting an explanation.

"I just quit my job in the UD as globally as I could. My side hustle—I make mixologist videos on YouTube. A few of them went viral recently," I explain, failing miserably.

"Can you make money from that?" He asks in all sincerity.

"Enough, I guess. I'm thinking of opening a bar in the mountains near where I like to hang out all the time." It sounds less shiny and amazing now that I say it. Sounds more like a pipe dream.

"You know that sounds a little suspicious considering the events." He looks at me solidly.

Oh. I know. I can see the timeline in his head. I—for some reason—got into a tussle with Dee two weeks ago. Knocked her brains out on the coffee table. Drug her to the dining room. Cut her finger off. Picked her up and put her over my shoulder.

I can dead lift her off the ground just as easily as lifting my fallen motorcycle. Kneel, put her over my shoulder. Use my quads and push through to my heels, stand up. I'd say I did that after I went to the bedroom and got the hat and gloves. The blood smears in the dining room were someone—in this scenario, in his head, me—putting her hands into a glove. Lifted her up and took her out.

Drive her somewhere. Dump her. Dump the car, maybe. Put the wrapped finger in an envelope addressed to me. All of this at the time I'm going through things at work with Robert. I get given paid time-off from work and head to the mountains.

On the way there, I mail the finger to myself. Pay someone to put the card on my door, or hell, even put the card on my door myself before I leave. We don't have a witness to say how long that card had been there. Somewhere I must have cut the security cameras. I've lived here long enough, I know where they all are.

Mailed the finger from Nashville. Caved. Rode motorcycles. Made sure I was seen. Made the viral "I Quit" video.

It was me all along. What's the motive? Pinning this on Robert from work.

My finger prints will show up on the Get-Well card. I had taken it from her to read the insides.

I'd think I was a suspect if I was investigating it.

'Damn.'

Agent Worthington looks at me harshly, "Sit here. You won't want to be moving out of town just yet."

Damn.

I text Mercedez, *"You won't believe what is going down."*

"?"

"That was Dee's finger! They're tossing her place now."

"H O L Y F U C K"

I couldn't have said it better myself. *"Might as well come over. They'll want to question you too."*

"I'll get some food. Mexican?"

"Yeah—uhhh, I guess?" Taco therapy. I can't imagine eating.

Was it just this morning I quit my job and handed in my gun and badge? Oddly, I don't feel in danger. You would think I would feel like the mad-man could break into my place anytime and get me. I had the finger. It came from someone that wants to tell me something.

What, though?

Shock and denial of the whole thing cover me like a wool blanket.

I wonder what they need to show the agent. I sit down and stare blankly at my open door. The sounds of the officers and agents are quiet but consistent. They murmur. Phones ring. Feet scrape.

Where is Betty? She wouldn't miss an opportunity like this to show her ass. She'd given the EMT's a tongue lashing once when they showed up for unit 210—at the other end of the hall—seizure. They had apparently let Satan in with them when they left the front door open. Or at least one of his lesser demons. She had been loud, pulled a lounge chair out and sat it in the hall so she could bear witness to the entire event.

"You can't stop me from sitting in the hall," she had shouted at them. "I have to keep the demons from slinking this way." She honest-to-God had a cross in her hands and held it up to ward off the EMTs and Satan or his minions.

The agent darkens my doorway. "Stay in here with Jude while we check out the next apartment," he speaks to a uniformed officer who enters my apartment and stands in the doorway, blocking my exit.

"I'm not going anywhere," I tell him, uselessly.

I can hear the jangle of keys as the superintendent finds the key to Betty's unit and opens the door. I imagined I can hear the door squeak on its hinges, but it is probably my imagination.

"*Here*," my phone chirps as Mercedez's text comes in. I look at it and then at the officer.

"My friend is coming in with dinner," I warn.

Mercedez appears behind him and quips, "Well, actually, I ordered it. The delivery guy should be here any minute." She eyeballs the officer until he moves enough to let her by.

I give her a hug, sit at the bar. She looks at me—at the bar. The finger was there. We can't eat here. I move towards the dining room table—never eaten here before.

"They're checking out Betty's place now," I tell Mercedez. "She should have popped out by now to yell at everyone. Maybe she's not home," I hope aloud.

The officer standing in the doorway turns to the side so he does not have to stare at us dead on. We sit on the couch and say nothing.

"That's creepy. Who do you think did it?" Mercedez whispers.

"You could have," I josh. "Not you. You drama-faint at the sight of blood."

"I do faint impressively," she says.

My brain disengages. If I'm not paying attention to now—then certainly I won't be a part of it. Yeah, that's called disassociation. Unfortunately, that is when dark memories return.

I don't think it was long after the time Jackson showed me the decaying animal heads and their separated bodies in the sewer. Maybe it was the spring after? He had asked someone out to the homecoming or prom or some ritual important to teenagers. Maybe it was just a date. She agreed to meet him somewhere first.

I heard the kids talk about it at school the next day. Jackson had spent the day getting a haircut, Dad's car washed, and otherwise sprucing up. That much I knew from witnessing the various changes in his appearance throughout the day as he came and went on errands. What I heard from the kids at school was he showed up at the place the girl had asked him to show up at: an old abandoned factory on the forgotten side of town. He did not know a handful of pimple-faced, beer-toting teenagers were inside positioned to watch the events.

Janet led him in and talked sweetly to him. Something Jackson had never experienced. He was a quiet outcast and kept much to himself mostly in school. He was actually forgettable on the high school scene, though many teens came to his funeral professing to be his closest friend. She was in high-flirt mode, running her hands up and down his back and the front of his pants, urging him to get inside the building where they could get it on out of sight.

She led him further back through the hallway and into an old office to a dilapidated desk. It was moldy and dank. Moss and weeds had crawled into every crevice of the building. The roof was not watertight and the water puddles housed water-bugs. Black mold clung to the sides of the puddles. Janet sat on the desk and ordered Jackson to take off his clothes. He complied and stood in front of her completely buck naked. Then she laughed. Though Jackson was completely naked and standing in front of Janet who had her shirt off, his Willie hadn't come to the party.

Little boys under the age of 10 were his thing.

Jackson got angry and came at her. Wrapped his fingers around her throat and squeezed. She screamed and tried to hit at him, scratched his face. Willie woke up then. As it turns out, hurting someone was also on the list of things to jack to.

He didn't have time to do anything. The teenagers who had been hiding in other rooms—peeping through the windows— came to Janet's rescue and beat the daylights out of Jackson. It was three on one. Janet cowered on the desk and yelled while three boys kicked, punched, pushed, and spat insults upon Jackson.

Jackson got one good hit in on a younger, skinnier kid from the group, Zack. Zack had a bear hold on Jackson while another boy got in a kidney punch. Jackson head-butted Zack and knocked him back on his heels and away from the group. Blood poured from Zack's forehead.

The teens tired and left Jackson to bleed on the floor. They helped Zack off the ground and hurled insults over their shoulder as they ran off.

Jackson didn't go to school the next day or for the rest of the week. Dad tried to get him to talk about what happened; tried to go to the police. Jackson refused to discuss it.

Zack actually came to the house after Jackson had been out of school for the week. It shocked me to see him when I opened the door. Lanky kid. More pimples than face. Dimple on his left cheek. Close cropped hair. Face was purple from his newly broken nose. He must have hit his head on something—a big angry gash pulsed above his eyebrows. I didn't care if someone came in and continued to beat up my brother, so I let him in. Kid just went upstairs. I heard later he had apologized. Jackson and Zack were thick as thieves for a while after that—until Zack's family moved away right after Jackson died.

With Zack as a friend, Jackson went back to school. Eventually the teasing died out. Though, he was a pariah from that day on.

I always expected people would shun me too, being related. Luckily, we were five years apart in age. The rumors and the kids that spread them had graduated by the time I got to the high school. I suspect Jackson got into more trouble at school than I know about. Dad didn't talk about it. The teachers remembered.

My algebra teacher gave me the stink eye once and asked, "We're not going to have any trouble out of you are we?"

A voice shakes me from my memory. "Delivery." A terrified young man stands at my doorway and cowers in front of the cop.

Mercedez saves him by taking the food. He nearly runs down the hallway back to the elevator.

We pick at the food, neither one of us is very hungry.

Agent Worthington comes back into view. He looks empty.

"We're going to need to take your prints," he says.

"You know they are already in the database because of my job," I answer. Probably isn't the best idea to get all technical with someone who thinks you committed a murder. Pragmatic—that's me.

He glares at me. His database doesn't talk to the UD's database. That's not how it works. He'll need a set to run through his criminal database. I stand up and Mercedez pats my arm.

"I'll take care of dinner." She closes the food containers, eyeballs the counter.

"Are you going to cuff me?" I ask. It is a serious question. He can bring me in on suspicion if he wants.

"Considering your service record, why don't you just accompany me to the field office on good faith." His scowls deepens.

I think his face is stuck in a constant scowl.

"Guess you won't tell me what you found." I look at Betty's door as we get out of my apartment. It is open. This time with agents going in and out. The medical coroner is going in, black field kit in hand. Shit. Something or someone-not-alive is in Betty's apartment.

***

They sweat me for six hours. Leave me in a room, question me, let me sit. The room is the type of dark, soulless room you would imagine. No big two-way mirror. Just a thick steel door with a small window. The interior of the room looks like someone took the uncomfortable steel chairs and raked them across the cinderblock walls. Multiple times. With vigor.

I think Agent Worthington went home and took a nap. When he comes back to question me—he is clean shaven. His eyes are a little glassy—that high-strung I'll never sleep enough look. He almost looks crest fallen when he tells me, "The time stamp and metadata on your Facebook picture puts you in Tennessee at the time of Betty's murder."

My mouth drops open. "Betty?"

"She was choked and had her neck broken two weeks ago, before Dee was killed," he answers.

I shake my head slightly in disbelief. Finally, my mouth engages, "Where?"

"They were both stored in storage freezers. Two of them were side by side in Betty's living room. Looks like Betty was killed and stuffed into one freezer. It was delivered two weeks ago by UPS. Dee had a freezer delivered to her apartment a week ago. Also by UPS, but ordered under her name. You weren't in the state for either of these orders, which occurred from their laptops in their apartments." Agent Worthington levels his deep scowling face at me.

I can see his face because of the scowl. All of those wrinkles. I can see those. I mean, this guy looks like he ate a cold prune.

"You are no longer a suspect. It looks like you *are* the target." He pauses for the words to sink in. "Can you think of anyone you might have seen that might be connected with this?"

I remember the guy in the garage "helping" Betty with getting things from storage and give Agent Worthington a description. "I only saw him the once."

"We searched her car. It looks like that's where the struggle occurred. She was killed in her car. Looks like she was there for a day or two, then transported to the apartment. Probably in the newly delivered freezer."

I think back to the flag on Betty's car when I was sure it was adjusted. The tip of the flag had been pointing in one direction and then the next time I looked it was pointing in the other direction. He must have been in the car. Betty's body too. Was he killing her right then? I missed it. I tell Agent Worthington my thoughts.

"You were U.D. not an agent. Don't beat yourself up," is his answer.

Shade much?

He's right. I think about the guy in traffic I had suspected "was off". Sent the feds to check him out—only to find he had shit his pants. Yep, I probably wouldn't have been a brilliant agent. Best I hang it up and go make drink videos for a living. Self pity—definitely my specialty.

Agent Worthington softens. He just informed me my neighbors are dead and frozen. And I'm next. "The question remains, why mail Dee's finger to you?"

"From Nashville," I whisper. "I guess I was being followed?" I say numbly. "Just to mail a finger? What's the point? Why Dee? It doesn't make sense."

"Tell me about what happened at work again," Agent Worthington says.

I go over the details about Robert at work, the porn magazines, and the bestiality magazines; how he lashed out at me and I ended up having to leave the UD. How today—well, in actuality, yesterday by the time we are having this conversation— was my last day. I packed my stuff up and headed home, only to find the feds searching for Dee and Betty.

"Fuck all, I wouldn't peg him for a killer type. A narrow-minded-big-ego-bully, maybe." I say. Needles of exhaustion cover my body.

"We'll bring him in and see where that goes," Agent Worthington says.

It doesn't feel right though. As much as I can see him keying my bike, or doing something chicken shit like that, he doesn't strike me as a killer. He has anger issues, so maybe I am being naïve. This feels much more personal. Meaner. More manipulative.

"We'll try to find this guy you saw in the garage too. Maybe he was a rent-a-helper or a volunteer that helps the elderly. We'll need a description from you before we take you home." Agent Worthington stands and walks to the door. He stops when I let out a snort.

"Well, that's going to be difficult," I admit, "I'm face-blind. I can give you general descriptions of hair and eyebrows, maybe some big features. But placement of eyes, nose and mouth don't get stored." I tap my forehead.

"How does that work?" he asks.

"Makes me pretty anxious when in crowd settings where I have to network and remember who I talked to," I answer. "It's why riding a motorcycle for a living is amazing." I pause, "*was* amazing."

Damn.

Agent Worthington turns to leave when a dour-looking woman approaches the doorway. She leans in close and says something low to Agent Worthington. I can't hear what she said. Before she turns and walks back up the hallway, her eyes meet mine and hold for a split second. I think I see pity there.

"What is it?" I ask, not knowing if they will answer.

"The old lady is missing a finger too," Agent Worthington says. He looks at his shoes briefly, raises his eyes to mine. "Someone will be in to take down what description you can give. We'll get you back home afterwards." I can see the defeat in his eyes. My descriptions will be of no use to him.

I think back to my spot on description of everything but the face of my best friend Darren when he burst into our training room all those years ago. I didn't know it was him, but boy, I could tell you what his shoes looked like.

They drive me home. I try to sleep. He promises to text when they have Robert in custody. They are awaiting a warrant. Seeing the investigation tape across Dee's and Betty's doorways is haunting. Worse is the countertop where Dee's finger was—it could burst into lava at any moment. Knowing I am a potential target makes me feel naked, helpless.

What a fucked up situation this is. What can I do? Yell at him? Empty words. I can't knock his block off. Empty threats. Due process will take its course and he'll get put away. Senseless. All because he thought I pranked him at work? Maybe he has some deeper psychological issues. Don't we all?

I can't sleep and I refuse to take anything that will put me under. If he breaks in, I'll be ready.

It is a sleepless night, and I keep replaying my life's events. Headless animals. Maggot covered fur. Burning Polaroids. Brains on pale-pink carpet. Severed fingers. Dimpled smiles like piranhas. Side by side freezers.

Facebook/YouTube/Instagram/Twitter post: *The Tippsy Kitty is taking a hiatus for just a moment to get a bigger kitchen. Stay tuned! For now, we'll rerun our greatest hits starting with this recipe for a Lady Finger! Enjoy!! #TippsyKitty #ChickMixologist #CaverCavolt #WhiskeyGirl*

"Nooooo! Don't go! What do I do with all of this Blue Curusoua?"—desultorylaurie

"Love the show!"— denise.likes.adrenal.cortex

"More Whiskers!!"—effectualliammeow

"Such a beautiful"—MumtaMumta

"I liked the Jolly Jello Shots. I saw a recipe where you make a shot glass out of ice"— wilhelmreiddoctor

"I have come to lead you to the other shore; into eternal darkness; into fire and into ice."—1825Salieri

"Are you still running the contest?"— deloriszphil099

"[knife emoji]" —KingBarbour90

"OMG I love Tippsy Kitty! You are my hero"—gilbertine.victorine

"You should make a drink in a cave"—cavemandigs

2.4K responses

LADY FINGER

Recipe notes from Jude's journal.

Mix in shaker with ice until chilled.
Equal Parts:

- Gin
- Cherry brandy
- Half part dry white wine

Strain into a chilled cocktail glass. Okra is also known as Lady's-finger, Mercedez says. Gross.

14 - DON'T DRINK AND UPLOAD

Don't drink and upload. It never ends well.

I honestly thought I had hit pause right after Blaine knocked the drink to the ground. Of course, I was laughing so hard, it's easy to see how I didn't press stop.

Uploading Jude in all of her honest glory leaning into the camera and proclaiming to the world that she quit is 100% my fault.

God, but she was in perfect form that night. Shining through as her: free, happy, not over-thinking anything.

Now this. A fucking finger in the mail.

I pick at a cooling burrito while FBI agents escort Jude out of the apartment.

How random? A finger.

Childhood horrors intrude into my thoughts. I jump.

She was missing three fingers. Her head hung at an impossible angle.

When they drag the freezers out of the apartment, I shut the door. The dollies scrape across the hallway carpet and clang against the freight elevator's walls.

I pull out a half-empty bottle of bleach and drench the countertop, hoping to erase the memory of everything. The stench makes my eyes water.

Memories, always close to the surface, haunt me.

His foot kicked the fingers on the floor. One rolled towards me and I jumped back so it wouldn't touch my foot.

My phone beeps. It's Jude, *"Betty is missing a finger too. WTF?"*

I text back, *"Holy Crap!"*

"Not a suspect anymore," she texts. The dots at the bottom of the app blink on, blink off, blink on, blink off. She's hovering over the keyboard, hesitating. *"Target,"* she finally completes the text.

"We can break our leases," I answer.

"They're getting the warrants for Robert now," Jude texts.

She trusts the system. That must be frustrating.

The next morning, I let myself into Jude's apartment. I also knock a little on the door before doing so.

"Don't shoot. It's me," I say.

"You up?" Jude asks sleepily and stumbles into the living room.

"Yes. No gym for you today?" I venture. It's seven o'clock. She should have run a couple of miles by now. But here she stands, looking like she got two hours of sleep.

"I can wait until he's behind bars," she says. "Coffee?" She holds up the industrial grade coffeepot.

"Of course." I set out coffee cups for us both. "I know it isn't the same. And I shouldn't even say it."

"You *have* to spit it out now," Jude says and misses pouring the water into the coffeepot. It spills onto the counter. "Fuck."

"Sit down. Let me get this."

"What you don't make mistakes?" Jude bristles.

We mop up the water together. She slumps against the cabinet. A sleepy Jude is a grumpy Jude. A sleepy Jude who wants to kick someone's teeth in but can't be a vigilante because that breaks the rules is a pissed off Jude.

"What isn't the same?" Jude asks from her seat on the ground.

"They'll get him. Find evidence. Put him away." *I hope.*

"What isn't the same, you were saying," she asks again, persistently.

I slide down and sit next to her, our backs on the cabinet. I gently lean my knee against hers and say, "I keep thinking about the Donut Shop." *'And other horrible things.'* "I ran away and hid from it. What if I told the police instead of hiding in my house? Would those kids—"

'The Jackson and Zack duo I never told you about.'

"—have been caught? Maybe kept them from doing it to someone else?" I feel guilty thinking about things from the past. "It's stupid. I don't know why I'm even thinking about it."

'Severed fingers, that's why. Reminds me of Janet—'

Jude presses her knee back against mine. "'Cause it feels like we're running away."

"I guess that's what it is," I answer quietly. "As long as he can't follow us, we're good."

***

"Just turn off the rack when you finish," Mr. Erdles called out as he shut the classroom door behind him.

I sat in the dark closet staring at the rack of equipment. What if I turned the tape over? Told someone? Instead of bending to Zack's requests.

I pressed record on the VHS unit. Then play on the SX unit. Yanked the patch cords so the output would not route through to a TV. Didn't need to see it on playback. It had already seared into my brain.

The night had been cold and rainy. Dressed in half-hearted costumes, the gang showed up to the abandoned car factory.

"This haunted house sucks," Janet said while peering at my hand crafted table of torture, complete with peeled grapes as eyeballs. She fussed with an arrangement of wilted black roses. "Are these real?"

"I dyed them black. Cool, right?" I pulled a rose out and smelled it. "It works better with white ones, but I could only find yellow."

"That's pretty cool," Janet agreed warmly. "Where did you get them?"

"Someone threw them out," I half-way lied. I pulled them out of the dumpster behind the funeral home.

"I've never got flowers before." She broke the stem and weaved the bloom into her hair.

"The lights need to be out. It will be scarier," I said and turned the battery powered lanterns out. Cheap wax candles cast warm flickering light against the rusted pipes and moldy walls.

"So lame. You put a 10-year-old in charge of decoration. What did you expect?" Jackson chuckled and grabbed Janet's hand. "Close your eyes," he said, and plunged her hand into the bowl of peeled grapes. He had dressed as a dollar store phantom of the opera.

"Ewwww," she said in protest but didn't pull her hand away. "Peeled gonads."

"Gross." Jackson pushed her away.

Janet's small dark tie came askew as she caught her balance.

"Are you a catholic school girl?" I asked.

"No. Mia from Princess Diaries," she answered and twirled to flare her plaid skirt.

"Never heard of…" I answered, but Zack interrupted me as he came into the room.

"Nice pink panties," Zack said.

He was already drunk or stoned. I couldn't tell. He wore a leather jacket and had greased back his hair. I hated when they talked about sexy things when I was around. It was happening more and more.

"I have to get back," I said and pointed to another table against the wall. Suddenly, my glued on cat whiskers and pancake make-up weighed a thousand itchy pounds. "The twins scored some beer. Janet brought brownies."

"Special ones?" Jackson asked.

"Duh," I said.

"Want a nibble?" Jackson asked as he handed one to Janet.

"They stink," I said.

"Like this haunted house." Jackson took a bite of the concoction. The sagging couch groaned in protest when he flopped on it.

"This is a bust." Zack pointed at the twins as they walked in, dressed as blood-soaked clowns. "Where are the kids you were going to bring?"

"Shit," Brad said then turned to the other, "We got the beer."

"Yeah."

"No kids to scare." Zack looked at me. "You bring the camera?"

I pointed to my backpack in the corner. A cold pit formed in my stomach. "Yeah. Over there." Zack and his trauma-filled home movies.

"Let's make a horror movie," Zack proclaimed.

"Oooh!" Janet cooed.

"We have fake blood!" the twins proclaimed.

Zack smiled and put an arm around me, squeezed me to his side, and said, "You make the best cameraman."

It was fun, at first.

"Stand there, keep everyone in frame," Zack directed.

I peered through the viewfinder at the black and white view of the world. "Got it," I said. I concerned myself with framing and following the twins as they hammed in front of the camera.

Brad pulled Janet to him and bit on her arm. He squeezed a packet of ketchup hidden in his hand. It oozed onto her skin.

"Ooooh my gawwwwd," she fake screamed and batted at him with her free arm.

Chad burst through the doorway and growled loudly. He shook a metal pipe from side to side over his head, like a chainsaw, and approached the "dying" blonde.

"Jackson, get in there," Zack called out from the couch. He had kicked back with his feet resting on the table while the play acting unfolded. "You could try to save her. Kill the clowns."

"With what?" Jackson asked.

Zack looked around. "Let's go to the assembly floor."

"It's cold out there. There're no windows," Janet whined.

"Or complete walls," Jackson added.

Zack grabbed the lanterns and said, "Come on. It will look neat."

We gathered on the factory floor. Rusted and bent tracks ran in an oval around the gargantuan room. Rows and rows of dipping tanks, ten feet deep, sat heavily on the left side of the room. Everywhere, metal doors hung askew in tilted doorways. Windows, removed long ago, became dark portals to nowhere. Pipes and steel struts cut by metal scavengers poked out at every angle. Bricks from the outer wall piled up against the tracks. Missing walls and long corridors pulled the cool night air through like a wind tunnel.

"Damn cold," Janet complained again. She scattered the black roses across the floor. "These will look neat."

Zack nodded his approval, set the lights down, and directed everyone to their places.

"Camera man. There." He pointed to a spot near the largest dipping pit. "Jackson, pull the mattress from the back office to here. The clowns can fall on it."

Jackson sneered a sick smile. That mattress. That back office. I hated the thought of that room and what they did there.

"Janet. The clown has pulled you to this vat. Lay down on that plank and hold your arm out over here," Zack said.

I looked through the camera; the sludge filled metal pit looked huge from this angle.

"Clowns. Jackson is going to swoop in and kill you. Jackson, pick up that thing there." Zack pointed to a pile of metal scraps. "Looks like a strap from a barrel."

Jackson handed the strap to Zack. He turned it over, wiped dirt globs off of it.

Jackson asked, "Hey, who wants to get pushed into the vat? That would be cool."

"No way, man."

"That sludge is fucking freezing."

Chad held up a handful of ketchup packets, "We can cut off my arm though. I can do this," he said and pulled his arm into his loose clown shirt. His elbow stuck out. "See? Then I can squirt ketchup."

"That could work," Zack said.

I positioned myself and recorded. The clowns dragged Janet to the top of the vat and flopped her down onto a plank of wood across the top.

She begged dramatically, "Oooh nooo, I'll fall!"

Jackson jumped onto the platform and swung the metal band at Brad. He turned his shoulder from the camera, screamed, turned back with only his elbow showing out of the armhole and spewed ketchup in a small dark streamer. Brad rolled off the plank and his foot slipped into the sludge. He submerged up to his crotch, one leg on the outside of the steel wall, the other leg on the inside.

"Shit balls!" he yelled, then pitched over the edge of the vat and landed with a thud on the ground.

I pulled the camera away from my face so I could see where he fell. He just barely landed on the mattress.

"Keep the camera going. He's fine," Zack instructed.

Jackson crawled up to the top of the vat and wrestled with Chad. I had to tilt the camera up to get them both in the frame.

Janet "fainted" and drooped her upper body over the vat wall's rusty edge. Arms dangled towards the factory floor where Brad sat off camera, nursing his hurt arm but too stoned to complain.

"Pause. Let's get a close-up. Jackson, you're going to punch the clown and he'll fall towards the camera." Zack pointed to where I should stand.

Jackson grinned devilishly under his cheap phantom of the opera mask. Janet stayed in her fainted position.

"Go," Zack said.

Jackson punched the air in front of Chad. He twisted and jumped from the platform.

"Aaaaaah," he yelled.

He barely missed me and landed on the mattress with a loud thud, kicking up piles of dust.

Then things got bad.

Jackson reached for Janet, but the plank wobbled under their combined weight. Her legs fell into the tank, followed by her body. She clung to the side and yelled wordlessly.

Jackson dove to the side to the metal platform. One foot hit the platform with a loud clang while the other hit the plank.

Through the viewfinder, the action appeared so small, minimizing the horror as it unfolded. The wood plank bucked and hit Janet squarely in the face. She lost her grip on the vat sides and slid down further, only holding on with one hand. Though dazed, Janet reached her other hand out towards Zack.

"Help!" she called.

He approached slowly at a saunter.

Jackson fought against gravity on the platform while Janet reached for Zack. Jackson fell backwards into a lever system. With a metallic screech, the lid of the dipping vat swung closed, bouncing heavily on Janet's skull. With a shudder it slammed shut, severing three of her fingers.

I pulled my face out of the viewfinder. What I just witnessed could not have happened. The lack of sound, no screaming, no cursing, no banging on the vat, was the worst silence ever.

The twins ran to the tank and tried to lift the lid.

Zack ignored them and instead bent to examine the fingers on the floor. I watched in horror as he casually picked up the nearest one and put it in his pocket. Absurdly concerned, I looked to see if he got blood on his pants. Instead, I saw the bulge of his arousal.

Alarmed, I turned to Jackson. His eyes were fixed upon the blood dripping down the side of the rusted green vat wall. A smile touched his face.

Sharks.

"Get her out!" I yelled to the twins. My voice sounded shrill and weak in my own ears.

They stood stone still in shock. The world turned into slow motion. I must have dropped the camera. I remember banging at the side of the vat with both fists while jumping as high as I could. My finger tips barely touched the metal lid.

Finally, Brad grabbed a metal pole and used it as a lever to open the lid. Chad pushed Jackson out of the way.

"Help us!" Chad said.

Zack climbed onto the opposite metal platform and secured the lid open with a large metal hook on a heavy chain. It groaned, but held.

Jackson knelt down and reached his arm into the dark sludge. "How deep is it?" he asked.

"Six foot metal walls, but look at that vat over there," Zack pointed, "there's another four feet pit in the concrete."

"Is she dead?" Brad asked.

No one answered. They looked at the surface of the water, no one daring to jump in.

Zack broke the silence. "Yes. The lid caved her skull in." His voice was flat. "Hand that pole to me."

Jackson complied then grabbed a pole for himself, "We can fish her out."

From opposite ends of the vat, they pushed their poles into the murk and towards each other.

"I got something," Jackson said. He put some weight onto his pole.

"Careful," Brad said.

I didn't realize I was crying until the saltiness reached my lips.

Her shoulder and the side of her head broke the surface, lolled, threatened to fall off of the pole and slide back into the deep.

Zack, not delicately, poked under her with his pole, keeping her from sliding away.

"Push towards me," he directed.

With some negotiation, her limp body came within reach. Zack grabbed her by the suspenders and hauled her upper body up over the lip of the vat. Her arms hung down like they did when she play-screamed for help in the recording. Except now, she was missing three fingers and her head hung at an impossible angle.

"Neck's broke," Zack confirmed. He looked at everyone directly and said, "It was an accident."

"Do we call the police?" Jackson asked.

"No. They'll find a way to make it our fault." Zack was emphatic.

The twins stared at each other from the top of the tank, fake blood dripping down their wet arms.

Zack continued, "We never saw her. If they come ask us, let's get our stories straight. We had a haunted house for kids. Nothing shady. No one showed up. So we left early." He squatted down and looked closely at Janet's mangled skull, delicately pulled the black rose from her hair and examined it. "She must have come later. Was high. Went up there by herself. Fell. The lid slammed shut. Broke her neck."

Zack pushed Janet back into the dark slime. He smiled as she disappeared.

"Our prints are here." Jackson pointed to the lid and poles.

Zack flushed angrily for a moment, then took a deep breath. "If you don't follow my lead, they will pin this on you. It will be your fault. You are all accomplices."

The twins climbed down the ladder and stood behind me. They each eyed the door.

"Kid." Zack pointed to me. "You should get out of here," he said and climbed down the ladder. His foot kicked the remaining fingers on the floor. One rolled towards me and I jumped back so it wouldn't touch my foot.

"There was no horror movie." Zack motioned to the camera in my shaking hands. A crack ran across the lens and case from when I dropped it.

"You broke it." Anger renewed, he backhanded me.

Stars blazed into my vision. Brad gasped.

Zack leaned in close and sneered, "If you tell, I'll tell everyone *what* you are."

15 - PANIC ATTACK

I take a sip of my coffee. Ice cold. I forgot about it. The microwave door makes too much noise, stabs into my head, as I warm the cup up for the third time.

Shit, I forgot about the guys and drinks last night. I call Darren.

"I was just about to call you," he says.

"Sorry I ditched you guys last night for drinks. I'm sure you can understand." I don't recognize my own voice. It sounds miserable.

"Boss gave us direct orders to not go over and see you or to wait for you at the field office." Darren's voice sounds like a warm blanket of comfort.

I'll never work with him again. We'd been through a lot together. My stomach turns sour, clenches.

Darren continues, "They arrested Robert. Found a bag with the cleaver in his trunk. Blood matched."

'Fuck me.'

"Wow."

"Had all sorts of weird things in his apartment too."

"I can't even imagine."

"That was the stupidest theory I had ever heard. You mailed the finger to yourself to frame Robert."

"Got to call them all," I whisper.

Darren asks, somewhat accusingly, "Why didn't you mention all the porn subscriptions you were getting spammed with. That's classic little-brain, limp-dick bullying. You knew it had to be coming from him, right?" He adds, "I'm just sayin'," to soften the accusation.

"I don't know. I guess it seemed like a stupid thing to complain about." In hindsight, it might have saved Dee's life.

"He was quite the hateful fellow. Had a stash of snuff films on a computer in his trunk. Quite a few printed articles about you too."

"What?"

"Yeah, remember when you were the second gi..., woman to join the UD? They did a write up on you two." Darren's voice quivers with anger. "He had that and just about anything you've ever posted online, printed out."

"Weird."

"Everything was in his car. Also, a key-fob to the building. And keys." Darren took in a deep breath.

Sounds like he is smoking. He quit smoking years ago.

He exhales.

"Are you smoking?" I ask.

"Fuck, Jude. He had keys to Dee's, Betty's, and your apartment." He pauses, then says, "This cigarette is stale, anyway. How did I like these?"

The phone slips from my hand. I look around.

'Was he in here?'

"They have him locked up now," he soothes.

"My apartment?"

I want to bleach everything. Burn everything.

"Those printouts were weird, Jude. Hold on a sec." Darren covers the phone, muffling his voice as he talks to someone else. His voice returns. "Every post, all the comments. There were printouts about your family from back when you were a kid. He even had printouts of your brother's obituary."

"What about Mom and Dad?" I ask, "did he have their obituary too? I mean, why not?"

"No. Just your brother's."

"Weird."

"This guy is a piece of work. It looks like he was following you. He took out Betty, moved into her place. Dee must have gotten in the way, so he killed her too."

"Why?"

Darren hesitates. I interrupt him with my own questions, "If he had a key to my place, why didn't he just come in and kill me?" I ask.

"Beats me."

"What did he do in my place? Yuck."

"Seems like quite the overreaction to his log book getting duct taped to the rafters," Darren says.

We speculate for a bit.

"Did you kill his puppy or something?" Darren asks.

Disturbing thoughts of severed dead animal skulls, oozing with moss and bugs—images that will never go away—invade my brain.

I ask, "Did he confess?"

"Nope. He claims he's innocent. Says the evidence was planted. Clammed up. Isn't saying a word." Darren said quickly, "Hey, I have to get back to work. Detail is getting ready. Call you later?"

We say our goodbyes.

"Thanks for filling me in," I say and tears spring to my eyes. I wipe them away angrily; causing more tears.

'God damn it.'

For the next six hours, I bleach my entire apartment.

A small knock on the door breaks through the lung-poisoning haze.

Mercedez peeks in, bright purple rubber gloves in hand, and says, "Good lord in heaven, open a window."

"He's in custody," I say and fill her in on the details.

"I hired movers." She dips a rag into my beach bucket. "We're out of here."

***

"Here, another cup?" I ask and hold out the coffeepot.

"I'm good," Mercedez says and looks deeply into her half-empty cup of coffee.

"No news is good news," I guess.

The sun streams in through the windows. Porn mags, freezer encased neighbors, bloody fingers, creeps with keys to my apartment are worlds away.

"Three weeks. He's being held with no bail. That's good." Mercedez pours the contents of her cup into the porcelain sink.

I top off my cup and say, "I like the quiet up here." The kitchen door squeaks slightly as I open it and step out onto the porch.

"Secluded is the word." Mercedez joins me on the porch. "They," she points to the right, "only visit on holiday weekends, I hear."

The neighbor's green metal roof is barely visible—2000 glorious feet away.

"And they," Mercedez points to the left of our porch, "aren't there. The place has been for sale and empty for a year."

"Ok. Don't have to worry they'll end up in a freezer," I say.

The woods are quiet as the sun kisses everything pink with its sunrise. I haven't seen a single soul for weeks.

I raise my coffee cup to the valley and say, "I love it."

"You need to meet the people I'm interviewing for editing the show," Mercedez announces from the kitchen doorway.

"I don't love it."

It's like nothing happened and Mercedez is business as usual, now mountain air flavored.

"He's going to have to visit the cabin and I suspect you'll want to meet him first to approve of him?" she crosses the wood deck and kicks at my slippers with her bare foot. Her nails, newly done, deep purple. "He's a caver. Susan recommended him."

"Fine."

I don't want to be 'out there' again showing my face and being visible. I want to hide. To disappear. To never be seen again. Since the CNN coverage, my site has blown up big.

"Odd no one connected the real you," Mercedez says, "with the Tippsy Kitty you."

"Besides Robert." I sulk.

"I mean the news. Both stories of you in the news at the same time. You a target of a murderer."

"Don't remind me." I sink into a rocking chair on the porch, pull my sulking around me like a cloak.

"And the famous unnamed Tippsy Kitty who quit in a viral video." Mercedez stands behind me and squeezes my shoulders.

"Whiskers was the connection for Robert."

"Hmmmmm. Just a few key questions and they could have linked those two stories together." Mercedez stares off distractedly.

"We will not link the stories for a marketing stunt," I say and pat her hand.

"You're hot now. Have to keep making the videos and move past this."

"Move past my neighbors getting mutilated and put in freezers? And I did nothing to deserve it." I'm angry and regret my tone.

Mercedez puts her head on top of mine and sighs. "We're up here. He's put away. We're safe."

"I know."

We rock together. A bird squawks and circles in the sky.

"Don't trap yourself in a box too," she says gently.

"OK." I point to the world around us. "I have to admit, that open kitchen, the gargantuan windows, a mountain view to die for—poor choice of words—are nice."

"Production value," Mercedez says.

"Meet me halfway. Can we still keep my face off camera?" I ask.

"Absolutely."

"It feels safer."

"Deal." Mercedez comes in front of me and leans against the porch rail, looks me in the eye. "Let's do a video today?"

I nod. "Get back on that horse." Suddenly flushed with warmth, I say forcefully, "God damn. Enough with the rent free creepy dude in my head."

"That's my girl. Strike while the iron is hot, puddin' pop," Mercedez croons.

An hour later and we're back at it. Making videos as if a gory finger and its frozen owner were never part of our lives. White bone peeking from bloody flesh. Blood drops on Dee's hallway, an abstract painting.

"I got a request to make a drink with juices. So here's a Fuzzy Bunny. You'll need the following juices: Pineapple Passion Fruit and Peach Mango." I make a face, gross—fruit juice. Glad my face is off camera. I speak to the camera jovially, "You can make this for your friends or enemies. They might like it too."

I pour the juices into a heavy, ornate punch bowl procured from a local thrift shop. Mercedez adjusts the lights to get a better reflection of the juice as I pour it into the bowl.

"Next, vodka and lemon-lime soda." I pour the clear liquids together and grimace again. "What do you think, Whiskers?"

Whiskers, who is enjoying the new woods life—as evidenced by the lineup of mouse tails on the back porch every morning—sits on a bar stool near the counter to supervise. She sniffs at the cilantro stalk I hold out to her, then curls up in a ball.

"She is not intrigued. Now you can garnish your drink with peeled, baby carrots and a stalk of cilantro. Use your noggin' and drink responsibly. Read the doobly-doo in the comments." I push the drinks towards the camera. Mercedez moves in for a close-up. "Follow Tippsy Kitty for more tipsy creations!"

"Cut," Mercedez says and turns off the recording.

"Brian is coming over in a few hours to say hello," she says.

"Who?"

"The part-time editor I hired. I have other clients, you know. I need help."

"Can I help do stuff?"

"You hate computers. Technology. You don't even trust an ATM."

She has a point.

Later, the house phone rings. Mercedez is in the backroom, her voice muffled, as she gives directions. "Your temp code is 1534. Come in the gate and drive back for about a mile. Take it slow. The gravel road has no shoulders to speak of. You'll see the gate light come on when you get close. Keep going until you come to our gate. I'll see you and buzz you in. It's another half mile after that." Silence as she listens to the person on the other end of the phone, then she says, "There is one neighbor, actually. They aren't in right now."

"Brian?"

Mercedez appears in the doorway. "Who else would it be?"

"I don't know. We have that live audience thing coming up soon." I pull out a large glass pitcher and pour the Fuzzy Bunny concoction into it. "I'm preparing myself for anyone to walk through that door."

I shouldn't lay a guilt trip on her. She's trying to do her best. She flips me off with a deep purple fingernail, smiles, and disappears into the back room.

This Fuzzy Bunny fruity mess stinks. I can't even take a sip. I pour it down the sink and stare at the drain.

I should take this jug of fruity slush to Caver's Heaven for the gang. I haven't seen anyone, haven't caved, haven't even ridden a motorcycle since moving up—or since the mail-order-finger arrived—depending on how you want to measure time.

The judge denied Robert's bail. He is behind bars, and I am thousands of miles away. I should feel safe. Will they need me to come back and testify?

As if reading my mind, Mercedez pops into the kitchen and leans over the sink to stare into the void with me. "Any caving or motorcycle plans yet, Anne Gables?" She points out the window to the steel building next door, "Everything is right there waiting for you."

Motorcycles, boxes of stuff, caving gear. Everything from my life—for the first time ever—in one place. Waiting for me to decide to live. Mercedez places a can of my purple Sparkle Shine on the counter. "You can polish them."

I rinse the glass and put it in the dishwasher. "Seriously, I've hit my quota of psychopaths, right?"

"Let's hope we both have, huh?" Mercedez walks out onto the porch to greet the car coming up the drive.

Brian steps out and waves. I am doing my best to ignore him but can avoid it no longer when he hulks into the cabin via the back kitchen door.

Brian fills the doorway. He is easily six foot three, maybe even more since he hunches over as if he doesn't want to be seen. Portly, a solid mound of padding like thirty pounds of pillows surrounds his middle. Hairy. His beard looks neglected and wild—dishwater brown striped with gray. Bushy eyebrows—like wayward caterpillars—rest atop of small wire-rimmed glasses.

I eye Mercedez flatly, not even hiding my concern. If Brian is a caver, I have never seen him at any of the local caving events.

Brian's voice is thin and reedy when he says, "I'm from Indiana. I moved here last month. Staying over in Trenton." Mind reader too.

He doesn't blink a lot. His eyes have a wet, large appearance magnified by the glasses. Perhaps—and I'll be the first to admit it—I'm not able to trust new people at this point.

Mercedez introduces us. I shake his hand and try to smile, or at least hide my cringing. They sit down at the kitchen table and talk nerd—cover the technical details of how to put together videos for Tippsy Kitty.

Thankful to be invisible, I tune them out and plunk into a rocking chair. Worn out from making the video, I work on feeling sorry for myself. I'm good at it sometimes. It's a healing process. Or something like that. I'll get moving again soon.

A week later, I announce to the kitchen, "I'm going into town."

Mercedez asks from the porch, "What for?"

"Shit. You scared me. I didn't know you were here." My damn heart races in my chest. Jumpy much? When was the last time I went for a morning run? Need more cardio in my life.

She leans against the French doors, both open to the porch, morning light streams through. "We have the practice recording tonight. Starts at 5. Remember?"

I had forgotten. Practicing for the live event. People. The energy I found upon waking up this morning drains out of me. I pour a cup of coffee and keep my back to Mercedez. "Maybe I'll just stay in."

"Go. Get out of my hair," Mercedez says, concern in her voice. "I have some details worked out with buying North Base Camp and setting up shop there. We can go over it when you get back."

"I want to go visit that cat café in Chattanooga and see how they wrangle all of those cats without," I turn towards her, "fur flying."

A small spark of energy hits me squarely in my chest. I continue, "This could work. A bar slash studio for Tippsy Kitty. Fill the place with cats."

"Focus forward, Jude Jewel."

"Focus forward," I reply but think, *'And forget that a crazy psychopath chopped up my neighbors and mailed a finger from Nashville. Did he follow us?'*

"He's behind bars," Mercedez says.

Her ESP is so good.

As if we haven't gone over this a thousand times, while packing, while driving here, while unpacking, while watching the sunset—a thousand times. But like a loose tooth, I poke at it again and say, "But it was him, right?"

"Who else would it have been?" Mercedez answers.

"His prints weren't anywhere."

"He was careful. He used to be a detective or something, right?"

"They did find the weapon and a bag of things taken from Dee and Betty's apartment at his car."

"Plus a hell-of-a lot of weird things about you."

"Circumstantial."

"Motive was there."

"It was him, wasn't it?" I'm talking myself out of leaving.

"You haven't left this cabin since we got here a month ago." Mercedez's voice is gentle. "Which bike you taking?"

"The beemer." It would feel good to be on the bike again. Good day for it.

"If you don't want to do the rehearsal tonight, I can call it off," Mercedez offers.

I bristle. "Fuck that," I say and grab my boots from the mudroom. Damn her, she knows how to push me forward. "Fuck him." I tromp to the detached garage and call back over my shoulder, "Fuck free rent."

Mercedez smiles at me and waves. "Love you," she calls out.

I blow her a kiss. Why does she have to know all of my buttons?

***

The ride and day out was magical. I can't wait to tell Mercedez about the Cat Café and everything I learned. I pull into the driveway and stop at the gate's keypad. Its keys are dingy and it is fairly obvious from the pattern of the dinge which are not used. I key in the code and wait patiently for the slowest gate in the world. It beeps as it grinds open. The gravel under my boot is loose and I replant my foot to keep steady. Warm heat from the BMW's sideways head bakes my other shin. Finally, it opens enough for me to slip through.

"Gosh that must have taken a full minute," I grumble.

A half mile later, I am at the gate to our place. This one does not have a keypad. The remote is in my jacket pocket. I fumble for it. Unbidden, the gate beeps and slowly opens. I wave to the camera at who I can only assume is Mercedez buzzing me in.

Ahead, the cabin is ablaze with light. Every outside light is on, bathing the woods in an artificial day. Twinkly lights around the porch blink through the trees.

The lights can't compare to the sky behind the cabin—an amazing array of purples and pinks with the brightest streak of yellow just at the mountaintop.

'Nice.'

My joy ends when I notice the cars in the driveway.

'Shit.'

I was so carried away with the ride and the cat café today; I forgot to worry about the rehearsal.

Delaying, I put my helmet away, stow my jacket. Maybe I should tidy up the garage. I could unpack a few things. I pat a cardboard box filled with items from my work locker. Sticking out of the box's crumpled top is a purple piece of webbing. I pull it out and smile, remembering when I climbed it to retrieve my can of Sparkling Shine.

My phone buzzes.

"You coming in?" Mercedez texts.

"Ugggh" I type, then erase it, type instead, *"Back on the horse."*

Inside, I find Mercedez with—

Three.

Complete.

Strangers.

My heart drops to my toes.

"This is Misty," Mercedez says. "She's from the next town over."

"Oh?" I try to see Misty but her features are complete blurs to me, blurs refusing to become cohesive. Going to have to fake it tonight and appear human.

Brian appears from the dining room. "Hello," he squeaks.

Mercedez continues to introduce me to the others. "This is James. He's a friend of Brian's. Also, a caver." Mercedez turns to a young woman sitting on a bar stool and staring into her phone. "And this is Maggie. James's daughter."

"She's not old enough to be on the show." I announce. Full of charm, I am.

Maggie doesn't lift her head from her phone while her thumbs move wildly across the screen. "It's his night tonight. Mom is out with her boyfriend." She stops and rolls her eyes expertly, then resumes her text conversation.

James laughs nervously. "Hi." He holds out his hand. "Nice to meet you." I shake it and he literally blushes. "I love your show."

Did he just blush? What the hell is that about? Misty bounds off the bar stool and holds out her hand. "Nice to meet you. I've not seen your show before."

I shake her hand and don't know what to make of that. "How did you all get invited to this?" I ask while locking eyes with Mercedez.

She smiles sheepishly.

Misty stares at me. Does she have resting bitch face or is she angry? Could just be her normal vibe. She crosses her arms and the charm bracelet jingles on her wrist. Does that bracelet have bones on it? Definitely bones—vertebrae. I look at Misty in the dark blurry patch that should be her eyes—so much black eyeliner. She looks like a poster child for goths-are-us with more piercings than digits—eyebrows, lip, nose, ears. She opens her mouth to speak and I see a tongue stud too. Bet she has a devil of a time going through a metal detector.

"I have a YouTube channel for my coven. My videos get three thousand views a day," she announces. She flicks those dark lined eyes at me and gives a I'm-better-than-you smirk.

Ah. Drama. Great.

I want to say, *"Listen chick. The shit I've been through would curl your hair. You'd cry that mascara down your face with just my morning exercise routine. Which I haven't done in a month, but that's besides the point."*

Deep breaths. There is the anger train pulling into the station. Misdirected. I am out of sorts, not exercising, and no longer in the high-stakes game of always being on alert. Fat-lot-of-good that did me. For the first time in my life I am not keeping my eye out for threats and my body is dishing up anger for having to relax. Poor Misty, it isn't her fault.

Instead, I say, "You must be proud."

"Mercedez helped me with hashtags and metadata to get a rise in rankings," she continues with words I don't understand. Trending. Scheduled. Blitz. Click-throughs. I tune back into her when her voice gets extra constricted and condescending. "I promote the understanding of chaos witches for the public."

I plaster a smile on my face—hoping it doesn't look as fake as it feels.

Mercedez intervenes, "Honey, Misty has an amazing following. The merch for that one is extremely unique."

I can't imagine.

Maggot covered bunny skulls.

She creeps me out. Not because she is a self-professed chaos witch. I'm sure I've met many people into that side of things before. She's pointy, like she has her claws out and isn't beyond poisoning someone.

My danger senses are working overtime, trying to find something where there is clearly nothing. Hard to turn off a habit, especially when it has something to prove, something to make up for—like totally missing my neighbors had been dead for weeks and stored in a freezer next door. No biggie.

The guests take their seats around the kitchen island. The phone absorbs Maggie, eyebrows bunch in scorn. Misty sits with her chin held high, looking down her nose at all with squinted dark-lined eyes. James looks at me wide-eyed and star-struck. Mercedez looks like the cat that ate the canary

"OK. I'm going to set up for tonight's video," I say as I pull bottles and things out and place them on the counter: rye, absinthe, sugar cubes, bitters, and an orange. "Mercedez, can you hand me the cider?"

She pulls the jug out of the stainless steel fridge and places it on the counter—a lovely counter that has never had a severed finger on it but is, unfortunately, surrounded by strangers.

I set out four shot glasses and place a candle near them, light it, look at Mercedez for her approval.

"Nice touch," she says.

Maggie clicks away and sinks lower in her chair. Misty leans forward at the lighting of the candle, a strange look in her eyes. James stares at me with big cow eyes.

Mercedez gives me a finger point, meaning I should start with the talking. I begin, "Tonight's drink is a new shake at a classic Sazerac and Cider that was posted on a fan's blog. It's called Panic Attack."

Mercedez points to the test audience. I say, "We're joined by a live audience tonight. Misty, Maggie, and James."

Mercedez pans the camera to each of them.

"We can't use this footage. She's too young to be in this," I protest.

"I'll cut that part out."

"Then why do it?"

"Practice. That way you won't stumble next week. 'Cause we'll do it live," Mercedez says.

I don't catch the meaning. "What's live? You mean in front of people."

"The video will stream live to FB. It's no big deal. You just keep moving, even if something goes wrong." Mercedez spins the camera back to me and points.

I put my hands on my hips. "We didn't talk about that."

"We did."

"Well, I didn't understand what you were asking me to do. What if I curse?"

"This isn't network television, you can curse," Mercedez explains.

Maggie raises her eyes and looks at me, gives a smirk and an eye roll as if to say "old people".

Mercedez points at me again. I take a deep breath and explain the drink.

"First, we'll add some Rye. Now this isn't my favorite rye, but I have a friend who loves it. Dickel Rye. It's made right here in Tennessee." I pour the rye into the shaker.

"Next we'll add this cider. I like equal parts. You can add a little extra if you wish."

Misty is more interested with the candle then the drinks, and James has more interest in my wee-cleavage. Mercedez holds her hand up for me to pause while she gets close-ups.

It's hard to take a breath. Shit. The air is too thick. This isn't...

The anger train pulled into the emotional station not fifteen minutes ago. Every train has a caboose. And the caboose of that particular brain-chemical train is anxiety or the special treat—panic attack.

Shit. Keep it together.

Mercedez points at me and I can't talk. Sweat forms under my boobs and drips down my belly. I take in a deep breath but can't fill my lungs. There isn't enough air in the room, in the world, for me to take in a breath. My heart pounds and the world in front of my eyes loses its color. A high pitched whooshing fills my ears. This must be what it feels like to die. My body is going to collapse.

This has happened before. I didn't die then. I won't die now. Just breathe.

Instead, I stand there squeezing the countertop with both hands, trying to ground myself. I concentrate on anything that isn't my body trying to kill itself with adrenaline.

Maggie clicking away on the phone. The sock in my left shoe has turned slightly and is uncomfortable. This smooth, cold counter has never-seen-a-bloody-and-severed-pink-nailed-finger upon it, is solid in my hands. The sound of the ice in the shaker clinking as it melts.

Misty turns her gaze from the candle flame and looks at me like I imagine she looks at bugs when she impales them with stick pins for her collection. She probably has a macabre collection of dead beetles.

James reaches out with concern to touch my hand. His hand gets closer. Closer. He almost touches my hand.

'Holy fuck and your horse too.' I barely make it into the bathroom before vomiting.

Behind me Mercedez says perkily, "I don't think she's feeling well. Rain check?"

Responses to the Fuzzy Bunny video upload:

"I can't believe you made my request! Thank you! It is my favorite. The first time I had it was when…"— gilbertine.victorine

"Lucky friends that get to help drink that!" —deloriszphil099

"Mangos are the best!" — desultorylaurie

"You can get the best Mangos in my country…"—freshcur45

"Hi beautiful. How re yuo?"—VicasRoyal

"Life is too brief to eat and drink poorly" —1825Salieri

"I make the same thing but use…"—reichelmichael

"[Gif of flowers]"—intrepidgoat

"Please like my page and follow me at …"—softskinnocrepe50

"Adopt a kitty for yourself at…"—hsoatn

"Tits!"— thswhtshesd22

"[Emoji of coffin]" —KingBarbour90

"Bet you would like a body shot."— FtGrlsNd0Apply69

"Ever use pears?"—effectualliammeow

FUZZY BUNNY

Recipe notes from Jude's journal.

- ½ bottle of Fruit & Vegetable Blends Pineapple Passion Fruit juice
- ½ bottle of Fruit & Vegetable Blends Peach Mango Juice
- Bottle of vodka (a fifth)
- Lemon lime soda
- Garnish with celery stick, mini carrot, or for those who like it—cilantro stalk.

Mix into an ice filled punch bowl. Serve into stemware and garnish. This is a take on a Mimosa. Mercedez suggested using frozen pineapple pieces instead of ice, like a party punch from the 1950's. Ick. If you like fruit juice then this might be the thing for you. I hate mangos, pineapples and passion fruit so—

THE PANIC ATTACK

Recipe notes from Jude's journal.

Place cubes in a glass wide enough to catch your fears.

- 2 sugar cubes

Soak with
- 2 dashes absinthe (Have any left from before?)
- 6 dashes orange bitters

Crush those fears and the sugar cubes. Add:

- Ice
- 3 oz Rye
- 4 oz Hard Cider

Stir and strain into stemware.

- Garnish with Lemon twist or burnt orange twist

This is a take on a Sazerac and Cider. I couldn't have been more prophetic with that one, huh?

16 - DEAD ROSES

"Is there anything I can do, Mercedez?" Misty asks while standing in the doorway, absently swinging one of the French doors. It squeaks gently.

"Nah. Thank you, though." I motion to the kitchen. "There isn't much to clean up, really."

"Here." Misty digs in a black pleather backpack and pulls out a small glass vial. "Peppermint essential oil."

The glass vial clinks into my palm. "What's that for?"

"I find it helps with nausea and migraines." Misty's dark eyes shine brightly. "Let me know if you need anymore."

I watch her leave on the security cameras. The gates open automatically as her red tail lights disappear over the hill.

The house is quiet. Every clink I make moving glasses and bottles is as loud as a chandelier falling. I hand wash a few things, and as silently as I can, place Jude's favorite silver knife on the magnetic strip over the stove. It snaps into place with a loud metallic thud, makes me jump. My elbow knocks into the fruit basket. Lemons, limes, and oranges spill everywhere.

"Clumsy Clara." I throw a free arm onto the counter to catch most of them. One rebel orange escapes and bounces across the kitchen's marble tiles and down the basement stairs. Its thumps echo into the darkness below.

'Damn it.' Jude had picked the lock last week, curious what was down there, hoping for a wine cellar. We must have not pulled it all the way closed.

I open the door. Worn wood stairs descend into darkness.

'This is when the light switch doesn't work in the movies.'

There is no light switch. A single silver chain dangles along the wall. I yank it and the naked bulb glows weakly. I take a few tentative steps until reaching the end of the dim light. Just out of reach, another silver chain hangs along the wall. I stretch forward, my foot slips off the stair and I lurch forward onto the next step.

'Damn, this is silly.'

I step heavily out of the light, onto the next darkened stair, grab the chain and yank. Dead bulb. A slim sliver of light streams across the basement from the far wall. Moldy dust floats in the beam. Ahead of me, across a chasm of darkness, a third silver string hangs down. As I take baby steps, shuffling my feet to keep from tripping, I kick what I hope is an orange. It or something skitters away, scuffling across the silted floor. It thumps and drifts away from me, scratching softly until I can no longer hear it.

'I don't need this orange that badly.'

I grab the third string, the gritty thin beads press against my thumb, and yank gently. It flickers, threatening darkness, then feebly illuminates the crowded basement.

Dark shadows grow and shrink along the walls in time with the swinging bulb. Bundles of something: plants, herbs, flowers, hang on a wire along the back wall. They obscure a back door. Its miniscule rectangle window covered in newspaper, no bigger than a tissue box. A single rip in the newspaper lets in light from the bright outside security lamps.

My eyes adjust to the dimness. A row of rusting tools hang neatly on the wall near me. I touch the flower shears nearest me, rust rubs off on my fingers. A forgotten gardening room.

The orange has lodged itself under a huge steel thing squatting to the right. No sense in leaving it here to attract rats. As I step towards it, perhaps a little too quickly; because creepy, I kick it solidly with the toe of my shoe. It lodges further under the—

'What is this?'

—rusted avocado-green deep freezer. I lean onto the lid as I squat down to reach the orange. A silver Frigidaire logo, hanging lopsided from one screw on the front, shifts and screeches a short metallic chirp. The lid closes further with a flump. Flakes of the lid's brittle seal fall down on my thumb, find no purchase on the shaking digit, and continue their path to the floor.

I stare at the freezer and think of—

Betty.

Dee.

Janet.

Jackson's funeral.

***

His closed coffin lid gleamed and reflected heaps of flowers. I hated the smell of them. Roses. Carnations. Ferns. Cloistered in mounds of affection shown by people who didn't know, who wouldn't look closely, or dared not look lest they see the monster he was.

I stood by Jude's side while she blankly accepted every hug and pat on the back offered by well-wishers.

"Sorry for your loss."

"If there is anything we can do."

They would glance at me, a gaunt, ashy, ignorable teen, then quickly look away; their eyes searching for something else to move their attention towards.

"Your family has lost so much," they told Jude and her father.

Someone cleared their throat. The small crowd stilled. Jude's father pulled at his tie.

"Amazing grace," a rotund woman with gray hair warbled.

The crowd took up the hymn and accompanied her. Jude and her father stared stone faced at the coffin as it sank into the ground. Once it had come to a stop, the preacher held his hands out, inviting the two family members to approach.

I hugged my arms tightly to myself, alone, as Jude and her father stepped forward, gathered small handfuls of dirt, threw them down onto the coffin.

A small pressure on my back, right between the shoulder blades, startled me.

"Don't turn around," Zack ordered.

The dirt fell almost silently onto the coffin.

"For you," he said and held a single black rose in front of me.

I froze. Cold sweat beaded on my forehead. Icy tendrils squeezed around my chest, threatening to pull the air from my lungs.

"Take it," Zack commanded, digging his fingers harshly into my shoulder.

I obeyed.

He enfolded his arms around me roughly, grabbed the rose in my hand and squeezed until the thorns bit into my skin, whispered, "You're next."

17 - DEJA VU

The next morning, I wake up with a headache as big as the collection of dead bodies Misty probably keeps in her basement.

She creeps me the hell out. Hell, everyone creeps me out right now.

I hear Mercedez—I hope it is Mercedez—moving around in the kitchen. I pull the weighted blanket up over my ears and cocoon even deeper into the warmth of the bed. The smell of coffee, bacon, and a mundane bladder urge me to get up.

"How are you feeling this morning?" Mercedez asks. She looks like she was up all night, dark bags hang under her eyes.

"I should ask the same thing. No sleep?" I point to her. "I could park a Mack truck in those bags."

She drinks deeply from her cup of tea and stares out at the view. The wind has kicked up and twists and twirls leaves with its force. It must be cold outside.

I want to go back to bed. I don't even want to exercise. The weight of the day is too much. The weight of me weighing her down is even heavier.

After forever, Mercedez finally says, "I'm sorry. I pushed you into having people over. I shouldn't have."

"It's silly…" I say, but she cuts me off.

"It's real. Feelings are real and you know that. I want people around to help me get through things. You want silence. We just heal differently and I tried to put my healing methods on you." She puts the coffee cup down. "Result. One panic attack and now depression. I feel so bad having done that to you."

Mercedez is taking it hard and I feel even worse because I just want to go back to bed. It is an overpowering feeling. Like the air itself is a lead weight on my head. It is too much to lift the cup of coffee. I stare at it. "It will pass. It isn't your fault. I got extremely angry at Misty last night and that's just part of the process." I hate the inflectionless tone of my voice.

"Misty?"

"She creeps me out."

"She comes across as intense. After you get to know her she's, well, still pretty intense with a dark, sick sense of humor." Mercedez inhales. "Oh, she left this for you."

"What's that?"

"She said it would help with the headache this morning."

I look at the label on the bottle. "Peppermint oil."

Mercedez puts an arm around me. "I'm sorry, sweet Sally."

I lean into her and we sideways hug, leaning on each other.

I sigh.

She sighs.

"Then James tried to touch my hand. He was all goo-goo eyed. I couldn't take it," I whisper. "What an overreaction." I look at her sideways. "Remember that panic attack, after…" I can't continue.

"I know." Mercedez pats my arm.

She knows.

"Mr. Morris, you okay with me staying over?" Mercedez stood in the kitchen's open backdoor talking with my Dad.

Despite the day being excruciatingly hot, Dad had every window in the house open. "Letting the house air out," he said.

No one walked in the front door anymore. We didn't want to walk by the sitting room. Even though, upon Dad's request, the cleaning crew had hung plastic sheeting over the doorway. I had peeked. A demolition crew had ripped out a rectangle of carpet and drywall, removed the couch. It was as if that section of the house had simply stopped existing.

"Sure thing. Rocket needs a friend right now." Dad turned towards Mercedez and added, "Thanks for being there for her."

Unsure what to do with the compliment, Mercedez made a noncommittal grunt and shrugged. I cleared my throat from my position in the dark hallway.

"Rocket." Dad pointed behind me. "Oh, why don't you two go on upstairs. The detectives are here."

Detective Anderson's and Officer Jones's long shadows slid across the stained linoleum floor.

"Evenin', Rocket." Officer Jones said to me. He looked at Mercedez and nodded. "We'll just be a moment."

Mercedez and I bounded up the stairs but kept close to the hallway in order to eavesdrop. Across from my door, Jackson's door was firmly shut.

"Look, Russell, we're ruling the girl's death as an accident." Officer Jones's voice was a husky whisper.

Detective Anderson added, "Jackson's prints were there and a dozen other prints. The kids hang out there and get into mischief."

"Did anyone come forward?" Dad asked.

"We received an anonymous tip a week before Jackson…" Officer Jones cleared his throat, "…died."

"It's been a year since Janet Watts disappeared without a trace. Then this tip comes in saying to look for her at the old car factory," Detective Anderson added. Chairs scraped across the linoleum as the men sat heavily.

"We suspect Jackson and a group of kids were there. Witnessed the death. Maybe he turned in the tip out of guilt and that contributed to his," Officer Jones's voice dropped to a mumble, "suicide."

"What about the other kid he hung out with?" Dad asked. "Dark haired trouble."

Mercedez had grown pale beside me. "He was at the funeral," she whispered.

"Who?"

"Zack."

"Shhhh. I'm trying to listen," I warned and leaned my head further into the hallway.

Below, the men continued to discuss the recent tragedies.

"Zack's family moved out of state right after Jackson's funeral," one of the men said. I couldn't tell who. "Out of our jurisdiction."

Detective Anderson cleared his throat. "Anyway, we're closing the case. Accidental tragedy. No sense in stirring it up, causing everyone grief."

"Family can find closure now they know what happened to her." Dad's voice was thick with grief.

Mercedez put an arm around me and hugged me. I didn't feel for Jackson's loss, but my heart ached for Dad's pain.

"I didn't know Janet," I said. It was suddenly hard to breathe. "Do you think Jackson had anything to do with it?" Cold spread through my body. "Maybe he…"

"Shhh. Get your head back in. They'll hear you." Mercedez pulled on my arm.

"I can't breathe," I told Mercedez.

"Count your toes," she instructed.

We sat in silence while I counted my toes and the men in the kitchen said their goodbyes. The squeeze box around my ribs loosened.

Dad called out from the bottom of the stairs, "Rocket, I'm going to head into work. Order some pizza."

"I know he was into some stuff." I told Mercedez. The empty pizza box sat between us.

"He was weird."

"I want to get rid of it before Dad finds it."

"Finds what?"

"I don't know. Weird stuff."

Mercedez frowned, then said, "OK."

The plastic sheeting crinkled as we walked into Mom's sitting room. A wall of obnoxious cleaner aromas stung our nostrils.

"Damn," Mercedez wheezed.

We stood at the edge of the ripped out carpet. Neither one of us wanted to step into the void. All traces of Jackson's brains and blood vanished with the couch, rug, and drywall.

"Dad's going to knock that wall down," I pointed to the wall where Jackson's brains once were, "and join this room with the breakfast area."

I couldn't move my eyes from the memory of him sitting there with Mom's ashes. I pointed to the opposite wall without turning my gaze. "He's going to put another bay window over there to make it brighter in here. Inviting."

I finally turned to look at the bookshelves. A slow rumble in my chest churned. I breathed deeply and counted my toes.

"Right before he, you know." I couldn't say it. "He glanced over here. I think there is something hidden in the books."

"Why don't you let me look? You don't have to find it," Mercedez offered.

"I have to get rid of his dirt. Dad can't find it. It would devastate him," I said as I stepped deliberately onto the bare section of the floor and crossed to the bookshelves. "I need to pack the books away before the construction starts, anyway."

When the first Polaroid slid out of the dusty Britannica encyclopedias, the tightness in my chest clutched hard. I gasped.

"Don't look at them," Mercedez instructed.

I couldn't avert my eyes. Couldn't explain to Mercedez I had to look. These kids were my fault. I should have said something when I walked in on him that time. Maybe I would have saved these kids from Jackson. We flipped each book upside down, holding them by their covers. Polaroids dropped to the floor. There were dozens of pictures involving three different kids. Nudes of scared little boys and a little girl. They looked like they were ten or eleven. Each of them looking at the camera, their eyes accusing me of failing them.

"Damn." I gulped. Bile rose in my throat. My sinuses stung from the bleach. "These were all taken in the same place. Wonder where this is? Some old looking building. Looks like an abandoned office."

Mercedez gathered the pictures together and put them in a shoe box, face down. She reached out and held my hand.

"Your hands are clammy," I said.

"The bleach is getting to me," she answered. "Let's tear this place apart and find every single picture."

Only the encyclopedias contained raunchy evidence. I rattled the shoebox at Mercedez. "OK," I said, "this room is clear. Let's toss his room."

An hour later we took a break and sat in the kitchen staring at a plate of brownies, neither one of us eating. The box of Polaroids sat between us like an armed bomb.

"I expected to find something in his room," I said, glad and worried we found nothing.

"Not even a porn magazine. Don't all red-blooded boys have those under their mattresses?" Mercedez asked.

"Do you?"

"Gross. Girls have cooties." Mercedez grimaced.

It made me smile for a moment and the fluttering in my chest quieted.

"He hung out in the shed out back sometimes. Let's look there," I suggested.

We found two collapsing, rat-eaten boxes filled to the brim with smut sitting at the back of the shed under an ancient bunch of scuba gear Dad had abandoned when I was a toddler.

"Doesn't your Dad come out here?" Mercedez asked. "All of this stuff is just sitting here."

"Nah. This shed sways in the breeze. Going to collapse any moment. We were never allowed to go in here. Guess Jackson thought it was safe from Dad."

"These magazines are old as hell. They could be your Dad's."

"Gross."

But Mercedez was right. I shuffled through the box to look at the faded covers. I could barely read the dates, which ranged from 10 to 20 years old.

"What's that under the box?" Mercedez asked, pointing to a deep green book tucked under the boxes.

Carefully, I pulled it from under the boxes without tipping them over. A few magazines spilled onto the ground despite my best efforts to contain them. One opened to a centerfold showing a woman sprawled on her back, hand displaying her genitalia for a man who knelt over her—erect penis held in his hand. I could only focus on how neatly trimmed her dark pubic hair was.

"Good God, no one wants to see that," I exclaimed and snapped the magazine shut.

Mercedez opened the scrapbook. "This is definitely Jackson's."

Newspaper clippings of missing kids, stories about serial killers, child molesters, and other monsters filled the scrapbook. Most were printed on stock paper. Some were actual newspaper clippings, brittle and thin. The earliest dated back to when Jackson was 7 and I was just a toddler. There was a dog collar taped on one page.

Maggot covered mounds of fur deep in a sewer.

I couldn't look at the crumbling pages too closely. I could picture young Jackson mooning over these heroes while camped out in the backyard. Taping down his latest newspaper clipping like a school girl dreaming over a celebrity magazine.

"What date is the last clipping?" Mercedez asked.

"About when Jackson was 14." I flipped the scrapbook to the last empty pages. "He got a Polaroid camera for Christmas that year."

We sat in silence. I suddenly didn't want Mercedez with me. I didn't want her to know this shame. My stomach rolled and my skin burst into a cold sweat.

"Let's burn it." Mercedez grabbed handfuls of magazines and the scrapbook. "Come on. You'll feel better."

We filled Dad's backyard burn barrel, doused it with lighter fluid and doused it again to make sure nothing remained—burning all the photos, magazines, and one putrid scrapbook.

She was right. Watching it all burn settled my nerves as if every spark sent towards the stars was a small bit of forgiveness.

On a whim, I turned to Mercedez and said, "I want to look in the shed one more time. Just to make sure."

"It's getting late," she warned. "Your Dad is going to be home soon."

"We need to hurry."

We searched. Our flashlights lighting up our faces in blue light. The shed creaked and moaned with every step we took inside. I leaned against a wall to get to the far edge of the small shed. A shelf collapsed noisily.

"Fuck Franklin," Mercedez swore.

"Look. There's something under that bag of mulch." I pointed to a half used mulch bag, leftovers from when Mom gardened.

"Probably a snake."

"It's metal."

Mercedez held the flashlight while I used a shovel handle to pull the metal box out. The green metal lid was worn, but not rusted.

"This isn't as old as everything else out here."

"Open it." Mercedez took the shovel from my hands and leaned it against the shed wall. It scraped across the tin wall, fell to the ground.

"You don't think he hurt those kids, do you?" I asked while wrestling with the lid. It protested with a shriek, then popped open.

My heart pounded and fluttered, this time with fury, when the contents of the box came into view: three video tapes.

"You don't want to watch those." Mercedez's voice was a horse whisper.

"Hold the flashlight still, let me see these labels," I requested.

"We should burn them too." Mercedez put her hands around mine and the box. "You don't want to see these. You'll never be able to un-see them."

"What if he hurt those kids?" I pleaded.

"He's gone. It doesn't matter anymore."

Headlights in the driveway stopped any further conversation.

"Dad's home." I slammed the box lid shut. The shed swayed with our hurried footsteps.

We ran up the stairs, our hearts in our throats, and dove into my bedroom just as he came in through the garage door.

"Rocket?" he called.

I gulped, slid the steel box under my bed, and answered, "Upstairs."

"Thanks for the pizza," Mercedez hollered.

He said goodnight and busied himself in the kitchen for a while before heading to the master bedroom downstairs.

When his door clicked shut, I turned to Mercedez and said, "I can't watch those with him in the house."

"You shouldn't watch them at all."

"I have to," I whispered and sat on my hands to hide their trembling.

Count your toes. One. Two. Three. Breathe.

I couldn't sleep at all. The covers were too heavy. The air too cold. The steel box under my bed weighed on my mind. An unstable nuclear bomb that might explode should the slightest tremor touch it.

Bright, searing sunlight streamed into the kitchen the next morning. Mercedez nibbled at a Pop Tart. I stared at mine, imagining what horrors hid in that box. Did he hurt those kids? What if he had something to do with Janet's death? Maybe Mercedez was right. He's dead now. It didn't matter.

My brain was twisting and whirling on fictional horrors when Dad simply asked, "Can you pass the orange juice?" and patted my hand.

Bam. Every small flutter of anxiety that had plagued me for the past day burst through me in a full-blown panic attack. But I didn't know that's what it was. I was exploding from the inside. The nuclear bomb hidden beneath my bed in that steel box had gone off inside of me instead. It would splatter me on the walls like my brother's brains.

Poor Dad. He called an ambulance, convinced I was having appendicitis or something. Mercedez melted into the background. In hushed tones, she told me to breathe.

The paramedics came in through the front door. The last time someone had opened that door was when Jackson's dead body was wheeled out. I found regained energy to puke. My aim was good, I hit the metal waste bucket. It reminded me of the metal box lurking under my bed. I puked again until nothing remained.

Later the doctors wrote it all off with one word, "stress". Dicks. They patted me on the head and sent me home. Stress of her brother's death, they said. No one was really into offering therapy back then.

Dad took a couple of days off to stay with me. He sent Mercedez home. I stared at the walls, the locked up remnants of a monster under my bed. I didn't sleep for a week.

Dad finally turned to me one night and handed me a Xanax. "Just one. You need sleep," he said.

He took them daily, I knew, to keep his moods even. He was explosive when he was angry. But never abusive, just loud. Since Mom's death, it had been slightly worse. I think deep down he blamed himself for Jackson's death, thinking his "emotional" gene had made Jackson weak. Now I was having anxiety attacks and he was even more concerned he had "infected" me as well.

I slept for 14 hours. The next day, he made breakfast for me. I actually felt much better, clearer. I had made my mind up. I would watch the tapes to rid myself of the demon under my bed.

The phone rang. "Be right back, Rocket," Dad said and patted my knee.

I tried to not flinch. Runny eggs stared back at me accusingly.

"It's going to get cold," Dad said while covering the phone. The long twisted cord dangled behind him like an alien umbilical chord. "Mmmm. Right here." He listened to the speaker on the other end of the phone. "Semi-Driver certification. Yup. Sam was supposed to be there."

I pushed the eggs around on the plate. Yellow oozed from the egg and soaked into the toast. I rescued the bacon from the surge.

"Called in. I see." He looked at me. "Flu."

I did my best to look upbeat and flashed a thumbs up in one hand and a half eaten chunk of bacon in the other.

"Sure. Sure. All good. See you in a few minutes." Dad hung up the phone. "You sure, Rocket?"

"I'm not going to break, Dad." I bit a piece of bacon to show my strength. "Promise to take it easy and stay in my room."

Alone, finally. The quiet in the house was wonderful and awful. I had to purge myself and the world of doubt. I could scan through the tapes. Prove to myself he did not hurt those kids or Janet or anyone.

Two horrible hours later, I called Mercedez. "Can you come over? I want to burn these tapes."

Silently, she held my hand as I burned the last of Jackson's sins.

When the last flame had died out she asked, "Did you watch them?"

"Yeah. With no sound and on fast forward." I flicked the lighter on, flipped the lid closed.

Mercedez poked a metal poker into the barrel and stirred the flames

"One was a horrible amateur S&M sex tape with hand written credits on cardboard." I said to the flames.

"Gross."

"I couldn't tell who was who. Mostly their faces didn't show. I fast forwarded to the end with my hand covering most of the screen." I lied. I knew who it was, and she was right—I would never be able to get the images of it out of my head.

"It wasn't Jackson, was it?" Mercedez asked.

"I couldn't tell. Two guys and a girl. One guy had a dimple." I pointed to my cheek to show where the dimple was. Zack has a dimple like that. "Consensual. All looked old enough. No kids." I hate sex.

"Was the girl Janet? Do you think?" Mercedez broke some twigs and put them into the burn barrel. They scraped against the metal. She cringed.

I smiled wryly. It was a girl; I knew that much. "Couldn't tell." I held my hands out to the flame. Shuddered. Those faces contorted in imitations of passion made them even more unrecognizable to me. Unforgettable. Disturbing. "After a bit of static, there was another amateur film. A stupid horror film. The twins were in it. You know, the ones that died in the car crash on New Year's?"

Mercedez turned to me, her eyes huge and her mouth gaping.

"What?" I brushed my hands together to get rid of the dirt. "It was a dub of a dub of a dub. Really grainy."

"Did you watch the whole thing?" Mercedez asked.

"Are you cold?" I asked. "You're shaking."

"Did you?"

"It cut to static after Chad fell off the tank. Then there was this creepy bit."

Mercedez rubbed her arms and stared at the embers. "What do you mean?"

"The very last bit was hand held, someone opened the lid of a metal pit and threw a mattress in there," I said.

A black-mold stained mattress slowly devoured by the inky water.

"The second tape was mostly empty with a walking tour of the office. No audio." I stopped. "Oh! I recognize the office. It's where those Polaroids were taken. Do you think it's the same place where they found Janet? Think there's more stuff there?"

I had almost convinced myself I had imagined those pictures. I stared at the ground.

Mercedez lifted the lid to the burn barrel and put it in place. "An old factory, the cops said. Nothing left in there now," she said and pointed to the barrel. "The cops combed that place pretty good. When they found Janet."

It was my turn to shudder. "Where exactly did they find her?"

"The police never said. What was the third tape?" Mercedez asked.

We turned and walked back to the house.

"That was actual child porn. I couldn't watch it. Asian girls under 16, the label said. I believed the label and did not watch it. Can't put those images in my head." I have enough of a horror show going on in there already.

Mercedez paused in the doorway and said, "So besides being nightmare fuel, no one got hurt on the tapes. Just sex stuff?"

"Yeah." I leaned against the closed door. "It's a weight off my shoulders." All evidence gone. Burned. Destroyed. No kids hurt. Teenagers making stupid horror films and a bad sex tape.

"Yeah," Mercedez agreed, "a weight off."

***

"Dad thought I was having appendicitis, remember?" I ask Mercedez. My shoulders droop as I let out a shuddering breath and imagine all of my "stress" leaving me. I take another deep one and let it out.

Mercedez pulls up a bar stool and sits next to me. We sit and breathe silently next to one another.

"Give me a little bit of time and then I'll be able to go at it again, okay?" I ask.

She nods and we sit a while longer in silence before busying ourselves with the day's activities.

I turn on the computer and grab a notepad.

"Recipes involving fruit as delivery methods," I write.

"How about I head to Nashville for a couple of days and give you some time alone? Would that be better for you?" Mercedez asks.

"You don't have to leave." I turn to her while adding "melon" to my list.

"I don't mind at all, Jelica Jude. You need quiet. I need people," she says.

***

I've been going nowhere for 24 hours. Doing nothing. It's good to talk to myself and Whiskers. She's a pretty good listener if you don't mind she sleeps through most of your confessions. I look online for different drink ideas and post them up on a bulletin board trying to clump them into themes. Fruit as cups, layered drinks, fun with ice, whiskey drinks, brown drinks, and various other colors, holiday drinks, etc. It is a fun distraction.

By the second day, I am ready to go out. It is slightly brisk for September, but that isn't a deterrent to me. Better than the snow of D.C. Funny, I haven't really missed my job as much as I would have thought.

I take the beemer out of the garage and plug my electric warming gloves—how super luxurious—into the designated plug under the seat. I don't want to go very far, so I drive back roads to a nearby waterfall: Foster Falls. A handful of cars grace the parking area. I grab a water bottle and a foldable walking stick from the luggage bags and head off towards the trails.

Leaves litter the ground and crunch underfoot. I stand at the overlook and watch the waterfall until my nose gets cold from the breeze. There are a couple of trails to choose from. I decide to hike down to the bottom of the waterfall. The rock steps are steep and muddy. I slip a little but use the walking stick to steady myself. One slip catches me off guard and I go down hard. Miraculously, I catch a rock on either side of me and my tailbone never hits the ground. I'd break more things with my gracelessness if I didn't have fast reflexes. It brings to mind the story I told the guys about falling upside down in the cave that night in the bar—three months ago, a century ago. I miss Darren and the team.

I pass a couple of hikers who are on their way out, one with a large tongue-out-drool-everywhere-dog pulling happily on the leash. The young lady at the other end of the leash—little backpack, hair in a ponytail, sweatband around her head, North Face vest, tight neoprene pants, spotless Nike shoes—unfortunately does a face plant when Rover pulls too hard at the wrong slippery rock. I grab the leash with one hand and her elbow with the other.

"You okay?" I ask while Fido sniffs my knees.

"Jackson," she scolds the dog.

'Excuse me?' I think.

I help her up and we both assess the damage. Scuffed shoes. Torn spot on the knee of her leggings.

"I'll be okay," she says after brushing off her knee, "Going to feel that tonight."

We exchange a few more pleasantries and then part ways.

Jackson. I smirk and watch her walk up the steep trail of rocks. Further up the trail, still on the boardwalk steps, someone is taking pictures. They unabashedly take a picture in my direction, then wave. A small wave.

Every hair on my body stands on end. Adrenaline surges through familiar veins.

'Who's that?' I wonder. *'No bad guys here.'* I remind myself. *'Robert is in jail. Jackson is dead. No bad guys here.'*

The photographer walks toward Fido—I mean, Jackson— and his limping owner. They must know each other. I command my nerves to stand down and continue walking down towards the base of the waterfall. Deep breaths. Count my toes. Listen to the waterfall.

I have the 60-foot waterfall to myself. Up above me, at the top of the waterfall, a couple of people stand at various points on the rock ledge path. I close my eyes to enjoy the solitude and the sound of the pounding water. My phone binks—complaining there is no service available.

I try to not think of panic attacks, live audience taping, Betty and Dee in side-by-side freezers not 100 feet from where I brushed my teeth, Betty's finger on my countertop.

'No bad guys here.'

The waterfall is soothing; the cool breeze, the numbness of my nose and cheeks—cathartic. I pull my knit hat further over my ears and smile.

On the way home, before heading up the mountain, I stop at the local coffee shop for a latte. We chat while the barista steams the milk.

"The co-op farmers' market will be here next weekend. Make sure to check it out," she says.

I eyeball the bulletin board—filled with local business cards and ads—on the coffee stand's outside wall.

"I'm working on opening a place over there where North Base Camp is. Mind if I put a flyer up for the opening when I get them?" I ask.

She turns the white payment screen towards me and asks, "Sure. When you opening?"

"Probably before Halloween."

In my current hermit state, I can't imagine opening a business and talking with people daily. But here I am—making plans. Healing. It's a process, and making plans is part of it. Taking control.

"What's it going to be called?"

"Tippsy Kitty."

She blinks a couple of times, then her face lights up in recognition. "Like the YouTube channel? Wait, is that you?"

I both loathe and love being recognized. It's no big deal. I make videos. It takes almost no talent. Just show up. Make the thing. Finish it. Have a cute cat and a talented Mercedez to make you look fabulous.

"Yes. It's such a silly thing. But I have fun making them. My business partner, Mercedez, does all the work. I just mix the drinks." I blow on the coffee cup's lid. The latte smells delicious.

"That's exciting! I don't even drink, but I like to watch Whiskers."

I tell her about the Tippsy Kitty being filled with foster cats that can be adopted and she literally squeals.

"It's not all signed and sealed yet. I'm working on getting the place now. Should close on it in a month."

It is exciting to tell someone about my plans and to see them excited about it. I can almost imagine a future.

Someone steps up behind me and I step to the side, nod my head to the barista and say, "I'll bring down a poster. Thanks."

The person behind me steps closer to me, my inner alarm goes up. I rarely scan people's faces closely, since it does me no good. I do scan for posture, intent, emotion, potential threat. Habits.

This woman looks creepy and intense, with unforgettable black mascara. It has to be Misty.

I take a chance and say, "Hi."

"Hi. What's your favorite drink here?" she asks. Her smile is large and warm.

"I'm a plain latte gal." I say. "The caramel lattes are great, I hear."

Those blue eyes rimmed with dark black eyeliner squint at me. This isn't Misty. She doesn't squint.

I know better than to trust my brain when it says, "Hey. We know this person." Also, this woman tilts her head differently when she speaks. My confidence sinks, but no one is the wiser. She's a nice lady enjoying a friendly chat.

The barista leans her head out of the window, "Jackie! The usual?"

"Yes, please," she calls back.

I say goodbye to both of them and sit on my bike while finishing the coffee. Jackie waves to me as she walks away, heading back towards main street where she probably works.

The parking lot around the small coffee shop is empty and the one next door to it has only a few cars. Out of habit, I scan the cars and street—taking inventory.

Nothing to see. Stop it.

But my brain keeps scanning. Red ford pickup, Ranger. Volvo van. Honda sedan. SUV. Banged up Chevy with a mismatched door. Two kids walking a dog.

Nothing to see.

No bad guys here.

I'll go work on my recipe for the show. Find something to look forward to. The bike hums as I take the switch-back curves up the mountain. By the time I roll up to the cabin's driveway, I am feeling more at ease. Things are okay and I am going to be okay too.

I park the bike and walk to the porch. The wind has died down, but the air has turned cooler as the sun slides towards the horizon. The last slivers of sun fall across the porch onto a beat up manila envelope leaning against the kitchen door.

I immediately vomit my latte onto the leaves. Lucky for me, I already have my helmet off.

Lucky—that's me.

Facebook post on "Tippsy Kitty" created by Mercedez:

"Next week two lucky guests will be the live audience at a recording session of Tippsy Kitty. We'll be live for this special event!"

7K Likes, Happy faces, Hearts, and Wow emojis.

5K comments

1.5K Shares

Comments:

"Hope you had a good vacation!"— gerrymander_alexander

"I can't wait!!" —rattyhattie

"When does Whiskers get a spin off?"— effectualliammeow

"I heard a rumor about a brick and mortar Tippsy"— jackiehasasecret81467

"Kitty? Is it true?"— mom62460

"You stole my idea." — karenu.wxkejt6l0

"[bony finger emoji] [dark flower emoji]" —KingBarbour90

"WTH? Is that a drink?"— matilda_jackson_australia

"I'd totally come visit your bar! I mean that in the most platonic, not-creepy way."—cliff93ozumvjfs

"Tippsy Kitty Bar with an Air B&B on the mountain would be rad!"—almondycelina

"With lots of cats!"— joseph.the.josef

"Watermelons for the win!"— denise.likes.adrenal.cortex

"You should try pineapples next!!"

New followers: 345

Joined group: South Field Mountain Residents

Joined group: Cavers R Us

Number of unread direct messages: 75

Unread message #67: *"I am disappointed that you did not talk to me. The waterfall is beautiful after a rain."*

Posted to South Field Mountain Residents by Darcy398: *"Did y'all see anyone hanging out around the fire hall? They were parked there when I left to go to work. Had a towel covering their window.*

Responses:

"Red Ranger truck? I saw them driving slow looking at driveways on Greenway Point road."—FranAndFrank

"Got a pic of the car on my security cam. License plate didn't come through though. One guy driving."— RebelYeller52

Ten more responses speculating on the nature of the vehicle and occupant.

DÉJÀ VU

Recipe notes from Jude's journal.

Pour over a big round ice cube in a square whisky tumbler.

- A simple drink:
  root beer
  vanilla vodka

Repeat.

18 - SNEAKY PETE

Crap. There is no way I am going to touch that envelope. It could be nothing. Maybe it is something Mercedez ordered. I use a post office box downtown. This is a rental and I don't give out the address.

Paranoid? Yes.

The envelope, creased and greasy—like it has ridden around in someone's trunk for a while—coils patiently on the porch. Images of bolt cutters dripping with blood spring to mind. Pink fingernails. Horrible, grainy VHS tapes of debauchery. Black mold mattress sinking into inky water. Its ghostly white glow still visible under the surface of the dark liquid like a horrid white floating die inside a magic 8-ball. Bobbing and surfacing to declare doom through a small round porthole: "fuzzy bunny", "sex tape", "Polaroids", "scared kids", "brain splatter", "eyeless skulls".

PTSD—that's me.

Anger boils in my skull. I am done giving free rent to monsters in my head. Fuck 'em. I damn well am not that frightened little girl being manipulated and tortured by a half-assed psycho anymore.

Hell, those Polaroid kids got it worse. And none of us got it like Dee or Betty. But god-damned. I'm stronger than this. Frightened at the sight of a manila envelope.

I'm going to get-the-fuck-over-this and this guy is going down. What's the worst he can do—kill me? Well, whoopdidoo.

Fuck. This. Shit.

I walk close to it and cautiously roll it over using the tip of my boot. The address is printed on a sticky label. Addressed to me. At this address. No return address. No post-mark.

I take a picture of the package without touching it and send it to Agent Worthington. *"This showed up on my porch. Ten bucks says you'll want to see what's in it."*

I watch the text box on my phone blink. It blinks forever. My anger boils even more.

"I'm done," I tell Whiskers in the kitchen.

Whiskers meows something noncommittal in response.

Agent Worthington texts, *"Don't touch it. Sending a field agent."*

"No shit." Eloquent with words, I am.

Whiskers rams her head into my arm, demanding love.

"I guess it is too late to tell you not to get on the counters," I tell her.

Hours later, my phone rings. A curt voice replies when I answer the phone, "I'm at the gate. This is Special Agent Miller. I was sent by Agent Worthington. What's the entry code?"

I pause for a second—what if it is Robert? He'd know someone would come to get the package. He knows the protocols. But he's still in jail, right? Just messing with me from afar? I hesitate a moment longer, then say the temp code.

"I'll see you on the cameras when you get to the next gate and buzz you in there," I answer and close the connection without waiting for a reply. I pull up the security app on my phone and watch the driveway.

A black Tahoe with two people rumbles slowly down the drive. Standard issue feds. I buzz them through. I can't tell if one of them is Robert or not. But he wouldn't go so far as to have a partner, I'd bet. So, I relax slightly.

Well, relax as much as one can with a suspicious package on one's porch you think contains Betty's missing finger.

I want them to open the package immediately, but I also want them to say they need to take it to a lab or something. Do x-rays. Schrödinger's finger.

The tech, I assume, places a white cloth down and other implements used to document the package. Meanwhile, the other agent asks questions.

My phone rings and I miss the opening of the package.

"I got us tickets to go see a concert at the Caverns! Warren Haynes. You'll go to that right? It's in a cave, for heaven's sakes. It is tonight. Got the tickets half off. Or is it too soon?" Mercedez beams on the other side of the phone, deep into how she heals—going into crowds.

It's beyond me why I don't tell her what is going on. I don't tell her I am witnessing a tech lift the manila envelope with a gloved hand. He pours out—a finger and something else onto the white cloth.

Wound around the finger is a small plastic bracelet, smeared with something icky brown. The bracelet spells out Betty with small crosses between the letters. In a universe thousands of years ago, a delusional woman told me they were jade.

Mercedez talks on in my ear, "I know you don't like crowds—but we can stand at the back."

"Sure," I say on reflex.

"Really? Some of your caver friends are going. Brandy will be there. It's how I heard about it—she posted it on Facebook."

The tech examines the finger with cold detachment. I look at Agent Miller then back at Betty's digit.

"I'm sure it will be fun," I tell Mercedez and somehow don't let any emotion creep into my voice.

"OK. See you tonight. Bye."

I hang up the phone.

Agent Miller shrugs, "It has her name on it."

"Robert is just fucking with me now," I say then ask, "He's still in jail right?"

"Yes."

"This place isn't rented in my name. I'm renting through a friend of mine. My name is nowhere." I puzzle.

"Security cameras?" he asks.

I open the tablet and call up the security cameras.

"See here?" I point. "Doorbell cameras on the front porch and back porch, cameras on the driveway gates. All show nothing."

I scrub the video back until you can see me leaving the house.

"Can't see the porch at the bottom of the door." Agent Miller points out.

"Where the package showed up," I add the obvious.

Agent Miller walks out onto the porch and looks at the camera, looks back at the door. "Not watching for things at ankle level with cameras."

On the porch, I attempt to look at everything with a cold detachment and desperately try to not freak out. How would I have snuck a package here? "Pretty sneaky." I whisper.

We toss around ideas of how Robert could have had it placed; each idea more unfounded than the next. All ideas are fair game when spit-balling. Eventually you turn up one that clicks.

Does he have a partner that followed me?

Phone tracking?

Lucky sleuthing? It isn't a stretch to find a rented cabin that is recently off the market. He knows where I like to go up here.

Robert could do it all from behind bars with access to a phone.

The delivery itself—could have been a courier, a buddy, not impossible to do.

We go round and round for what seems like hours. The tech packages up the remains and stands in the doorway.

"Look," Agent Miller says as he walks towards the car, "I can't assign anyone else to this case, to watch this place. My manpower is limited as it is. And according to the records, we already have our guy in custody. He's probably still fucking with you from behind bars. I'd like to know how, but I'd also like to close some other cases on my desk."

I can empathize, but his bedside manner could use some improvement. He doesn't have to come out and tell a girl she's not his most important case. Lie to a girl, dammit.

"I'll let you know if anything else happens," I promise and watch the Tahoe bounce down the long, gravel driveway.

I bleach the countertops anyway and hose down the porch.

Do I tell Mercedez?

No.

Why on earth do I not tell her?

Denial.

If I don't admit it out loud to someone—it didn't happen. Besides, Robert's just messing with me from behind bars. Maybe he packaged Betty's finger and sent it to a friend for safe holding. Message the friend my new address, ask him to do a stealth drop—and boom—special-digit-delivery.

The friend could be none the wiser. *'Hey, old buddy. I'm pulling a prank on a colleague of mine while they are on vacation. Would you sneak this on their porch? No trace. Just a harmless prank. Thanks, pal.'* The UD is always pranking its own. What's a prank between friends?

No free rent.

Going to stop thinking about him.

Right. Now.

To distract myself, I look up Brandy's post about Warren Haynes appearing at The Caverns and post a reply, *"I'm looking forward to it! He's my favorite."* I'm so proud—I learned how to add a gif.

"I'm going to get us a beer!" Mercedez yells into my ear.

"Whisky?" I yell back.

"I'll see if they have it!" she says over her shoulder and disappears into the crowd.

We are inside The Caverns and the pre-show is warming up the audience. I am doing my best to blend into the rocks and disappear while simultaneously enjoying the people watching.

The place is literally a cave, a large cave room with a built-in stage and padded folding chairs set up for the audience. Lights hang about the place and a dimly lit audience packs inside the void. I'm not sure how many people are here. Two-hundred seated, maybe? Another hundred in the standing room section— most of them dancing.

The cave air is damp and cool. Occasional drops of water fall from the rock ceiling. To most, this is an amazing, unique place. To me, this is home. I love the dark of it, the chilly dampness, the way the air moves through to passages beyond. I find a place on the back rock wall where a rock ledge juts out. If you sit on it without something under you—you'd end up with a cold and damp rear. I place a small football stadium cushion and perch myself. It is a great vantage point. I can see the stage well enough, stay out of the traffic, watch all the people, and literally be a wall-flower.

Brandy, having a ticket for a padded seat vs my standing-room-only ticket, follows the usher past the red-velvet ropes and melts into the seated folk. I don't expect to see her again until after we file back to the parking lot.

"Did you hear they give tours of the Big Room cave just up the dirt road? I've never been. Want to go?" someone in front of me says.

I jump.

"Oh, sorry," she says and pats my hand reassuringly.

I look at her for a moment—not sure who is speaking to me from the darkness. The dark doesn't matter since seeing her face isn't going to help me. She sneaks a piece of hair behind her ear while tilting her head to the side. Dark hair, shoulder length. Sidewise smile. Battered long-sleeved t-shirt with a skull on the front. She is waiting for me to recognize her—in my fashion. So, she knows me.

"Brandy. Why aren't you in your nice fluffy seat?" I ask, recognizing that chipper dork anywhere.

"When Warren starts singing—everyone is probably going to stand," she says and gestures to her five foot five frame, "I'm not going to be able to see over them. Besides," she points to the rock I have claimed, "this looks like a great place to sit with good company."

She boosts herself up to sit on the ledge next to me. Not having anything to sit on, she immediately regrets it, "Oooh—moist."

I smile. "Sorry I don't have any extra cushions." I point to my comfortable derrière.

"I'll survive," she answers.

Just then, the lights dim even further and the headliner walks out on the stage. His soul-filled voice reverberates throughout the chamber. "Hello Tennessee," he says while the band members take their place on stage.

Warren licks out a stream of heart-wrenching notes from his guitar. The crowd jumps to their feet and cheers. Some in the standing room section with me dance. I enjoy the whole spectacle, from my safe perch, out of the way.

Brandy leans against me and smiles. Mercedez appears with huge beer cans.

"No whisky. Sorry," she mouths.

We enjoy the music together.

After their first set is through, they take a break. The lights come up and the crowd thins out a bit as many go outside for a smoke or to enjoy the warmer night air. I don't dare give up my coveted spot on the rock, so stay put while Brandy and Mercedez go to stand in line at the restroom near the entrance of the cave.

The entrance to the cave is very impressive. When we arrived I posed for a picture with Mercedez in front of it. The PR person for The Caverns was taking pictures. Mercedez gave him a card and discreetly from PR person to PR person said, "This is her handle on IG. Tag her." That's never not weird.

Sure enough, as I wait for Mercedez and Brandy, my phone pings. I have one bar of reception—just enough for this notification to reach me.

The picture was posted to their Instagram, and they tagged me, "*@TheTippsyKitty visits The Caverns to enjoy Warren Haynes!*"

I cringe to see myself in a photo, thinking of security clearances and bosses who would complain. Old habits. I guess I can show my face now. This is what I do. Who I am. Out there. Can't hide. Snail-mail-bloody-digits-be-damned. I try to put the thought of—was that less than 12 hours ago?—the severed finger on the porch out of my head.

The Instagram post registers likes and comments as I look at it on my phone.

'Gosh.'

Someone bumps into me, nearly knocking the phone out of my hand.

"I am so sorry," he says—grabbing the phone and my hands to steady them.

I can't see much of him in the dim light—dark hair, Dr. Strange goatee, tall—just at or over six feet. He leans towards me so I can hear him over the piped-in music.

"Looks like you have the best seat in the house." He turns and points to the chairs. "I have a standing room only ticket."

"It sold out fast," I answer. "Fun venue. I can see great from here." The lights from the stage pulse as if to prove my point.

He turns towards the stage and smiles. Dark bangs fall across his forehead, pulsing light highlights his dimpled smile and a slight bump on the crook of his nose. Then the house-lights flicker, telling everyone to take their seats: the band is about to take the stage.

He holds out his hand, "Kurt. Sorry I almost broke your phone. I wasn't watching where I was going."

"You ever been underground before?" I ask.

"No. It's cooler than I thought it would be." He looks at me and continues, "I mean, like, colder. Also cooler. I mean, neat." The words fumble from him and I think he smiles again, though it is hard to see in the dark. I imagine a dimple briefly showing itself, disappearing.

Saving him from further bumbling, Brandi and Mercedez approach with a second round of giant beer cans. Mercedez eyes Kurt with suspicion, looks at me with that best-friend do-I-need-to-maim-this-guy-for-you look. She squints at him in the dark, trying to make out his face.

I give a miniscule shrug that conveys, *'Nah-he's okay. Put the knives away—for now,'* and almost introduce Kurt, but the soul-warming voice of Warren Haynes singing "Soul Shine" ends all further conversation.

His voice fills the rock chamber and for a moment, for me at least, the world falls away. I don't think of fingers in the mail, the fact I have not told Mercedez yet, and how she will take it when I do. Betty can't get any deader, and Robert has run out of fingers to mail. Resolving to enjoy the moment, I sing along with Warren. Mercedez squeezes my hand and we sing and sway together.

Kurt stands nearby, but removed from us. I notice he does not sing along. To each his own.

The sound dies down and Warren changes guitars. In the momentary silence, I introduce Kurt to Brandy and Mercedez.

"Oh hey!" Mercedez points at Kurt with recognition.

He looks surprised and says, "From the gun range?"

"Still on that gig?" she asks.

"Last night. Heading out tomorrow."

I follow the friendly exchange and add, "Small world."

Brandy quickly pulls her ticket from her back pocket. "Trade you. I'm not using the seat. You can have it." She holds the ticket out to Kurt.

Lights from the stage dance about the crowd as Warren approaches the microphone. Kurt looks at the ticket Brandy holds out to him and for the briefest of milliseconds, I swear, he looks like he is mad. Not confused. Not irritated. Blazing mad. Then his face splits into a wide smile.

There is the polite back and forth of gestures and shouting, "Are you sure?"

"Absolutely."

"Wow! Thank you." Kurt takes the ticket. Before he bounds off, he pulls out a business card from his wallet. He hands each one of us one, gives a thumbs-up, and disappears into the crowd.

I can't read the card in the darkness, so tuck it into my back pocket and promptly forget about it.

By the time the show is over, I am elated beyond belief and have thoroughly forgotten about Kurt. My elation dies when we drive up the cabin and the headlights fall onto the porch.

Fuck. I'll have to tell Mercedez about the digit-delivery. What a buzz kill.

I hesitate on the porch and look at the barren spot where the thing had been.

"Mercedez, I have to tell you something. Let me make us a drink."

Fifteen minutes later, Mercedez whispers into her empty glass, "That's a buzz kill."

I pour a pink-slushy concoction into her glass and mine. It is pre-made and the easiest thing to grab.

"I don't think I could sleep through the night if I wasn't honest with you. Hate ruining a great evening." I stare at the Sneaky Pete drink, then sip it.

Not bad. Needs more cranberry fruit cocktail to offset the grapefruit Fresca. Or maybe there's something else besides Fresca could work?

Even in my darkest hour, I'm critiquing the recipe. I'm not sure what that says about me. Well, not the darkest hour—I guess I've seen worse. That's what it says about me. A severed finger or two is not the worst thing I've been through. Well, maybe the worst thing Dee and Betty have been through.

Damn. What did they ever do? What did I ever do?

"Did you check the security cameras?" she asks.

"Yes. That's the creepiest part of it. The doorbell cam doesn't see the porch floor. No other camera picked up anything," I answer, deflated, creeped-out.

Mercedez flips through her phone and makes harrumphing noises to herself. Finally, she sighs. "No missing footage." She looks at me and summarized the same thing Agent Miller had outlined, literally, this morning. Hell, was that just this morning?

"So, someone drove up the mountain and parked somewhere on the road, walked through the woods—not on the driveway—to avoid the cameras. They came up to the side of the house, out of the woods, and climbed the fifteen-foot rock outcrop—no cameras there because it's a rock drop into said woods. Then they slid this package to the door, out of sight of the doorbell camera."

"That's exactly what Agent Miller said." I'm not helping. Mercedez glares at me.

"And he can't spare any agents to keep an eye on us?" She isn't asking me. I think she's directing her question to Agent

Miller. The middle finger upheld in the general direction of "north" is a clue. She turns to me, sincerely sad, and says, "I wish you had told me earlier."

"And ruin the concert?"

"I understand. But..." She gestures towards the front door and porch beyond. "That's messed up."

I nod and we sit in silence for a while. I busy myself with putting the rest of the slushy filled plastic bag back into the freezer. We barely made a dent in it.

"Maybe we should hold off on the Tippsy Kitty Bar opening?" She walks to the sink and turns on the faucet. "The closing is next week. We should delay the opening for a while. Let this get resolved. You think?"

"I suppose. What about the live-audience show?" I venture.

Mercedez stops washing her glass and stares out the night-filled window. "I've already made all the arrangements. We'd lose money. You'd lose money." She washes again. "It would be horrible for your brand."

I don't answer. I know the answer already. It is all so surreal.

"I promise to hyper-vet the people. No psychopaths allowed." She puts her glass in the drying rack and dries her hands.

"You're right." I down the rest of my drink, not even appreciating the sweet and tangy flavor, then take Mercedez's place at the sink. "Robert is behind bars and he paid somebody to black-ops drop off the package. Some cop-buddy or an old military friend. They know how to get around the cameras. Hell, I know how to get around the cameras."

"We need more cameras," Mercedez states resolutely.

"This place is a rental. We can't add to it."

The gleam in Mercedez eyes warns me to stop being logical. Technology is her battle-ground.

Facebook posts:

"Tonight at the Caverns! Warren Haynes. Contact Karlee for a special caver 50% deal. She's only got a dozen standing-room only tickets held aside. See you there!"—CaverBrandy

5 likes. 5 comments.

Replies:

"Thanks! Message sent."—Mercedezzzzz

"I'm looking forward to it! He's my favorite. [gif of raccoon quietly clapping]"— TippsyKitty

Reply to TippsyKitty: 45 likes and 35 comments.

"I hope you have fun!!"—Rachel382

"[skull emoji][guitar emoji][skeleton hand emoji]"—KingBarbour90

"I saw him once in Atlanta!"—little.miss.chockablock

"I like this place and could willingly waste my time in it."—1825Salieri

Instagram Posts:

'The Caverns' Instagram post for Warren Haynes' concert tagging @TheTippsyKitty"

1,634,490 views

977 comments:

"I wish I could have gone to that concert! I'm so bummed."— Max_Angel

"I saw Tippsy Kitty there! In the front row!! Great show."— Rjluzzi

"Sono colui che viaggia non visto."— 1750Antonio

"__@funkyflizer33"— Toray

"I can't wait to go to the live recording!"— _kali_kali_ka

SNEAKY PETE

Recipe notes from Jude's journal.

Basically a spiked slushy.

I pre-make it, pour it into a sealable plastic bag, place the bag flat in the freezer. It won't freeze solid. Scoop out as much slush as you want. Serve with another liberal dose of Vodka, Rum, or Gin—whatever you used originally in the recipe.

- 2 quarts cranberry juice cocktail
- 1 can frozen lemon concentrate (thawed) – that's an oxymoron
- 1 can thawed-previously-frozen orange concentrate
- 1 quart grapefruit soda (I need to play with this ingredient. What else could be used?)
- 1 quart vodka, white rum, or gin—if you prefer
- 1 - 1 ½ cups sifted powdered sugar (I use Splenda.)
- Garnish with a lemon or orange twist if you have time and aren't trying to break it to your best friend another phalange-post has found us.

Cut down the recipe, if you don't have an army with you.

19 - SWEAT THE SMALL STUFF

I sort through the stacks of folders and sticky notes, cross reference them with my analog journal.

With a few clicks, I send a quick message to Brian. "I need some help with the cameras for the event. Let's do multiple go-pro type cameras. Thoughts?"

Coordinating a live event, now with extra security, vetting, additional cameras that would make the White House impressed, is challenging. Add, arranging the closing on the brick-and-mortar bar and turning it into something on brand.

Another couple of emails sent to coordinate last details on the closing and my morning to-do task is complete.

With all of that, I have kept my mind away from crazy Robert, Betty and Dee in freezers, and fingers in the mail. Plural.

First off, fingers in the mail. Who does that? What type of sick past does Robert have? Second, why did she keep that a secret from me? Says the queen of secrets.

I add in calendar reminders for Jude to pick the recipes for the event. She has notifications turned off on her phone.

The screen glows and I drift off. Fume. Robert. How is he terrorizing Jude from jail? How unhinged does one have to be to go through all of this just to terrorize her?

"You're next," Zack said as he squeezed my hand around a black rose.

Zack moved away before he could make good on his threat.

Does Robert have something in his past like Zack? Dead school girls dressed in Halloween costumes floating in a sludge filled tank, half their skull caved in.

Poor Betty and Dee. If Robert did that to them, this wasn't his first time. He must have a history, red flags somewhere. He just didn't start off by killing neighbors and stuffing them in a freezer.

In the browser, I open an incognito tab. I could check, do some data diving to see what he has out there. He's behind bars—what does it matter?

To quote Jude, "No free rent."

We've got things to do, least of which is figuring out the details of a kitty-cat inhabited bar. My favorite type of thing to keep my mind busy and away from dark places where the Zacks, Jacksons, and Roberts prowl.

After an hour of making lists and more lists of things to do, I stretch and pour a hot cup of tea to accompany the sunrise as it kisses the tops of the far mountains. Something jangles in the kitchen behind me.

"That you?" I call out.

"Nope. Boogy man," she answers. Sleepiness cracks her voice.

"I made a pot of coffee. It's in the thermos."

"I love you," she calls back.

"I know."

While she clinks and clanks in the kitchen, I open up Tippsy Kitty's Facebook messages and Intagram direct messages. Most of these are useless messages from weird creeps. I haven't cleaned these out in a while.

The warm sun slides down the wall and birds chirp merrily outside. The valley in front of the cabin stretches forever. You can imagine there isn't a soul in sight.

Jude leans in the doorway behind me. I know better than to engage in conversation before the first cup of coffee, but can't help myself.

"Do you ever look at these direct messages on the Facebook and Instagram?" I asked.

"No. I muted all of that stuff. Should I?" She sounds defensive.

"Not your job. Just wondering." I delete a few more weirdo messages from the inbox.

"Do you think there's something in there?" she asks, sounding slightly alarmed.

"I don't think so. Well, nothing in there besides the normal internet trolls." I delete another couple of messages with a satisfying click. "The only thing we get is the typical 'Hey beautiful', 'Hello friend', and a bunch of gifs filled with flowers, teddy-bears, cats, etcetera."

"Don't forget the dicks," she adds.

"You don't see any boobs. Just dicks." I turn to Jude and she shudders.

"We could change that." Jude walks back to the kitchen to get a second cup, calls over her shoulder, "Tippsy Titties. A whole new clientele."

I don't answer; keep deleting messages.

'When do we see those titties?' one message reads with an x-rated gif attached.

Well, there is a call from *that* clientele, I think as I delete the barrage of bullish messages from men in dark places. Safe behind keyboards, away from the rejections or the warped things that put them there—needing to reduce others, particularly women, to feel superior.

Cringe. I report it as spam, block them, and move on.

I delete message after message, seeing the patterns separating the honest to goodness actual messages from the creeps.

So many creeps.

Facebook direct messages, unread, deleted:

'Hello darling. Thank you for being my friend.'
'Hai beatiful.'
'I see you."
'You STOL my idea. I have a kitty bar!'
'Hello. Howe are yu?'
'For the sun every morning is a beautiful spectacle and yet most of the audience still sleeps.'
'I hope these flowers make you smile.'
'I have information. The FBI won't listen to me.'

20 - PAIN KILLER

"Hey, I'm going to go down the mountain and get some fruit at the co-op farmer's market for the live recording session," I call out from the kitchen to Mercedez.

No answer. She's muttering and plinking at the keyboard in her bedroom.

I text her, "Saw your calendar reminder. FYI"

"Hmmm?" she calls back.

"I'm going to try a take on the 151 Ways to Die recipe, and put it in a watermelon," I reiterate, over enunciating every word as I lean into her bedroom. "Want anything?"

Mercedez has her laptop open and is staring at the Tippsy Kitty page intently. She hovers a finger over the keyboard. From my vantage point, flower gifs adorn the inbox. She turns to me and simultaneously clicks her mouse button.

"Oops," she says and looks back at the monitor. "Hope those weren't important."

"Oh gosh, sorry I distracted you." I'm good at interrupting her at the worst of times.

"They'll write back if it was." Mercedez looks at me, getting all serious, and says, "This is a good thing—doing this recording. Carrying on. We have to keep going."

"I agree. So, what's the heavily-vetted-don't-creep-me-out guest list look like?" I ask and sit down in the loveseat next to the desk.

Mercedez gives me a wry look as if to say, '*You rarely get into the details—but okay.*'

She continues, "So, I kept to a few *strangers.*" She holds her hands up and wiggles her fingers in the air to emphasize the boogy-man potential of strangers, then continues, "only two."

"That's not a very big audience." I can't believe I said that— like, I'd like no one for an audience, thanks.

Whiskers walks in, needing to be a part of this important business conversation. She aggressively rubs against my legs until I pick her up. Being a shoulder cat, she immediately drapes herself over my shoulder and purrs. Her long whiskers tickle my neck.

Mercedez lists the guests for me. Each name makes me shrink inside. "Alexander and Brandy said they would drop by."

"OK. I know them. Well, I know Brandy. Alexander, not so much. But if she likes him, I like him." My coffee cup is dangerously close to empty. I stare at it.

"The two VIPs from Kentucky who won the online contest," she adds.

"Do we know what type of people they are? Did you do background checks or something like that?" I'm sure they are nice people. Not everyone is evil, right?

"They run a nursery. Like wine. Post all the time about the beauty of life. Seem like pleasant people. No kids. Mid 40s." Mercedez reads their stats from a digital note pad. "Phil and Deloris Newls."

"Well, you can't be an evil person and care for 3000 plants." I empty my coffee cup then add, "unless you are burying people under the plants. Good fertilizer."

"You are turning morbid."

"Better than a freezer."

"Valid point."

We both turn quiet. Too soon. We shouldn't joke about it just yet.

"Anyone else?" I ask, hoping the answer is no.

Mercedez pauses.

"Damn it. Who else did you invite?"

"Misty."

"The goth gal?"

"She loves your show and has helped me connect with the local pet rescue people for the café."

"She's probably a pussy-cat at the center of her pitch-black heart," I add.

Mercedez smiles, accepting her win. "She gave you peppermint oil for your migraine."

"I guess that's not too bad. I'm overreacting. These people didn't send me severed fingers in the mail."

"We gotta keep putting ourselves out there pretty-puddin' or he wins." She looks back at her screen and clicks a couple of buttons, then adds quietly, "All the sharks win."

***

The morning is too bright, the sun too high, the wind too much. I can feel a headache starting at the base of my brain. Consciously, I tell the muscles around my neck to stop climbing to my ears. Relax. Count toes. One. Two. Three. Breathe.

I browse quietly, trying not to be seen at the co-op farmer's market stand. It's a small place with a footprint smaller than a convenience store. Five tables with produce stacked on them. A pole barn type awning, with the lumber-yard stickers still stapled to their sides, perched above them for shade.

People lean over the produce and talk to one another. Small town, everyone knows everyone. I am the outsider and that is fine. I don't want to talk to anyone.

The stand of watermelons squats at the farthest end from the parking lot. I make my way around a couple of gossiping ladies with a polite nod.

They each eye me, then return to their conversation.

"Whatcha looking for today, sweetie?" a bent man with a beard to his chest says. He smiles and looks at the watermelons. "I'll make you a deal."

I smile in return. He is a kindly-looking fellow. Sun-baked and wrinkled face covered in a moppet of unruly beard. Gosh, that must be hot.

"Thanks. I need two." I point to the largest ones. "How much?"

I pay what he asks. His face droops, denied a good barter. He slaps stickers on the watermelons, pats them, brightens and says, "Sounds like a party!"

"I'll take this one with me." I point to the largest melon. "Be back in a sec for the other one."

He is about to say something—I assume an offer to help me carry the watermelons—when one of the gossiping ladies calls him to answer a question.

"Settle this for us, Gus. Isn't this a boy bell pepper? Which one is sweeter?" the lady asks.

"Gus? Can you help us here?" the other lady calls.

He nods my way, a twinkle in his eye, and walks towards the ladies to settle the disagreement.

I get a good hold on the one watermelon and consider if I can handle two. Maybe. Nah. I'd rather not drop them in front of everyone.

Near my shoulder, a voice speaks, "You having a party?"

I turn and stare at the person standing next to me. "Uhhhh." Articulate—I told you.

There is an awkward pause while the man standing in front of me, head tilted to the side, dark bangs over his forehead, goatee, looks at me like I should recognize him.

I'm used to this look. He smiles. A dimple appears.

Absurdly, I think about ice cream.

I smile bigger in return—as if I do recognize him and wait for him to say something, to move somehow, to give me a clue as to who they are.

He pauses a little longer and then says, "I'm so glad I ran into you. I didn't get a chance to say bye at the concert the other night."

The goatee: Kurt. There are a lot of goatees around, you can't go on that marker alone to recognize someone.

"How did that seat work out for you?" I ask and rest the watermelon on the stall's tabletop.

"Great! I mean, the concert was great. The seat too. That was nice of your friend…"

"Brandy," I finish his sentence.

"Brandy." He smiles. "Can I help you with the watermelon?"

"Sure." I point to the other watermelon. "That one there."

Kurt picks it up and walks me to my motorcycle. "Are these going to fit?"

"You'd be surprised what you can fit in these side bags." I unfasten the left bag and ungracefully slide the watermelon inside. It tries to rebel. I catch it with one knee and it complies. I hold the right bag open and Kurt places the watermelon inside. "They shouldn't get too warm over the pipe. Look funny in the soft bags though."

"Kind of like..." He latches the bag and steps back. "Um."

"Yeah. Balls." I am already putting on my helmet. Dang it. I forget people like to stand and talk. Mission accomplished—watermelon purchased. Now I want to go home and chill them. "Thanks for the help."

"You have a short ride?" he asks, smiling and blinking in the sunlight.

"Oh. Yeah. Just up the mountain." I point in a general direction towards a range of mountains in the near distance.

He smiles and stands there awkwardly as if he wants to say something else, takes a breath, then smiles a tight smile.

The sun glares off my keys as I put them in the bike's ignition; the reflection sparkles briefly across his face, his dark curly hair hanging over severe eyebrows. Part of me—irrationally—wants to invite him to the recording session. Why? He looks lost. I guess? He looks like he needs a friend. I want to help him. Weird.

"Well, see you later," he says, turns towards the tomato stand.

"Wait up." I can't believe my mouth is engaging without running the words up for approval.

He turns and waits, one foot still pointed towards the fruits and vegetables. "What's that?" he asks.

"I do these YouTube videos." I roll my eyes in a self-deprecating gesture, belittling the weird words coming out of my mouth.

"Tippsy Kitty. I know." He looks at the ground and studies his shoes.

"Ah." I say and nod my head slightly.

He knew who I was all along. I might have misread 'needs a friend' for 'I'm a fan and don't know how to say it.' That might explain the split second flash of anger I saw at the concert, when Brandy offered him her tickets. He wanted to stay and talk to me? Maybe?

"That's what these watermelons are for." I pat the side bag nearest me then continue, "So you know about the live recording session on Friday?" I ask.

"Yeah. I saw that on Facebook," he answers, turning back towards me. He adds, "I like your videos. Whiskers is hilarious."

"We're setting up the cameras and things tonight. It's a different setup than normal. I'm going to test it when I get back."

'Shut up,' my brain screams. Who cares about that? I blurt, "You should come up for the show on Friday."

Socially awkward—that's me.

He looks hesitant.

"It's a small group of friends and two Facebook people who won the weekend stay at the cabin next door," I add.

"All right. I'd love to. Thanks," he answers, then adds, "Is there anything I can bring?"

"Nothing at all but your appetite. Mercedez has gone overboard for this one." I laugh.

A micro-expression of discomfort crosses his face, his mouth turns down at the edges, just briefly. Is he uncomfortable with groups, maybe? Or—oh—the mention of Mercedez. He's wondering if she's my girlfriend. Friend zone, dude. Friend zone.

Overthinking—that's me, always.

"It's Friday at 6pm. Get there at 5 if you can. Message me on Facebook and we'll send you the address," I say.

"Thanks. I will." He waves.

I throw my leg over the bike and stand her up, kick the kickstand up with my left heel. "Umm," I twist back and add, "What's your last name? So I know to look for it."

"Salls. S. A. L. L. S. Kurt Salls." he spells out his name.

"Roger that."

I wave and just as I am about to rollout my phone beeps. I flatten the tank bag slightly, so I can see the phone through the clear plastic bag. Darren is calling. I pull it out, click the green icon, and shove the phone inside my helmet. It presses against my ear.

"Darren?" I ask.

"Hiya" His voice is distant and tinny.

"I can't talk too long—just about to drive home." Best to set expectations. I hate phone calls. If it had been anyone else but him, I wouldn't have answered. Let them leave a message. They can text like any human being under 60.

Kurt wanders through the vegetable stalls looking at carrots, his back to me.

Darren gets right to the point, "Robert keeps trying to call me. He wants to reach you, swears he's innocent."

"I got another finger on my doorstep here at the cabin," I tell him.

"Holy shit," Darren whistles. "The old lady's?"

"Yeah."

"That's messed up." He pauses, then adds, "I got a copy of the file—all the evidence they got from his trunk. I didn't know if you wanted to see it or not."

'*Yuck,*' I think but say, "I guess so. Email it to me?"

"Done."

Against my better judgment I ask, "How weird is it, Darren? Do I want to see it?"

Kurt pays for a bundle of carrots then walks towards his truck, a small red truck. Ford Ranger. Dent in the dark red side.

"...weird, right?" Darren asks.

"Sorry—lost you for a second. Can you repeat that?" My focus must have shifted.

"He was very obsessed with where you came from. He had pictures of you and Mercedez in high school, pictures from your brother's funeral, that article about you joining the UD. Pictures of your brother and his friends. Weird, right?"

"Yeah. Weird." I don't want to see the evidence at all. "But they have the murder weapon, right? It's not just circumstantial." I know, but need to hear it again.

"The knife was found in his trunk along with the ski-hat and gloves covered in Dee's blood," Darren says then adds, "Hearing date is getting announced tomorrow."

"I need this all to be over with." I say.

Kurt drives in front of me and gives a brief wave. I wave back. Fleetingly, I remember that guy at Foster Falls—that little wave.

"I'm looking forward to your show on Friday. Me and the guys are going to watch it at the bar."

I want to crawl into a hole but say, "That's sweet. I miss you guys. Well, not all the guys, but some of you guys."

"Yeah. It's not the same here without you."

We say our goodbyes and I think about how weird my life has become. I hope for closure. Robert will get sentenced, go to prison. There are no fingers left to mail. Shit, I'll need to testify. Fine. Then I can get back to caving and hopefully this will be the last of the live recordings. It stresses me too much. I'm done with stress. I have to learn to say no.

On my way home, I swing by the post office and pick up the mail. Amazon boxes, probably something for Friday's event, and some Neanderthal bills I can't pay online.

At the cabin, the sun is near setting, and the back porch is gorgeous. Mist fills the surrounding trees and valley. The setting sun breaks through in rays bathing everything in a warm glow.

"I guess that's what they mean by golden hour." I take a mediocre picture of it with my phone.

I am frowning at my phone when Mercedez yells from the back porch, "I need your body here to get the chest cam right."

Mercedez isn't a yeller—in fact, I've never heard her raise her voice, so the odd command is even odder given the articulation.

"Chest cam?" I ask while stepping onto the back porch.

Mercedez and Brian are setting up lights and tripods, putting tape on the floor to mark places, and adjusting chairs.

"Here, put this on." Mercedez says as she puts a weird-looking tube around my neck. Attached in the center is a small GoPro camera. "I know. It's weird." She adjusts the camera and looks at me.

My face, I'm sure, says it all.

"It's going to get in the way of your drink mixing." She looks at the camera and holds out her hand. "OK." She turns to Brian. "New plan. Hang a mirror."

They haggle over the mirrors, the lighting and shadows they might cast, views they might obscure. Eventually, they settle on a guide wire with the small cameras hanging off of it.

I pull Mercedez to the side while Brian fixes a gazillion cameras in place.

"Do you think this might be a little overboard?" I ask her, hoping not to hurt her feelings.

"Look big to be big," she says and beams at me. "This is going to look amazing."

I point to a small rock grouping on the bluff's edge. "What's the rock pile there for?"

"Fireworks."

"Of course." Mercedez can't be left alone. "When do the fireworks go off?"

"At the end of the show," Mercedez answers matter-of-factly.

I blink. She is enjoying this. The least I can do is not fight her. "Ok. I trust you."

"I love you, Sweet-Sally." Mercedez kisses my cheek and bounds off to work with Brian on light placement now that the sun is setting. I hear her mutter, "Thank heavens there is no rain tomorrow. It's going to be dry as a bone."

I split the mail into Jude and Mercedez piles and leave them on the dining room table. Mine is one tenth the size of Mercedez's stack. After a few trips in and out of the house, I have watermelons in the refrigerator, and nothing left to do but worry about things.

"When you're done, I'll make you a drink," I call out to Mercedez and Brian.

"I got some pizza coming," Mercedez says as she waltzes through the door. She's glowing with excitement. "Brian is going home. He'll be back tomorrow."

I look at the concoction in my hand with freshly poured rum in a pre-mix of pineapple and orange juice. All topped off with a touch of coconut cream. "I made too much then. Oops. No one delivers pizza up here, right?"

Mercedez looks at the table, "Misty is coming by with the Pizza. Mail?"

I told you she has problems with obvious things, "Yup. Hand me that nutmeg, would you, please? Is she hanging out with us?"

"Nah. She was on her way up the mountain to visit her aunt. Asked if we needed anything." Mercedez unconsciously moves a stack of glasses around and takes pictures of them for Instagram and social media posts unknown to me. "She's very nice underneath all of that mascara."

I sprinkle nutmeg on top of the drinks and admire the color.

"Your Pain Killer," I say with a flourish.

We sip our drinks in silence. The sun sets in a glorious display of colors. The sky fades to a burnt orange.

"Split Brian's drink?" I ask and pour the remaining bit into our glasses.

Lighting bugs flit about. Who can worry when life is this beautiful?

"This is good," Mercedez lifts the near empty martini glass. "You should do this for a living."

"I should open a bar."

"With cats."

"People will need to take a breathalyzer test before adopting a cat," I say.

"Can you imagine? Waking up with a hangover and asking, *'How did I end up with this kitty cat?'"*Mercedez laughs—a sad laugh.

I take her glass and mine to the kitchen. Mercedez phone beeps. She looks at her wrist. Types in a temporary gate code—I assume. Within minutes headlights pierce through the woods. Mercedez clicks the device again on her wrist and the headlights make their way to our door.

"That smart watch is pretty neat." I point to her blinking wrist.

I didn't know she could do that with her big honking watch. Mercedez sits at the dining room table and opens her mail, unaware of how she astounds me with her technical know how.

"Right? Upgraded me when I upgraded you. Did you order anything from Amazon?" Mercedez asks, holding up a small Amazon box.

"Nope."

The doorbell rings, which is silly. This cabin is fairly small. You can hear anyone walking up to it on the gravel driveway from 200 feet away. And Mercedez just beeped open the gate for her.

I lean around the kitchen wall and look out through the open screen door. "Is that a mystic pizza?" I call out, finding myself incredibly humorous and slightly buzzed.

Misty doesn't even crack a smile. Her alabaster skin glows in the dark. "I brought you a bottle of gin too."

I am interested now. "Oh? That's very nice of you." I have found people often have leftover bottles of something and give them to you once they know you'll give the liquor a good home. I try to make a cocktail for them with it, proving the said alcohol can be good—if done right. Usually the donated bottles are the garden variety, but occasionally something unusual arrives. Those are the most fun.

"Gin." She hands the bottle to me. The gin inside is purple.

"Where did you get this? Nice." I hold the bottle up for Mercedez to see. "Empress 1908 gin." I turn back to Misty and help her with the pizza. "You can deliver pizza anytime with gin like that!" I give her my thanks.

Misty might have smiled—difficult to tell. She personifies resting bitch face.

From behind me, at the dining room table, Mercedez whispers hoarsely, "Mother Fuck."

Misty's face bursts into a radiant smile. "Oh, cool!" she says, "phalange bones!"

Facebook/Instagram post:

"Phil and Deloris from Kentucky have won the VIP treatment. A glorious weekend mountain cabin getaway and a seat at the bar for the Tippsy Kitty's live recording. Tippsy Kitty has an announcement to make! You won't want to miss it!"

65K 5K Likes, Happy faces, Hearts, and Wow emojis.

7K comments

2.6K Shares

Comments:

"I'm so excited for them!"— Rachel382

"Beautiful."—1825Salieri

"You're not a real bartender." — thswhtshesd22

"More WHISKERS!"— craft2cardsMe

"Gin Gin mule"— mom62460

"So close. [skull emoji, gravestone emoji]"—KingBarbour90

"What's the announcement? Here's my favorite drink...."— roRollins8

+4.2K more comments

PAIN KILLER

Recipe notes from Jude's journal.

You're going to need this after opening a phalange delivery. Mix in shaker with ice:

- 4 parts pineapple juice
- 1 part cream of coconut (or Coco Lopez)
- 1 part orange juice

Strain into a traditional martini glass.
Float this on top instead of mixing it in for a real punch:

- 2 parts Pusser's rum
- Garnish with 1 pinch ground nutmeg (optional)

21 - CALM BEFORE THE STORM

"Of course I'm not going to—we're not going to—touch anything. No one *wants* to touch it," Jude argues into the phone with Agent Miller.

Misty excuses herself once she realizes we are not as excited about receiving finger bones in the mail as she is—after she ate some pizza.

"Do we have other dead people missing fingers? What the actual fuck is with the finger thing?" Jude spouts everything my brain screams.

I sit quietly at the table, unable to move, staring at this fleshless bundle of bones. An Amazon box. I didn't even think twice about opening it. I thought it was a new LED light I ordered recently.

The box looks normal from the outside: addressed to me—not Jude—to ME. The return address is blank. Inside the box is a small red velvet ring box, wrapped in bubble wrap. No card. No letter. Just the tip of a finger bone sticking out of the center of the box like a sick Tim Burton engagement ring. I can't tear my eyes from it.

This isn't Robert's doing. He doesn't know me. I saw him that one time at the bar.

Jude's voice from the kitchen sounds defeated. "I don't know." She pauses, then adds, "No. He didn't even know Mercedez."

My brain buzzes and my hands are a thousand miles away, shriveled and useless. I'm reduced to that small kid, afraid of everything, afraid of the angry teenagers who punch and hit, afraid of the looks of disdain, afraid of those I allowed to be close who then turned against me—sometimes with violence, becoming ashamed and revolted at seeing themselves like me— afraid of being alive, drawing breath, being different, a weak and horrible burden to everyone. Then long buried dread, the dark and gruesome depths that hold memories of Janet's bashed body, swells around me. Every dark abyss I ever crawled out of threatens to swallow me whole. The weight of my smallness makes it hard to breathe.

Jude places a hand on my shoulder. I startle. A sob escapes from me.

"Sorry," she says and removes her hand.

I grab it and hold it in place on my shoulder. "Jumpy." I motion to the red-velvet box in front of me.

"Come on. Have some pizza while it is hot," she says.

We move to the kitchen and after vigorous washing of hands sit and watch the pizza grow cold.

Headlights move through the woods, pause at the gate. My phone beeps from the kitchen table, next to the finger. I glare at it, dial the app on my smart watch and open the gate. The headlights continue towards us.

Jude looks at my wrist with curiosity.

"Gate connects with my phone," I explain.

Agent Miller steps out of his Tahoe. His feet grind loudly on the gravel as he walks towards the porch. Jude lets him in.

"In there," she says.

I stare at the pizza. Twiddle with my smart phone and rename Agent Miller's contact. "Want some pizza?" I ask.

The next morning we awake and go about our day as if nothing weird has happened. Neither one of us goes into the dining room.

"Good thing this is a rental," Jude says over her morning coffee.

"He's got to run out of fingers eventually, right?" I am trying my best to be logical about the situation. Something isn't clicking right about all of this.

My phone rings and I glare at it. I finally answer on the third ring.

"Agent Miller here," he says unnecessarily.

"Yes." I have him in my contacts—but don't want to expel any more words than necessary and explain I know who he is. As if fewer words would make all of this less real.

"We've had an agent in internet forensics combing through the social media accounts you provided for us."

"Uh-huh," I articulate.

Jude's phone rings and she glares at it, then me, like my phone call is contagious or something. She answers it and walks out onto the porch.

"There are plenty of weird messages. Many unread." Agent Miller clears his throat, continues. "I'm to understand neither of you read the finger messages."

"What on earth is a…" I pause and look for Jude outside. She is out of earshot, "…finger message?"

"Did Jude see any of these messages?"

"No. Neither of us did. I clean out most of them and manage the accounts."

"The bone is old, obviously. It has been treated. Bleached," he says. "There are messages you two have been getting with Halloween emojis—skeleton fingers—in them."

"For how long?"

"A month. On their own, we'd think nothing of them. But the content of the messages are odd. Taunts of sort."

Jude is walking back and forth on the porch, one hand on her hip, the other waving around emphasizing her agitated conversation.

I sigh. "You want me to look them over and see if it makes me think of anyone?"

"Exactly."

"You don't think it's Robert just fucking with us?" I know the answer before he even says it.

"Robert's charges have been dropped," he says quietly.

"Why?" My brain continues to rail, '*Why the actual hell would you drop the charges?*'

"These messages and posts all link through three accounts. Some images have embedded location data and dates," Agent Miller says.

"It's not Robert?" I refuse to believe it.

"He has been helping in the investigation."

"To save his own ass." I raise my hand in exasperation.

Jude, on the porch, turns and looks at me with her mouth agape. She mouths, "What the fuck?"

I suspect we are getting the same information. Darren must be on the phone with her.

I shrug and ask Agent Miller to repeat his last sentence.

"I said, he's been released, Robert has," he repeats.

"I don't understand. There was a third finger and now you're just letting him go?" I walk towards Jude on the porch and she towards me. We meet in the dining room and hold each other's free hand, each one of us talking on the phone to a bearer of doom.

With a metallic screech, the lid of the dipping vat swung resolutely shut. For a split second it bounced heavily on Janet's skull, then slammed shut, severing three of her fingers.

It's not Robert. It was never Robert.

"Well," Jude says, "we have the closing of the bar today. A show tonight. I don't know what else to do. I'm sick of this terror in the mail bullshit."

I can almost hear Darren on the other side being descriptive about what he'd do to the guy if he ever gets his hands on him.

"And it isn't Robert. Are we sure?" she asks.

Agent Miller asks if I can take the time to look at the messages and see what jumps out. They are starting from scratch and building a profile of who they should look for.

"Sure." My voice falters. "Um." I don't want to consider that long ago demon.

"You're next," he said.

I squeeze Jude's hand for a second. She is still talking to Darren, "Thanks. I get it. I'm glad you updated me." She listens for his response. "We'll keep things buttoned up here. After the closing and show today we'll hunker down and the agents will find him."

Agent Miller says in my ear. "Call me anytime if you see or hear something. Nothing is too insignificant."

"Gotta call them all," I answer. Jude always says that.

Jude side-eyes me with a questioning glance as she hangs up her phone.

I hang up as well.

In unison we tell each other, "It's not Robert."

"I have something to tell you," I say to Jude. My heart sinks.

***

Doing our best to keep a brave face, we go to the real estate closing. The sellers aren't present. They signed earlier. We're alone with the lawyer in the cozy legal office. The lawyer must be from Mississippi, I assume, based on his long drawled out accent.

Jude and I sign where the lawyer points in a thousand places. No one speaks. Papers slide across the table. Pens click. We are on auto-pilot. I expected the event to be more upbeat or jubilant. Not detached.

I pause mid-signature. "Are you sure?" I ask, my question loaded with meaning.

Jude and I have said little since I confessed about Zack, making a dupe of the horror film, Janet's death on the tape, Zack and Jackson beating me up at the donut shop, and Jackson's passes at me. I told her almost every secret I kept from our entire childhood, except I couldn't tell her I was there. I didn't tell her I was the one that recorded the horror film and Janet's death.

"Did you watch the horror film and see her die?" Jude had asked.

"Yes." I evaded by telling a half truth. "And I didn't tell anyone." It still boiled down to me not telling. I don't want to list what other tapes I made.

Both of us kept our secrets. Who else was hurt because of that?

And now, how can she want to open a business with me? My secrets have brought Zack, not Robert, to us. All of this is my fault.

Jude squeezes my hand. The lawyer eyes us with a look we are very used to receiving.

"We should have done this a long time ago," she says.

"Even with everything going on?"

Jude pulls the last of the papers towards her and signs with a flourish. "I wish you had told me before. I could have been there for you. But, later is better than never."

The lawyer, Fetty, hands a manila envelope to us. We both flinch in unison as if a snake, or a severed finger, is going to pop out of it.

"It's the keys," Fetty says with a hint of surprise. "You can begin occupation of the bar now." He leans back into his oversized leather chair, laces his fingers on top of his girth.

Jude reaches for the keys and looks at them closely, then at Fetty. "We'll send you an invitation for the grand opening." She manages to sound upbeat.

"Let's go imagine the possibilities," I tell Jude.

We bid our goodbyes to Mr. Lawyer Fetty.

I imagine fingers piled up on his desk. Past traumas, repressed memories, all of which I paid good money on therapy to deal with, pounce around in my brain and tie me in knots.

My personal repressed memories "Donut Shop Beat-down", "Teenage Horror Film", and "You're Next" occupy my thoughts on replay.

"Red light," Jude informs me as politely as she can.

I almost blew through one of the three red lights in this town. The bar is up ahead on the right.

"You okay?" she asks.

"Demons from the past," I answer and wait for the light to turn green. A tractor pulls into the intersection in front of us. He waves and smiles.

"Right? Why would Zack show up now?" Jude asks.

I pull over in front of the bar and we look at it. The lights are out and it looks unloved.

"Needs paint."

"Needs bigger windows so people can see in."

"Enclose the patio for the cats."

"A big sign."

"Motorcycle parking."

"Cavers welcome sign."

"This is the right decision, right?" Jude asks.

"What are we going to do, hide on a mountain top?" I answer.

"Dipshit can just come get us and stop sending stupid fingers in the mail," Jude grumps.

"I was just thinking the same thing."

I turn the ignition off, and we walk up to the bar. Jude unlocks the door and we each hold a hand up for the other to walk through. I gently push Jude through the door and she giggles.

"You should publish your book of recipes too."

"Proceeds go to the animal rescue society."

"Of course."

We grab hands in the center of that dusty place. It is going to be a project. But what a great feeling to look at something that needs love, care, attention and know it will exhaust you, try you, but ultimately it will be wonderful. I love things like that.

"Yeah," Jude whisper and spins to look at every corner at the same time. "I love it too."

***

It's a busy day. Secrets spilled. Bars purchased. Live show to run. A psychopath tormenting us. We'll see him coming, now that we've figured out who he is. I'm bone weary, I can't imagine how Jude is holding up through everything. But there she is, making a new drink and testing out the cameras with Brian as if nothing is wrong. She's a far cry stronger than she was during the panic attack night.

I sit in the dining room and look through all the deleted messages. Agent Miller had highlighted a thread of them I apparently had been oblivious to all of this time. The warnings were clear. All this time, this crazy f-er has been sending weird messages under the name KingBarbour90.

I scroll through them, getting more mad with each click. I take a deep calming breath and glance through the window.

Jude is in her element, making a drink, talking to the camera, and smiling. Such an enormous smile. I don't know what this drink is—but it involves an umbrella.

Whiskers stands by patiently, as if awaiting her cue. Jude holds the drink to her and after some sniffing and twitching of her nose, she bats the umbrella out of the drink and chases after it.

Jude and Brian erupt into laughter. She hands the drink to him and he sips at it politely.

I walk out onto the porch as Jude says, "Yeah, I'm not a fan of fruity drinks either. Some people love them."

"I can help clean up and set up for the evening's event," I offer. "Not wielding the cameras makes me feel useless."

"I have all the cameras feeding to the control board over there." Brian beams.

"What you looking at in there?" Jude asks.

"Agent Miller asked me to look through the direct messages and see if there could be anything there that stood out to me." I answer, trying to not let any emotions show.

"Serious? Has he been sending messages?" she asks while carrying the leftover drink into the house. "I'll put this extra Chrysanthemum tea in the fridge for later. It makes a nice dessert drink, I think."

"Oh crap. I need to put the hors d'oeuvres in the oven." I open the fridge for her and the freezer door for me.

"You avoided my question." She glares at me while I arrange the frozen spinach puffs on a tray.

I don't look up, intent on getting the spacing just right, and lie through my teeth, "No. Just the normal creeps."

What good would extra stress do her right now? Messages with emojis. Ooooh. Oooogidy boooogidy. Stupid passive aggressive spineless tactics.

Betty and Dee might disagree. Stuffing dead people in a freezer and cutting off their fingers, that's not passive aggressive. That's the definition of fucking aggressive.

"Hey." Jude says, breaking my reverie.

I look at her.

"We'll get through this. We always do," she says and smiles.

My phone rings and my wrist watch lights up with a text from Brandy, *"We're here early to help set up!"*

"Brandy and Alexander are here to help," I inform Jude then add, "Yeah. We'll get past this." I'm not sure I believe me. Zack is coming to get me. I'm next. Don't get Jude too.

Facebook messages, unread:

"[Emoji of skull] [Emoji of skeleton hand] [Emoji of gravestone] [Emoji of knife] [Gif of severed monster finger] [Gif of severed monster finger] [Emoji of girl with blond ponytail] You're next."—KingBarbour90

"Please. I have to talk to Jude. I was an asshole. But I'm not the guy."—RobertTheLoud

CALM BEFORE THE STORM

Recipe notes from Jude's journal.

Blend all ingredients:
- One and a half part Rum
- Half part Blue Curaçao
- One part Chrysanthemum Tea
- One part pineapple juice
- Half part (or more) lime juice
- Half part orgeat syrup
- Garnish with orange or pineapple slice

Pour in a tropical tall glass and garnish with fruit slice and umbrella. Don't forget to smile for the camera.

CHRYSANTHEMUM TEA

Boil 4 cups of water, remove from heat.
Add 6 tbsp of Chrysanthemum buds.
Let sit for 10 minutes.
Strain.
Stays good in the fridge for 2 weeks.

22 - DEVIL'S MARGARITA

Headlights approach the cabin. Behind me, Mercedez buzzes people in through the second gate.

"Misty is driving up," she says.

Brandy and a fellow I haven't seen with her before walk up to the porch. She is beaming a smile from ear to ear.

"Bitch!" she says pleasantly and grins.

"Bitch!" I answer and we hug.

Long story, there's a group of us caver bitches and that is our greeting.

I hold Brandy at arm's length. She was in an accident recently. The scar over her eyebrow is barely pink. I point at it. "You heal quickly. I thought you were in a nasty accident."

She smirks and points towards the gentleman with her. "Alexander is an excellent nurse. All better now." Brandy tugs Alexander's long sleeve shirt and pulls him towards her for a kiss on the cheek. "Alexander, this is Jude. Mercedez is over there."

I shake his hand, strong grip. His leather driving gloves creak.

I've made all of this noise about being face-blind, but I can see this guy. When someone's face actually dials in for me—it's embarrassing. I look at them a little too long. I have to stare because I can see them. All the pieces align, and whatever part of my brain allows for that pattern to record—it clicks.

He removes his hat, makes a slight bow and says, "How wonderful to meet. Brandy speaks highly of you." Dark curly hair, mischievous smile, not quite six-foot, angular frame, and a voice that makes you want to listen to him all day long.

"You must be a radio announcer or something," I blurt out. "So formal."

He raises an eyebrow and says, "Construction."

Brandy lets out a small laugh. "Indeed," she says. "Where can we jump in?" She looks over my shoulder, "Mercedez, we're here to help. Put us to work."

They receive their orders from Mercedez, and the kitchen becomes a whirlwind of activity.

I seriously think we are making too much of this event, but Mercedez is the boss.

Another car drives up. Footsteps on the gravel approach the porch. I open the door for Misty, though I can barely see her behind the flowers she carries.

"I thought you might want these for the show," she says and places an oversized vase overflowing with two dozen roses onto the kitchen counter.

Mercedez stops in mid-sentence and turned towards Misty.

"Those are…" Mercedez's voice stutters.

"Are they dead?" I ask.

Tactful—me.

"Dyed black." Misty adjusts a rose in the arrangement and seems satisfied with her manipulations.

It looks the same to me.

"Oh."

Before I say anything snarky Mercedez interrupts me a bit manically. "They would go great with the theme!"

Misty might have smiled slightly, a twitch of the jet-black lips. "What's the drink for the show?" she asks.

"151 Ways to Die," I answer.

Mercedez is already moving the flowers around, getting the best angles to take pictures.

"Perfect," she says and then sniffs the air. "Brandy, would you check on the cherry tarts in the oven? I think they are ready."

"On it!" she hollers back. Clanking and movement from the kitchen indicates things are ready.

I want to crawl into bed and take a nap—already over people and things.

Brian appears behind me and whispers in my ear, "It's quiet outside."

I hadn't really looked at him before: nearly bald, dark eyes. He slouches like he wants to be five-foot tall but is forced into a 6 foot 5 inch hulking body. You can feel him wanting to disappear—a kindred introvert spirit. I get him.

The sun is over an hour away from setting and a layer of cool air drifts through the trees. The valley stretches in front of us. Distant bright green meadows visible through the haze covered trees.

"It's a good spot up here," Brian says. "I used to fish up here before houses were built."

"I like the camera setup you have." I point to the guide wires where six cameras hang.

"Those two are for seeing you mix the drinks." He points out the small silver boxes. "Front and side. That one." He points to a camera on a higher guideline. "Looks down on your hands.

Normally you'd use a mirror, but the sunset was going to get in the way."

"Oh," I say. "I appreciate all the work going into this show."

I would have been happy with one camera, but I also could eat PB&J sandwiches for every meal. Discerning taste—not me.

"These two see the audience's faces and that one over there is a wide shot for the sunset and fireworks," He says proudly.

"Wow." I stand at the bar as if I am about to make a drink.

The bar sits on a stone patio, surrounded by trees and tiki torches. The breathtaking bluff view of the valley is behind me for the cameras and audience to enjoy.

"Seriously. You all have outdone yourselves with this one," I tell him.

He smiles and we lean against the bar and watch nature in introverted bliss—silence.

"Oh," He breaks the peaceful bliss of reserve but hesitates.

"Hmmm?" I ask.

"You'd be interested in this." He walks towards the bluff and peers over the drop.

The bluff drop isn't sheer, not a straight drop. A sharp slope.

Brian continues, "There's a small cave down there. You cave too, right?"

"Yes. Mercedez doesn't. But I do." He has my full interest. "How big is the cave?" I look out at the top of the plateau across from us. "We're too high up for anything more than a shelter cave here."

"It can't be more than 40 feet long before it peters out."

"How far down the bluff?" I ask.

"Not even twenty feet."

"Hang on."

I jog to the garage and grab my trusty webbing, bring it back to Brian.

"That will reach it." He holds out his hand for the webbing and like little kids getting into mischief we wrap one end of the webbing around a small tree and dangle the rest down the bluff. He leans over, holding onto the webbing. "Just reaches it." He points. "See that old tree rotting there?"

"Yes."

Behind us, Mercedez calls my name.

"It's to the right of that." He smiles and turns as Mercedez approaches.

"What are you two looking at?" She stands behind us, hands on hips, her light-pink blouse billows in the breeze. Mercedez's fingernails and suede pumps match her blouse.

How much time that must take to put together. Wow. I'm dressed up if I spend a moment to condition my hair.

I smile at her. "A cave."

"Good heavens."

"Just a little one," I whine.

"I'm going to get the VIPs. You ready to pre-game?" she asks.

"We can go see it tomorrow," I kid.

"Nothing is getting me in a cave, and you know it, Missy Mary." Mercedez pats Brian on the shoulder. "Are you crazy enough to go in them?"

He drops his eyes and answers, "Yes."

"I'll get the pre-game drink setup inside," I say.

"Wait for me. We'll do a normal one camera setup in there," Mercedez calls out as she gets into her car.

Her phone rings as she shuts the door.

Inside, I juice some limes for the pre-drink and pull the pre-made watermelon drink out of the fridge.

"Here. I will help you with that," Alexander says. He stops in front of the watermelon and looks at it pointedly. "What is it for?"

"This watermelon will get filled with tequila, whiskey, rum, and Everclear," I answer. "You won't want to drink much of this."

"Indeed," Alexander says.

"Put it right there on the counter next to the other watermelon, please," I instruct and set my bowl of fresh lime juice at the other end of the counter.

"Why two watermelons?" Brandy moves the black roses out of the way to make room for the second watermelon on the counter.

My phone beeps. I fumble with the app to open the gate. "Backup in case I drop the other one," I answer.

Alexander pats the watermelon solemnly and says, "Someone is coming up the drive."

"I invited this guy I met in town named Kurt." I open the door and watch the red truck drive up and park.

As Kurt walks up, Mercedez drives up with the VIP guests. All four ascend to the porch in almost unison with introductions all around. Kurt smiles at Deloris and Phil, who are positively beaming.

"Hi there, come on in. We're about to pre-game with a drink called The Devil's Margaritta. With two ts." I say and motion towards the open door.

"I love your show!" Deloris gushes and introduces me to her husband. "Phil does too."

He smiles sheepishly.

Deloris is mid-fifties, round, exuberant, and wears bright colors. Phil is beanpole thin with matching thinning hair, watery eyes and a non-existent chin. He smells of Old Spice.

"Get some food, make yourselves comfortable. We'll do the first recording at the kitchen counter," Mercedez hands them each lovely linen napkins.

I note they are monogrammed with the Tippsy Kitty logo. Well, heavens. Monogrammed linen napkins.

Brian holds the camera up and points to it.

"We're going to do a recording of this drink—it isn't live. Just something we can package later. Get you used to the camera," Mercedez informs the audience.

I barely have time to say hi to Kurt. "Thanks for coming to the madness. Did you have any trouble finding the place?" I ask and hold my hand out to shake his.

He pumps my hand twice, without missing a beat, and smiles gently. "Nah. It isn't that hard to find. There's a lot of cameras." He points to the porch.

"Mercedez needs to work for HBO or something." I point to the dining area across from the bar. "You okay off camera?"

Kurt meekly takes his seat and says, "Happy to be off camera."

I take my place at the bar and instantly forget about the cameras, the strangers, the crowds. I want to show them how to make this drink. They need to see how cool it is.

"I've squeezed some lime juice and made a simple sugar syrup by boiling sugar into a cup of water." I hold up the lime juice for all and the camera to see.

Mercedez picks up her phone and takes what must be B-roll, getting close to the two dozen black-as-Misty's-heart roses then walks backwards to get a shot of the whole crowd watching while I explain the drink. She looks at the roses, pauses, frowns.

Black roses.

Jackson's funeral.

Misty *would* like black roses and that has nothing to do with anything—just a coincidence. I keep my game face on and talk to the camera.

"I'll shake together some tequila with the lime juice and simple syrup." I pour three shakers full. The shakers match and have the Tippsy Kitty logo engraved on them.

The copper shakers glisten with condensation. I hand a shaker to each VIP and show them how to shake the contents.

"There's a thing with the type of ice you use, how you shake it so it mixes but doesn't bruise the drink." I show them a good rhythm of how to shake the mix.

"Like this?" Deloris asks.

"Ease up just a smidge on the force," I instruct. She is shaking it like her life depends on it. "And maybe a little more umph on your shake, Phil." He is barely moving his shaker—as if it might explode.

They adjust their shaking as Misty stage whispers in a deadpan voice, "It's almost like maracas."

"Shake. Shake. Shake, senora," Deloris sings.

Mercedez and Brian both react to the magic happening on stage and push in for close-ups of the audience, Brian on the left and Mercedez over my shoulder.

The crowd sings that song from Beetlejuice. I don't entirely know it and even if I did, I'm not singing. So, I just stand there and smile a thank-God-the-cameras-aren't-on-my-awkward-face smile.

"Now we use a strainer and pour," I say, bringing the shaking—and singing—to a halt.

Kurt looks relieved the singing is over. Alexander has a smirk on his face—as if this is all oddly enjoyable to him. Weirdo.

After straining the drinks into small margarita glasses, I pull out a long handled silver spoon. "Now the fun," I add with bravado.

I pour a stream of red wine down the spoon on top of each drink. The red wine floats on top of the other liquor, causing a two-toned drink.

"Cool!" Deloris exclaims.

"Garnish with a slice of lime."

I push a drink in front of each audience member after anointing the glass with a lime slice. Brian gets close to Phil for a close-up of the glass. Phil leans back to be out of the way.

Having Brian and Mercedez buzz around us with cameras is less distracting than I thought. It's like a dance. We're all doing well, I guess, since we're all so used to taking pictures with our cameras. Well other people are, I barely know how to work the thing. Everyone gets it and flows right with the recording.

I take a glass to Kurt at his safe position off-camera in the dining room. He sits right next to where the latest finger was.

"You okay?" he asks.

"Yes. Yes. Here's your drink," I answer.

"Sorry, I don't want to be on camera. Not my thing. Cameras. Sorry." His nervous voice drifts off with the apology. He pulls at his earlobe.

"Not to worry." I turn back to the group who are all awaiting the invitation to drink. "I have to get back."

He nods and holds up his drink.

"Now for a toast." I hold my drink up to everyone and towards Kurt. "We just closed on the brick and mortar location of Tippsy Kitty today. I invite you to our grand opening in two months! Tippsy Kitty!"

Everyone clinks glasses and cheers. They sip tentatively at the drink, then more readily. I have one shaker left over since Brandy and Alexander don't drink. Discreetly, I cover the shaker and open the fridge door.

"Brian. There's enough for you. Want one?" Mercedez asks.

He shakes his head.

She laughs. "Best to not drink and upload. Been there. Done that."

The shaker slips from my hand, almost dropping to the floor. "Hell fire."

Brian lunges forward, "Oh!" He reaches for the drink but is too far away to help.

I flinch from his sudden movement and almost drop the shaker again. "Got it. Swear." My voice is high pitched in my ears.

He clasps his hands in front of his hulking chest, whispers, "I scared you. Sorry."

"Didn't want to wear it. Thanks for trying to help me. Really." We speak in hushed tones.

Brian meets my eyes, smiles. "I don't drink, sorry."

"I'll make you a non-alcoholic drink next time. Okay?"

"Sure." He smiles again and returns to the porch.

Mercedez shuts the fridge door for me. I tell her, "I'll save that for us. We'll toast after the show wraps."

"Agreed," she says. "You're crushing it, by the way."

"Thanks."

Behind me everyone comments on the drink.

"That's good."

"I wasn't sure—but, I like it."

Mercedez instructs everyone, "While we get setup for the live recording outside, grab some food and make your way out to enjoy the sunset."

Brandy comes up and says, "Hey, I hope you don't mind, but we'll stay in here for the recording. Is that okay?"

"Brandy, you should go," Alexander calls from his place at the kitchen counter. "I will stay in here out of the way."

"I'll keep you company." Kurt holds up the empty glass and says, "That was magnifico!"

"Thanks. Oh hey, would you dial in some music for us? I have speakers in here and out there," I ask Kurt and point to my phone on the living room table. "That's the one thing we didn't think of. Spotify us?"

"Absolutely. Do you need the watermelon out there?" Kurt asks.

"Just the one. I'll keep the other in the kitchen. I probably won't need it for the show and will make something with it tonight. Less 151 Ways to Die and more daiquiri." I pick up my bottle of tequila, which is needed for the next video.

Kurt asks, "Are you going to cut a hole in this second watermelon? Can I?"

"Sure. Grab that knife there and…"

Mercedez interrupts me, "Ready, Jude?"

"Be right there!" I call to her, then say to Kurt, "After the show maybe?"

Kurt has my favorite silver knife in his hand. "I'm looking forward to it." He stabs the watermelon with a thunk. The knife projects from the round orb like a tropical sword in the stone with a too-happy sticker stating, "Enjoy Summer!" The dim shadows, cast by the overhead lights, overlap and all point towards the porch behind me.

Facebook post to Tippsy Kitty's discussion page, pending approval.

"[Emoji of skull] [Emoji of girl with blond ponytail] [Gif of severed monster finger] [Emoji of boy] [Emoji of boy] [Emoji of bomb] [Emoji of boy] [Emoji of gun] [Emoji of girl with blond ponytail] [Gif of severed monster finger] [Emoji of old woman] [Emoji of headstone] [Emoji of knife] Tonight."— KingBarbour90

DEVIL'S MARGARITTA—WITH TWO TS.

Recipe notes from Jude's journal.

Do not do a salted rim

I call this Blood on the Water, myself.

Mix in shaker with ice until chilled. Strain into margarita glass:

- One and a half part tequila
- One part lime juice
- Half part or more simple syrup

Using a spoon, float the wine on top creating a red layer.

- Half part red wine
- Garnish with lime wheel

23 - 152 WAYS TO DIE

"Oh. My. God!" Deloris exclaims. She holds up the small stemware filled with an amber liquid. "This is strong!"

"But really good," Phil all but whispers next to her.

The sun is setting behind me as we sit on the rock patio. Pinks. Purples. Oranges blaze across the sky. I can't imagine a better show. Everyone is enjoying themselves.

Deloris and Phil are lightweights and sway a little on their bar stools. Misty looks unphased. She scowls and fusses with the black roses, which were moved to the outside patio for set decoration.

Brandy leans over to her and points to the roses, "Those are fun. Great pairing with the drink."

Misty pouts slightly, "I don't know who sent them. They *are* perfect."

Mercedez and I hear the comment. Our eyes meet.

"The roses," Mercedez mouths from off-camera.

"Fuck," I mouth back.

She looks around as if someone might jump out at us. I conceal my concern by turning to face the sunset and raising my small glass. "And that, my friend's, is 151 ways to die—tropical style."

This fucker needs to come out into the open. What does he even look like now?

"Cheers!"

"Salud!"

"Chin-Chin!" everyone agrees and sips.

Whiskers sits on a bar stool and watches with little interest. Mercedez places a small cat treat on the counter to encourage her to jump up on the bar. She complies, hints of pink and orange reflect on her fur.

"Raise shields," I instruct.

Those in the splash-zone, which is everyone, hold up plastic ponchos—branded with the Tippsy Kitty logo, of course.

I place a shot of 151 Ways to Die, garnished with a small chunk of watermelon, in front of Whiskers. She sniffs at it and even nibbles at the watermelon. After a few moments of contemplation, she hits the drink to the side, splashing it on Deloris mostly and a little on Phil.

"Huzzah!" I say and ruffle Whiskers' long fur.

Deloris giggles and Phil even lets slip a small laugh. He looks around hoping no one heard, looks at a camera perched on the guide wire to his right, then twists his beet-red face away.

Mercedez picks up Whiskers and moves her to the house. No one notices, they are happy and all talking. Mercedez hands the cat to Alexander, says something, then comes back out.

Alexander nods in my direction and cuddles Whiskers.

"Another round?" she asks.

"Absolutely!" Deloris says.

I fill the shot glasses again and look at the camera trained on my face. Brian has set them all to rolling at the same time. He is busy at a small but intricate looking computer station doing something magical that ends with a multi-camera feed going out live to Facebook and YouTube. His face tenses as he focuses on his magic box. The lights reflect off of his bald dome.

'Wait. Could he be Zack? What do I remember about Zack?' My heart beats faster.

Mercedez points to me from off camera—my cue to wrap the show up.

"Everyone at home watching, thank you for supporting Tippsy Kitty and having fun with us. Special thanks to our VIP guests Phil and Deloris for being with us this weekend. Hugs and love to my ever supportive best friend Mercedez who makes all of this magic. To you: Don't be a bad kitty. Don't drink and drive. Live Happy!" I raise my glass. In the fresh darkness behind me, fireworks erupt, overtaking the dark purple sky.

After eating more finger food, all the guests file towards the door. Mercedez escorts Deloris and Phil to their guest cabin next door.

"That was a fun show," Brandy says. She and Alexander stand in the doorway.

Alexander holds out his hand for me to shake. No gloves this time. His dark brown eyes are so intense they almost twinkle.

I must have drank too much. I am still mesmerized I can *see* his face. Trying not to be awkward, I look at our shaking hands.

He brings my attention back to him by saying, "Jude," with warm emphasis he continues, "You two are going to get through this."

"Thanks," I mumble.

"I look forward to visiting your new bar," he says, then releases my hand.

"We'll be there," Brandy adds. They leave with another wave and shouts of goodbye.

Misty carries the vase of roses into the kitchen and places them on the counter.

"Oh, you should take those back," Mercedez says.

Brian peeks his head in through the back door and calls out, "I've got to run real quick. My mom locked herself out of the house." He points behind him. "It's not going to rain—so, I'll come back and get the gear tomorrow?"

"Sure thing," I tell him.

"Are you sure about the roses?" Misty asks, a hopeful faint smile on her frowning lips.

'Oh my god, you need to take those roses away,' my brain insists.

"They were great for the show. Those are yours. Take them home and enjoy them." Mercedez says tactfully. "You never told me, where did you get them?"

"They were a gift," Misty says, smiling even larger—her mouth did not smile, but the muscles around her eyes did.

"A secret admirer," I say and smile tightly.

Zack knows where you live too, I see.

Kurt walks into the kitchen and places a stack of dishes into the sink. "Where do you want these dishes?"

"Right there is fine. We'll clean up in the morning," I answer and look at him hard.

'Could he be Zack? He's so nervous. Afraid of his shadow. Not the cocky dick we knew as kids.'

Mercedez gets a faraway look in her eyes as she watches Misty leave. I tap her elbow and ask, "Everything good?"

She jumps then recovers, "You saw what I saw, right? Black roses from a secret admirer."

"Yeah."

We keep our voices low.

"I'm jumping at everything. Tired, I think. Post party plods." Mercedez regains her composure and smiles, wrinkling her nose slightly. "All good. We're jumping at shadows now."

Kurt crosses the kitchen and stops in the doorway. "Great show. Thank you for inviting me." He turns to Mercedez.

She looks at him expectantly, waiting for him to say his goodbyes.

Kurt purses his lips slightly, as if tasting a lemon, nods, then walks through the door.

Mercedez shuts the door and asks, "What the hell was that?"

"Maybe the drink didn't agree with him?" I guess. "Or he's Zack, ready to chop off our fingers."

"We'd know that smug fucker a mile away." She turns off the porch light.

"Did Agent Miller get back to you?" I ask.

Mercedez checks her phone. "Says they have come up with the same conclusion. No leads on Zack. Not since high school."

"I liked things better when it was Robert," I grump and smack the counter with a dish towel.

Mercedez looks out the kitchen window. "I guess those cameras and things are going to be okay."

The glasses clink together loudly as I pick them up and move them to the sink.

"We can clean up in the morning," Mercedez says.

I open the fridge and retrieve the martini shaker filled with the last of the *Devil's Margaritta* from earlier.

"It is still cold, probably watery. Want to finish this off?" I hold up the copper shaker and gave it a shake. Ice clinks inside. "Look at that, there's still ice."

"So much tequila. I'm going to regret this." Mercedez holds her head in one hand and grabs a clean martini glass with the other.

"I'm surprised we don't have engraved silverware," I say as I strain the drink into the glasses. It doesn't look too watery.

"Are you making fun of my branding efforts?" she says—half kidding.

"No. Serious comment. It would look nice wouldn't it?" I float the wine on top of the drinks with a spoon from the silverware drawer.

"That's a good idea," Mercedez says.

Something in her voice makes me look at her. "You already have some don't you?" I ask.

Mercedez points to a single black rose on the dining room table. "Did Misty leave that?" she asks.

"I suppose so."

"Those gave me the obvious PTSD creeps. But they looked great on the show," she says. Her face droops into a grimace.

"What?" I ask.

"Nothing."

My phone, forgotten on the counter, vibrates. Robert. Good heavens, what does he want? God damn. I don't want to think about him or weird killers right now.

"What?" Mercedez asks.

"Nothing." I answer and turn the phone off.

"That reminds me. I should do a few posts to wrap up the evening's live event." She looks across the patio to Brian's editing station. "I need to get some footage from that contraption," she says.

"First." Still in a toasting mood, I hold my drink up. "I want to say thank you for making all of this magic happen."

"To us and Tippsy Kitty," Mercedez says and holds her glass high.

We clink glasses and sip our drinks.

"I'm thinking of one more event for tomorrow," Mercedez ventures.

"I know when you are up to something."

"We could take the VIP guests down to the bluff to that little cave you two were looking at. I asked Brian. He says it isn't very far."

I think about it. It could be fun. "I'd have to teach you how to hasty repel down."

Mercedez wrinkles her nose.

I continue, "It's just holding a rope or webbing around you, nothing complicated. Who else is going to take pictures?"

She thinks about it, then resigns to her fate. "In for a penny. I suppose. For you, I would slide down a rope to a cave." Mercedez looks at Whiskers. "I don't think she's going though."

We finish our small drinks. I take Mercedez's empty glass from her. "I'll put these away. You go do the camera things you do."

"Thanks."

Mercedez is slightly unsteady on her feet, but not too bad, as she goes over to decipher the controls on Brian's box of magic. She presses a few buttons, bending close to get a good look at the geekness only she and Brian can decode.

The tiki torches are burning low—but have not completely guttered. Their flickering lights, the red dots from the cameras, and the glow of Brian's stack of computer things give the patio an eerie quality. It makes me think of King Kong, where the lady gets tied up as a treat for the furry beast. Maybe it is the rocks and the flickering tiki torches.

Imaginative and macabre—that's me. Misty might beat me at that game. One black rose on the bar. Weird. She must have left a few of them everywhere. Perhaps feeling guilty she wanted to take them home, so she wanted to share?

The clink of the glasses as I put them in the dishwasher seems excessively loud. I search the kitchen for more dirty dishes and look at my favorite German knife sticking out of the unused watermelon. I'll put that back in the refrigerator and make a daiquiri out of it for the VIP guests tomorrow for their goodbye.

On the kitchen counter, a single black rose sits next to the watermelon. How many Goth roses did Misty leave? My vision blurs as I reach for the rose.

Black water greedily sucking at a mattress as it sinks to the bottom of a pit. A dead rose thrown in after it.

My phone vibrates. I failed to turn it off earlier. Clumsily, I hold it close to my face. Hard to focus on it. Robert again. I try to answer. What does he want? Why now? My thumbs won't listen to commands. They hang like numb weights. The phone stops vibrating.

Maybe Mercedez can help. I turn towards the patio. The phone vibrates again. This time it is Darren.

"What is so urgent?"

I try again to answer but cannot even hold the phone. It slithers from my hand and clatters to the floor. Waves of ephemeral darkness push in at the edges of my vision. A numbness spreads throughout my body.

The world slows down. Every detail recording for me as I fall to the ground. My head bounces. The universe spins. The watermelon on the counter gloats over me.

Somewhere in the back of my head a voice asks, *'Remember Darren busting in with that toy gun? Yeah. This is not a training exercise.'*

A handsomely manicured hand grabs the knife; yanks it free.

Incoherent memories swirl. Memories of a heavy cardboard box. Its rectangular lid flopping with each step.

The pulp in the air smells sweet. A drop of juice—not yet mixed with the tequila I intended for it—falls onto my face.

My brain issues one last somewhat coherent thought before checking out and plunging me into darkness, *'151 Ways to Die? Well, here's to 152. Heh.'*

24 - SOBRIETY SAVES LIVES

Jude is jumping at shadows, thinking every man in the room could be Zack. I'm so glad I didn't tell her about the weird messages and comments on the social media sites. Finger bone emojis, Jesus wept.

I need to add in a cave adventure to the VIP's agenda. I'll have to sort that out tomorrow.

Walking across the porch, I stumble just the teensiest bit. I'm mostly sober. Can't get hungover. Tomorrow I have a slew of follow up tweets and Instagram posts to make. Have to thank everyone for watching the show. I need some screen grabs from the recordings to personalize the posts. Don't forget we're going to slide down a rope and see a cave.

'Gosh, why did I suggest that?'

It will look great. I trust Jude. She wouldn't put us in a dangerous situation. It's just a few feet down the slope.

Brian's box of magic for the multi-camera recording is intricate. Oodles of dials and buttons litter the surface. Having touched nothing like this, I'm more curious than afraid. I twitch the mouse to turn off the screen saver. The screen blasts my eyes with overly bright light, making me squint.

The browser on the computer shows the output which was streamed to Facebook, YouTube, and Instagram simultaneously. The live session has ended, but the cameras are still feeding to the browser.

The camera feeds capture the beautiful patio, tiki torches, bar, and empty bar stools.

The last camera points towards the barstools where the audience sat. Now, it sees past the barstools and directly into the kitchen. A watermelon sits on the counter. Jude's precious chef's knife sticks out of it. On camera, a shadow walks across the patio into the kitchen.

'That isn't Jude.'

The world swims. I didn't drink that much. With all the excitement, maybe it's hitting me hard? The shadow stops in the doorway. Jude stands at the sink, her back to him. He is tall. Maybe it's Alexander or Kurt? Did they forget something?

The world blurs a little further and my legs are growing into blocks of ice, numb. This isn't drunk.

Inside, Jude sways and drops to the floor. The man from the doorway walks in, yanks the knife out of the watermelon. He tests its weight. Says something. Raises the knife overhead. Lunges towards Jude.

I try to yell, to scream, but my face has gone numb. My body is a ten-ton weight sinking to the ground.

My phone? On the kitchen counter. I set it down when we had that last drink. My purse? My gun? In the dining room.

Arms droop and become unresponsive. It is difficult to breathe. I can't call for help. The security panic button is inside the house. What the hell can I do? A lean towards the computer. Slump against the side of the metal cart it sits on. Thank God it's sturdy. I struggle to reach the mouse. My arm misses. My hand plops on the metal like a dead rat. I try again, this time using both hands as one. I can barely see the bright screen, my vision fills with circles of fuzzy gray bricks. Using both hands to click and move the mouse, I click twice.

Did I click the right buttons? Did it work? I can't see the screen to tell.

My knees buckle. With a twang, my chin hits the sharp edge of the metal cart.

'That should have hurt.'

25 - DEAD WOMEN TELL NO TALES

Red blinking camera lights, red-eyed dragons in the dark, glow dimly around the patio.

He drags Mercedez by the heels across the patio. Her cut chin leaves a swatch of blood. He stops to regain his purchase on her legs. A pink shoe falls off and tumbles across the patio, falls to the ground below with a soft thump.

He tugs again and pulls her towards the kitchen, passing Jude's still form without pausing. The door to the basement sticks. He places Mercedez next to Jude, freeing his hand to wrestle with the willful door. One by one, he pulls them down the stairs into the basement.

Outside, the red-eyed dragons dim. One by one, their batteries give out. Their all-seeing eyes grow dark.

***

I don't open my eyes at first. In the dark, I will my head to stop throbbing. The sounds of the world come to me from thousands of feet away, under water, with airplane engines roaring, and possibly bobcats screeching. My teeth chatter. The movement of them causes my head to pound more. I try to stop them by dropping my head to my chest. The chattering turns into shivering and my body twitches and spasms without my consent.

Sounds around me sharpen. I am not alone. I attempt to still my body; it ignores me.

Shoes walking on dirt covered wood. The air smells still and damp. Clinking: metal on metal. A moan in front of me. Mercedez!

Did my breathing change? I try to keep it slow and steady. Do unconscious people shiver? Probably not.

"You're awake." A deep voice above me croons.

'Damn it.'

"Five more minutes," I whisper back. Cause, fuck him. He's going to do whatever he's going to do. I will not give him my fear.

Unbidden, flashbacks of Jackson's smirk come to my head. "I'll tell all your friends at school you pee the bed," he stood over me while I played dolls in my room. That fucking sideways grin, I would grow to hate plastered on his face. He hadn't even hit puberty yet and barely outweighed me. But how is an eight-year-old to know she could have tackled him to the ground? She didn't. She didn't learn that for a long time.

"I don't pee the bed, you do!" I dared to retort.

He grabbed my upper arm and twisted harshly with both hands, burning and bruising the delicate skin.

I cried out and that "I'm better than you" grin widened, an evil leer lit his eyes with heat.

Visions of that grin breaking through the suicidal grief— when I had taken a step back from him in Mom's sitting room— looms in my head. He saw me cower. That lit him up.

Rough hands grab my short hair and yank my head up, bringing me back to now. Pain shoots through my back and joints as they try to accommodate the strange contortions. I wiggle, testing the size of my bindings. Against my chest, my knees compress me into a small, unyielding, cold, plastic box. I smell ozone in the air, just underneath the sweat, mold, dirt, blood.

"Always the sarcastic one." He spits the words, anger seething. "The perfect princess. Thinking you're better than everyone else."

A fan. All righty then. The voice sounds familiar, but not. I attempt to open my eyes. The world swims in an unfocused sea of fuzzy grays and piercing white.

Mercedez next to me stirs. Her knees press up against my knees. Warmth. I wiggle my toes, which I suspect are underneath her butt. They are too cold and obstinate to move much.

"Jude," she calls out hoarsely.

"Shhhhh. Right here," I whisper in what I hope is a consoling manner, but it comes out as a croak.

I press my knees against hers. She presses back. The side of the thing we are in bites into my left knee in protest.

My hands, tied under my legs, are as distant as DC. I reach my fingers, barely brush the calf of Mercedez's leg. She hasn't shaved recently. That's unusual. The party must have stressed her out. Not quite the thing to focus on right now. I feel bad anyway. She's usually so meticulous.

"Shut up. You will both listen to me," he hisses.

Great, now he's got to monologue. Is that real? Do they always monologue? My brain drifts to Jackson on the couch, whining in some delirium he had prayed Mom dead.

With flat eyes, Jackson raised the gun and said, "I could take you with me."

I hate that Mercedez is here. She shouldn't have to get hurt.

My body shivers and shakes. A numbness creeps up my legs and arms, working its way towards the central mass of my body. Hyperthermia. Mercedez is smaller than me. She must be worse off. I lean forward and try to touch her ankle with my fingers, feeling for a pulse. Mercedez's fingers touch my arm and tap. She's here. Weak. But here.

"Let Mercedez go. She's got nothing to do with this." My voice comes out as a shivering whisper. Words clink against my teeth.

"Head up your ass, as usual. This has everything to do with Mercedez," he hisses, then grabs Mercedez's hair, yanks her head back.

She yelps and her body spasms, feet kicking.

I will my eyes to open—only see dim-blurry-adjust-the-brightness shapes.

He hisses in her face, "I need to erase my past. Mercedez knows all about that." He lets her go, takes a step back.

The single dangling naked light bulb—required for creepy basements—swings on its exposed wire. The harsh shadows it casts fall across Kurt's face, twisted into a sneer.

Kurt. I am sure of it. The guy I invited to the party. The guy who I met at the fruit stand, at the Caverns. Except this guy isn't mousy, tripping over his own words. This guy towers with self-confidence and power. Kurt.

"Kurt?" I blurt. "What the fuck?"

He dangles a single black rose upside down over Mercedez's forehead. She shivers and drops her gaze to mine. Hurt and sorrow filled eyes. A soul-wrenching acceptance of what is coming fills them.

Kurt pushes his manicured hand across his forehead. Dark bangs pull back, revealing a single white scar above his eye.

Like a zap of electricity from tailbone to head, his scar fills my vision. Dirk, carrying boxes in the garage, talking about helping Betty. The hair on my neck standing on end. Shivers. A gut wrenching need to not be near him. My body sensing danger but not knowing where it was while we stepped into the elevator. Dirk, the guy who we suspected put Betty and Dee in side-by-side freezers. Macabre frozen drive-in theater patrons awaiting the show. Dirk had lifted his head to look at the motorcycle ramp suspended from the ceiling, and that scar was visible under his wavy-floppy bangs.

"Dirk," I say with as much disgust as my hoarse throat will allow.

'Kurt is Dirk.

Is he Zack?'

"Keep going kid, you haven't bottomed that rabbit hole yet."

***

"Kurt?" Jude speaks with realization, but she doesn't know. "What the fuck?" she adds, eyes glaring.

I can't see much in the darkness. Blood blurs my vision. My chin throbs with each heartbeat. A shadow falls across me and a single black rose flashes in front of my face, caresses my cheek, soft petals like searing knives.

Looking at Jude, I try to convey my deepest sorrow for failing her. One mistake I never owned up to. I was just a kid. I couldn't stop him. I could have told. Could have made a duplicate of the tape and turned it in. Instead, I did what he asked. Got beat to hell for it. And never told a soul. Not even Jude. And now, we are both going to die, shoved into a freezer together.

I don't even recognize him. Stood right there at the gun range with him. Brought him right to us. I drop my head, not wanting to see her eyes, not wanting to see her hate me for my lies.

"Dirk," Jude whispers hoarsely.

She still doesn't see him. Can't recognize him. How could she? I couldn't see him for who he truly was. I can see faces and tell one person from another.

"Keep going kid, you haven't bottomed that rabbit hole yet," he says, then drops the rose on our legs. It tumbles and falls— thorn lodges between my bare ankles.

I bury my face in my knees, hoping to hold back the tidal wave of unwanted memories, and fail.

***

Kurt, who helped me carry the watermelons to my bike. Kurt is Dirk, the same guy who carried boxes in from Betty's car in DC. Now the images of those two men merge via one single scar on his forehead. A white thin line puckering at one end. Should have received stitches to minimize scaring.

He's Zack? I can't connect it.

My mind reels, as it does when I realize I've mistaken someone. Tightness squeezes my chest, a you-wouldn't-recognize-your-own-mother fear creeps in. I fight against the useless direction of thought. Focus on the issue. Focus on the small steps, not the bigger picture. Who cares who this dude is. Dirk. Kurt. Fuck-tard who likes to put people in freezers. God, what did Dee do to earn a popsicle death? Do you freeze to death or run out of air first?

His cocky preening pierces through my mishmash thoughts of *fuck 'em* and *'when will they find our bodies?'*

"Don't recognize me?" he turns from Mercedez, head buried between her knees, and says, "I can always count on you to not see past the surface material."

Kurt holds out a hand to indicate his khaki pants and sport shirt. He draws in on himself and moves like Kurt. Slightly mousey, horrifically adorably self-conscious. "Body movement can be changed." He nervously pulls on his ear and continues, "Noses, chin shape, jaw line changed."

Kurt stands tall and loosens into his joints, someone comfortable in their skin. Athletic. Dirk. He smirks. Self-confidence, but not too much, radiates from the tilt of his chin. Dirk says, "You were always fun to fuck with."

Softly, Mercedez pushes her knee against my knee. The smallest touch of her fingertips tickles my calf. I reach towards her. One finger stretches until it reaches her fingertip. A bondage-E.T-phoning-home-minus-the-glow. We hold there on the warmth, our shaking bodies making the task difficult.

Kurt/Dirk absently smooths out his hair and pats his bangs as if taming a life long cow-lick to cover his scar, though now the bangs are short and held flat with product.

He says, "Most identifying marks can be hidden. I kept this one though." He taps the small white scar. "A good memory." A wide grimace, not one unlike Jackson's, spreads across his face showing pearl white capped teeth. "Found the bottom of that rabbit hole yet?"

I see it then. The cow-lick of dark hair—untamed—covering an angry scar, years ago on a driver of a panel truck looking over his sunglasses and saying, "Never mind them. They aren't worth our time."

Jackson sitting next to him grinning his stupid grin months before he blew it off with Dad's retired service revolver.

That dark hair, drenched with sweat, falling over his eyes while making an amateur S&M tape with Jackson in a dimly lit, rat infested, abandoned warehouse.

***

"Zack." My voice is a whisper.

"Mercedez. Loose end number one gets the gold star," Zack/Dirk/Kurt and who knows how many other false faces he has says.

"Jude doesn't know," I plead. "Let her go." Copper tasting blood fills my mouth. Uncontrollable jittery teeth cut my tongue as I speak.

***

Oh, I know what you did to Janet. You turned in an anonymous tip that ratcheted up the stress on Jackson. So he killed himself. I'm not mad about that, I helped talk him into it. You took out the twins, probably. Jackson. Now Mercedez. The fuck you will.

Please, don't let my face tell him what I'm thinking.

I reach for Mercedez's fingers again, press my knees against hers, probably smooshing her legs too hard against the freezer wall. She shifts her shoulders to the side so she can reach her arms further under her legs and touch my fingers. She taps my fingers, one, two, three. A consoling gesture. Or Morse code? Hell, I don't know that. Or did she just tap to me, 'be quiet, kid. Let the adults take care of this.'

Am I being super paranoid? How hard is it to not be paranoid at a point like this? My mind slows down and takes in every hyper-detail again as adrenalin drowns everything else out. I'll only have this for a little bit before it drains me. Then I'll, we'll, die—frozen, gasping for breath.

Focus. He hasn't shut the lid yet. Not freezing to death, just cold. Plenty of air.

"You know she can't identify you. Let her go," Mercedez says. "How did you…" She stops and spits, very un-Mercedez like, leaving a red splotch on the side of the white wall. It dribbles down into the darkness. She continues, "…find me?"

She's getting him talking to buy time. Why? We're in the god-damned middle of nowhere. If we yell, shoot off guns, fireworks, cannons, the neighbors further down the bluff, or across the valley, would just listen to the echoes of the shots fade out, shrug and say, 'Well, guess we have some city-folk on the mountain feeling a little wild,' and go back to their satellite TV or bitching at each other on Facebook about the latest mountain-top-whose-goat-is-this-and-why-is-it-in-my-yard scandal. The VIPs, 2000 feet away, wouldn't even know what address to call the police to.

***

"I had to assume you two were glued together at the hip still." Zack leans against the wall, puts his foot up, looks like he could light up a cigarette at any moment. Smoking behind the gym. "Jude's easy to find. That write up in the paper about being the second woman on the motorcycle presidential thing."

I wiggle my toes further forward under Jude's butt and push the rose thorn out of my ankle. The rose falls to the side.

Zack drones on about the YouTube videos, the CNN coverage, beacons over Jude's head, like he needs a trophy for finding Jude and then me. It's not hard to find people nowadays. All he needed to look at was the owner of the TippsyKitty website and he'd see it was me. Public access. But he doesn't know that. Thinks he's smart. Hell, look at most photos and they have the longitude and latitude embedded in the metadata. Smart, my ass. Let him keep telling me how smart he is. Talk. Talk. Talk.

His eyes grow cold and he stops talking.

'Fuck.'

"What's that noise?" he stands up, tenses.

"Why kill Dee and Betty?" I ask and move my weight over to lean on Jude. Sorry, babe, trying to slide these hands forward.

He looks up at the ceiling. Shadows obscure his eyes, like a skeleton, when he lowers his gaze. "Betty was easy, and it got me just down the hall from you two."

"Well, I didn't really live there."

He ignores me, liking the sound of his own voice. "And Dee? Did you not notice how much she looked like Janet?"

Jude goes rigid next to me.

He continues, "I had to for old time's sake. This time I wasn't stupid enough to record it. Old lady had a peephole between the two apartments. I had to see what was in there." He shivers. "Creepy. A peep hole."

I want to shut out the image of Betty in her frozen coffin. Eyes staring into nowhere three feet from Zack as he leers through a hole in the wall at Dee preparing for her daily jog. Putting her hair back in a ponytail, oblivious to the monster on the other side of the wall.

Waited long enough for the FedEx driver to deliver another freezer. Strangled her. Cut off her finger. Bundled her up and put her next door, like a drunken sorority girl. Folded her into her freezer tomb.

"Why the fingers?"

"You know," he answers.

I know. With another slow push I slide my bound hands out from under my feet. The electric tie bites into my wrists and scrapes along the soles.

"And the tape?" He leans in close to see what I am doing. I freeze.

Jude flops over my feet, covering my hands with her torso. Her cheek bounces on the side of the freezer. She flinches and glares at him.

"I burned it." Shakes chop her words into a staccato.

"Jackson's tape." I clarify. Jude's missing the point.

"That wasn't a full dub." He glares. "You didn't make others?"

How can I convince him? "No." My voice sounds thin. "I was a kid. I gave you the tapes."

He sneers. "I should have used a tire-iron on you instead of a 2x4."

I flinch at the memory of Zack and his group of goons jumping me at the donut shop.

Zack looks up, pride in his voice. "I made that VHS dub for Jackson. A special tape just for him. Put the mattress in the pit with her. Had his DNA on it."

I never saw the sex tape. Jude did. Damn, that has to mess you up.

"Gave the VHS to him right before he shot himself? Threatened to turn him in." Keep talking, Zack. Tell us how you like fucking with people.

He eyes me hard. "Jude, did you watch when she made the dupe?" He chuckles and reaches for the freezer lid, swings it on its hinges, looks for a reaction. Getting nothing more than a double dose of hate radiating from her eyeballs, he turns to me. "Guess she didn't stay to watch the credits."

Jude doesn't look at me. I'm so glad she doesn't. I will fall to pieces. Memories burn through my skull like white phosphorus acid.

Jude continues to glare at Zack. He opens a thermos and places it between our feet. The smell is sickeningly sweet and overpowering. He steps away quickly.

Jude kicks my butt and eyes me strongly. She puffs out her cheeks, a childish mimicking holding your breath. Her cheekbone bleeds where she split it on the freezer wall. She turns her head up, gets a good gulp of clear air. I follow her lead.

Zack adds, "Ask Mercedez who the cameraman was." He swings the freezer lid closed. "You'll want to duck your heads. Wouldn't want this to smash your skull."

A metallic, heavy handle clicks into place.

Darkness.

I lift my tied arms and beat at the freezer lid. It won't budge. Jude is busy doing something with her hands.

***

I know this smell.

With wide glistening eyes, Jackson invited me to his room. "Come see my mouse."

I must have been four then. He had a small dusty bottle and some makeup sponges from Mom's bathroom.

"That's Mom's. I'm going to tell," I whined as any little sister would.

"Shut up and watch." Jackson pinched my shoulder—not hard enough to make me cry, but hard enough to know there'd be another one that would leave a welt if I didn't keep my mouth shut.

Jackson held the sponges to an open bottle and tipped it. A strong, sweet smell filled the room. It was strong enough to make your eyes water and push you back a step. He put the sponges in a mason jar with his white mouse and screwed the lid shut.

"What's happening?" I asked, not understanding.

"Wait. It takes a couple of minutes, dumbass," he hissed and leaned in closer.

The mouse sat there, his whiskers twitching, unaware of the chloroform soaking into his bloodstream.

Jackson became impatient and grumped, "You must have done something to the jar lid. Made it leak." He pinched me hard. "If you make a sound, I'll take your baby dolls and put them in a dark place where no one can find them. They'll cry and cry."

To a four-year-old, that's harsh stuff. I pressed my lips together and tried not to whimper—angrily wiped away the tears.

The mouse fell over on his side, his eyes wide, his breathing fast. After a minute—his breathing stopped all together.

Jackson tapped at the glass. "Too much. I just wanted to knock him out." A ravenous look filled his face.

I didn't stay to see what he did with the mouse. I ran out of the room to protect my dolls and refused to eat dinner that night.

That sweet smell.

It will knock us out in five minutes. I don't know if it is enough to kill us—but knock us out in a freezer running low on air. So many ways to die.

I almost don't hear Zack's last comments. I am taking my sock off, or trying to take my sock off as best I can without him noticing.

"Ask Mercedez who the cameraman was," he says.

I freeze. The tapes I hid. A sex tape with Zack, Jackson, and a young teen girl. Maybe Janet? Mercedez wasn't the cameraman for that, was she? Or the hokey horror film? The camera had paused and moved. It wasn't on a tripod. Zack wasn't in that film. Holy shit, was Mercedez there when Janet died? God, I can't imagine what a brain fuck that was.

"You'll want to duck your heads. Wouldn't want this to smash your skull."

I don't duck in time—still thinking about Mercedez holding a camera as carnage plays out in front of her innocent eyes. The freezer bangs my head, almost causes me to take a breath.

Can't think about Mercedez and her secret right now.

Focus. Step one. Get my sock in the thermos of chloroform. Thank heavens he didn't pour it on us. I pull at the sock, it refuses to come off. Mercedez bangs at the locked lid. We'll get to that problem next. Finally, the sock releases its grip on my toes. The force sends my arms (still bound behind my legs) into the thermos. It tips. I imagine it spilling in the darkness.

Mercedez pushes against it with her leg and together we pin it into a vertical position. I flap the sock against her leg and she doesn't react. We need to work on our ESP.

My body burns for air. I can't take in a gulp. One or two probably will just make me dizzy. This stuff takes a few minutes to work, but I am not risking it. I lift my legs—concentrating like a yoga master—maneuver the sock into the thermos mouth. If I can get it in there, maybe I can slow down the process.

Mercedez gropes in the darkness to inspect what I am up to. We clasp hands around the thermos, push the sock into the neck. Our fingers fold over top of one another, holding the sock and searching for any air holes. Don't soak up the liquid and become a Molotov cocktail, I beg the sock.

Thirty endless seconds. We hold our breath. I break contact first. Slip my hands out from underneath my legs. Lift my shirt over my face.

I dare to speak through the filter, "Breathe through your shirt. Chloroform."

"Air won't last," she whispers back. "Door's locked."

There is nothing to do with the electric ties around our hands. I have nothing to rub against them, no shoe strings, no belt, no hard edge.

"Listen," I urge. My head spins.

Outside, we can hear the scraping of his feet on the concrete floor. A phone buzzes sharply on the lid of the freezer. We both jump. It vibrates and rattles as if it will drill through the steel to us.

Zack ignores it. The buzzing continues. Mercedez's smart watch lights up to tell her she has an incoming call. In the glow, I can see her smile. She stretches and reaches her fingers around her left wrist to touch the contraption.

She bends her wrist to show the caller id. Bright blue glowing letters spell: Pizza Guy.

'What the hell?'

She rolls a small dial at the side of her watch and presses a button on the screen. The screen blinks once and then goes dark. I hear a click and the screen lights up again, illuminating our small-and-cozy-freezing-coffin-for-two. The shakes have run their course through our bodies, only to be replaced by a heavy sluggishness. Mercedez rests her head against her knees. The chloroform vapors probably don't help.

Above us, the phone scrapes across the lid loudly.

Muffled, but still audible, "Who delivers pizza out here?"

He's expecting us to be unconscious soon. We will eventually succumb. Not as quickly as he wants. I'll bet Zack doesn't like for things to go off schedule.

"Oh man, would you get that for us?" I holler and press my lips close to the rubber seal of the lid. It flakes when I touch it. Using the end of the electric tie around my wrist, I poke at the seal until a small hole appears. The barest whisper of fresh air and temperature change registers on my forehead as the hole lets in the outside oxygen.

I motion for Mercedez to do the same. Raising our bound hands, we poke holes in the brittle seal. Old freezer. The seal is brittle and crumbles. I turn my head to the side as much as I can and suck at the air there. I don't realize how groggy I am until the gray fog lifts off my brain.

Mercedez must feel better too. She calls out, "Don't you eat all of my pepperoni!"

You can almost hear Zack take a step back—wheels spinning. His prey—who should be nearly incapacitated—is asking for pizza.

Mercedez reaches for the thermos. Her watch's glow casts erratic shadows everywhere and lights her face from below. She looks like a crazed demon. Our ESP clicks and I know what she is planning: Get him mad enough to open the lid.

I jab the small opening with the zip-tie tie. Bending my hands in awkward positions to get the tail to poke out so Zack can see. "This works, Mercedez," I say for Zack's benefit. "Run this back and forth along the lip for some fresh air."

Zack smacks the lid. "Stop that." He grunts something under his breath. "It won't be enough to counteract the thermos of..."

Mercedez interjects, "You mean this thermos I plugged shut with my silicone falsie?"

The lid shudders above our head so loudly it makes my ears ring.

I wish she did have a silicone boob we could plug the thermos with. While hers are definitely silicone, they are not easily removable. Zack doesn't know that. The sweet smell is getting to me, and I'm sure Mercedez. She presses her lips to the light coming in the freezer and breathes. We have to keep it up.

I jab again at the seal and make a frantic slashing with my arms, breaking away more of the seal. It feels good to be defiant.

"Stop it, damn it," he bellows. Then the sound we have been waiting for—a clink of metal—as he reaches for the lock.

Mercedez and I lock eyes. Shift our weight onto our toes. Ready to spring. Mercedez pulls the sock out of the thermos.

The lid opens. We jump. Fall up, really. We tumble out of the freezer like drunks. Mercedez throws the thermos towards Zack. We land like rag dolls and roll away. Gulp at damp basement air. It burns my throat.

I can barely see Zack as he stumbles back, wiping liquid out of eyes.

That's got to be bad,' I think. 'Good shot!' I attempt to say. No words actually come out of my mouth.

Zack drops to his knees, shoves a finger down his throat. He wretches clear bile onto the dusty floor.

Bonus points, Mercedez! You got it in his mouth.' My tongue is too thick and heavy to speak.

Mercedez stands and blinks. A trail of dried blood covers her from chin to belly button. The basement looks like an abandoned gardening area. Old pots, shovels, shears, hang forgotten on the wall. She grabs a rusty pair of shears from a hook. I find a small serrated hedge trimming blade. Zack is still retching and trying to yell at us at the same time.

In any other situation, his failure at producing words while trying to vomit out poison might be funny. I can't find the energy to do anything but keep moving.

Feet untethered, we bounce and stumble off the walls and into each other while we climb the stairs into the kitchen. There we stop and help one another unbind our hands.

I turn and shut the basement door, throw the bolt—a small useless brass trinket. "Not going to hold."

The kitchen is so bright. It has been centuries since I stood right there. Smiling into a camera and pouring a drink for the man who would try to kill me. Poisoned my leftover Devil's Margaritta drink? How many years since I bought that watermelon?

I measure the distance from me to the counter. Tumble towards it like a toddler taking their first steps. Hands outstretched, ready for a crash landing. Three steps. My body gets heavier with each step. I make it. Exhausted, drenched in sweat. Hug the watermelon to my chest like a life preserver.

"Purse?" Mercedez is going through the same efforts to reach her handbag. With effort, she pulls out a small gun. Holds it to her chest.

Where is my knife? Not in the watermelon. I eye the melon. That would make a poor weapon—round liquid filled orb. Maybe not.

Sounds of Zack moving heavily up the stairs spark another spike of adrenalin into my system. I throw the watermelon at the ground in front of the door. It spatters with a satisfying thunk, sending chunks of watermelon all across the tile. Maybe he'll slip and break his neck.

"Go." I point out the back door.

"Move," Mercedez orders. She is in a shooting stance, leveling a 9 mil at the door. Love that gal.

Zack bursts through the door. His face is a greenish hue. The door swings open, smearing the watermelon. A piece of rind breaks and sticks under the door. It squeaks in protest against the tile. The door stops halfway open. Zack's momentum keeps him from stopping. He hits the door hard with his shoulder. His foot slips on the watermelon.

I want to kick him down the stairs, but Mercedez has her weapon trained on his center mass. I don't budge. Not going to cross in front of that barrel.

***

The gun is heavier than I remember. My vision swims and warbles. *'Jude, stay back.'* Just need to aim at the blurry, dark angry thing. The crack of bone is loud when he lands on his knee. Zack's green face is pale. For sure, he's going to pass out now.

I can't keep my mind straight. We were just in a box. Freezing, dying. Now we're here. My watch beeps. The gate is open. Is someone coming?

"Shoot him!" Jude yells, shaking my mind from drifting.

You want to say so many things at a moment like this: something valiant, pithy, courageous. I can only grunt, "Stop," in the general direction of this demon man who has manipulated, cajoled, beat, and scarred me; and tried to kill my friend. Hold my breath. Place my finger pad on the double trigger. Squeeze.

***

Mercedez pulls the trigger. An insignificant firing pin click. Empty chamber.

She looks at the gun in disbelief.

Damn it. Nothing in the pipe.

"Fuck. Chamber it!" Backseat shooting. I slowed him down with the watermelon, didn't I? I contributed.

Zack lets out a roar. Dives towards Mercedez. Knocks the gun out of her hand.

I grab her arm and pull her towards the back door. "This way," I urge.

Everyone does that—forgets to chamber a round. I mean, let alone when a childhood killer is coming at you from a basement of near-death. Understandable. No time to tell her now.

We run sluggishly. A loud clank of Zack chambering the gun. Our pace quickens with another spike of adrenalin.

"This way. Duck." I lead Mercedez towards the edge of the bluff and think, *'Be small. Be invisible. Don't see us.'* My bare feet scream at the sticks and stones underfoot.

"Where are we going?" Mercedez asks.

"Over the edge." I hand webbing to Mercedez.

***

"What?" I take the webbing from Jude. One-inch wide. Thin. Flat. Insubstantial bit of nylon. What the hell do I do with this?

"Watch," Jude urges. She pulls the webbing behind her, holds onto it with both hands like a hula hoop. "Remember

Disney? In line for the Pirates of the Caribbean? Mom yelled at us for leaning and sliding on the ropes. Just like that."

I nod numbly. *'Dead men tell no tales.'*

Except I'm not dead and I saw what Zack did. I was there. I was a witness.

And I did nothing.

He assumes I told Jude. He won't let her live either.

Jude snaps in my face. "Focus." She grabs my left arm and points it down the bluff. "This arm points down. Got it? Point down. Go."

"Down. Go."

"Don't let go of the webbing."

She pulls my left arm to my body. Pushes my hand and the webbing to my chest. "This is your brake. Pull in. Stop."

"Pull in. Stop."

Jude looks down the slope. The full moon barely illuminates the steep angle covered in trees and undergrowth. 1800 feet to the valley floor. Sheer twenty feet rock drop-offs scattered across the mountainside. "It's a slope. Slide if you have to."

Where are my shoes? I hold the webbing tightly and stare at my toes. Jude snaps again. Damn, but she's annoying.

Jude pulls her downward arm and the webbing across her body. Leans into it. It creaks. The webbing around me pulls up with her weight. "It's wrapped around that tree. You have one end. I have the other. Don't let go. We will fall."

"I don't know if I…" My knees won't stop shaking.

Above us, Zack stomps out onto the porch.

"Go!"

We hurry sideways down the hill. Webbing rubs quietly along our backs. Bramble cuts my feet. I slip and yank my arm to my body. The flat webbing pinches my waist, stops me. Gravity wins. My backside hits the ground. But I do not roll.

Jude shushes me and we both sit still. Listen for sounds above us.

"Just a little further." Jude descends. She is nearly silent.

I try to stand, nearly fall over again. The webbing leading up the bluff thwacks against the ground as I flail.

At the top, the tiki lamps blaze, a full moon behind them. Like a scene from King Kong. Except the gorilla is Zack.

"I hear you!" Zack steps in front of the tiki flames.

'A moving target is harder to hit than a sitting duck.' A stone outcropping sends a shock of white pain through my knee to my teeth.

"Stop," Jude hisses. "In." She grabs my webbing and pulls me towards her. Disappears into a dark void.

I grab at her hand and blindly follow her voice. A shot rings out. The bullet ricochets nearby with a dull twang. The report echoes through the valley. Before the echo falls away, another shot. A meaty thwapping sound.

Can't catch my breath. Fall into the dark hole. A high ringing sound fills my ears. What is Jude saying? She needs to let go of my arm. It hurts. Let go of my arm. Maybe the webbing has me.

Let go.

***

Mercedez tumbles into the cave opening behind me.

"Are you shot?" Stupid. I heard the shot. Saw her twist as if suddenly pushed. "Where?" I grab at her. Grope for the warm wetness. Upper arm, straight through. Can't tell how much it bleeds.

"Damn." Mercedez slumps against me.

Where is Zack? How far? The cave opening forms a barrier around us. Can't hear him. I pull at the webbing. *'Don't get caught on a rock.'* Silently, hand over hand, I pull it to me. *'Good luck getting down here now.'*

"Who is the Pizza man?"

"I'm shot."

"Your smartphone in the freezer. You opened the gate."

Mercedez touches her arm, winces. "The FBI are here."

"Are you delirious right now? Is that the pizza man?" I'm pulled into the wall. My tooth clinks against the rock. *'Shit.'*

"YOU CAN'T HIDE…" Zack's voice rings above us.

The webbing yanks out of my hand. I grab the end whizzing by me. Double wrap it around my body and arm. Lean into it. An absurd tug-of-war.

"…FROM ME!"

'Can't let him have this webbing.' I pin my knee against the rock. Push back. Lean out to see where he is.

"Don't do that," Mercedez warns.

He's at the top still. Webbing in one hand. Gun in the other. The torches behind him blaze, highlighting the webbing as he wraps it around his lower arm. It trails below him towards me. If he puts weight on it, I only have to let go of my end. He'll fall down the bluff. Come on down dumb fuck. Or better yet—

Someone yells. Zack turns towards the voice. Headlights shine on his face. He's smiling.

I want to yell. Shout something glorious. Tell him to F himself. Instead, I growl with rage and think, *'You fucker.'*

With all of my weight, I throw myself to the ground. Yank the webbing with me. The webbing around his arm snaps with my weight and spins him off balance. His arms pinwheel. The gun in his hand waves wildly in the air.

Two shots ring out. Dull hollow staccato thwaps—thunk, thunk. A cloud of pink erupts from Zack's upper torso. He falls over with the momentum and disappears from my sight. A high-pitched scream wails. Flames erupt brightly, sending writhing shadows down the hillside.

"What the..." Mercedez leans around me to see.

A fiery figure appears on the bluff's edge. Zack ablaze. No screams. No sound. His mouth frozen wide open. He turns. Fire crackles. Slowly, he falls to his knees.

"He's going to fall on us." Mercedez yanks me back.

Instead, he flops onto his face. Flames greedily lap up the still carbon form. A downdraft pushes the stench to us.

"He won't do anything to us ever again." I plop onto the ground and shake.

DEAD WOMEN TELL NO TALES COCKTAIL

Recipe notes from Jude's journal.

Mix in shaker with ice until chilled. Then shake it some more, 'cause why not. We got frustrations to get out. Equal parts:

- Jolly Rancher infused vodka, raspberry (still have some, right?)
- Spiced rum
- Blue Curacao
- Half part sweet & sour mix
- Double part lemon lime soda
- Garnish with this trick: soak a lemon slice in rum, light the rum on fire, throw a dash of cinnamon into the flame. Sparkles!

26 - TIKI TORCH ON THE ROCK BLUFF

Darren is the first to raise his glass, "To the Tippsy Kitty!"

Everyone raises their glasses and cheers, except for Mercedez, who has her right arm in a sling.

The bar is half-full with my friends from the DC UD unit and caver friends. It is an interesting dynamic to watch. Laced-up g-men on one side. Adventurers and perhaps a good number who like their Type II controlled substances on the other side.

We are having a special private opening party for Tippsy Kitty a month before the grand opening. The place is still a wreck but slowly coming together. A healthy helping of older cats and a few kittens lounge in the cat patio. The kitchen grill isn't working. I don't expect us to have any food items beyond things that are microwavable for another two months.

I couldn't be happier.

"We were all watching the live show and cheering Jude on," Darren explains to the crowd.

"How long ago was this?" Susan, from the far end of the bar, asks.

Busy pouring drinks for everyone, I answer, "Been a couple of weeks."

Darren continues his story, "In the background, I recognized Zack in the kitchen from the photos Robert showed me. Right when the fireworks went off, Zack went to the window to watch them."

Robert leans in and takes up the story. "I found the link between Zack and you two while I was trying to get myself out of jail." He looks at me sheepishly, "Sorry about the..." He gestures with his drink. "...you know."

"Water under the bridge," I say. "Unless the porn mags was you."

"Zack," Mercedez answers.

"We called Agent Miller. He tuned into your show and wasn't buying that Zack was up to no good," Darren says.

Robert adds, "The show ended, and we were still arguing. Then the feed came back. We saw him dragging you across the patio."

"I could barely see straight. Glad I clicked the right buttons." Mercedez, tired, leans over the bar. "Brian had left everything going. Had a family emergency. I just had to click the 'go live' button and hope I had picked the camera facing the kitchen." She touches the bandage on her chin. "Stout metal cart."

"That got Agent Miller moving," Darren says.

"I opened the gate for them with my smart-watch." Mercedez pointed to her wrist.

"Oh—I thought you were texting while we froze." It did light up the freezer for us pretty well.

"Wish I could have taken him out," Mercedez says quietly— probably obsessing over that empty chamber.

Robert looks at her pointedly, "No. You don't want to live with that."

They lock eyes, and something passes between them. A silent warning. Mercedez nods and says, "You're right. I have enough baggage from Zack, don't need more."

"How did you know Kurt was Zack?" I ask. We'd given our statements, they had de-briefed, but Mercedez and I were still catching up on the missing pieces.

"Well, I knew about the finger," Mercedez says. "That third one was to me. It was personal."

"She told the Agent about the same time Robert was figuring out the finger connection too." Darren adds.

I interrupt, "Hold up. Fresh beer for everyone." I pour a handful of pints and set them on the table. The microbrew sparkles in the dim lights.

"I used to be a detective." Robert looks at his feet. "Got asked to leave the unit years ago. Chain of command bullshit." He shrugs. "Dusted off some old contacts to help find something to get me off the hook for those DC murders."

Agent Miller walks into the bar, an old-fashioned bell over the door jangles. He looks at it with fierce eyes, as if it might need to be dispatched before leveling an iron gaze at us. "Sorry. I'm late. Paperwork."

"Come on in. Robert here was just getting to the part where he figured out the finger," Mercedez says.

"I probably annoyed the hell out of Agents Miller and Worthington," Robert continues.

Agent Miller nods his head in agreement.

"The finger was personal, like Mercedez said. I looked into your past, where you two came from." Robert stops to take a sip of his beer. "Good," he adds, tipping the glass towards me.

I place another beer on the counter for Agent Miller, expecting him to decline. He takes the amber liquid without hesitation.

"Janet, the young girl that was killed in your hometown," Robert proceeds gently, dropping his eyes to his beer, "right before your brother killed himself."

My throat clenches. Mercedez shifts close to me and puts a comforting hand on my arm.

"They found her sunk to the bottom of a filled in pit. A mattress and some junk on top." Robert picks his beer up to sip, hesitates, puts it back down.

I stop breathing. On the tape, the mattress. Watched it sink into a pit. On top of Janet. I had no idea.

"I didn't know where she was found," I say.

"They kept a lot of details out of the press. It was easier to do that back then," Darren adds. He scoots down a bar stool so he can be closer to Mercedez and me. He continues, "One detail, besides that she was found in the automotive pit was..."

"Three fingers were cut off. But only two were found." Mercedez whispers.

Silence fills the bar.

Agent Miller picks up the story. "When Mercedez received the third finger in the mail, meant for her, she called me."

Mercedez holds up a hand, it trembles slightly, "I knew whose finger that was."

"Before the show, you knew? Heavens," I blurt.

"I never told you or anyone. What does a ten-year-old know?" She shrugs her shoulders. "I was there. I recorded the whole thing." Mercedez leans against me. She is cold to the touch and trembles. "He threatened to expose me to everyone and back then that was more horrible than death." She takes a deep breath and continues, "The horror film. We were having fun. It was an accident. What happened to Janet. But Jackson and Zack, they were into it."

I rub her shoulders and pull her close to me.

"Zack wanted a dub of the tape so he could have it. The original was some old broadcast thing no one could play. I made him the dubs. Wasn't smart enough to make a copy for the police."

"You were just a kid," I hoarsely whisper.

"Zack and his cronies jumped me at the donut shop that afternoon," Mercedez adds.

The story pauses. I replay every moment we had been together. Imagine how she could have told me this secret.

I want to ask her about the sex tape—but no one here knows about that. We burned it. Watched the flame devour it, just like it engulfed Zack's flesh.

"I shut those images away and never spoke of them again until that finger showed up. I called Agent Miller and told him." Mercedez places an arm around my waist and squeezes back, "Told Jude some, not all."

"I looked into it and the story checked out. DNA matched. Robert was off the hook." Agent Miller adds, "I hoped he would stop calling me."

He drinks deeply from his glass, wipes away a small bit of foam from his lips, continues, "The forensics team started combing through your social media channels and could trace three different accounts all back to one person. The location data in the photos put that person near you. Tracking you."

Robert says, "I was combing through the posts as well. It was a long shot, but I noticed the black rose picture."

"Emoji," Mercedez helpfully corrects.

"That thing, in the comments. It made me think of the picture from the paper—your brother's funeral," Robert says.

"I hate that photo. Hate they printed it in the paper. All of us around the casket," I add.

"Zack brought spray-painted black roses. They were weird," Mercedez says.

They were weird. I remember my dad eyeballing Zack like he was a leper.

"He looks so different now. No one would be able to recognize him," Darren adds, stressing the words *no one* for my benefit. Good guy, Darren.

"That made him cocky. He felt invisible," Robert adds. "The emoji-things and comments were everywhere. Including a picture of you at the caverns."

"Where he was! The Kurt version of him anyway." I remember that flash of anger on his face when Brandi gave him her ticket.

"Forensics scoured the pictures. Found him in a couple posted by the Cavern's PR team. Hard to go to an event and not get photographed," Robert says.

"After a court order, we could find the owner of those accounts. He even had a profile page with his picture on it," Agent Miller says. "The metadata in the photos on his account pinpointed him to locations of a string of bodies we have, all missing fingers, stuffed in freezers. There was an open investigation on him in California."

"Then he saw the article about me in DC," I say.

"He knew I'd be close by and I could..." Mercedez falls silent.

I try to lighten the mood, "Finger him for Janet's death."

Mercedez glares at me. Too soon. She smiles half heartedly. "This is all my fault," she says.

"I can't believe you lived with that secret all this time." I take a swig of my beer, not my favorite, but this is not a time for cocktails. "Zack must have turned in the anonymous tip about Jackson, putting pressure on him. Gave him a VHS tape of the horror film minus the death. Added in the mattress getting put with the body."

"Zack wasn't on the tape. Just Jackson. They would have pinned him for it," Mercedez says.

"He couldn't take it and…" I can't finish the sentence aloud. Too busy replaying the scene in my head where Jackson tried to make it my fault he wanted to blow his head off. "So you saw the video feed." I point to Darren. "And you were 90% sure Zack was Kurt when you saw him in the kitchen."

"We called Agent Miller and hopped in the car for the long drive here." Darren says.

"I got the honors of taking that guy down," Agent Miller says flatly. "Fire was a bonus."

"Chloroform. Flammable." I raise a glass and everyone else does as well.

"The Dirk/DC connection can't be proven. There was no DNA and he wasn't caught on camera. But he was linked to all of those porn magazines you were getting," Darren says.

"And I'm the only one that saw him." I give a half-hearted shrug. "Doesn't matter now."

"Damn, he had access to the fridge while we were making the show. He was all alone when Alexander was putting Whiskers away," Mercedez says and looks at me.

"Doctored the leftover Devil's Margaritta. I said we'd toast after the show," I add.

The room grows silent. Each one of us processing the ordeal in our own way.

A bell jangles as the door opens. Brandy and Alexander walk in.

"Are we too late for a drink?" she asks. "Actually, I'm just here to see the kitty cats."

"I only have a few, so far. They're out on the patio through those doors." I point behind me.

Brandy leans over the counter and squeezes me with a bear-hug. Alexander squeezes Mercedez's good shoulder.

"This will certainly make a splash in the papers for this small town, will it not?" Alexander smiles.

Mercedez looks at him, wide-eyed. There's the Mercedez I know. She says, "Let's own it. An exclusive post on our social media platforms. Submit it to the local papers. They'll pick it up." Mercedez eyes Agent Miller and continues, "Leaving out many key items that are not public knowledge."

She paces. We all watch as Mercedez plans and strategizes aloud. "Of course, mention this opening of the Tippsy Kitty. Free publicity. Spin this. No bad guys left to come after you." She pauses. "Us."

"I hope," I say.

"Ready to give a statement?" She holds out an upside down pint glass as a microphone for me to speak into.

I look at the people around the bar that saved our lives, smile and say, "This started with Mercedez."

"What?"

"When you gave me that new phone."

"She's a Neanderthal," Mercedez says into the pint glass while looking at Darren. "I also bought myself a smart-watch which saved the day."

"And Whiskers knocking the drink over—also your fault," I add.

"Cat has opinions."

Uploaded video to the Tippsy Kitty Café's Instagram account.

35K likes

1K comments

25 creepy dude DMs.

In the audience: Darren, Scotty, Robert, Brandy, Alexander, Susan, and Misty.

Jude and Mercedez are both in front of the camera. The bar glitters behind them. A bank of glass windows behind the bar shows a room of kittens and cats in various forms of catness. Patrons sip on cocktails, beers, sodas, coffee while being in audience with royal felines.

"Y'all come visit us," Mercedez says to the camera.

Jude leans towards the camera, "You can adopt a kitty and take it home with you."

"As long as you aren't creepy," Mercedez says.

"Pending background checks," Jude adds.

The camera cuts to a close up of Whiskers sniffing a cocktail. A lime wedge hangs on the side of the small martini glass. She takes a tentative lick of the lime wedge, her face screws up with displeasure.

Mercedes's manicured hand reaches in with a long lighter and sets the lime alight. Whiskers squints at the flame. Sniffs.

Another hand reaches in and pets Whiskers. Jude's voice from off-camera says, "We got this one, Whiskers."

She knocks the drink towards the camera.

The video fades to black.

TIKI TORCH ON THE ROCK BLUFF

Recipe notes from Jude's journal.

Mix in shaker with ice until chilled.

- 2 parts Campari
- 1 part coconut rum
- Splash of pineapple juice or—gasp, peach schnapps
- Pour over one large square ice cube in a short tumbler.
- Garnish with a rum soaked lime, set that lime on fire, throw a dash of cinnamon into the flame. Sparkles!

APPENDIX

The settings and places Jude visits are inspired by my favorite places. You'll recognize them if you are a caver from Tennessee. The small cave towards the end of the book is the cave under my house. It tapes out to 50 feet if I really push it—with a Chihuahua holding the measuring tape. One day I'll draw a map of it.

Moonshine

Recently, while climbing a hillside to get to a cave, I commented that I needed an Apple Pie Moonshine recipe. One of the cavers not only had one committed to memory which he recited as we trekked forward, he had some to sample upon our return from the cave—don't drink and cave. I live in a sublimely synergistic universe. Moonshine recipes are very guarded. If you really want to make moonshine take a look at this website: moonshiners.club.

The Naughty Cat Café—Chattanooga, TN
https://www.naughtycatcafe.com/visit-us
Reserve an hour spot to hold court with the royal kitties while enjoying coffee, beer, and bakery goods. You can even adopt a kitty.

National Speleological Society (NSS)
https://caves.org/
If you are interested in caving, this is a great place to start. From their website: *"For over 70 years, the National Speleological Society has promoted safe and responsible caving practices, effective cave and karst management, speleology, and conservation."*

Panic Attack recipe used by permission from Imaginibus: https://www.imaginibus.com/blog/the-panic-attack-sazerac-and-cider

SCCI (Southeastern Cave Conservancy) —
https://saveyourcaves.org/

A group dedicated to protecting and preserving caves through conservation, education, and recreation. They currently own and manage over 170 caves. You have climbed through a few of them with Jude in this book.

Lastly, on a serious note.
If a child expresses hesitation to visit, kiss, hug, or be near someone. Even a family member. **Listen. To. Them.** https://www.rainn.org/articles/protecting-children-sexual-abuse

LAST WORDS FROM THE AUTHOR

This all began because I am an unimaginative drinker surrounded by people who love a beautiful cocktail. Order Jack neat and get a side eye. I set out to understand their love and kill a few of my personal demons along the way.

Dragon Con & LGBTQ: I went to Dragon Con 2019 to stalk my favorite author, Chelsea Quinn Yarbro, and get a picture with her, as you do. Mission accomplished. Check out my Facebook page—look for the picture with the biggest geeked out smile. I'm not good in crowds, but a good friend went with me and tolerated the full day it took me to gain the nerve to talk to Quinn. While there, I saw a LGBTQ group holding signs begging for representation in fiction. They are right. I did my best, and that is how Mercedez—a quiet, powerful and poised black transgender woman—walked onto the page demanding her own point of view in this book. She did not tell me her full story, keeping many secrets to herself. We also taught Jude about the term Ace, 'cause, I wanted a book without sex.

Caving & Motorcycles & Prosopagnosia: Many of these situations are my own. Though I put Jude into the circumstances and she handled them much better than me. The W road—that's word for word me, except I can't lift my bike off the ground. *"Hell fire!"* It was hilarious. I've never said those words before until that very moment when I didn't fall over the bluff's edge to the cars below.

Seriously, caving: Caving is a very dangerous sport. *Never* cave alone. Follow safety guides. Don't do what Jude does. Learn more at caves.org.

UD: I took creative liberties with the Uniformed Division of the secret service and their security clearance process and training. That was fun research. They do have to be able to lift their bikes off the ground as part of their entrance test. Jude is badass.

ABOUT THE AUTHOR

Tina O'Hailey is an animation professor, a caver, and an occasional mapper of grim, wet, twisty caves (if she owes a friend a favor or loses a bet), whose passion is to be secluded on a mountain and to write whilst surrounded by small, furry dogs and hot coffee. Tina was once struck by lightning.

She has served as an artistic trainer for Walt Disney Feature Animation, Dreamworks, and Electronic Arts. Any movie credit she has is minimal and usually found in the special thanks section. The meager credits do not account for the great honor it was to teach talented artists who worked on numerous feature films and games.

She has authored animation textbooks "Rig it Right", "Hybrid Animation" published by Focal Press, and the Darkness Universe novels "Absolute Darkness", "When Darkness Begins" published by Black Rose Writing.

Her favorite motorcycle is her BMW R1200C—mathematically perfect for her short legs, turns on a dime, and is the ugliest bike ever.

Follow her adventures. Social media links on:
https://coffeediem.wordpress.com/

NOTE FROM THE AUTHOR

Word-of-mouth is crucial for any author to succeed. If you enjoyed *Dark Drink*, please leave a review online—anywhere you are able. Even if it's just a sentence or two. It would make all the difference and would be very much appreciated.

Thanks!
Tina O'Hailey

We hope you enjoyed reading this title from:

Subscribe to our mailing list— *The Rosevine*—and receive **FREE** books, daily deals, and stay current with news about upcoming releases and our hottest authors.

Scan the QR code below to sign up.

Already a subscriber? Please accept a sincere thank you for being a fan of Black Rose Writing authors.